I0822623

The Princess of Perizidon

The Perizidon Series

Book One

Matthew D. Moore

ISBN (hardcover): 979-8-9898754-0-5
ISBN (e-book): 979-8-9898754-1-2
Library of Congress Control Number: 2024907240

First hardcover edition April 2024
First e-book edition April 2024

Developmental Editing by Hannah Gokie (reedsy.com)
Copy Editing and Proofreading by Shannon Cave (reedsy.com)
Cover Art by Lisa Dunaway
Map by Catherine Pallotta

Printed and Published by MD Moore through IngramSpark
Indianapolis, IN USA

To Christine, who encouraged me to write and gave me the time and space to do it;

To Jonathan and Rachel, for being better children than I deserve;

To Bill, whose storytelling helped fuel my imagination;

To Lisa and Catherine, my awesome artists and troubleshooters;

To Jeff, for being the best Dungeon Master ever;

To Courtney, Dawn, Jonathan, Becky, Rob, Holly, Shane, and Andy, for putting up with the original Sarl;

To my father, David, who opened my eyes to good literature and good wine;

To my mother, Nancy, for a lifetime of support and lots and lots of prayer;

And to my sister, Deborah, who made me believe that Narnia was as close as our childhood backyard.

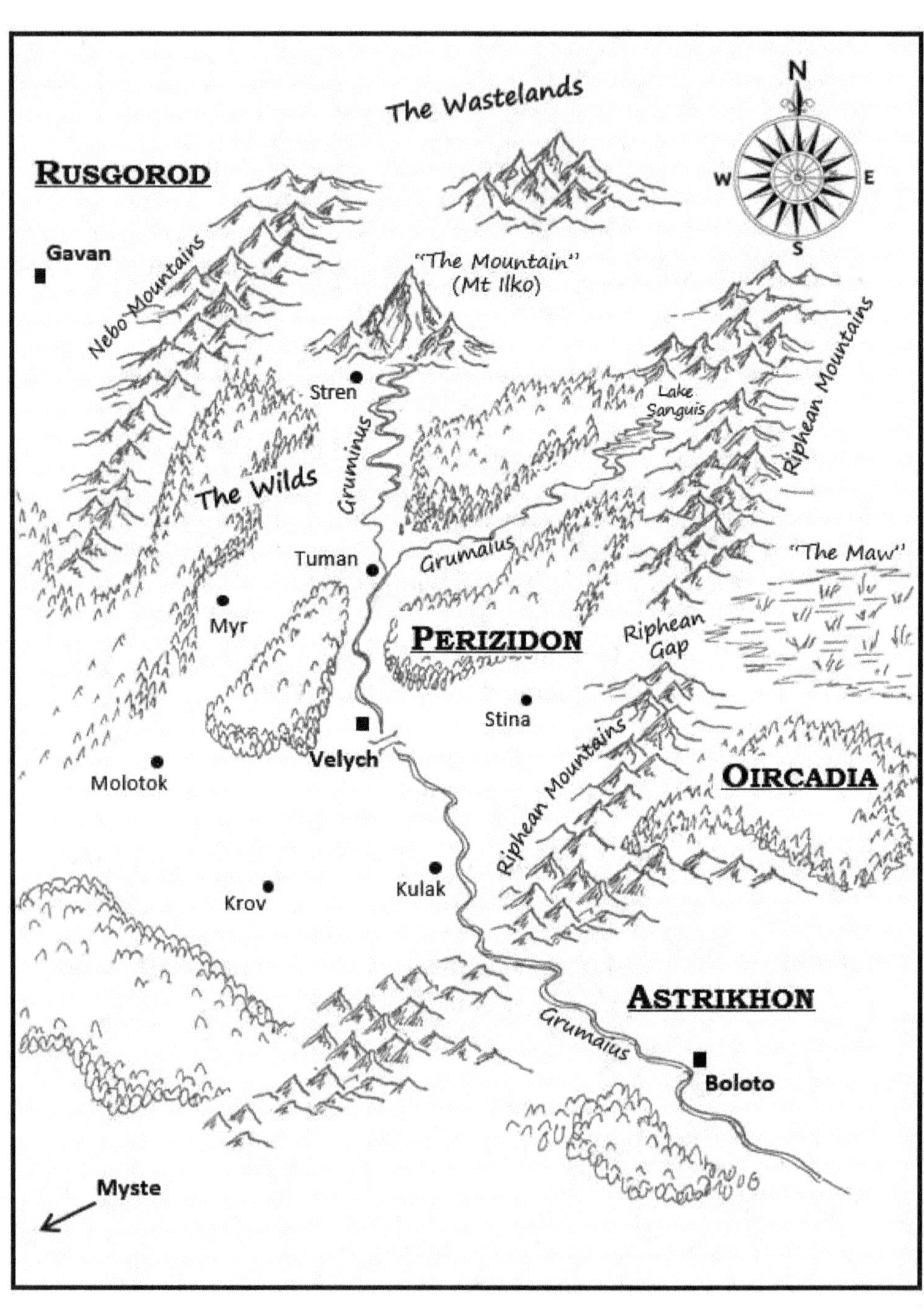

The Wastelands
N
W
E
S
RUSGOROD
Gavan
Nebo Mountains
"The Mountain"
(Mt Ilko)
Stren
Lake
Sanguis
Riphean Mountains
Gruminus
The Wilds
Tuman
Grumaius
"The Maw"
Myr
PERIZIDON
Riphean
Gap
Stina
Velych
Riphean Mountains
OIRCADIA
Molotok
Kulak
Krov
ASTRIKHON
Grumaius
Boloto
Myste

PROLOGUE

The Mountain

It was always cold on the mountain. The simple folk who toiled in the lowlands beneath it only knew it as "The Mountain" for it was the only one they had ever seen up close or cared about. The *pontifex maximus* supposedly sat in a golden city perched upon another impressive mountain far away, but none of the locals had seen this other mountain, let alone the pontiff. For most, the only part of the great, wide world that mattered was centered around their town of Stren, which stood some five leagues from the foothills of The Mountain and perhaps a league beneath its peak. Nobody really knew for sure the actual height of The Mountain; in their collective memory, nobody had ever climbed to the summit to look down upon everyone else. There was nothing up there but cold and snow, and they already had enough of both during the winter months. Nobody thought there was the need to waste a lot of time and energy just to experience more of the same.

To be sure, there were many more mountains to both the east and west; on a clear day, you could just make out some of the other peaks on the edge of the horizon. But only the orc trappers ranged that far away, and other than the pelts they brought back with them, there was nothing much of interest to report. Besides, what were mountains in the distance worth if the townsfolk didn't even care about the one on their doorstep? Not even half a copper denga.

Stren was fairly isolated from the rest of the known world, but it did receive some visitors beyond the trappers. Timber and pelts were sent down the river, while tools and wine came back the other way. But all of the shipments were handled by the longshoremen who came and left with their flat-bottomed barges, and on the whole, they were a taciturn bunch who kept to themselves. They rarely dealt with anyone but the dockmaster, who was an expert at giving orders and keeping secrets. The mayor would sometimes receive royal couriers, but she only interacted with the sheriff and stayed as far away from the rabble as she could. It was said that she had angered some noblewoman in the kingdom's capital and had been assigned an administrative post as far away from civilization as possible without being formally exiled. Regardless, the mayor relayed no stories of mountains, court intrigue, or anything else to the local populace and kept most of the imported wine for herself. The only real news of the outside world came from the priest, and he only came to the town approximately once a month to hear confessions and collect taxes.

Rumors, however, could be provided by anyone with half a brain and a tongue in their head, the former being of secondary importance to the latter. And the latest rumor to make the rounds was that there actually was more than just cold and snow on The Mountain. The few people who lived in the foothills outside of town spoke of strange lights on the slopes and shadows flitting back and forth among the trees, whoever (or whatever) was creating them staying just out of sight. Even the orcs who came through town had been mentioning the shadows recently. Usually the greyskins didn't scare easily, but some of them seemed a bit on edge when talking about what they thought they had seen. Whatever it was, it wasn't natural.

Tongues had wagged more than usual over mugs of ale at the Wild Boar tavern throughout the spring and early summer. But nothing bothered the town guards as they dozed at their posts, and the sheriff maintained there wasn't a reason to mount a formal investigation into old wives' tales. The priest always listened closely to the stories on his trips through the area, but other than taking notes in his ledger, did and said nothing about it. The mayor, if it was possible, drank more wine than usual. And so, the rumors stayed just that, and life maintained its difficult but peaceful pace.

The priest had brought one bit of important news with him this past month: the following spring, there was to be a celebration for the investiture of the heir apparent to the throne of the Kingdom of Perizidon, Princess Lianne. As her birthday was on the 16th day of Martius, the third month of the year, the priest had referenced the date as it related to the holy scripture of Ivan deliberately during his homily, so that the significance of the event would not be lost on even the simplest of the gathered host. The fact that the church would be paying for the festival helped generate interest as well. After the announcement was made, a few brave souls grumbled that they would prefer that the church pay for better roads, as opposed to roasted boar and cherry wine, but they were quickly hushed. If there was an inquisitor in the crowd, nothing came of this minor blasphemy.

Harvest was still several months away, but as always, there was much work to do. Thoughts of shadows in the trees and royal celebrations faded into the background as the people of Stren returned to their labors. The Mountain, as always, watched impassively from a distance.

CHAPTER ONE

The Princess Of Perizidon

The Mountain did have a real name, several in fact. But the only name that mattered to Her Royal Highness Princess Lianne Kalchik of Perizidon stood out in crimson letters on the royal map she was currently studying, stylized in almost unreadable calligraphy that had been quite the fashion several decades ago. Mount Iklo stood near the northern edge of her father's kingdom, which itself was a patchwork of counties of varied size that took a good rider with fresh horses over a week to cover. She had only ever seen paintings of the mountain, and from what she knew, nobody of import had seen it in person for several years.

The county that the mountain was located in paid its taxes on a regular basis, and there were no enemy armies to contend with in the barrenness to its north, and that was enough for it to be largely ignored. The army, small as it was, had other issues to deal with, and frankly, could have used several other peaceful border counties to ignore as well. The church could draw upon the local population for acolytes as needed; there was no need to send the archbishop north from the capital to create additional religious fervor. Finally, her father was a sound and just ruler, but he was extremely busy and had no time to travel anywhere, even in his own kingdom, just to go sightseeing. Apparently, there was nothing more to know about the mountain or the region around it that wasn't already known.

Still, Lianne wondered why the mountain and the area around it didn't generate more interest. The Grumaius River that flowed past the very palace she was standing in had only two sources, one of which started as a spring bubbling up from the depths of Mount Iklo. Surely that and the goods that flowed south on that leg of the river were of some strategic importance. However, it was the other source of the river, also to the north, but farther east, that was considered important, albeit for a different reason. That area of the country had been a longtime favorite destination of the royal family during the summer months. A picturesque castle had been built by Lianne's great-grandfather, overlooking Lake Sanguis, a body of water that had formed in ancient times from glacial runoff; it was this lake's discharge that marked the official start of the Grumaius.

Over time, a small village had sprung up along the lip of the lake to provide services to the members of court who would travel with the royal family, even to this desolate spot, in an attempt to curry favor. Lianne's father, in a moment of vulnerability, had once told her that he actually hated the lake due to some argument with his uncle that transpired there many summers ago. But the king went just the same, for tradition's sake, and also to make various courtesans suffer through sunburns and horsefly bites. Lianne smiled mischievously at the thought of various lords and ladies suffering in silence with blisters on their faces and welts on their arms.

There was even a church that had been built on the small island that protruded out of Lake Sanguis at the end opposite its outfall. You could take a boat to the island and pray to the Almighty, giving thanks that the kingdom was blessed with such a great natural resource as the river. The ferrymen charged a rather hefty sum for the trip, although they only demanded payment for the ride back to the mainland. You could always swim back through the ice-cold water if you didn't want to pay them, but very few ever took up this challenge. Not that Lianne ever had to pay when she visited the island. Besides, she rather suspected that the ferrymen themselves only saw a small percentage of the toll, her father and the church taking the majority of what was collected as tithes to the lords on earth and in heaven respectively.

Lianne wrinkled her nose at that image of Lake Sanguis on the map. She didn't necessarily mind going there like her father did, but she and her younger brother, Lucas, had long ago explored as much of the surrounding countryside as their bodyguards would allow. Last month's annual trip had passed without incident, meaning it had been a tiresome and boring affair for both of them. There was much more to see in what was to be her kingdom, and Mount Iklo seemed both an imposing and intriguing place on the map spread out before her. She had daydreamed about it constantly as a child and had told Lucas somewhat impertinently that she would travel to see it as soon as she became queen.

Using both hands, she traced the two tributaries of the mighty river from their sources until they met, a couple days' hard ride to the north of the capital city of Velych, where she was currently standing. The leg coming from Mount Iklo, deemed lesser by royal society many years ago, was called Gruminus, so at least some ancient cartographer had not been lacking a sense of humor. It subjugated itself to Grumaius, at least in name, at the confluence.

Lianne drummed her fingers absentmindedly on the map as her eyes wandered back to the mountain. Yes, there was much more for her to see and do. She was turning eighteen in less than a year and, despite Mother's protestations, was already sitting in on Father's council meetings. He didn't allow her to speak, but she wasn't there to talk anyway; she was there to listen and observe. She was, rightly or wrongly, already forming opinions about his advisors and who she would like to promote and, more importantly, who she would replace when it was her turn to reign. There were, of course, court politics to navigate, and in this subject, she was wise enough to know that she was barely a novice. So, she kept her thoughts to herself for the time being, while she attempted to learn the rules of the game. Her life was going to change soon, whether she liked it or not.

It had been an easy life to date, she could admit to herself, and not just because of her royal status. Her parents loved each other, or at least tolerated each other's bad habits, and this love or tolerance had been extended to her and her brother. While there had been reprimands and punishments meted out by both parents throughout her childhood, most had been earned. There had been no lecherous priests or abusive masters to contend with as part of her upbringing, no assassination attempts, no major outbreaks of the plague within the kingdom, and no large outbursts of civil unrest. The only minor family scandal she was aware of was one she had initiated herself when she had insisted, at the age of twelve, that Father allow her to be trained in the arts of war. This demand had arisen from her discovery that her brother, some four years her junior, was already being taught to use real archery equipment. Why should he have all the fun, especially if it was normal for men and women alike to serve under the king's banner?

Father had listened to Mother's histrionics about how no daughter of hers was going to ride into battle at the head of an army and then had ignored her completely by summoning the castle guard commander to start Lianne's training that very day. Mother had immediately left for Lake Sanguis in a cold rage and had not come back to the capital for almost four months. Bad weather and an outbreak of banditry were the reasons given for the extended absence, and Father had not pressed for her to return. When the queen finally did return, it was with much fanfare, for as far as the general populace knew, she had been off on official state business. Life within the royal family circle more or less returned to its previous state after that, although Lianne could sense a tinge of sadness in her mother's voice and eyes whenever they were alone together.

Things did change later on when her sister was born, and Lianne suspected that Mother had not argued against her sitting in on council meetings as strenuously as she might have if she did not have another daughter to dote upon now. Lianne loved her mother dearly and was glad she had inherited her common sense and air of quiet strength. However, she was eager to rule, or rather to lead, and this was something her mother could not provide lessons in, nor did she care about in the first place. And so, Lianne had set about learning how to shoulder her father's load directly from the source.

Lianne heard the faint sound of chimes coming from outside the room and down the hallway, signaling Sext. She straightened up from the table and stretched, raising her hands towards the ceiling and slowly tilting her head from side to side. It was not at all a ladylike pose, but it made her neck muscles relax somewhat and helped her refocus. It was almost time for her geography lesson, and she had snuck into the library early to take a look at the maps. She knew that Master Gregor would find some minute island or village that she knew nothing about to drill her on, so she needed to have her wits about her. She glanced at the map again and rather hoped the lesson would be about Mount Iklo or the county in which it resided.

A slow, somewhat unsteady gait could be heard coming down the hallway, punctuated by the sharp retort of a walking stick hitting the stone floor. Lianne's maidservant, who had been standing unobtrusively in the corner of the room the whole time, slipped forward to arrange the princess's cape as she sat down in a large leather chair next to the map table. Lianne smiled faintly and nodded at Melina, who disappeared back into the corner as quickly as she had emerged. The princess assumed a stately pose and waited for the old master to appear around the corner; the mental jousting was about to begin, and she was eager for it.

CHAPTER TWO

Brothers In Name Only

Bainor looked up from pouring drinks as the two orcs walked into his tavern. It certainly wasn't uncommon to have greyskins stumble into Stren from time to time and rub shoulders with his regulars, and most of those gathered barely gave them a second glance. It was true that there was now a slightly higher risk of a brawl breaking out, but their copper denga pieces were worth the same as anyone else's money. As far as Bainor was concerned, business was business; if both the Shade of the Abyss and the Almighty strolled into his establishment, so long as they paid their tabs, he would treat them equally.

The orcs that had entered on this late summer evening might have been a bit more worse for wear than the typical trapper, but overall, they did not stand out from others of their kind. A cursory inspection revealed they had weapons, but nothing that wasn't required for their trade or for protection out in the Wilds. As Bainor watched, his enforcer persuaded the greyskins to put their larger blades in the weapons locker, the same as all the other patrons did. They did so without too much protest, after which they made their way to a table in the back corner of the main room.

Bainor nodded at one of his barmaids, and she immediately made her way towards the two orcs to take their order and engage in small talk. He continued to study them as they ordered a round of ale; he thought he might recognize one of them from a previous visit but couldn't remember any details. That was a good sign as far as Bainor was concerned, since that meant the orc hadn't caused too much trouble or done anything memorable. *Maybe it's not the same one? Eh, I can't tell, they all look the same to me. We'll find out soon enough if they're worth any extra hassle.*

Before getting back to the business at hand, Bainor gave a quick nod to Ernest, the hulking enforcer seated at the end of the bar, who had just interacted with the orcs. Ernest had worked at the tavern long enough to know the meaning of the subtle gesture; to watch the newcomers, but to not get involved in their business unless a tavern guest (or more importantly, tavern property) was at risk. Ernest glanced back at the two trappers, shrugged indifferently, and went back to his own drink. The orcs just sat silently at their table for quite some time, drinking ale and apparently lost in their individual thoughts.

***

Umuk had already been in a foul mood when he had entered the tavern, and his mood only got worse as the evening wore on. He was tired and hungry, and the place didn't look like the easy knock over he had thought it would be. If more of the original group were still around, then a heist would have been child's play, but that was a nonstarter; everyone was dead except for the surly oaf across the table from him. *An' he's a beaten dog, that one.*

Umuk motioned for another round and glowered at his companion. Uptar was of good size for an orc, almost as big as

Umuk. He grudgingly admitted to himself that Uptar had certainly proven himself capable in the various skirmishes they had become entangled in over the past several months. His hunting and tracking skills had helped keep them alive for a time, but now he was out of arrows and had no scraps left for bait. The duo had been reduced to petty theft and basic foraging for the past two weeks, an ignoble end to a journey that had started out with such promise.

He's prolly thinkin' 'bout that bitch of his again. If that doxy cunt an' tha others hadn't died, then everythin' woulda turned out different. Truly, tha gods hate me!

There had been an argument outside the town's main gate. It was a tired and familiar argument, full of days-old bile and rising hatred between the two orcs. Uptar had made it clear he was done with wandering. The promise of starting a new life west of the mountains was gone, and it had been gone for some time. Now that they had reached a decent-sized settlement on the river, he wanted to head to the docks and find work that would take them south. Although winter was still several months off, he wanted to at least start heading towards where it was warmer. Umuk had played along and agreed that they would talk with the dockmaster first thing in the morning. But as they had entered Stren and walked towards the town's main tavern, one last desperate plan had started to formulate in his head.

The tavern would definitely have money, and in a remote community such as this, it should be easy pickings. Never mind that the last time he had tried this, it had ended in lots of blood and little money. The prospect of some quick coin still sounded much better than weeks of hard labor on a barge. But Umuk hadn't counted on the enforcer; a place like this usually couldn't afford one. Not that Umuk didn't think he could take the large human out, but it would take long enough that someone would be able to go alert the town guard before he was done shaking the place down. And on top of that, he knew he was going to have to act alone.

Umuk hadn't mentioned the possibility of stealing the money box to Uptar because there wasn't a chance in the abyss the other orc would go along with the idea. Not now, when so many of his other recent ideas had gone awry. But it didn't matter, as Umuk had made up his mind several days ago; he was going to rid himself of Uptar one way or another and strike out alone. The chance of grabbing easy money, slim as it might be, would just make it easier to start anew. The odds didn't really matter to Umuk anyway, because he was a survivor. He had survived fighting the Shinajin in the far east; he had survived the Choros penal colony; he had survived the plague; he had survived this descent into nothingness; and he would survive whatever came next.

Okay, okay, no worries. I can always change tha plan. 'Sides, if this place can hire that hulk, it just means there's more ta take! See where tha barkeep keeps goin' after a tab gets paid? Yeah, tha money box is right there behind tha bar. Just get a room for tha night, sneak out an' grab tha coin when everyone is sleepin', and hop it outta here. They'll be so mad in tha mornin'! They'll arrest this git bastard sittin' next ta me 'cause, of course, they'll think he was in on tha nick! He was just too slow or too stupid ta leave is what they'll say. They think we're all stupid anyways. Worst case, they lock him up for a few days, an' I'm clear gone by tha time he gets out. Best case, they hang tha dumb shite an' he gets ta sard his whore in tha afterlife as much as he wants.

***

Uptar silently stared into his mug, ignoring his companion and everything else around him. The drinking was only giving rise to dark memories, not drowning them as he had hoped. Try as he might, he could not help but relive every painful step of the journey that had brought them to the tavern.

When their large group had originally broken out from the Choros penal colony and escaped west, the plan had been to find some remote area in the vast wilderness of the north where they wouldn't be bothered and could start anew together. All had been hardened by their time in that hellhole; surely if they could survive there, then they could survive anywhere. But that assumption had proven tragically wrong.

Westward flight had taken them to the edge of the Great Inland Swamp, or the Maw, as it was known to the orcs. They had planned to use it to lose any pursuers, as the group's leader, Harah, claimed she knew a way through. Between her memory and Uptar's tracking skills, they had found the right path and disappeared into the marshlands. They had quickly shaken the posse formed to hunt them down, but their success came at great cost. Over half of the fifty-odd fugitives had contracted a mysterious fever while wading through the fetid muck. What feeble attempts that could be made to treat them failed, and the sick had died miserably, one by one.

What was it? Tha Black Death? A shaman's curse? Does it really matter? Uptar closed his eyes, accepting the inevitability of the memories rushing up to meet him, and he let the accompanying darkness wash over him one more time.

The group's only apothecary had lingered a bit longer than the rest of the sick, but she, too, had succumbed in the end. Uptar's hands tightened around his drink as he remembered burying his beloved Vesna. He had failed in his promise to bring her peace and happiness, and now she lay rotting in a shallow grave alongside her kin. She would be consumed by the creeping marsh, forgotten by everyone except him. She deserved so much better than that.

His right hand drifted to the pendant Vesna had given him that he wore on some coarse thread around his neck. It was a small, roughly cut, red stone set in gold, and it contrasted wildly with everything else he owned. He suspected it was some minor piece of jewelry she had stolen from the warden's wife when tending to their sick child. But he had accepted it in good humor from her the night before the breakout, and he had initially worn it to honor his allegiance to her. Now, he wore it in her memory and as penance. It felt cold against his flesh, hidden from view by his tunic.

After Vesna and the others had died, Uptar hadn't cared what he did or where he went. Nobody in the remaining group cared, really; most of their hopes and dreams had died with their compatriots. But there was no turning back, and the survivors had pushed on out of necessity. Harah had led them further west, through the gap in the Riphean Mountains towards the Kingdom of Perizidon. They had snuck past the few guard towers located along the border with Oircadia without issue, a rare instance of fate looking favorably upon the group. From there, they had struck out to the northwest, still ostensibly looking for a place to settle. But Harah had drowned herself in a creek after stumbling into it while drunk, and the group's fortunes had gone steadily downhill after that. Umuk claimed leadership of the shrinking band since he was Harah's second, but he had turned towards raiding the countryside as opposed to attempting to lay claim to an empty piece of it.

They had survived for a while by obtaining supplies with the sharp end of a sword and by sifting through the ashes of burned-out homesteads. But this rash approach had finally caught up to them on their last raid, where the homestead defenders turned out to be much more than some ragtag farmers. A handful of longbowmen had cut them down from well-fortified positions as they had rushed in, and only three out of a dozen orc raiders had managed to limp away.

The third orc had succumbed to his wounds just a few days after that. Umuk hadn't even buried him, just stripped him of what weapons and clothing could be sold or bartered and left his corpse for the wolves. Uptar had just stood and watched, silently trudging after Umuk when he was done desecrating the dead. Now, they had barely garnered a second glance from the guards at the gate as they entered town; they were just two more greyskin trappers down on their luck.

What little coin they had left, they were drinking through now. There was no plan. There was no future. *An' if I know this clown at all, he's thinkin' of robbin' this place. At least I'll probably be dead at tha end of his stupid plan.* Uptar opened his eyes, revealing what his memories had left him with. Nothing.

CHAPTER THREE

The Diplomat

Symon sat at his desk, comparing his mental notes of what he wanted to bring against the written list sitting in front of him. For once, his assistant had used her head and was assembling the correct equipment for an autumn trip to Boloto. When he got to the end of the list, he could only think of two items to add. *Not too bad, and quickly done as well. I must remember to thank her for a job adequately done now that she's finally headed in the right direction! Her mother will be thrilled.*

"Symon?"

Symon kept his head down and pretended to continue to look at the list. He had sensed the other man staring at him from the doorway for a while now and had ignored him thus far. *Not now, Jarek, not now!*

"Symon?"

Jarek entered the room and approached the desk, making to come around it so that it would be impossible not to notice him.

God's bones, Symon. You talk with royalty every day. Why is this so difficult? He looked up and smiled, but he did not move to get out of his chair.

"Ah, good morning, my dear! You caught me at work, as always. I will be up for lunch soon, I promise."

His partner stopped short of walking around the desk and

instead halted next to the lantern that sat upon it. The light shouldn't have been needed at this time of day, but Symon's eyes had been more tired than usual recently. Jarek noticed the royal document that had been casually tossed on top of several others at the corner of the desk and turned it slightly for a better look. He glanced up at Symon, surprise showing on his face.

"It's done? Already?"

Symon nodded. "His Majesty signed it last night as soon as I presented it to him."

"Ah, wonderful!" Jarek bent over and inspected the strong, bold signature of King Elric Kalchik II. "No flowery calligraphy for our king, that's for certain."

Symon gave a short laugh. "Never! Straight and to the point, as always." They looked at each other, both wondering if the other had noted the irony in the comment.

"So, what now?" Jarek asked.

What now, indeed. I suppose I should tell you sooner rather than later. Symon cleared his throat. "I have been commanded by our king to return to Boloto at once to present the signed document to King Haldir and complete the agreement before winter is upon us."

Jarek took the news quietly, although Symon knew he was seething inside.

He hurried on as nonchalantly as possible. "And perhaps just as importantly, the princess will accompany me this time."

That seemed to do the trick, at least for now. Jarek had

always had a fascination with Lianne, to the point of obsession. His mood brightened visibly when she was mentioned.

"Ah, really? Is this the court introduction you've talked about in the past?"

"It is. She will be requested to go by her father tonight, and she is not one to go against his wishes."

"But won't that mean a delay in your departure? Surely her retinue will need to be enormous! And the schedule will need to be detailed out exactly!"

Jarek had lived through any number of official court visits, and Symon knew that this would sound rushed to him. *Because it is rushed!*

Symon grimaced slightly. "You would think so, yes. But His Majesty has already told the council that he wishes this to be an informal introduction, not a state visit. A squad of soldiers for her bodyguard, perhaps a few ladies-in-waiting, and that is most likely it. We were planning to leave with the year's final caravan headed south to buy us a bit of cover from any watchful eyes, but I think using the river will provide more flexibility in the schedule. It will make for a much faster transit as well."

Jarek looked agitated, and Symon knew the issue now wasn't just his rapid departure after coming home so soon. His young partner was certainly one for protocol, and Symon could already tell this trip was beyond the pale as far as Jarek was concerned.

"But, Symon, this all seems so sudden. And forgive me for

saying so, a bit improper. Quite improper, actually!"

Symon sighed but smiled appreciatively at Jarek. *You always did have a good sense of propriety.*

"No, no, your thoughts echo mine. But His Majesty insists that his daughter be introduced to the House of Sokolov and the Astrikhon court prior to the investiture. He feels the gesture will build upon the goodwill created by this agreement. He is probably right, but the timing... Well, the timing could be better."

"Wait, wait, wait. Back up a bit. The investiture, is it really happening? When?" Agitation had been replaced by excitement in Jarek's demeanor in an instant.

"Yes, it is happening. That was decided while I was gone." *Blast that Gregor! I know he was behind the final push. The council knew I was against it being held so soon, but they made the decision all the same. I was gone far too long, and yet Elric pushes me out again immediately. And as a babysitter, no less!* Symon fell silent, staring blankly at the far wall. There was an awkward pause before Jarek tried again.

"Ah, I see. So, it must be happening soon?"

"On Princess Lianne's birthday, no less."

"Oh my! That is very soon. So much to plan in so little time." Jarek looked as though he was contemplating how to navigate the intricacies of the ceremony while Symon struggled to keep his true feelings to himself.

Discussions about the ceremony had been going on for some time in the king's council, and what frustrated him the most was that there should have been at least a year to formally plan the event. Someone or something of importance was bound to be overlooked now that everything was being rushed. He could not understand why the king was insistent on the schedule.

And of course, all of the major decisions will be made while I am gone. This damn trade agreement. Everything would have been fine if Haldir Sokolov and his fool of a chancellor understood simple arithmetic! Four months wasted on diplomatic negotiations, when it should have been less than one! And now I pay the price for Astrikhon stubbornness and stupidity by having to miss planning the largest ceremony our kingdom will see this side of a coronation!

Jarek folded his arms across his chest. It appeared he was waiting for Symon to say something else, but he could think of nothing that would lighten the mood. The silence between them lengthened into an uncomfortable interlude.

Eventually, his partner sighed in resignation. "Well, I suppose if there is to be an introductory trip to Astrikhon, then it must occur now or not at all. But, dear..." Jarek paused briefly and looked up with watery eyes.

Please don't say it, please don't say it, Symon thought.

"Must it be you that accompanies her?"

Symon felt like screaming. Such a simple question, with much too complicated an answer. He felt he was trapped between losing his king and losing his loved one, and all the diplomacy in the world wouldn't help him appease both parties. He looked down at the list of supplies again, the lines blurring in his vision. He wanted to stay, for very selfish reasons, but knew he could not.

"I...I'm sorry, Jarek. I must go where the king commands."

Jarek did come around the table now and placed his arms around Symon's shoulders. Symon leaned into him, resting his head on Jarek's stomach. He could feel Jarek's heartbeat echoing anxiously through his body, merging with his own until there was only one steady thrumming in his ears. He closed his eyes, remembering for the first time in a long time how good it felt just to be held. *Why is life so complicated?* All of a sudden, their time together flashed through his mind, and it pained him to see how many blank spots there were.

He felt tired, all the way to his bones.

The moment passed. Jarek leaned over to kiss the top of his head and then released him. "Well, Symon, I am glad you are still the King's Man." He walked back around the table and made to leave the room.

Even if it means I'm not your man? Now Symon did rise from his chair. "It should not be a long trip, my dear. A proclamation, an introduction, a party or two, that is all. I hope to return within a month."

They looked at each other from across the chasm that had grown between them.

Jarek smiled. "Good. Now, please come upstairs soon, as you definitely need sustenance and rest before you set out again."

"Yes, I am almost done here. I will be up in just a few moments." They both knew he was lying, but neither wanted to stop pretending just yet.

Jarek bowed his head to his soulmate and turned to go.

"Jarek?"

"Hmm?"

Symon paused briefly, but then he spoke clearly. "I love you."

"I know, Symon. I know." The warm flicker in Jarek's eyes was hard to see, but it was still there. "Just come home to me as soon as you can."

***

It was later the same day when Symon hurried through the streets of Velych towards the Kalchik castle. A sharp wind was blowing, seemingly a portent for the winter gales that were still several months away. Usually, he felt changes in the weather in his arthritic knee several days in advance, but this cold and blustery day had caught him off guard. Fortunately, the guards at both the outer and inner gates of the castle recognized him, even when wrapped tightly in a hooded robe, and they made no attempt to stop him. There was much to discuss with the king about the upcoming trip back to Boloto, and he rather hoped His Majesty could find some time for him alone before Vespers.

The main hall was much quieter than normal, but Symon was so absorbed in his thoughts that it took a few moments for it to register that there was almost no one present. In fact, except for a few guards and a servant who was cleaning some spot on the floor, the only other person in sight was young Lord Titus. He appeared to be asleep in the far corner, but as Symon approached him, he saw the bottle and could smell the wine. *So, passed out rather than sleeping. He'll be dead in two years if he keeps up his current pace!* Symon shook his head in disgust and waved a hand dismissively at the sot before looking around for another familiar face. He undid his outer covering and wished, not for the first time, that the hall had a fireplace.

One of the guards at the far end of the room by the throne had been passively watching him, but now he came hurrying over when it was clear Symon was looking for assistance.

The guard gave the king's salute, clearly knowledgeable about Symon's status with the king. "Dragoman Chumak? Might I help ya, sir?"

"I certainly hope so. Where in the blazes is everybody?" Symon suddenly had the horrible thought that today might be Niedziela and everyone was at the cathedral to celebrate the Sabbath. *But no, I would have heard the bells. God's bones, am I becoming both deaf and daft?*

"Ah, sorry, m'lord. I thought ya already knew. The king dismissed court early for an emergency meetin' with some special diplomat."

Sard me! It was all Symon could do to maintain his outward composure. "What...what did you just say?"

The guard, being older and wiser than most, paled just a bit. He understood the reason behind the instantaneous cold anger emanating from Symon. "It was very sudden, m'lord. Everythin' was normal-like, as tha king was hearin' petitions like any other third Witorek of tha month. But then one of tha pageboys came runnin' in an' made some sort of hand signal, an' the king—"

Symon interrupted the guard sharply. "What hand signal? Did you see it?"

"Erm...somethin' like this?" The guard stuck his halberd under his right arm and then crossed both arms across his chest with his thumbs interlocked.

The movement surprised Symon. *A church emergency?* "How sure are you of that?"

"Quite sure, m'lord. Tha boy came in through tha same door as you, so I had a clear view of him. He rushed in so quickly that he caught me eye, so I was lookin' straight at him when he made tha sign."

Symon got himself back under control. *Annoying that I wasn't told, but perhaps unavoidable given the circumstances.* "Thank you, Guard...?"

"Guard Kushnir, m'lord. Ivan Kushnir." Ivan had his halberd in hand again, and he stood at attention as he gave his name.

"Thank you, Guard Kushnir, for being alert."

"It's my duty, m'lord."

Symon smiled and put his right hand on Ivan's shoulder in a friendly manner. "Well, sirrah, you would be amazed at how many people cannot even do that."

"As you say, m'lord." The guard allowed himself a quick smile and bobbed his head in deference.

"Did you see this special diplomat?"

Ivan shook his head. "Most peculiar, m'lord. They didn't come through here. They musta been shown up tha back way."

"I see. Do you know if the king may be disturbed?"

"He directed that any of his council members be shown through only to tha inner stairway, m'lord. Justinian should be there with a message for any of ya. But he said no one was ta disturb him directly unless tha castle was on fire."

"I see. And have any other council members made an appearance?"

"Tha master builder, m'lord, 'bout a half hour ago. When I told her that she'd have ta see Justinian, she just stormed off in a huff without goin' further in."

Symon did his best not to laugh out loud at the news. *So, the king is too busy even for his doxy. Interesting indeed. And I doubt I rate above her in his desire to see anyone while he entertains this stranger. But since I am here, I might as well listen to what young Justinian has to say.*

"Very well." Symon gave a short bow, and they walked together back towards the guard's post. When they reached the doorway, Ivan wheeled and resumed his duty, while Symon passed through without another word.

Justinian was exactly where the guard had said he would be, standing at the foot of the stairway that led to the royal family's private chambers. However, he was not alone, as two knights in full armor, and with swords drawn, stood with him, one on either side of the stairs. Symon slowed his pace and kept his hands at his side. The additional guards were curious at best, and he was unsure of the situation he was walking into that required their presence. That, and he had an aversion for anyone in a suit of armor, because he never knew when they might take a swing at him. Knights inevitably had almost no line of sight when fully done up, and they certainly didn't have the mental acuity to distinguish friend from foe when not on a battlefield with banners and colors carefully laid out for all to see. Swing first, ask questions later seemed to be their standard mantra.

Justinian was alert to Symon's entrance and moved forward to meet him, a concerned expression on his face. Not even twenty, the lad had already been in his position as retainer to King Elric for over five years and had acquired the skill and grace of someone twice his age. Symon had mentioned to Jarek on several occasions that when he looked at Justinian, he saw his future replacement. They halted a pace or two apart from each other and bowed, the younger man taking pains to ensure he stooped just a bit lower than Symon. He then closed the remaining distance so that he could speak to Symon in a conspiratorial tone.

"Dragoman Chumak, I am so glad it is you and not one of the others that has arrived first. This situation is most unprecedented, and I am unsure of what to do!"

A lie, as I'm sure the king told you exactly what to do. But an appreciated lie all the same.

"The guard told me of the signal used. Is it indeed a church emergency?"

"Aye, my lord. No less than a grand inquisitor is with the king!"

Symon's eyes widened, surprised yet again. This was completely unexpected and somewhat alarming. None of his spies within the rectory had warned him that the inquisition was sniffing about the capital.

Justinian must have been thinking along the same lines, as he leaned in even closer and whispered, "My lord, it is my belief that the inquisitor came here without Archbishop Dorjan's knowledge!"

What? Is Dorjan in trouble? No, it cannot be that. He's old and harmless. He's certainly not prone to sin, either heathenistic or hedonistic.

"I see. Did you happen to catch a glimpse of his face?"

"Her, my lord. And no, not really. She was wearing the normal uniform of the inquisition, and she had a hooded cape on as well. Similar to yours, my lord, only black, and it completely hid her face. Once I showed her into the king's study, His Majesty immediately gave me my orders and dismissed me. As I was closing the door, she lowered her hood, but her back was to me."

Symon consulted his memory. *I only know of a handful of female inquisitors. Are any worthy of being called a grand inquisitor?* He had a strong suspicion he knew who it was.

"Tell me, Justinian, did you see the color of her hair?"

"Black as coal, my lord, the same as her attire. It appeared to be cut short, almost like a pageboy."

"And what was our king's reaction when she entered?"

Now it was Justinian's turn to widen his eyes. "Now that you mention it, my lord, he *smiled* at her!"

That cinched it for Symon. *It has to be her!* "Moirne. Moirne Koval!"

"You know her, my lord? When was she last here?"

"Before you started in your service to His Majesty, good sir. She is, indeed, a harbinger of momentous occasions, be they good or evil." Symon looked about the space they were in. It was obvious to him now that he wouldn't be able to see the king immediately and would need a place to wait. Unfortunately, there was nowhere readily apparent that wouldn't involve being under the steely gaze of the knights. That, and the council chambers were no doubt off limits, since they were on the second level. "I don't suppose you know how long they will be?"

The king's retainer shook his head. "I do not. Although, His Majesty ordered wine and food be brought up at Vespers, so I take it they will be a while."

Momentous occasion indeed. Symon stood silently, pondering his next move.

After a few moments, Justinian politely cleared his throat. "Beg pardon, my lord. Might I inquire as to why the grand inquisitor was here previously?"

Symon understood what the younger man was trying to do; he would have done the same in his position. He responded truthfully, at least as far as he had to.

"It was almost a decade ago now. The situation involved a delicate court matter involving a former chancellor skimming treasury funds. The inquisitor handled the issue quite exquisitely, actually."

Justinian put a finger to his cheek, tapping it as he thought. "The Chancellor Madvarious story?"

"Ah, you have heard of it. Yes, indeed, Chancellor Madvarious." Symon hadn't thought of him in a very long time, and he rather hoped it would be an even longer time before he had reason to think of him again.

The young man grew animated. "But this is an interesting new wrinkle to an old story, my lord. It is certainly not common knowledge that the church was involved in resolving the matter! Why keep it quiet?"

Symon put his arm around Justinian and turned so that it would be impossible for the knights to read his lips, even if they were capable of such a feat. He spoke in a low voice. "It was what the chancellor was spending the money on that drew the ire of the church. Although, if memory serves, the inquisitor was quite the detective and helped obtain the proof needed to accuse and convict Madvarious. The involvement of the church was kept quiet to reduce the amount of shame borne by the chancellor's wife and children, by order of the king." *Not that it did them any good in the long run.*

Justinian's eyes sparkled for the briefest of moments; he

clearly wasn't above a bit of rumormongering. "Wasn't Madvarious thrown into one of the bridge excavations and buried alive?"

Symon chuckled. "I love that little legend! It only grows better with time. No, he was strung up like a common thief, but the king did have his body cast into one of the cofferdams and buried in the silt next to one of the pier foundations. The masses loved it, as it was the building fund that he was taking money from to feed his, ah, warped proclivities. So, it was true justice in their minds."

"Next to, but not *in*, the foundation? That seems rather specific."

"Master Builder Kitko would not allow the body to be thrown into her forms. Something to do with 'unacceptable voids in the concrete' or some such nonsense."

"That woman..." Justinian hesitated, seeming unsure if he should go on.

"Yes, that woman." Symon sniffed and wrinkled his nose, as if the mere thought of her was a malodor. "She has been a stubborn mule since the day she arrived, especially when it comes to *her* bridge." Symon didn't really care what the retainer thought of the master builder, since everyone already knew of his own disdain for her, but the expression on Justinian's face was priceless. He was definitely no ally of Darnaya Kitko.

Symon took his arm off the retainer, adjusting the sleeve of his cloak. "Well, I shall need to come back later. There is no sense in waiting here."

"I will send word when the king is available, my lord.

Although it may be quite late." There was just the proper amount of regret in the young man's voice.

"Thank you, Justinian. Yes, please. Send a messenger when you can, no matter the time." Symon nodded his head slightly and turned to leave.

"Dragoman Chumak?"

"Yes?"

The retainer paused, collected himself, and then formally bowed. "Thank you for taking me into your confidence, my lord. I shall not forget it."

Symon smiled and returned the bow. *If I am indeed losing stature with our king and the rest of the council, soon it will be your confidence that I must take advantage of instead of the other way 'round.* He turned to make his way back through the throne room.

He had failed to mention to Justinian that the inquisitor was practically a family friend to the king, as strange as that sounded. This despite the many rumors that made most avoid contact with her if at all possible, even more so than the normal inquisition. *It's those damn eyes of hers,* Symon thought. *It feels as though she is looking at your naked soul the entire time you are with her.*

He had the sneaking suspicion that the inquisitor had seen the king clandestinely several times since the Madvarious incident, but there was no way to prove it. That she was a harbinger of momentous occasions was no exaggeration, and her service to the church was long and storied. So long, in fact, that no one seemed to be able to place the first time she had arrived in Velych. *Perhaps*

Dorjan knows, or at least knew at one point. I fear our archbishop has outlived his usefulness. All Symon knew was that Grand Inquisitor Moirne Koval had been making impromptu visits to the royal court of Perizidon for longer than he had been in service to King Elric. And that was longer than he usually cared to admit.

The walk back to his residence was cold, but Symon did not feel it; there was much to ponder.

CHAPTER FOUR

The Mercenary

"Sir! Sir!" Denis burst unannounced into the back room of the town hall, skidding to a stop in front of the cluttered table that Absalom had been trying to nap behind. "Ya need ta come with me at once!"

"Wha-What?" Absalom managed to not fall out of his chair as he was startled fully awake. Bleary-eyed, he looked up at the young watchman, who was breathless with excitement.

"Sheriff, please! You have ta come see what's goin' on!"

Absalom managed to gather a few thoughts together. He glanced behind the teenager, who appeared to be alone. "Come now, sirrah, what exactly is so important that you can't tell me what it is?"

"It's tha greyskin that just came in through tha north gate, sir!"

Absalom stifled a yawn, starting to become annoyed at the rude disturbance over a seemingly routine matter. "And what exactly makes this one orc so different from all the others that grace our lands?"

"It's tha body he's carryin', sir!"

"The what?!" This time, Absalom did fall out of his chair as he stood up too quickly, banging his aging knees on the table and slipping sideways to the floor as his chair scooted away to one side.

Cursing at himself, he quickly sprang up and started searching for his sword. "Nobody stopped him and asked him what his business was?"

"'Course we did, sir! But he said he was wantin' ta go to tha town hall straight away ta meet tha sheriff, so Fenris decided he'd escort him an' sent me ahead ta warn ya."

No doubt leaving the gate completely unattended! Absalom had found his sword but suddenly stopped buckling it on and looked over at Denis. "Wait a moment. You said the orc is coming here?"

"Yessir!"

"So, if he's coming here, why do I need to go with you to see him?"

The watchman paused before answering, looking confused. "Sir?"

God's teeth, they give me simpletons to work with! Absalom sighed and ran his hand through his thinning grey hair. "Never mind, Denis, never mind. I want you to go to the barracks immediately and call out the reserve. Three men are to go secure the north gate until Fenris returns, and I want the rest back here with you. Double-quick now, lad!"

"Yessir! At once, sir!" The watchman turned and ran out as quickly as he had run in.

Two scribes poked their heads around the doorway, confusion mixed with curiosity on their faces.

Absalom waved them away. "Back to work! Back to work!

Nothing to see!" He finished putting on his sword and rubbed his eyes with the palms of his hands. *What in the Almighty is going on? Regardless, there's sure to be a crowd soon if that orc is coming here.*

Making sure he also had his cudgel, Absalom walked out of his office into the main hall of the building. Being midafternoon, it was fairly empty, but he either heard or anticipated a buzz from outside.

Shite, I nearly forgot! "Pasha!" He motioned at one of the scribes he had just dismissed. "Yes, you, come here please. Go and get Sister Elise. We may need her services here. Hurry now!" *If there really is a body, she's going to need to see it.*

The public square outside the building was relatively small, only about fifty paces on each side. If it had been a bit later in the year, the space would have been packed full of local farmers selling bounty from the fall harvest, but today it was relatively free of people despite the nice weather. However, Absalom had indeed heard the murmuring of a crowd, and only a few moments after he had stepped outside, a motley rabble swung into sight, approaching from the north.

There had been little rain recently, so a light cloud of red dust hung above the crowd as they approached. At the forefront came Fenris and the other two watchmen who were supposed to be at the north gate. They were pretending to escort a large orc who was striding confidently forward, directly towards Absalom. Slung over the orc's right shoulder was a good-sized mass swathed in burlap, rope tied around the middle and both ends. The greyskin was obviously enjoying the attention.

Absalom hitched his thumbs in his belt loops and assumed an authoritative stance. He could already tell the orc was taller than him by at least half a head, and the arm that held the burlap sack in place looked muscular enough to mean business. But the guards seemed more nervous than afraid, and the noise from the crowd was one of curious anticipation as opposed to anger or fear. As the orc drew closer, he unslung the body-shaped sack and tenderly cradled it in both arms.

The stranger suddenly shifted his gaze to his left. When Absalom looked in that direction as well, he saw Denis entering the square at a run with three other watchmen trailing behind him in various states of readiness. *Good lad, that was quick indeed!* He made a quick motion at them, and the quartet moved to fall in behind him. They and the orc arrived in front of the town hall at the same time, and when everyone stopped moving, there was the briefest moment of complete silence. To Absalom, it was as if the Almighty had paused the world to paint the unfolding scene.

The orc coughed politely, and Fenris, a tad red in the face, stepped forward. "Watch Commander Undross reportin', sir! This here 'gentleman' entered tha north gate just now with a request to see tha sheriff straight away. He'd like ta report a dead body, sir!"

A ripple of murmuring went through the crowd at the last statement.

Absalom smiled at the orc and addressed him politely. "Well met, good sir! Absalom Morrow at your service. I am sheriff of Krov. Now that you have seen me, pray tell me your name and how I can help you."

The orc smiled back, showing his sharp teeth. He slowly advanced a few more steps before carefully setting the burlap sack down on the ground in front of the sheriff and his retinue. Standing back up, he bowed his head briefly and gave the king's salute, his right fist over his heart.

"Sarl Blackmoor, Yer Honor. Found this here body 'bout two leagues northeast of yer town, an' it bein' a young woman, I assumed that she might—"

"Marina? Marina!" A middle-aged woman, clearly distraught, pushed her way through from the back of the assembled mass and approached the sheriff. "Please don't tell me it's her ya found?"

The murmuring of the crowd increased, questions and comments flying. "What's that? Marina, found dead? By this stranger? Where was she found? How long she been missin' now, almost a week? Someone go an' get her uncle! How do ya know it's her in that sack? Oh, poor Yulia!"

As the woman made to kneel by the silent form, a female priest suddenly emerged from behind and to the left of the sheriff. She had the gait of a young girl, but her eyes were filled with wisdom beyond her years. Her white vestments were almost blinding in the midafternoon sun, and she made to intercept the older lady before she could put her hands on the rope entwining the bundle of burlap.

"Yulia, please! I know, my dear, I know. We are all distraught over Marina's disappearance, but we must let the sheriff do his duty. Let us hear the orc out before jumping to any conclusions!" the priestess pleaded with the other woman, holding her at bay from the body.

Yulia allowed herself to be led back a few steps as she cast a pained look in Sarl's direction. As soon as she was distracted away from the body, the priestess quickly nodded at Absalom, and he took his cue from her. He motioned to the guards behind him, and they advanced to surround the silent form laying on the ground. The sheriff noted that, if it was a dead body, there was a distinct lack of bloodstains on the burlap wrapping. He looked back at the orc, who himself was looking intently at the two women as the priestess continued to comfort Yulia.

Absalom cleared his throat. "So, Sarl, was it? You said this was a young woman?"

The orc's eyes snapped back onto him. "Yessir, that's right. Tall, flaxen hair, wearin' a dark blue gown. She had a couple thin copper bracelets on her—"

A long wailing sound erupted from Yulia as soon as she heard the description of her daughter. She could not be consoled as the crowd noise rose with exclamations of sorrow and surprise, drowning out the rest of the orc's words. Two men broke from the rest and relieved the priestess of the older woman, escorting her away. Several others surged towards the body, but Absalom immediately barked out a command. The four guards surrounding the dead girl took defensive stances, cudgels out, while Fenris and the other watchmen made to grab the men attempting to get closer.

"Good people, please! We must have order! We *shall* have order!" Absalom shouted above the noise.

While some cries continued for a bit longer, his command was heard, and the boiling mass pulled back from the edge of becoming an uncontrollable mob. The priestess had gone to the lifeless body and was now kneeling beside it, soundlessly praying. Slowly, the crowd quieted, the pushing and jostling against the watchmen lessening as the moments passed. The orc stood passively in the midst of the turmoil, arms crossed, looking at Absalom the entire time.

Absalom addressed the gathering calmly but firmly. "Thank you, my friends. Be assured, Sister Elise and I will question this stranger and determine the truth of the matter. I shall have an update for you and the mayor, hopefully yet this afternoon. If there is foul play at hand, my men and I will not rest until the issue is resolved, I swear by the Almighty! Please, now, let us do our jobs!"

A few in the crowd started to slowly disperse, but most broke into smaller groups, who stayed huddled near the center of the square. Nobody else attempted to get near the body as the priestess completed her prayers, and the watchmen visibly relaxed. The crowd was full of friends and family members, and none of them wanted to hand out bruises and bloodied noses if they didn't have to. However, they were surely as curious as the rest of the townsfolk as to what had happened. Marina had been a very popular girl, with several suitors vying for her hand, and her going missing over a week ago had been the cause of much consternation and gossip around town. The fact that none of her suitors had disappeared with her was of noted interest as well.

Absalom approached the orc, who looked down at him with a bemused look on his face. The greyskin was dressed similarly to other trappers in the region, his garments roughly made but suitable for long days in the Wilds. He only had a small satchel at his side, which made Absalom assume he had a campsite somewhere nearby. This was strange in that he couldn't recall seeing the orc before now, either drinking at a tavern or trading on tannery row. However, what invariably drew his eye was the large battle-axe strapped across the orc's back. Absalom hadn't seen it from the front as the orc had approached him, but now it was quite obvious. *Not really a trapper's first choice of a blade, that one.*

"Well, good sir, you certainly know how to make an entrance, I'll give you that. And as you just witnessed, it appears you may have solved a recent disappearance of ours in an unfortunate manner. I have some questions for you, and it'd be best if we had this conversation privately. If you don't mind, of course."

The orc's gaze drifted around the square, and he seemed to be silently counting the number of guards. Finally, he looked back at Absalom and shrugged. "'Course I don't mind! Lead the way, Yer Honor."

He grinned, showing his teeth again, and Absalom managed to keep his face calm and his stance relaxed despite the fearsome visage being quite close to his own. *Steady on, he's just trying to put you and the boys on edge. He seems smart enough not to try anything too rash.*

Fenris, who was the closest watchman to Absalom, coughed nervously. He was obviously getting skittish at being around the greyskin for an extended period of time, as if he was worried a feral dog was about to snap its leash.

"Uh, sir, what about tha body?"

"We must move it," the priestess replied for Absalom. She stood up, still inside the quartet of watchmen surrounding the corpse. She bowed slightly at Sarl. "Good sir, would you be so kind as to carry the body into the town hall for me?"

Absalom almost stopped the orc to say that some of the watchmen would carry the body instead, but then he thought better of it. Elise's idea of keeping the orc's hands full was a good one, and he watched quietly as Sarl picked up the burlap sack again.

The orc held it in both arms and looked at the priestess. "Lead on, Yer Holiness, an' take me ta where ya tend yer god's flock," he intoned.

Elise frowned. "The town hall will do for now, sir." She gestured at the building behind her and continued. "But know that all are welcome in the Almighty's house. If you care to seek solace there later, I will be happy to hear your confession."

"Well, only if ya want yer god's house hit by lightnin', Yer Holiness," the orc replied in jest, and he smiled yet again. However, he didn't show his teeth this time, and he bowed politely to her.

Elise smiled warily back at him and led the way inside the town hall.

Absalom dismissed most of the watchmen, but he kept Denis and one other with him as he hurried into the building after the priestess. As he entered the main hall, he motioned at Pasha again, who came over immediately.

Absalom addressed him quietly. "You know Artem Beligne, the tailor? Please fetch him for me, quietly if you can. That's a good lad." Having set this in motion, Absalom led the two watchmen into the back room that served as his office, after the others.

The body had already been placed on the long table, with various papers, candles, and other paraphernalia having been pushed hurriedly to the side. *Or onto the floor,* Absalom noted, somewhat vexed, but with Elise present, he did not voice his consternation. The trapper and the priestess stood opposite each other on either side of the table, and the young woman appeared to be angry or embarrassed at something the orc had just said.

"Stop it, I say!" Absalom heard her mutter in a low hiss, but he was too late to hear what had transpired.

"Is everything all right, Sister?"

"Oh, she's fine, Yer Honor," the orc said lightly. "She just don't like me sense of humor."

"Joking about defiling the dead is *not* humorous!" Elise retorted and turned away from the table to compose herself.

Absalom sighed. *Wonderful, we have a court jester to deal*

with. As an act of faith towards the orc, he took off his sword and put it in its rightful place along the back wall. When he turned back around, all eyes were upon him. The room was quiet and stuffy, and it felt isolated from the rest of reality. He bowed his head in deference to the priestess. “How would you like to proceed, Sister?”

She gave him a quick smile. “Thank you, Sheriff Morrow. Well now”—she turned towards the orc—“let’s get your particulars out of the way first. Sarl Blackwhore is your name?”

He snorted in apparent good humor. “That’d be an improvement, Yer Holiness. Nah, Black*moor* is tha name. Ya know, after a swamp an’ not a brothel.”

Denis coughed in an attempt to hide his laughter at the crude joke but then immediately went pale as he found the priestess staring directly at him. He stood at full attention, fear in his eyes.

Elise laid into him. “This is not a game, Watchman. We are dealing with a crime against one of your neighbors, one you are sworn to safeguard! I cannot guide and protect the souls of this town if we cannot also protect their earthly vessels! Would you have the death of this woman on your hands?”

“Yes, Sister! I mean, no! No, Sister! Please, Reverend Sister, I meant no insult, I—”

Absalom stepped into the conversation before the poor lad wet himself. “Denis...Watchman Kovacs! C’mon lad, you weren’t stationed a couple leagues out of town where the body was found, now were you?” He frowned at the priestess. *It’s fine to reprove him for impropriety and not knowing his place, but it's not a reason to call the wrath of the Almighty down on him! If anything, you should be sharing your ire with the bloody orc.* "Here now, take Watchman Melva with you and stand guard outside the door. You may let Artem Beligne enter, but keep those scribes and anyone else out. I'll call you if anything else is needed."

"Yessir!" Denis had recovered somewhat, but he would not look at the priestess as he made his exit.

The other watchman silently followed him out, closing the door behind him. Absalom remained looking at the door for a moment, rubbing his face. *Do not let these distractions overwhelm you when there is a death to discuss.* Settling himself, he turned to face the two remaining people in the room and addressed the orc.

"Very well, Sarl Black*moor*, you've had your fun at the expense of my man. I'd appreciate you giving your story straight and narrow so that Sister Elise and I can ascertain the truth of it."

"I got no reason ta lie, so yer work will be light," replied the orc. "Where do ya want me ta start?"

"At the beginning, of course," rejoined the priestess, somewhat testily. "Where do you hail from, and what brings you to our region?"

"I'm from tha Choros tribe, born some forty leagues east of tha Riphean Gap in tha lands of me forebearers. I learned tha ways of tha hunt as a lad an' became a trapper when I was old enough ta leave home. I've plied me trade on both sides of tha mountains fer some time now. Do a bit of paid sword work now an' then as well.

Well, axe work, really." He smirked at them, his arms crossed in a somewhat defiant pose.

"How far do you normally range?" Absalom asked.

"Eh, don't rightly know. I usually stay north an' east of here, though. An' I always stay outta Rus territory ta tha west. They don't exactly like me kind."

Absalom nodded. It made sense that a trapper would stay north for beaver pelts and other quarry. *And nobody likes dealing with those Rusgorod thugs, human or orc.*

"So, what brought you down here if it's not your normal territory?"

"Strange beasts in yer woods, Yer Honor. Them that ain't supposed to be there."

Absalom frowned. "There have been rumors of wargs nearby the past few months, ranging closer than they have for quite some time. You believe this to be true?"

"Aye, Yer Honor, I do. Seen tha wargs with me own eyes, among other things. Dangerous bastards, ta be sure. Good skins though." The orc showed his teeth again, accompanied by a dangerous-looking leer. "Fetch a nice price, with that thick fur they got. An' nobody 'round here seems ta know how ta deal with 'em, so good huntin' is what brought me south."

"So, you've been hunting nearby our town this whole summer?"

"Aye."

Absalom narrowed his eyes slightly. "Strange, then, that I

haven't seen you here getting supplies or sustenance."

The orc shrugged. "Brought what I needed fer supplies with me. As ta whatever ya mean by 'suss-tah-nahnce,' I either don't need it from ya or I can get it on my own. I weren't plannin' on comin' ta town 'til it was time ta trade pelts."

"Isn't it hard to trap wargs?"

"Why do ya think I got me warg killa strapped ta me back?" Sarl gestured at the axe with a grin, and Absalom could have sworn he flexed at the priestess in the process.

Whether or not this was true, Elise showed no visible reaction. She had been following the conversation between the two of them closely, hands folded together in front of her.

"So then, how are you doing with your hunting?"

Sarl looked at him blankly. "Well enough," he answered after a long moment.

Absalom smiled. *He must really be a trapper, or he knows enough to act like one.* "Fair enough, orc. I guess we'll see how many pelts you've collected when you come to trade." He paused, reflecting upon something Sarl had said. "What did you mean by seeing 'other things' in the forest just now? What else have you seen besides the wargs?"

The orc coughed and looked embarrassed. "Well, Yer Honor, not ta play inta any local gossip or tha tales ya tell yer young'uns, but..." He trailed off, as if debating what to say.

"Out with it, orc! We must have the full truth!" intoned the priestess. She crossed her arms and scowled at him.

"That's just it, Yer Holiness. I'll tell ya what I think I saw, an' you'll have ta decide if I'm knocked in tha head or not." He paused, then said firmly, "'Cause I'm pretty sure I saw a *vovkulaka*."

"What did you say?" A chill ran down Absalom's back, and it seemed as though the afternoon sun filtering through the high windows dimmed for a brief moment. *May the Almighty preserve us from such evil! We haven't had reports of shapeshifters in this region for several generations!* He glanced at Elise and noted she was studying the orc closely, as if trying to ascertain the status of his soul.

The orc remained silent, as if he thought Absalom's question had been rhetorical.

"Are you sure?" Absalom pressed.

"That I saw a warg stand on his back legs an' walk around like one of us? How sure would ya be?"

"He's not lying," the priestess said. "That's what he thinks he saw, at least. I believe that much."

God's bones! Could this day get any worse? Absalom looked up at the ceiling, took a deep breath, and exhaled slowly. "You saw just the one?" he asked after a few moments.

"Far as I could tell, yeah."

"How far away were you from it?"

"Not that close. 'Bout a hundred paces downwind. Tha pack knew I was huntin' them by then, so it was gettin' harder ta get close without spookin' them."

"What was it doing?" Absalom asked.

"It was pacin' back an' forth, like it was thinkin' 'bout somethin'. Then it scribbled in tha dirt for a bit with a stick 'fore it walked away into tha trees."

"And when was this?"

The orc thought for a moment. "'Bout a week ago. Maybe ten days?"

Elise broke in with her own question. "Did you go see what it wrote on the ground?"

Sarl looked at her and nodded. "Yeah, but I couldn't make out much. Might've been a map of some sort."

Absalom frowned. He didn't like this news one bit. The information wasn't nearly enough to go on and pretend it was a serious threat. But he also remembered the stories the old men would tell when he was just a boy about a supposed shapeshifter that terrorized the region for an entire summer some fifty years ago. Livestock was slaughtered every night by some unknown evil, and the search party that had been sent to investigate a vovkulaka sighting to the east of town had disappeared without a trace. Eventually, things had calmed down and the killings had stopped. He didn't rightly remember why, other than nobody had ever claimed to have gotten rid of the monster. He didn't want to start a panic, especially with the girl being just being found dead. *The girl! Shite, the girl!*

Elise must have been thinking along the same lines, as she spoke up again, this time a bit more gently. "Sarl, we must know how you came upon the girl. I assume she was already deceased when you found her?"

The orc looked down at the table that held the silent form, and for the first time, showed a bit of sadness in his features. "Aye, Yer Holiness. Poor thing was dead an' half eaten when I found her. Had figured out which one of tha pack was tha alpha, an' he kept circlin' back ta one dense hollow. Turned out his mate was there, 'bout ta give birth ta a litter of pups. That's when I saw tha body, tucked away almost out of sight. Girl musta been caught recently, seein' how wargs like ta feed their newborns fresh meat, but I guess Mum or Dad couldn't wait. Her face was eaten off, limbs torn asunder; it was a mess. There were other bones scattered about that weren't hers, so if yer missin' other folks, I imagine they wound up in tha same place." He paused, but neither human said anything about other locals potentially being dead, so he continued.

"I killed tha alpha an' his mate an' it seems like tha rest of tha pack scattered, for now at least. If that vovkulaka is real, I assume it's travelin' with them. Anyways, I figured someone would be missin' tha lass, so I wrapped her up an' brought her here."

Absalom broke his silence. "How did you know she was from here?"

"I didn't. But from what I could tell, tha girl weren't dressed like no trapper, or no trapper's woman, for that matter. She coulda been a runaway, or been kidnapped an' escaped, or was just ridin' somewhere an' lost her horse. Any number of reasons ta be lost in tha woods, right? Just hard luck tha wargs found her, I guess. But this bein' tha closest place ta where I found her that might have a lawman, it's where I aimed ta go." He looked at the priestess and grinned. "I dunno, Yer Holiness. Her bein' from here, too...maybe that's yer god guidin' me along tha right path."

Elise ignored his light taunt. "When did you find her?"

"Yesterday. Wrapped her up last night, started walkin' here this mornin'."

The priestess looked over at Absalom, her body language indicating that the overall gist of the story made sense to her. He had to agree with her unspoken thought that Sarl's narrative fit within the timeline of Marina's disappearance. All the same, by now he had observed that, while Common obviously wasn't the orc's native tongue, the trapper seemed to be using his accent to hide a certain degree of intelligence and cunning. *He's definitely playing up the role of the dumb brute. Probably gets away with it all the time. But, even so, what was Marina doing up in those woods in the first place? The orc wouldn't know that. Let's hope her uncle can shed some light on the situation.*

As if on cue, there was a minor disturbance outside the door, and an instant later, it burst open. Another grey-haired man, not quite as old as Absalom, but somewhat worse for wear, pushed his way past the two watchmen into the room. He stopped short when he saw the orc, and his eyes darted back and forth between Sarl and the bundled corpse on the table.

"What's all this about a body being found out in the Wilds? My sister-in-law is in hysterics about it being my runaway niece!" He spat his words at Absalom, completely ignoring the priestess.

"That is what we are attempting to ascertain, Artem. Sister Elise and I have been questioning this orc here, who brought the body in just a bit ago."

Artem snorted derisively. "What would this dumb-looking brute know about my niece? He's not from around here, is he? How would he even know what she looks like?"

Sarl stared back at the newcomer calmly. When he spoke, it was in his strong native tongue. "Mozhe, ya tupa, ale ty obrazhayesh chudovys'ko z velykoyu sokyroyu, suko."

Artem squinted at him. "Eh? What's that? Can't you even speak Common, dog?"

Absalom, who knew enough of the dialect the orc had used to understand "axe" and "bitch" hurried to step between the two. "Artem! Even if this isn't your niece, it's important to know who it is and what happened to them! I asked you to come to help identify the body. If it isn't Marina, then you will be free to go."

Artem waved his hand dismissively at the room. "Fine, whatever. Let's get this over with, then."

Absalom waved the two guards back out of the room and then turned to the priestess. "Sister, would you please perform the necessary act?"

"Dvadtsyat' denga, staryy vyrve, koly pobachyt' tilo!" the orc said while smiling wolfishly at Artem, his teeth fully on display. The tailor, despite the brusque bravado displayed until now, paled somewhat and took a step back.

"Tykho, vin stane v nahodi teper, koly vin tut."

Absalom raised his eyebrows in surprise as Elise calmly reprimanded the orc in his own tongue. All he had been able to process from the orc's second statement was that the greyskin wanted twenty denga for something, and he rather hoped that it wasn't for the tailor's skin. *Thank the Almighty that Elise can understand him!*

Sarl, who didn't seem quite as taken aback at the revelation that the priestess had understood him, turned back to her and formally bowed from the waist. "Yak khochesh, Sestro."

"What are they saying?" Artem hissed angrily at Absalom. "You tell her to tell him to stay away from me! That thug's got no right to threaten me, especially if he's the one who did the killing in the first place!"

Absalom wanted to slap the fool. "Do you really want your head lopped off?" he hissed back. "Do you think I could stop him from doing unspeakable things to your person if he wanted to? You are here for *one* reason, to help identify the body! Otherwise, keep your thoughts to yourself, and I will get you out of here as quickly as possible!"

Artem's face had changed colors several times as Absalom admonished him. He obviously wasn't used to being treated like this. However, this time when he glanced at the orc, the tailor apparently caught sight of his large axe for the first time. Whatever insult he was about to hurl in Absalom's direction became stuck in his teeth.

Swallowing hard, Artem instead crossed his arms and

refused to look at either Absalom or the orc. "Just get it over with," he muttered.

Elise said another short prayer over the body and then bent to undo the ropes that bound the burlap surrounding it. The knots were formidable looking, and she didn't have any tools with her. She paused to look around the room to see what Absalom might have handy. Without waiting to be asked, the orc stepped forward and, with a straight-edged hunting knife that had been strapped to his thigh, quickly cut the ropes on either end of the bundle covering, as well as where it wrapped around the middle.

The priestess wordlessly nodded her thanks, but before she could start to unravel the burlap, found her wrists being gently held by the trapper. She looked up, surprised at the action, to find him staring into her eyes.

"Careful, Sister. It ain't a pretty sight," Sarl said quietly, and then he let go. He offered up his knife to her and stepped back after she accepted it.

Having taken the knife, Elise decided to cut the burlap rather than unroll it and made an incision near where she thought the head of the corpse was located. Peeling the rough fabric back revealed there was a linen sheet underneath. It had been tightly wound around the body and was heavily mottled with dark red stains. The rusty smell of dried blood mixed with the light putrid odor of flesh just starting to bloat came wafting out into the room. She slowly cut the linen and pulled it back to reveal a nightmare.

To say it was a body was generous, as they all stared upon

chunks of flesh torn asunder, with barely any skin or whole bones left. The only semblance of this once being a human was that the remains were more or less contained inside a homespun dress, the blue color visible only in a few places. A few patches of blond hair were matted down on what they could only guess used to be the head; the entire visage had been ravaged such that only the back of the skull was in one piece.

Elise took a step back, crossing herself as she whispered a quick prayer in Latin, "Omnipotens nos protegat et haec anima caelum inveniat!"

Artem had pushed forward as the priestess worked, but when he saw the full horror being displayed, he staggered back, gagging.

Absalom had seen far too many dead bodies in his lifetime, but never one like this. He closed his eyes and recited his own prayer for the deceased under his breath. Sarl, who had bound the monstrosity up in the first place, had assumed a neutral pose with his hands in front of him, as if he was also praying for the girl. When he heard the noises coming from Artem, however, he looked up and grinned mischievously.

Absalom, recovering, went over to the tailor, who had turned away and was bent over, hands on his knees, trying to recover some sense of propriety. "Artem... I'm sorry, Artem, but we must attempt to identify the body."

"What? How in the abyss are we supposed to do that? There's nothing left to...oh..." Artem had made the mistake of looking over at the table, and he heaved again. The sour smell of regurgitated wine quickly overtook any odors coming from the corpse.

"Will these help ya?" Sarl approached them. Digging into his satchel, he produced three copper cuff bracelets and handed them to Absalom.

Accepting them, Absalom turned them over in his hands. Somewhat bent out of shape and discolored with blood, he could still see that the two thinner bracelets had a twisted pattern but otherwise were rather indistinct. The third bracelet was thicker, and it had a stamped design on its exterior. He recognized the interlocking pattern of the meander. It appeared there had been an inscription or name etched on the inside of the bracelet, but it had been scratched out.

Artem, still bent over, glanced up at Absalom and noticed the bracelets. "Where did you get those?" he asked hoarsely.

"Off tha body, or rather next ta tha body, when I recovered it," said the orc. He leaned over so that his face was level with Artem's and whispered loudly, "Please say I was tryin' ta steal them. C'mon, *suka blyat'*, say it!"

"Ah! Good sir, please!" Artem practically squealed, and he stumbled away from the trapper. "Forgive me, I meant no...it's just..." He fell to his knees in the puddle of his own spew, whimpering.

"Zalyshte yoho v spokoyi, Sarl!" Elise barked out a command from behind the table. She appeared to be trying very hard to keep her composure, and Absalom assumed she was ordering the orc to behave himself.

Sarl straightened up and took a few steps back, but he kept his eyes on the man on the floor. "Dvadtsyat' denga!" he said to no one in particular, and he slapped his open palm with his other hand as if demanding payment.

Absalom again approached Artem. He crouched down, carefully avoiding the filth on the floor, and held up the bracelets. "So, you recognize these?"

"Yes...they're hers."

"Marina's?"

Artem nodded and closed his eyes, oblivious to what he was kneeling in. "Yes, the smaller two were gifts from her parents, right before her father died. The large one, she wouldn't tell me who gave it to her, but she started wearing it a few months ago."

"Maybe one of her suitors?" Absalom hypothesized.

"I don't know, and the stubborn girl wouldn't take it off, even though I threatened to beat it off her..." Artem's voice trailed off.

A pit had formed in Absalom's stomach. The girl's death had indeed been unnatural, and if he were to bring any justice to the situation then he risked panicking the entire town. *I truly pray that she was killed quickly and did not suffer. Oh, her poor mother, she cannot be allowed to see this!*

"Who...who did this?" Artem asked. He was starting to recover his senses, as well as his rude demeanor. "She was to be married soon. I have been negotiating her dowry with Vladimir Ingvar, and he will demand answers!"

"Wolves killed her," the orc replied shortly, looking directly at Absalom as he spoke. "Pack of wolves 'bout a day north of here. They musta been rabid or just hungry, poor girl. I heard tha screamin' but they were... Well, let's just say she was dead before I got there. I killed tha wolves an' brought her body ta tha nearest settlement I knew about."

Absalom had glanced over at the priestess as the orc was speaking, and she met his eyes and nodded briefly. *Bless this orc for thinking quickly. A story based on the truth is always better than an outright lie.*

He turned to Artem to confirm the statement. "Yes, ah, that's what the orc was telling us before you arrived. Now that we know it's Marina, what we still don't know is what she was doing so far away from home. Do you have any idea?"

"How should I know?" Artem snapped as he stood up. Despite the filth on his boots and pantaloons, he was fully back to his normal, bitter self. "Head always in the clouds, never in the work at hand! Why, just the other week, she completely bolloxed up my books and would have cost me several dozen kopeks if I hadn't caught it! I didn't see her again after I banished her from my store. Maybe she decided she would run away to punish me."

I'm sure your "banishment" came with several good licks to her back, if even half the stories about you are true. Maybe she'd had enough of that, Absalom thought. "What do you mean, to punish you?" he said aloud.

The tailor snorted again in disgust. "She knew I was trying to marry her off so I wouldn't have to deal with her anymore. She certainly made no bones complaining about living under my roof, so you would have thought she would have been more grateful about what I was trying to do." He looked meaningfully at Elise as he said this, then sniffed dismissively and turned back to Absalom. "About the only trait she had that I could bargain with was her looks, though. I'm sure she thought me not being able to finalize a match for her would somehow make me lose face in the community. Ha! Just shows she had no idea about how business works."

"Yes, not a clue," Absalom said sarcastically. "And because you treated her like common livestock, instead of your own flesh and blood, she ran away, and now she's dead."

Artem turned red. "How dare you insinu—"

"Enough!" Absalom shouted the man silent. "You have done what I brought you here to do, and now I am done with you! But before you go, you will swear to the sister and the Almighty that you will say nothing of what you have seen to anyone, especially Yulia! Your niece will be buried with full church rites and will be remembered for how she lived, not how she died. Do you understand?"

"Well, I—"

"*Do you understand?*" It had been a very long time since Absalom had been this angry. He gripped the cudgel at his side as if he were going to break it over the other man's head if he did not comply.

Artem's eyes bored into him, and for an instant, it seemed as though he would attempt to tell him off. Absalom glared back until the tailor finally looked away and bowed his head.

"Yes, I understand," he said grimly. "I won't say anything about the little shrew!" Without looking at anyone, he turned and scuttled out of the room.

Absalom slammed the door behind him, still fuming. *The worst part of this is that, once he calms down, he'll realize he can keep the dowry money that Marina's father left her as his own. The bastard will make out regardless.*

Sighing, and forcing himself to be calm, he turned to face the room once more. Invariably, his eyes were drawn to the human remains on the table. He shook his head at the sight and then asked the orc a question that had been bothering him ever since the linen sheet had been pulled back.

"How could you tell this was a woman, let alone a young woman?"

Sarl actually rolled his eyes. "I assume ya ain't got too many men 'round here wearin' dresses, do ya?"

"Well, no, but—"

"An' she wasn't wearin' a bonnet or wimple, least as I could tell. So, she was either an unmarried lass or a whore, an' I figured I'd be nice an' not call her a whore in front of everybody when I brought her in. Unless you're missin' some whores too?"

"That's enough!" Elise snapped. "I will not have you denigrate the deceased!"

"He started it!" The orc protested as a child would.

"Enough! Let the dead rest in peace!"

Absalom remained calm. *The orc's lying about something, but no matter. He didn't kill the girl, that much I believe. Almost everything else about this situation smells wrong. But Elise obviously doesn't see the need to press matters, and that wretch of a man, Artem, doesn't give even two denga about his niece. A sad state of affairs all around, and we still have the wargs to deal with.* But as he continued to look at the corpse, a way forward was forming in his head.

"As you say, Sister, let us put Marina to rest. I would ask that you visit Yulia as soon as possible and break the news as gently as you can. You must find a way to convince her that she should not view the body. It would be the death of her."

Elise nodded. "Yes, I will go to her immediately. And you are, of course, correct. She cannot see the body."

Absalom turned to the orc. "Good sir, I have no real sway over you, and I would ask for your assistance, rather than try and threaten your compliance. Would you be a partner with us in a game of deception? Your wolf story is as good as any that I could come up with, although I suggest a slight modification. We should say that, after closer inspection, we believe the girl broke her neck in a fall, and then you came upon the wolves savaging her corpse. I prefer that over causing undue panic with stories about wolves attacking humans directly, let alone saying anything about wargs and shapeshifters." He glanced at Elise. "I can handle that imbecile, Artem, if he dares say anything to the contrary."

Sarl shrugged. "Sure, I'll follow yer lead. That *malen'ka pyzda* that ya brought in deserves a beatin', so what do I care what he thinks? Doubt he'll say much 'bout anythin' after flayin' all over himself."

Absalom sighed inwardly, greatly relieved. "Thank you."

The orc continued. "Besides, it's not like anyone 'round here will be able ta pester me 'bout what happened. I'm gone as soon as we're done here."

"But what shall we do about the wargs, Sheriff Morrow?" asked the priestess. "They are still a real threat, are they not?"

He thought for a moment. "Well, we can use the wolf story to our advantage. Even they could cause problems if they are hungry enough. We will have patrols extend out from the town into the adjacent farmlands for safety. I'm sure I can muster some volunteers to provide extra manpower, at least until the harvest season is upon us. People will just need to tend to their livestock a bit more carefully for the time being. As for the vovkulaka…" He thought for a few moments more and then looked at the orc.

"Your story is not strong enough for me to raise the alarm about a shapeshifter being in our midst. But"—here he turned towards Elise—"I would ask that you provide protective wards that can be placed on the town gates and also on the doors of any homestead within half a league of town. We can say they are just a precaution against the wolves, in case there is a greater evil that drives them. That, I am afraid, will have to do for now, and I will pray that it is enough."

Elise nodded again. "I will think of something to say on the matter to the townsfolk and will prepare the wards on the morrow."

"Very good," Absalom said wearily, and he turned back to the orc. "I assume you intend to continue to hunt the pack for their pelts?"

"Aye, Yer Honor, least until I know they've left tha area, or if there really is a shapeshifter runnin' around with them."

"So be it. I will have papers drawn up that indicate a bounty has been issued by the Town of Krov for dealing with the wolf threat. That will provide support to our story if anyone does ask about what has happened here."

Elise cleared her throat. "Actually, Sheriff Morrow, if you do not have an objection, then I would instead make it a holy order. That would allow our trapper here to request aid from the church in hunting down the wargs, regardless of what county or parish he finds himself in."

This seemed a bit much to Absalom, but he reasoned it couldn't hurt if the rumor of a prowling vovkulaka gained traction. "Very well, Sister. You will handle this?"

The priestess nodded. "Yes, I can have the warrant drawn up yet today."

"Good." He eyed the orc once again. "I do not have any further questions for you. Do you have any, Sister?"

The priestess seemed about to say something, but then looked away and simply said, "I do not."

"Very well. Sarl Blackmoor, you are free to go, as soon as Sister Elise provides you with the documentation we have just discussed. May I ask, will you head back to your camp as soon as possible, or will you spend the night in town?"

"How's tha tavern by tha north gate? I might stop there for a drink before leavin' town."

"Ah, the Dancing Bear. The ale is good enough there. Actually," Absalom said, smiling cordially, "tell Master Beringer that Sheriff Morrow sends you with his compliments and that your meal is on my tab. Uh, within reason, of course."

Sarl grinned, and he didn't show his teeth this time. "That's mighty proper of ya, Yer Honor." He bowed deeply to both of them. "I'll be headin' there now."

***

That evening, Elise made her way to the front of the church sanctuary, kneeling at the altar rail. She was tired from the day, both physically and spiritually, and she was truly eager for respite. The meeting with Yulia had not gone well, but in the end, she had been able to deliver a modicum of closure for the poor woman. She bowed her head and began to recite an ancient prayer of petition.

"Almighty One, Thou alone art good, just, and holy; Thou canst do all things, Thou accomplishest all things, Thou fillest all things. Remember Thy mercies, and fill my heart with Thy grace, Thou who wilt not that Thy works should be void and in vain. Turn not Thy face away from me; withdraw not Thy consolation, lest my soul become as a thirsty land to Thee..."

In time, she completed the ritual and rose to retreat to her chambers. As she turned, however, she caught sight of a large, dark mass sitting in a pew, just outside the light of the candles near the altar. Her heartbeat quickened just a bit, and she immediately walked down the aisle until she was abreast of the interloper.

"You came..."

"I did, Sister. Just proves yer right, yer god lets anyone inta their house." The orc looked up and around. "I'm still waitin' on tha lightning, tho."

She let the gibe pass. "I am happy to see you, Sarl. And to speak with you alone." She expected another sarcastic response, but this time, there was only silence in return. After a few awkward moments, she continued. "Thank you for all your help. I don't know what we would have done without you. Were you able to see Marina on her way?"

The orc leaned forward, but it was still difficult to read his features in the low light. "Yeah, this mornin' before I came inta town. She an' Ruga should be far ta tha southwest by now. With luck, they'll disappear inta tha crowds in Myste within a couple weeks."

"I hope that they continue their flight even farther away from here. Ruga promised me he had secured passage all the way to Kostantine."

The orc nodded. "Mmm, good. More of me an' Ruga's kind

there, nobody'll care at all 'bout them bein' a mixed couple."

"And with any luck, Ruga leaving two weeks ago keeps any rumors at bay about her being alive and them being together," Elise mused.

"I don't think anybody knew he was sweet on her. Tha girl, on tha other hand, from what I could tell, she was a sardin' mess and could barely keep her mouth shut 'bout him."

Elise nodded. "Something like that..." Marina had confided with the priestess several months ago that she had a secret orc lover and that she thought her uncle was getting suspicious. When Artem had boasted to the girl about the arrangements he was making with the Ingvar family to marry her off, she had come to Elise begging for help. *Her urgent cry for assistance started the chain of events that has now unfolded fully. But I can't tell anyone that, not even you.*

It was as if he read her mind. "Don't worry, Sister. I won't try an' make ya break yer vows. Least not that one." There was a low rumble of a chuckle, and Elise blushed in spite of herself.

She rushed on, hoping that he couldn't tell that he had rattled her. "The body...what did you wind up using?"

"Tha corpse of a warg, like we talked 'bout. It was a mess skinnin' it an' makin' it look human, tho. I'm glad tha others didn't get too close."

"Yes, the Almighty was with us. I do feel badly for leading Absalom astray, as he is a good man. But he would not have understood the situation." Elise knew she would have to atone for deceiving the honorable sheriff at some point in the future.

"Mmm, if ya say so."

She paused and then asked a completely frivolous question. "So, I must know. What was harder for Marina to give up, her hair or her bracelets?"

The orc gave her one of his familiar smirks. "Whaddya think?"

"Her hair!" *That girl is too vain for her own good!*

He laughed heartily. "Definitely! Poor Ruga, he had ta hold her hands so she wouldn't grab tha shears away from me. Prolly didn't help that I told her that she would look good bald when I—"

"Sarl! You did not say that!"

"What? I was just jokin' with her, but then I guess Ruga shouldn't have laughed. I may have cost him a night in tha sack."

"You're incorrigible."

"Aye, Sister, that I am." He looked at her and started to say something, then seemed to change his mind. "Anyways, she got happy again when she knew for sure she was leavin' here. She wanted me to thank ya for all ya done for both of them."

"I just told her to follow her heart," Elise said without thinking.

"So, do as ya say then, an' not as ya did yerself?" There was a sudden edge to the orc's voice.

Elise visibly winced. *I deserve that.* She desperately wanted to put herself in his arms and hide from the world, but she was afraid of what he would do. *Am I more worried that he would push me away or that he would carry me off with him?*

"Sarl..." She couldn't go on.

He looked at her intently for a few moments and then sat back in the pew, staring at the front of the chapel. She stood silently next to him, not knowing what to say, feeling very small.

The orc finally broke the silence. "So, Yer Holiness, looks like yer still married ta yer god, eh? Not sick of them yet?" His tone was nonchalant, but even in the gloom, she could see the tightening of his chest.

Elise sighed deeply, feeling guilty about the situation she had created so long ago. She slowly reached out and gently placed her hand on his arm. His skin was cool to her touch. He visibly shuddered but did not pull away.

"Sarl...my dear *Siryy Vovk*, we both know I cannot give you what you want."

He placed his hand over hers, cupping it tenderly. He didn't look her in the eyes, and when he spoke, he couldn't say her name. "I know, *Soloveyko*, I know."

She smiled faintly at the childhood nickname he had given her many years and many leagues away from the here and now. But the memories just made the moment that much harder. *My father is dead, and my mother doesn't even remember my name, yet I still bind myself to the oath I swore to them.* She felt like screaming until the roof of the church collapsed in on them both. Instead, words started rolling out of her mouth in a rush.

"I'm so glad you were already nearby, Sarl, and that you

would still heed a message from me, but I am truly sorry to get you involved in all this. I understand if you feel like I'm using you, but I just didn't know where else to turn when Marina came to me and— Ow!"

Sarl had squeezed her hand tightly, then let go as soon as she protested. He rose quickly to his feet, his looming size threatening to overwhelm her. When he looked down at her, she could only see the outline of his head, the darkness surrounding them making it impossible to discern the features of his face.

"Please, *Soloveyko*, you'll only make it worse if ya keep talkin'."

She knew him well enough to know he was not purposefully trying to shame her, but she looked down and away all the same. *Surely, he knows how special he is to me? That I long to see him happy and whole? That if the world was different… Oh, go sard yourself, Elise!* She looked back up at him. "I'm sorry, Sarl," was all she could say.

He sighed, adjusting his satchel as he spoke. "No worries, Sister. Ya know me, I'm always yers ta command. Besides, if I didn't have any hope left in us workin' out, I wouldn't let ya find me, now would I?"

"I know that…" *And I also know that someday you will rid yourself of that talisman I gave you, along with your thoughts of me. When that happens, I will have to bear that pain as my penance for all the suffering I have caused you.* She hated feeling sorry for herself, but the mood enveloped her.

"Ya got that warrant ya mentioned to tha sheriff ready ta go?"

"The... Oh! Yes, I do." She quickly went to retrieve a small document from a lectern that was between the altar and the pews, quietly handing it over to Sarl when she came back.

He placed it in his satchel without looking at it. Elise nervously played with a loose strand of thread on her tunic as he made ready to leave.

"Where will you go now?" What she really wanted to ask was *When will I see you again?*

"Back north, most likely. Gotta see if I can find that vovkulaka an' then—"

"Wait, what? That part of the story you told Absalom was *true*?" She looked at him in complete shock.

He looked back at her, the candlelight from the altar making his eyes shine in the dark. Elise imagined she was looking at the red eyes of a warg instead of Sarl's pale green ones and shivered at the thought.

"Don't rightly know, Sister, but I'm pretty sure I saw what I saw. I do think that somethin' or someone is drivin' those wargs. I'll track 'em ta see what I find, an' if need be, I'll get word back ta ya an' that sheriff of yers." He patted his satchel. "Yer paper may come in handy more than ya thought."

"Yes." She bit her lip, worried about old wives' tales coming to life. *And here I thought dealing with wargs was bad enough! But the shapeshifter might be real as well?* She subconsciously crossed herself.

Sarl continued talking, apparently oblivious to her rising fear. "I do have pelts ta trade; that part of tha story is also true. If I can't find nothin' else out there, I'll take care of them shortly. But I figure I better head ta Velych ta trade 'em instead of comin' back here, in case someone gets suspicious. Better prices in tha capital, anyways."

"Very well. I..." She was at a loss for words. There was just too much to digest. Finally, she blurted out, "Just, please take care of yourself. You know I worry about you." Her statement sounded flat and lame, even to her, but she didn't know what else to say.

"You too, Yer Holiness. You too." He took her hand and kissed it, bowed deeply, and then turned away.

"Sarl!"

She called out to him after he had taken just a few steps, unable to contain her longing for him. He stopped and slowly turned as she ran to him and, like a small child, held out her arms. He bent over to embrace her fully, inhaling deeply as he did so, as if he meant to consume her very essence. She had purposely worn lavender oil in the hopes of seeing him tonight, and he could hold her forever as far as she was concerned. After a time, her habit fell away, allowing her long, tawny hair to collapse around her face, strands tickling his nose. Her tears were hot, and her eyelashes fluttered against his cheek as she tried to blink them away.

Finally, Elise broke her grip around Sarl's neck. He released her gently, but before he could straighten completely, she quickly kissed him on the cheek. “Thank you,” she said huskily, and then she turned and hurried away, back up the aisle towards the altar of her master.

CHAPTER FIVE
The Inattentive Soldier

Dane stifled a yawn and thought again about how much he hated guard duty. Yes, of course it was an honor to be picked for a royal posting, especially for someone his age. If the season was a bit farther along towards the Koleda holiday, then he would be grateful to be out of the cold. But the day was unseasonably warm, and he longed to be outside and doing something, anything, besides guarding an empty room. Bohdan was probably slacking off in the stables right now, gambling away whatever money he had at passe-dix or some other dice game. Dane didn't mind if his friend lost all his denga, but he did mind if Bohdan was losing it to someone other than him. He pulled at the high collar of his jerkin and wondered if, by chance, he had missed hearing the bells at Sext that would have meant his shift was more than half over.

"Ssst! Steady on, ya idiot!" Caleb, the guard on the other side of the entryway, had noticed Dane's squirming and was now throwing an evil glance his way. "The cap'n catches you goin' on like that, we're both in for it!"

Caleb, several years older and infinitely better at standing still than Dane was, wasn't wrong. The captain meted out punishment equally on the guilty and the innocent when it came to minor offenses. His rationale was that either everyone was guilty and he had only caught one person in the act of transgression, or the supposedly guiltless individual hadn't tried hard enough to stop whatever misdeed had transpired. There was always armor to polish or chamber pots to clean, and the maids were quite happy to let some poor guard take over their duties for a spell. These forms of collective punishment did have the desired effect of incentivizing the soldiers to police themselves regarding such issues as hygiene and petty theft, but it also led to the more clumsy or stupid individuals being ostracized.

Dane was neither clumsy nor stupid, but he was known to be caught with his mind fixated on anything other than what he had been told to do. This made him a huge liability to the other soldiers when it came to pulling duty with him, as they would invariably pay for his inattentiveness. Lots had been drawn that morning to see who would stand guard with him, and Caleb had lost, despite protesting this was the third time in less than a fortnight he had been stuck with Dane. The first two assignments had not gone well, and Caleb had loudly announced to everyone in the barracks that he would be damned if the little piece of shite made him do extra chores for a third time.

"He's gonna stand at attention for tha whole shift if I have ta impale him on a bleedin' poleaxe!"

Dane sighed. He had been sitting just two beds down from Caleb when the threat was made. He didn't hold any additional animosity towards his irate partner, mainly because he knew everyone else felt pretty much the same about him. If only the army could see some real action instead of just parading around the city and standing in front of doors, he knew he'd be the best soldier in the entire brigade. After all, wasn't he the best swordsman in his company? Give him a shot at fortune and glory, and he'd be a knight in no time!

He nodded slightly at Caleb and attempted to straighten himself into position again. He grasped his halberd with his right hand more tightly, wedging the butt of the weapon into a worn groove in the stone floor and leaning into it slightly for support. Another guard had showed him this trick the first time he had been placed at this particular station, and it certainly helped take pressure off his back. Dane didn't necessarily care if he got the older boy in trouble or not, but personally, he had better things to do this afternoon than waste time being disciplined by the captain. If only he could shut his eyes for a brief moment, he might be able to endure the boredom.

It didn't help that he didn't know what the point was for having guards at this location inside the keep. The two of them were on the second floor, roughly halfway down the main hallway with stairs at one end. The throne room was immediately beneath them; it would take only a few moments to run there if an alarm were raised. But there were always at least two knights already in the throne room when court was in session, and they could certainly handle any issue more quickly and efficiently than anyone at this location. Moving ever further out, there were guards at the entrance to the keep, guards at the main gate to the castle, guards at all of the city gates, and guards along the city walls. Guards everywhere, and in Dane's opinion, nowhere were they less important than where he was standing right now.

The king's council room, which also served as the royal map room, took up most of one side of the second floor of the keep, and it was at this doorway that Dane and Caleb stood on either side. Dane reasoned it made sense to post guards here when a meeting was ongoing with the king or other important officials. But then, the one time he had been present when the council was in session, the guards had been moved away from the chamber to the end of the hallway near the stairs. This was supposedly to keep anyone from entering the floor unannounced, but Dane suspected it was also to remove the temptation to eavesdrop. Regardless, the fact that guards stood immediately next to the chamber when it was empty, and not when it was in use, made no sense to him at all. Barely anyone came to this floor anyway.

Dane knew there were probably even more guards higher up in the keep. There would definitely be guards up there at night when the royal family took their rest. But he had never been higher than the second floor. Only the longest-serving and most-trusted soldiers were allowed access to the upper floors. They, at least, served a purpose in keeping assassins and lovers out of the royal bedchambers. Dane smirked inwardly. *Unless the guards themselves are the lovers.*

A thin film of sweat covered his face. If only there was some movement of air. On some days, there was a nice breeze from the window openings in the chamber room, but today the warm sun outside had not brought any wind with it. Dane quickly wiped his brow with his left hand. Luckily for him, the gesture was on the opposite side of where Caleb stood motionless, and he did not appear to see it. *Maybe he's dozing off too?* Dane wondered. He knew some soldiers could sleep at attention, somehow maintaining both their balance and cadence of breath so that they weren't caught. He licked his lips and fought the urge to shout obscenities at the top of his lungs.

Maybe a spy or an assassin could gain entry to the throne room unobserved, past all the other guards? Or perhaps some noble was up to no good, colluding with an unsavory character from afar? When all others failed, perhaps this post was to be the last resort, the final bastion of protection from the kingdom's enemies.

That must be it! He saw it in his mind's eye now... *He would be called upon to save the king from a plot most foul. The Kingdom of Rusgorod, desperate to sow disorder and ruination, would send a most beautiful and charming lady to call upon the royal court of Perizidon. All the courtiers would swoon at her feet as she moved gracefully through the room, her perfume acting as a pleasant distraction, dulling senses and reaction times. She would put out her hand to one of the smitten knights as she approached the throne so she could mount the steps more easily. The king would be frozen in place, mesmerized by her flashing green eyes and her supple breasts, all the while wondering where such a wonderful creature had been all his life.*

Too late, the knights would realize the scheming wench was reaching for a brightly colored hairpin, not knowing, but perhaps sensing, it was coated with the deadliest of poisons. And now she leapt at the helpless ruler, wielding the hairpin like a dagger and bringing it down, down, down towards the exposed neck of her victim!

But, somehow, he, Dane Oldenfeld, alone had sensed something was wrong and had already dashed downstairs. He would ignore Caleb's surprised oaths and the trail of the assassin's perfume that had rendered all others helpless in its wake. Entering the throne room, he might stumble over a collapsed lady-in-waiting, but somehow would maintain his balance as he lurched towards the throne and the would-be killer. At the last moment, he would reach for her wrist and stop her blow from—

"Ya sardin' cock! What's wrong with ya?!"

Dane was rudely brought back to reality as the shaft of Caleb's halberd hit him squarely across his nose. Immersed in his daydream, he had almost let his own halberd drop to the floor, and now he fumbled at it with both hands as searing pain shocked him fully awake.

Blinking back tears and red in the face, Dane whirled to face Caleb, who had already returned to attention, his own features as pale as ghost. "Why'd you do—" Dane started to yell back at his antagonist but then froze midsentence. He could hear the footsteps and female voices coming from the stairwell, no doubt what Caleb had been attempting to warn him about. *God's nails!*

Dane arranged himself as best he could and came to

attention just as two figures rounded the corner.

It's the princess! Dane's emotions somersaulted over themselves as he caught sight of her out of the corner of his eye. He continued the struggle to maintain his composure, albeit for a reason other than having been just smacked in the face. *Steady on, boy! Remember, she's above your station. Way above your station!*

Love was a dangerous word, but Dane knew that *any* feelings he might have for the princess were dangerous due to their respective ranks in life. He rarely saw her, even when he was assigned to duties in and around the castle, but he had been infatuated with her for over a year now.

At the brink of womanhood, she was perhaps two years younger than him, but he had felt like a helpless child the two times he had been in her immediate presence. He was embarrassed to admit to himself that the beautiful assassin in his flight of fancy had been an older version of the princess. *Ah, Almighty One, get a hold of yourself!*

He swallowed hard and tried to focus on nothing but the grey stone wall opposite him.

Both men remained motionless as Lianne approached. She was in deep conversation with her female companion, and the two of them ignored the guards completely as they came down the hallway, stopping just outside the door to the council room.

"Do you understand me, Mel?" the princess asked.

The other girl, who appeared to be near the same age as the princess but was obviously a servant, nodded her head vigorously.

"Yes, m'lady. Ya wants me ta—"

Lianne coughed sharply and glanced at the guards for the first time, shaking her head slightly, while acknowledging their presence. She looked back at her servant, and Dane could have sworn that she winked at her.

"Yes, Your Highness," her companion immediately rejoined, grinning widely. She curtsied to her mistress and then stepped past the guards into the room.

Neither one of them thought to challenge her.

Princess Lianne looked squarely at the two soldiers now, inspecting them both in turn. As she took in Dane, he couldn't help but blush as her eyes flashed across his countenance. If she noticed his red face or the welt he could feel forming on the bridge of his nose, she made no mention of them.

"I don't know you, Soldier. You are...?"

It took a moment before Dane realized she was addressing him directly. The color instantly drained from his face, and it was all he could do to keep his eyes looking forward.

"Part of the first brigade, Your Highness, assigned by Captain—"

"Your name, Soldier," Lianne broke in gently. "I would just like to know your name."

"Uh..." For the briefest of moments, his mind went blank, but he recovered before making a complete fool of himself in front of his future queen. "Dane Oldenfeld, Your Highness!" Unsure of what to do next, he erred on the side of formality and performed the king's salute. "I live to serve!"

The princess bowed slightly at the waist in response. Her face remained calm, but there was a twinkle in her eye as she addressed him again.

"Well met, Guard Oldenfeld. Tell me, is this your first assignment within my father's castle?"

"No, Your Highness!" Dane hesitated. He wasn't sure if she wanted a detailed accounting of his postings from the past several months or if she wanted to be reminded that he had been part of her security detail in the past. He rightly decided she did not.

"I see. Well, I shall endeavor to remember your name for the future, Dane Oldenfeld."

Dane wasn't sure what to say in response to this, and he was somewhat tongue-tied by the fact that her perfect lips had just formed themselves around his name. He said nothing and continued to stare straight ahead.

After a brief pause, Lianne turned towards Caleb. "Guard...Taykas, is it not? Caleb Taykas?"

"Yes, Yer Highness." If Caleb hadn't been standing fully at attention already, he was doing so now.

Lianne smiled. "Excellent. Guard Taykas, remove yourself and your companion to the end of the hallway by the stairs. Master Gregor will be arriving shortly, and you are to stay at that position until we are done in here." She gestured at the room behind them. "We are not to be disturbed unless there is a dire emergency."

"As Yer Highness commands." Caleb bowed his head briefly,

as did Dane.

Lianne didn't bother with formally dismissing them and instead walked gracefully into the chamber room without another word. After a brief pause, they both turned and marched in unison down the hallway.

How does she know Caleb already? He's barely had any more assignments in here than I've had! Dane reached the stairwell and did an about-face, managing to find another groove in the floor where he had come to attention. *And what would be considered a dire emergency, anyway?*

Suddenly, he smiled to himself. *Perhaps the dirty Rus have sent a handsome rogue to kill the princess instead of her father. They intend to murder the heir to the throne of Perizidon! Maybe this scoundrel, Caleb, is the assassin! That's it, I'm here to watch him! I may yet save the day and the kingdom...*

CHAPTER SIX

The Not-So-Good, The Bad, and The Ugly

Uptar sat by the fire, warming his hands. Glancing behind him briefly, he noted the mountains to his east were caught in the rays of the setting sun, their peaks tipped with the dazzling whiteness of perpetual snow. It wasn't too cold just yet where he was sitting, but the clear sky overhead foretold a chilly night. At least there wasn't much wind, just enough to ever so slightly sway the copse of fir trees where he had set up camp.

Turning back to face westward, from his vantage point he could see several other campfires dotting the hillside all around. Each fire formed an individual dome of light within the gathering darkness. It was as if the entire party had decided they had had enough of each other's company during the day's hike and needed to be alone with their own familial groups. Uptar assumed all the singles had gone off to get drunk together by the stream at the foot of the hill. As long as they kept quiet, he didn't care what they did or where they were. It was too nice of an evening to worry about anybody else.

The coneys he had caught earlier that afternoon were just about ready to eat, the fat dripping from them into the fire, creating small flareups every few moments. The makeshift spit was almost charred through, and he had to be careful removing it from above the flames, so as not to drop any of the meat into the coals.

Unfortunately, they had run out of potatoes a few days ago, so the berries that Vesna had foraged would have to do as their only side dish.

There was rustling in the underbrush to his right, and he knew without looking that Vesna was returning from her evening toilet. She had been uncharacteristically quiet during the last hours of hiking and while they set up camp, but she graced him with one of her crooked smiles as she approached, her eyes looking appreciatively at the rabbit meat. They ate in silence, content with each other's company.

As the night closed in and the fire burned low, Uptar's eyes adjusted to the darkness and he laid back, looking up at the stars and attempting to establish the group's location. They had hiked a few leagues northwest that day, still hugging the mountain range on their right. He and several others had scouted ahead, and no settlements, or even lone homesteads, had been discovered. Harah, the group's de facto leader, had decided that additional scouts would be sent out tomorrow while the group held fast where they were. They might have just found a piece of wilderness they could call their own. There was quiet optimism around all the campfires tonight that the group was on the cusp of transitioning from fugitives to settlers.

Vesna laid down next to him, snuggling close and putting her head on his chest. He absentmindedly stroked her hair, bringing strands of it close to his face. It smelled like pine when he inhaled deeply. She shifted slightly, and her weight made the talisman tied around his neck press into his chest, caught between their bodies. Wincing at the minor irritation it made on her cheek, Vesna lifted her head, and with her long fingers deftly undid the top of his tunic so she could root out the stone. It seemed to throb with a reddish hue as she raised it up to look at it in the dying light of the fire.

Winking slyly at Uptar, she kissed the glowing gem and let it drop back onto his chest. It felt so hot on his skin that he could have sworn it was part of the sun. He moved to pluck it away, but she intercepted his hand and pushed it up and away over his head, her hand encircling his wrist like a manacle. The intensity of the stone's pulsations was encompassing him, penetrating him, burning him, but rather than flinch away, Vesna moved on top of him to envelop herself in the heat that was emanating from his body. He could taste her as she kissed him deeply and desperately, undressing both of them as she did so.

Her hips shifted, and now Uptar was inside her, the whole world suddenly ablaze. She was all he had ever cared for, and everything else was lost in the blinding light and searing heat that cascaded outward from their union. Vesna swayed above him in ecstasy, wanting more of him, wanting all of him, and he laughed and cried at the joy she brought him in return.

Lightning flashed in the hot, white sky above them, and it stretched to the horizon, creating jagged lines like cracks in a sheet of ice. Suddenly, the sky started to splinter around the cracks, flecks of black appearing amid the brilliant light. As the darkness grew rapidly, they both looked up in alarm, all blissful thoughts cast aside. Shards of the sky began to rain down around them, and Vesna raised her hands to protect her head, her mouth open in a silent scream. Uptar tried to shield himself, as well, but found he was fused in place, as if his body had melted into the ground beneath them. He struggled to unpin his shoulders as he stared helplessly into the forming void.

Time stood still, and the world turned upside down. They began to fall into what once was the sky, their bodies wrenched apart by some force stronger than gravity. Uptar could move again now that he was free from the earth, and he desperately grabbed at Vesna as she fell away. She was moving so much faster than he was, and she reached up back toward him, panic in her eyes, her mouth still open, as if she was calling his name. He couldn't hear her, and then he realized with a sickening shudder that he couldn't remember what her voice sounded like. His own screams tried to bridge the growing distance between them and failed.

Vesna hit the surface of the void and disappeared beneath it with barely a trace, only ripples expanding outward from where she had entered. The ripples grew until the surface was surging with foam-tipped waves, making it impossible to see where she had entered. The dark waves reached out to Uptar as he accelerated downward into their midst.

The cold water hit his face like a stone wall. He gasped for air, not knowing which direction to go. If he could just find her, then all else would be bearable. He struggled towards what he thought was the surface and—

"Hit him again!"

Uptar heard someone give the order immediately before a wave of water overwhelmed him. He spluttered and choked, coming back to the land of the living. Only now did he realize it hadn't been a wave, but rather the remains of a bucket of filth.

He shifted to his side, looking up at the two forms he could vaguely see standing over him. Soiled straw mixed with the now-muddy floor that he lay prostrate upon, caking him in grime. The dream had felt so real this time, and he struggled to return to reality.

The forms came into focus, revealing themselves to be a male and female human. They looked to be soldiers of some type, and it was then that he realized he was in a fetid jail cell.

The female smirked at him. "Awright, he's finally awake! Sorry ta wake ya so rudely, yer highness, but tha sheriff wants ta see ya!" She waited for a beat before sticking a well-aimed toe of her boot into Uptar's solar plexus. "C'mon now, luv, we ain't got all day."

The spasm of pain brought him fully back to consciousness, and he rolled away from the humans holding him captive before raising himself into a sitting position. He looked at them warily.

"Well, c'mon, up ya go! 'Less ya wanna real beatin' now?" The woman, clearly the jailer in charge, made a sign to the other human as she spoke, and he dropped the bucket and made to take out an ugly-looking cudgel that was hooked to his belt.

Uptar knew he could take them, but what good would it do? Some momentary satisfaction, followed, no doubt, by a bunch more guards laying into him with their clubs and swords. He needed to figure out why he was stuck in jail before deciding he needed to break out of it. *An' where's that shite Umuk, anyway?*

Glowering, Uptar slowly rose to his feet, wiping some of the muddy straw off his body. At full height, he stood a good head over both humans, and the male guard subconsciously took a step back.

The jailer apparently hadn't been on duty when Uptar had been unceremoniously dumped in his cell the night before, and she paused for a moment as she literally sized him up. "Right...Borys, get tha shackles fer this one."

"Yes'm! Ya want 'em fer 'is ankles, 'is 'ands, or both?" The guard's Common was almost guttural, and Uptar could barely understand him.

"Go with hands only. We'll see if his highness wants ta play nice." The jailer had seemed to guess correctly that he was unsure of his current status. "Let's see what tha sheriff wants done with him."

Gods, it would feel so good ta crack some skull! Uptar did his best to look placid.

In due course, he was restrained and led out of the small cell. He couldn't tell exactly where he was, although he assumed it was somewhere in the town hall of whatever settlement he and Umuk had stumbled into the night before. When they had walked through the main square, he had been surprised that the building was two stories, not to mention that it was constructed out of stone. It meant local money, craftmanship, or both were present at a level higher than expected this far out in the Wilds. *Prolly what made Umuk think makin' a play for tha tavern's money box was worth tha risk, sardin' idiot that he is.*

He was led up a set of stairs onto the second level of the building, passing several soldiers who gave shoddy salutes to the jailer. At the top of the stairs, Uptar found himself in a large room with four windows that opened out towards the town square. He was indeed in the town hall, and he guessed it to be sometime early in the morning based upon the angle of the shadows being cast outside.

A middle-aged man of average build was looking out of the far-right window, arms folded across this chest. He turned towards Uptar and his keepers as they entered, and he looked Uptar up and down with a sense of familiarity.

Uptar was halted in the middle of the room several paces away from the man, who he assumed was the sheriff. The jailer and Borys saluted the man and stepped back, staying in the room between Uptar and the door they had just come through.

"Name?" The sheriff's voice was mild-mannered but expectant of receiving an answer.

Uptar just stared back at the man, noting the long sword on his right hip and short dagger on his left. His leather jerkin had seen some action in the past, but overall, seemed to be in good shape. This was no one to be trifled with, as it was clear that he expected trouble.

"Kira, don't he speak Common?" The sheriff looked past Uptar's shoulder at the jailer.

"Think so, sir. Report says he an' his friend were orderin' ale well enough last night at Bainor's. That an' he followed instructions good enough just now."

The sheriff returned his gaze to Uptar. "Look, orc, I could give a rat's arse if ya want ta cooperate or not. There's two of ya, an' either one or both of ya can swing for what happened during tha brawl last night. Right now, that's up ta what either of ya tell me."

Uptar snorted in protest at the threat of a lynching and decided to break his silence. "Ya give folks tha noose just for drinkin' in peace an' gettin' caught up in a bar fight? We didn't even start tha fight!"

The sheriff smirked in return. "Well now, thank ye for decidin' ta converse with me after all. But ya got it wrong, orc. Tha charge ain't for disturbing tha peace. It's for attempted murder."

Uptar's eyes widened. *What the shite?* "What are ya talkin' 'bout? Whose murder?"

"Why, Ernest, of course!"

Uptar stared at him blankly; the name meant nothing to him.

The sheriff waited a beat before huffing in exasperation. "Tha enforcer at tha Wild Boar? Ya don't remember tryin' ta kill 'im during yer rampage last night?"

Uptar tried to think back to the night before. Now that he

could put the name with an ugly face, he knew who the sheriff was talking about. He could have sworn the burly human was alive when he last saw him, swinging a chair at another patron's head as the brawl escalated. But then someone had clubbed Uptar from behind, and he couldn't remember anything after that, until the putrid filth hit his face this morning. *'Cept for that shite dream.*

"That's...that's impossible," he finally said.

The sheriff shook his head, almost apologetically. "There's at least one witness that claims an orc went after poor Ernest. That an' one of yer big knives was stickin' out of his leg when I got there. He's lucky ta be in one piece this mornin'."

"Musta been Umuk?" Uptar muttered to himself, questioning more than accusing the other orc. *But if he did it, then he wouldn't have stopped there. This Ernest fella would be dead.*

The sheriff leaned forward "What's that ya say? Umuk? Ya thinkin' yer friend did it?"

"He ain't my friend!"

"Whatever. Ya came with him, so ya can be twins, for all I care."

Uptar just glowered at him.

The sheriff sighed. "Fine. Let's start over. Name?"

"Uptar of tha Torghut Clan."

"Thank ye kindly, Uptar of tha Torghut Clan. My name is Yuri Fa—" The sheriff looked at him sharply. "Wait, ya said yer friend's name is Umuk? Umuk and Uptar? Seriously?" He snickered, obviously amused. "Well, if ya ain't twins, are ya brothers at least?

Nah, probably not, only one mother I know of is that stupid with names!" He looked past Uptar and winked at the jailer behind him before continuing.

"So what are ya then, some kinda band, or a bunch of misfit minstrels? There's got ta be more of ya skulkin' around here, right? Where are yer sisters, *Ulia* and *Ulyana*? Oh, I know! With my name, can I join yer singin' troupe? Ya got any *unique* rules I should know 'bout? Ya know, before I have ta pay a *'uge* fine fer breakin' one an' ya get all *uppity* or *ugly* 'bout it?" He grinned widely at Uptar, obviously pleased with himself and his alliteration skills.

Uptar wasn't sure what to say. "I got no idea what yer goin' on about."

"C'mon now, fess up, orc! Which one of ya is tha lead singer? It's *Umuk*, I'm guessin'. Nah, wait, I bet y'all sing in *unison*, right?"

Uptar shook his head incredulously at the man who, in his mind, had clearly been hitting the wine early today.

"What's tha matter, *Uptar*? Are ya *unsure* of how ta answer? Are ya *utterly* stunned inta silence, or are ya taking *umbrage* with all my *unusual* questions?" The sheriff had to turn away and grab hold of the windowsill for support as his entire being gave in to his unique brand of humor.

Uptar looked around the room in total confusion. Borys also looked completely confused, and he glanced over at the jailer for instructions. She just shook her head and rolled her eyes, apparently having witnessed the sheriff's act in the past. She crossed her arms, but to Uptar's chagrin did not appear to let her guard down.

The sheriff slowly regained his composure. He did a farmer's blow out the window and then turned back, wiping his nose on his sleeve. "Umuk and Uptar..." he muttered to himself, and he giggled a bit more at some private thought.

Uptar, having no idea what was so funny to the human, remained silent.

"Right, where were we? Oh yeah, introductions. Thank ye kindly, Uptar of tha Torghut Clan. My name is Yuri Farkas, tha sheriff of Stren. Yer hostess there behind ya is Kira Toth, tha jailer of Stren an' my second. An' that ugly cuss with her is—" He paused. "What's yer name again, son? Oh, never mind, it don't matter to tha orc. Sorry, Uptar of tha Torghut Clan, we got new faces on tha dole that I ain't had time ta learn yet."

This wasn't starting off like any interrogation Uptar had ever been in before. *What's this sheriff playin' at? Or is he just totally gone in tha head? Shite, if he's that crazy, this could go anywhere!*

Yuri looked out the window as if searching for something out in the square. "Well, Uptar of tha Torghut Clan, I'm guessing you ain't a musician since ya got no instruments in yer gear. So, what are ya then?"

"Trapper."

"Ah, I see. A trapper with no arrows an' no traps?"

"I'm outta arrows, and why would I have me traps with me?

They're back at camp. Came ta town ta buy supplies, includin' arrows. Outta bait, too, if you're askin'." Uptar mixed lies with half-truths to create a somewhat plausible backstory, perhaps enough to delay matters until he could figure out what in the abyss was happening.

The sheriff turned around. "Kira, does tha report say anythin' 'bout what tha twins had on 'em when they were brought in last night? Any supplies or money?"

"Nothin', sir. Story that was told ta me was tha fight at Bainor's started 'cause this pair wouldn't pay their tab."

"Wouldn't? Or couldn't?"

"Don't rightly know that, sir."

"I'm askin' our friend here, Kira, not you. So, Trapper Uptar of tha Torghut Clan, ya ain't bought no supplies yet, but ya ain't got no money neither? What's tha real reason the two of ya came inta my town?"

Uptar sighed in exasperation. "Ya got me, Sheriff. I confess, we was here ta rape an' pillage tha place."

Yuri narrowed his eyes and looked at his subordinates. Uptar barely had enough time to brace himself before the blow from a cudgel took out his left knee. Even though he knew the hit was coming, the location came as a surprise. The first one usually went to the back. He staggered forward, barely catching himself before he sprawled out on the floor. He bent over in pain, refusing to yell out in front of his captors.

Yuri took a few steps forward and bent over slightly so he

could look Uptar in the eye as he struggled to recover. "Before yer arse gets jealous of yer mouth spoutin' shite, why don't ya tell me what's really goin' on?"

Out of laziness or stupidity, Uptar's hands had been shackled in front of instead of behind him, and now he could barely contain himself from reaching out and strangling the sheriff. But Yuri couldn't stop glancing behind where Uptar was doubled over, and Uptar could sense more than two people were now hovering outside his field of vision. *They're just waitin' for tha command ta administer a bit of frontier justice, ain't they? Sard 'em. I ain't gonna give tha bastards tha satisfaction.*

Instead of attacking the sheriff, Uptar let out a long, slow breath and straightened back up. His knee was throbbing, but it didn't feel like there would be any lasting damage. If Yuri was disappointed with the outcome, he didn't show it as he stepped back to the window and waited for a better answer from his prisoner.

Uptar, wincing, gave it to him. "We're just trappers, like I said. Down on our luck, stopped here for tha night, meant ta look for work at tha docks today. We were just mindin' our own business at tha tavern, an' tha fight started on tha other side of tha room. It just sorta, I dunno, moved over towards us." Uptar omitted the part about why the brawl had shifted towards them, with Umuk making a play for the money box behind the bar and getting into a tussle with the bartender. He figured if the sheriff didn't know about that already, there was no sense in giving up the other orc, since, of course, everyone would think they were in it together.

"Ya didn't start tha fight over yer tab?" Yuri persisted.

"I just told ya, we didn't start no fight! 'Sides, we had enough ta pay tha tab. Guess one of yer boys failed ta report that they nicked our money when we got hauled in." Uptar braced himself for another blow, but Yuri just smiled.

"Fine, fine, but what about Ernest? Why'd ya try an' kill 'im?"

"There ain't no why, 'cause I didn't try an' kill 'im! Last thing I remember, that big oaf was swingin' a chair at somebody. But then somebody else jumped me from behind. Which is pretty much like what yer plannin' ta do right about now, I'm guessin'."

Uptar looked behind himself as he spoke and, sure enough, the jailer and her assistant had been joined by a couple of soldiers, blunt-headed maces in their hands. The newcomers and Borys all leered at him, but Kira remained strangely calm.

Uptar glanced back at Yuri, trying to keep everyone in his field of vision in case they decided to act. "An' I don't know nothin' else."

The sheriff had a thoughtful look on his face, and he shook his head ever so slightly so that the soldiers lowered their weapons. He studied Uptar for a few moments and then crossed the room to a table that had been shoved up against the far wall. His and Umuk's equipment, such as it was, was piled there, seemingly at random, and Yuri pushed a few odds and ends out of the way before picking up a long hunting knife. Roughly made, but of good weight, Uptar recognized it as Umuk's.

"So, what about this knife, orc? This here is what was stickin' out of poor Ernest. It's yers or yer twin's, ain't it?"

Uptar answered slowly, trying to keep any emotion out of his voice. "Ya mean one of tha knives we stuck in tha weapons locker when we first came in?"

Yuri grinned widely and mockingly bowed. "Ha! Kira, I think we found us a smart one! Glad yer askin' tha same question that she's been thinkin', orc. Because I'll admit, tha folks sayin' ya went after Ernest with a knife sure ain't sayin' nothin' 'bout ya breakin' tha weapons locker open first."

"Then why—" Uptar started to protest but stopped immediately. There was clearly some game being played that he didn't know the rules to, and getting mad at this point wouldn't help. Forcing his anger into his gut, he seethed in silence.

Yuri tossed the knife back onto the table and turned back towards the group. "Trapper Uptar of...wherever, I forget...just one more question for now. Tha person ya said that Ernest was swingin' a chair at, can ya describe 'em?"

Uptar thought for a short moment. "Human...male...'bout yer height...brown hair with a beard, red shirt...dumb look on his face..."

Kira spoke up immediately. "That's gotta be Andriy, sir."

"Hmm, yeah. Why don't ya send some men over ta Andriy's shop an' ask him ta come over here. Ya know, just ta hear his story again."

The jailer nodded and turned to Borys. "Go tell Olena ta round him up an' then come back here."

He saluted her and quickly left the room.

Yuri motioned at the other two soldiers, and they followed Borys out, closing the door behind them. Once they were gone, the sheriff turned to address Uptar again.

"Glad ta see ya got more sense than yer friend, orc. He wasn't as forthcomin' with me. Didn't say nothin', not even his name, so Kira here had ta send him back ta his cell with some lumps. I bet, right now, he's thinkin' over what he did wrong."

Uptar had been wondering where Umuk was, and it appeared he had already had his turn with the sheriff. He very much did not believe that the other orc was thinking over what he did wrong, but he kept that to himself. *Surprised he didn't give me up, the dumb shite.*

Yuri wandered back towards the window as he talked, and at first, Uptar couldn't tell if the sheriff was addressing him or the jailer. "I'll tell ya that ol' Andriy's yarn spinnin' didn't make sense ta me soon as I heard it. He ain't never been much good at nothin', an' story tellin' sure ain't a strength of his." Now he addressed Uptar directly. "But tha fact is, orc, since ya ain't from around here, ya stick out like a sore thumb. It's easy for even dumb folk ta blame ya for somethin' they've been wantin' ta do for a long time. It's just whether I choose ta believe them or not, right?"

Uptar remained silent, and after a few moments, the sheriff continued.

"Fact is, nobody would care if a couple o' strange orcs got hung. Shows I'm doin' my job, right? But ol' Andriy, he's gone an' pissed in too many drinks lately, so I imagine I can get a couple people from tha bar ta tell me tha truth sooner or later. That is, if I want 'em ta do that." Yuri crossed his arms and looked directly at Uptar. "So, where does that leave ya, orc?"

Uptar shook his head. He knew what game was being played now. "I'm guessin' at yer ever-lovin' mercy, Sheriff."

Yuri exchanged looks with the jailer, and he grinned mischievously. "We really do got a smart one here, Kira! You're right, orc, at my ever-lovin' mercy. I know you likely ain't up ta no good 'round these parts, seein' as there have been reports of orc raids on smaller settlements comin' in for some time now. If that ain't you an' yer twin, then it's someone just like you. Either way, it's a good enough reason ta lock ya up, if not string ya up. But I can be reasonable, if yer reasonable too."

Uptar knew when the jig was up. "Whaddya got in mind?"

"Ya said ya want work at tha docks? Well, I got some need along tha same lines. An acquaintance o' mine runs tha docks an' most o' tha flatboats that come an' go this far north, an' there's been some trouble with smugglers on tha river. Either takin' on loads they shouldn't or stealin' his loads outright. Tha longshoremen are blamin' me friend instead of lookin' inside their own for who's helpin' tha smugglers. So, he needs some more help, either on tha dock or on tha boats, so he can move some of his current staff ta guard duty. It'll be shite work at first, as part of a loadin' crew or wrestlin' timber in tha river, but if ya work out, then someone like you should move up quick. I won't pay ya, o' course, seein' as you'll be workin' off yer debt to society, so ta speak. But, who knows, there might be coin in it for ya after a while. But workin' for free is still better than, well, ya know..." Yuri made a vague gesture that implied a noose being tightened around his neck.

Uptar thought about it for a moment. What choice did he really have? He could rot in a cell, or he could be strung up, or he could participate in whatever shady deal the sheriff was selling him. It just sounded too good to be true, to be handed a job he probably would have been begging for this morning if he hadn't wound up in jail. He'd just have to lay low and stay quiet while he figured out what was going on.

"Sure, sign me up. Better than dyin' anyways."

"Glad ya see it that way. What about yer friend?"

Uptar shrugged. He really hoped Umuk would be too dumb to figure things out on his own. "Up ta him, Sheriff. He ain't my brother, an' he ain't my friend, an' I got nothin' more ta say 'bout him."

Yuri gave a short laugh. "Spoken like a true mercenary! I think you'll work out fine." There was a knock at the door, and he turned to face it. "Yes, come in!"

Borys came back into the room. The sheriff appeared to make a brief attempt to remember his name but then gave up and just issued him an order instead.

"Okay, lad, take our new friend here downstairs. Put him back in his cell for now, but take those shackles off an' give him somethin' decent ta eat. Oh, an' some clean water ta wash up with. Uptar, make yerself presentable, an' we'll head ta tha docks later today for an introduction with tha dockmaster. We'll see if yer twin comes along or not." He laughed when Uptar growled in frustration at the joke. "C'mon now, it ain't my fault y'all look tha same as one another! Get outta here, we'll talk soon enough!"

***

Yuri let the door close behind Borys and Uptar without further comment. He returned to looking out the same window he had been at earlier, lightly drumming his fingers on the ledge. Kira stood silently while he collected his thoughts.

Finally, he spoke. "Whaddya think? He's a smart one, for sure. But is he too smart?"

She furrowed her brow as she thought this over. "I dunno, sir. Weaved some truths inta his story, smelled out tha ambush ya set for him, an' he caught tha trick with tha knife I told ya ta try. So he's pretty cunnin' an' thinks on his feet. He probably is part of tha group that's been muckin' things up out in tha Wilds, just like we thought. But that also means he probably ain't from around here, so there ain't no way he can know what we're drivin' at with this job you're offerin'."

"Fair enough, Kira, fair enough. Right, that works for me. What about tha other one?"

She sniffed dismissively. "Stupid as they come. But if he

agrees ta come along, he'd make fer a good meat shield inna fight. An' I'll always take another meat shield." She smiled at this, and not so nicely.

"Ha! Yer ruthless! Don't ever change!" Yuri chuckled. "Right, tha other one may be stupid, but he can't be stupid enough ta choose a hangin' over a job. So, assumin' both orcs say yes, let's get 'em on tha dock with Bartosh an' see how they do with a bit o' manual labor. If they can follow orders an' don't try an' run off at tha first chance, we'll work 'em inta tha boat crew. Even if they figure out what we're doin' at that point, I doubt they'll care."

"True enough, sir."

"Good. Give Bainor tha regular amount of coin for spottin' tha twins, an' throw in a bit extra ta help Ernest's woman out while he recovers." Yuri shook his head in disappointment. "He should've known better than ta let Andriy get that close! Now we have ta make that bastard swing for stickin' him."

Kira was unmoved. "Andriy's a piece of shite, sir. I'm sure he deserves hangin' for somethin' else, even if it ain't for stickin' Ernest."

"Ruthless, Kira, just ruthless! All right, get outta here, I'll be by tha house later on."

"Yessir!" The jailer smiled, gave a half wave of a salute, and left the room.

Yuri was lost in thought for a while longer. If the two orcs worked out, his overall crew would be nearing three dozen. Certainly not enough on their own to act outside of Stren, but he was sure his contact had other cells sprinkled throughout the kingdom. So long as the mayor stayed drunk on her wine, local operations should continue to run smoothly. He was glad that Kira seemed content with playing his second and feeding him intelligence. Hopefully, they would both find out more about the overall plan soon enough. *I just don't wanna have ta climb halfway up that blasted mountain for another meetin' any time soon.*

CHAPTER SEVEN
The Interloper

Night was falling as Kozel entered the clearing surrounding the homestead. Although some light shone out through holes in the chinking, he couldn't hear any voices or sense any movement from within the log building. Even though he knew the wargs were somewhere to the north, he still sensed something evil was afoot here. Quietly, he unsheathed his long knives and crept forward.

The darkening shadows hid his approach. All was eerily silent, as if even the insects knew how tense he felt in the moment. He made it safely to the front of the building and attempted to peek through one of the larger gaps between the logs, but it was too dim inside. He couldn't make anything out in the low, flickering light coming from the fireplace, other than it appeared to be only one large room inside. The front door was shut tight, and he didn't want to try the latch, at least not without knowing what was waiting inside.

Taking a second look through the gap in the chinking, he noticed a dark space along the back wall directly across from where he was. *Probably another door, and that one appears open.* He could smell blood, and his pulse quickened.

He recalled that the farmer who had requested his assistance had a number of young ones, but he didn't know exactly how many. Not that it mattered. Only one had been promised to him. Kozel hoped it wasn't too late for the overall family, as they had seemed like honest, hardworking folk, but he admitted to himself that he was only really concerned about Dovira. He pushed all thoughts of her out of his mind. He first had to figure out what was happening and who, if anybody, was inside the house.

Fields ripe with grain fanned out behind the house as he cautiously worked his way around the corner. The last rays of the orange sunset caught the barley spikes just so, making them look like a roiling mass of flames as the plants swayed in the light breeze. Kozel guessed that harvesting the ripe crop would start any day now, if it had not already been started in some of the more distant fields. He didn't think the plants were tall enough to hide anyone crouching within them, and no paths had been trampled into the nearest crop. Nevertheless, he tried to keep an eye on his right flank as he worked his way towards the second door.

The back door was indeed open and fell inside the shadow cast from some nearby oak trees. Pausing at the frame to let his eyes adjust, Kozel still could hear nothing from inside. Looking down at the door sill, he could tell that someone or something had been dragged out of the building and away to the left. There were faint markings on the ground indicating which way the party had gone.

First things first. He stealthily crossed over the threshold, as if but a shadow himself.

The smell of blood had indeed been an omen of what lay before him. At least four bodies lay about the room, all still. Kozel slowly took in the scene, and with a touch of sadness, noted that the farmer was among the dead.

He saw that the corpse closest to the back door was human, unlike the farmer and his family. Dressed shabbily, the man held what looked to be a butcher's axe in his right hand. Kozel flipped him over with his boot. A small knife, perhaps not even a dagger, had been run perfectly through his heart. There was a look of surprise on his death mask, and Kozel nodded grimly at the dead farmer. *At least your family took one of them with you, my friend.*

As Kozel approached the next body, he could feel the slight tremor of a heartbeat calling to him through the dirt floor. It was an older female orc, who he knew to be the farmer's wife. As tenderly as he could, he turned her onto her side. It was immediately obvious where the butcher's axe had been employed, as massive, deep cuts were evident on her thighs and stomach. Blood still pulsed weakly out of her body, but he knew there was no saving her.

As he attempted to prop her head up with a blanket that had been next to her on the ground, her eyes fluttered open. Weakly, she shifted so she could look at him. He made no attempt to hide who he was and calmly stared back at her.

"Traitor," she hissed, with a look of pure hatred. "You...you did this."

Kozel wanted to caress her hair, but he knew the gentle action would mean nothing to her. "No, my dear, I did not want this. I would have stopped them had I been here."

"Knew...he...shouldn't have dealt with you." She wheezed as she grasped helplessly at the archaic crux immissa that hung about her neck on a coarse string.

Kozel idly wondered how long ago she had received the bauble from a church missionary. He didn't know of many orcs who believed in the Almighty. *Not that your old gods could help you either.*

"Go in peace," was all he could think of saying. He had told her the truth in that her death and the death of her family made no sense to him in the grand scheme of things. Belief in the Almighty, or anything else, couldn't change the fact that fate was sometimes chaotic, and he loathed that it was this way in this world.

She slipped into the next as he watched, and he made no attempt to stop the process.

Kozel didn't bother to check the farmer, but he quickly looked around at the other bodies. There were, in fact, two more. One of the children lay by his father, and the other had crawled under the table in a vain attempt to escape. This angered him, because he saw no reason to slaughter the innocent young. Not when they had so much potential in front of them. But his Dovira was not among the bodies, and as he hurried out of the menagerie of death, Kozel hoped he could find her in time.

The trail leading away from the back door would have been easy to follow, even if he couldn't smell the blood, as the bandits had made little attempt to hide where they were going. They had made camp some distance from the homestead, and Kozel understood why they had selected their location as he made his way quietly through the underbrush towards them.

On top of a small hill, the site afforded a good view of the surrounding area and was within a league of several homesteads. He assumed that "his" farmer's location was the first one they had attacked. It was by far the biggest target, and they would have assumed it to be the wealthiest. Also, if multiple attacks had already occurred nearby, the rest of the farmers would have been on high alert. Potentially, even the town he knew to be several leagues away would have sent out a patrol or two in an attempt to mollify the locals and safeguard their food supply.

Kozel could see four figures gathered around a small campfire, but he had to assume there were a few more. Based upon the amount of blood left on the trail, at least one was grievously wounded, which would help the odds. Not that he was worried about a fight. That would come soon enough. His primary concern remained Dovira and whether they had taken her with them. It was difficult to pick out her scent from among the others for some reason, but he was fairly certain she was still in the area.

He was still about fifty paces away when his keen ears began picking up pieces of their conversation, and he started to circle around to his left to stay downwind. No telling if they had dogs with them or if they weren't all humans.

"...not bad...attack..."

"Are ya blind, ya shite?! Look at—"

"Keep it down! We dunno..."

"...Sergei...bleedin' out an'...has broken ribs! Not ta mention...is dead on tha floor back at tha farm!"

"Okay, okay, we didn't think this suka would have more...her old man. But if ya didn't wanna sard her so bad, she wouldn't...ta knife Sergei, would she? Next time, stick to tha plan!"

"Oh, like I'm tha only one here that wanted to sard tha little grey whore! If that's true, then hows come everyone 'cept Matvey here drew lots for their turn ta have her?"

"That don't mean we shoulda took her in tha first place!"

Kozel had already quickened his pace. He could make out the form of someone kneeling, just outside the ring of light. All sounds of the men bickering by the fire faded into the background as he could finally hear Dovira's stifled groans. He could smell the seed from three of them inside and around her, and his vision tunneled into the back of the head of the one with her now. A pig of a man, he was too busy sodomizing his victim to notice Kozel approach. Not that it would have made a difference.

He grabbed the man from behind, putting one hand over his mouth as he pulled him back. In an instant, one blade was out, and with a quick upward motion, the rapist's still erect genitalia was shorn off. If there had been time, Kozel would have stuffed it down the man's throat and choked him with it, but his rage was already settling in.

His knife continued upward, gutting his victim instantly. Blood was everywhere now, and it only served to heighten his already fine-tuned senses, almost to the point of overload. Kozel threw the still-quaking body to the side and turned to face the others, who stared at him and their dying compatriot in shock. Both blades were out now, and he strode forward into the light so they could clearly see him as he challenged them to a fight they could not hope to win.

"I am your destruction, you miserable worms! Come and meet your death!"

There were five of them, but one was lying by the fire, unconscious and bloody. Only three drew their weapons in response to his challenge, while the last one, whimpering, stumbled backwards and fell to the ground. The leader of the gang, a large man with a bulging neck, motioned to the other two to spread out. Kozel didn't give them a chance to do so as he charged headlong into their midst.

The clashing of steel ended well before the screaming did.

Once the men had been incapacitated, Kozel immediately went to Dovira's side. The girl was in deep shock, and he didn't dare to try and rouse her. He gently moved her closer to the fire and tended to her physical wounds as best he could, but he knew he did not have the power to remove her mental anguish. Now she lay under a blanket, eyes open but not seeing, her future unknown to him. With smoldering anger, he turned his attention back to the bandits.

He took his time deciding what to do with each one in turn. After a bit of rummaging through their packs, he was able to find enough rope for what he wanted to do with the three that had attempted to stand against him. He had kept them barely alive on purpose, and he meant to exact a bit more earthly justice out of each. While he worked on them, he cast his eyes about for the others.

The last rapist's body still lay where Kozel had thrown it, and there was nothing more he cared to do to him. The unconscious man by the fire soon went to his death on his own, soaked in blood from a knife wound to the neck. Whatever sins he took to the grave, they were now someone else's problem to judge. That just left the one who had refused to fight.

This particular bandit had never moved from where he had initially fallen. It puzzled Kozel why the sorry fellow had neither fought nor fled, and it was somewhat annoying that he would have to be dealt with at all. Kozel couldn't smell his seed anywhere around the campsite, so he assumed this was the one called Matvey by the others. *That might afford him a quick death, if he's cooperative.*

Finally, when he had reached a good stopping point in his work on the trio, Kozel sauntered over to the prostrate figure, grabbed him by the shoulders, and hauled him into a sitting position. The young man screamed in pain as he was moved, and Kozel assumed it was due to the broken ribs the group had mentioned before he attacked them. The injured man pivoted himself onto his knees, bracing his upper body with his arms to try and keep any pressure off his torso. He tried to breathe in small sips as tears slipped off his cheeks and onto the hard-packed ground.

Kozel decided he could afford to wait a bit for the man to compose himself.

After a while, the young man slowly exhaled, opened his eyes, and glanced at Kozel for the first time. A look of fear crossed his face, for Kozel refused to show his true self. All the man could see was a dark-skinned figure with jet black hair. Any detail beyond that was hidden, as Kozel's features seemed to bleed into his clothing. The effect created a shifting mass that was impossible to focus on, except for his eyes. Based upon similar encounters in the past, he knew that the reflected flames from the fire would make them glow red in the surrounding darkness. It had been an unexpected byproduct of hiding his true self, one that he was rather fond of now.

"Hey, Matvey. You realize you're already dead?"

The would-be bandit closed his eyes and nodded his head, leading Kozel to believe he had guessed correctly on the man's name.

Matvey's voice was low and tearful when he answered. "Yeah...we all deserve death for what we did today." He shivered and began to cry again.

"Stop that!" Kozel crouched down next to Matvey, slapped him in the face, and then grabbed hold of his chin. He squeezed until the young man cried out and opened his eyes. "Answer my questions truthfully, *kytsya*, and I shall send you on your way quickly. Unlike your friends over there." He nodded in the direction of the fire.

Matvey stole a look, long enough to see three naked bodies splayed out on the ground, their remaining limbs tied to crude stakes fashioned from dead tree limbs. He didn't look long enough to decipher what body parts were missing from each body.

Kozel released Matvey's chin and leaned back. "You're fortunate that you still have something of a conscience, otherwise you would be laid out like your friends there. Now, tell me quickly, *kytsya*, as I smell blood on your hands, who did you kill at the homestead?"

"Tha...tha farmer... Please, good sir, nobody was supposed ta die! It was just supposed ta be a quick hit, we grab whatever coin tha—"

"I don't care," Kozel said brusquely, cutting him off. "Why did you kill him?"

"He was actin' like a lunatic an' refused ta submit! He was wavin' about some sort of axe an' kept goin' on 'bout how he was protected from all misfortune, that we was damned tha moment we stepped inta his house."

Well, he was half right, at least, thought Kozel, but he didn't interrupt.

"He...he just wouldn't stop. He was practically beggin' us ta attack him, even though his wife was yellin' for us ta just take their money box an' go. Igor finally went for him just ta shut him up, an' he called out some name three times all at once. Then he—"

"Whose name did he call?"

"I..." Matvey's face went white with terror, as if saying the name just once would immediately conjure up a demon.

"God's bones, man, *speak!*"

"Marchosias." Matvey choked the name out in a rush, as if it was forcing its way out of his mouth, and the word hung in the warm night air.

Kozel stayed as emotionless as he could as he absorbed the powerful name. It disappointed him greatly that the farmer had thought to call for aid from a marquis of the abyss. *Did he really think he was that important in the grand scheme of the universe?* After a moment's reflection, he came back to the present and looked up at the sky, where several stars were already shining. It was still several days until the full moon, and the waxing gibbous orb wouldn't rise into the heavens for several hours yet. *I'll have to stoke the fire to see what else I'm going to cut off those three on the ground*, he mused thoughtfully.

Matvey was shaking almost uncontrollably in the dark.

Kozel turned his attention back to the broken man. "But no one...no *thing* came?"

"No. We all froze in place when tha farmer called out, but after a few moments, Igor just laughed an' swung his axe at him. But he missed tha farmer an' hit his wife instead. There was screamin' all around, an' tha farmer just went crazy! He rushed me, an' I... All I did was raise my sword ta defend myself. It was as if he impaled himself upon it! Oh, what have I done? What have I done?!"

Kozel had heard enough. He could either imagine the rest

of the miserable story himself or pry it out of the girl, it made no difference. "What you have done, my friend, is earn yourself a quick death. I will honor my word." He drew his knives again, and the sharp blades flickered cruelly in the dim light of the fire.

Matvey closed his eyes but remained in an upright position on his knees, head held level.

Kozel leaned in to make the death strike when... *What's this? What is he whispering?*

"...Hallowed be thy name. Thy kingdom come, thy will be..."

Kozel paused. The man was praying for forgiveness from his death bed. The Unholy One would not wish to lose a soul, but rules were rules. He waited for Matvey to finish his prayer.

"...And lead us not into temptation, but deliver us from evil. For thine is the kingdom, and the power, and the glory, forever. Amen."

The blades flashed, and Matvey's head rolled to the side. Kozel tilted his own to look at it where it had fallen, and he could have sworn that the man was smiling and appeared to be at peace.

"Well, my friend, I hope, for your sake, you will be judged fit for purgatory. The abyss is not a welcoming place, especially not the burning sands your friends are bound to go to. Or maybe it will be immersion in the River Phlegethon for some of them? Ah, decisions, decisions. I am glad I am not the one who must rule on such matters!"

As Kozel talked, he slowly walked back towards the fire until he was standing in front of the three living corpses he had staked out on the bare ground. He poked at the largest brute with the pointed end of one of his knives. He wasn't sure if the man was conscious after having most of his intestines ripped out, but when the blade entered his soft flesh, he cried out in pain.

"Mercy! I beg you. Mercy!"

"Ah, you're asking the wrong person for mercy, my *durnyy m'yasnyk*! Maybe you'll be a penitent man at the last moment like your recently departed brother-in-arms, but somehow, I doubt you will be judged in the same light as he will be. Regardless, I have given you a nice view of the night sky, so cast your eyes and your voice to the heavens if you would ask for forgiveness! Well, while you still have your eyes and your tongue, at least."

Suddenly, from the north, Kozel heard the baying of a wolf, with several others quickly joining in. No doubt the wargs had sensed the scent of so much blood wafting on the night breeze and were coming to feed. They would be at the campsite soon, and he couldn't afford to be here with the girl when they arrived, as crazed as they would be.

He turned to address the bandits again. "It appears we will have unexpected guests arriving soon! A pity, as I had such a night planned for all three of you. But wargs like their meat fresh, so I will leave you to them. Just don't do anything rash before they get here."

Sheathing his knives, Kozel quickly crossed over to the dying fire. He gently lifted the girl, cradling her in his arms, and was gone.

CHAPTER EIGHT
Head North, Young Orc

Why did they come south at all if they're just goin' back tha way they came? The question kept repeating itself in Sarl's mind, keeping time with his steady pace. His pursuit of the wargs that had started out cross-country in a haphazard manner had steadied when the pack reached an old logging trail that headed north in a fairly straight fashion. They seemed to be keeping mostly to the tree line, but their footprints were clear and their strides measured. There was no apparent attempt at concealment.

Stranger still was that, rather than shying away from contact, the pack seemed keen on visiting every settlement this side of the Grumaius as they headed back north. They would break away from their general route whenever they got close to a village or hamlet, circling the community in question, as if making sure the occupants didn't leave until the pack's business was complete. The wargs would spend a day or two in the general vicinity of each settlement and then be off again, always pushing north. Their continued loitering was the main reason Sarl had been able to keep in contact with them, given they could travel much faster than he could if they chose to.

The settlement visits were not going unnoticed. Usually, it was only local livestock that would suffer at the mouths of the pack, but at least twice now, the wargs had feasted on human flesh. Both times, they had attacked a homestead set some ways out from the nearby village, and both times, it had been a slaughter. More disturbing to Sarl than the human deaths was that the pack had also caught several trappers out in the Wilds, eviscerating the poor orcs and leaving little behind.

Sarl had stopped long enough at two settlements for a hot meal and to catch up on the local gossip, and both times, he found that hysteria was bubbling just below the stoic surface of the populace. News of the attacks was traveling faster than the pack itself, and nobody knew for sure what sort of evil was stalking the land. At least one village council had dispatched a courier to the nearest garrison town to plead for assistance, and many prayers of petition were being offered up in advance of the traveling priest's next visit. The growing fear and discontent had been especially palpable at Sarl's second stop.

For his part, Sarl had commiserated with patrons and bartenders alike, but he had shared very little information on what he knew and no information on what he suspected. He had not shown his church warrant to anyone, as there had been no need. However, he was all but certain now that the vovkulaka was not only real but was driving the warg pack before it, perhaps even using them as an escort of sorts. There was a specific scent he had picked up just east of Molotok that had persisted as he pushed north after the wargs, an unnatural metallic odor that seemed to catch at the back of his throat whenever it was at its strongest. He had attributed this scent to the shapeshifter due both to its uniqueness and to where it led him.

From his tavern visits, Sarl knew that whoever or whatever was creating the scent was entering the settlements themselves as the pack circled at the fringes. He had caught the barest hint of the lingering aroma during both of his stops, and he assumed it was because the shapeshifter had loitered in one place for a long period of time. The brazen shite had sat at the bar of the first tavern Sarl had visited and at the corner table in the second, most likely for hours on end.

What's it up to? Is it meetin' with someone at each stop? Or is it just takin' tha time ta drink ale an' whore it up?

It bothered Sarl that he didn't know what the shapeshifter looked like when it was in human form. He thought he had caught sight of it several nights ago, but the moon wasn't high enough in the sky to be sure, and he had seen little more than just a profile. It had seemed to be aware of his presence, even though he was downwind and hidden in the underbrush. The figure had quickly melted into the dark, and he hadn't been close enough to the pack since then to try and investigate further. At least its scent remained easy to follow, meaning Sarl hadn't needed the warg tracks to stay on the correct heading.

That was, until yesterday evening, when the metallic odor had disappeared completely.

Sarl had wasted quite a bit of time circling in an ever-wider radius, hunting for the scent or any other sign of the shapeshifter. He was much more interested in following it than the wargs, especially if they were parting ways. But it had been to no avail, and it was as if the monster had vanished into thin air. That left the wargs, with their clear path continuing north. Sarl reasoned, or at least hoped, that the vovkulaka would rejoin them at some point. He could either follow the pack or give up the chase, and he wasn't keen on the latter choice.

For the better part of the morning, he moved forward at a trot. At his current pace, he could easily cover a league in an hour on clear ground for an extended period each day. He knew the pack could travel much faster than that, but for whatever reason, they hadn't been pushing themselves, even when they weren't stalking prey around the outskirts of villages. He had even started granting himself a few hours of rest each night, as they appeared to be doing the same. Based upon their droppings, he estimated he was less than a day behind them, even after following them for such a long time. Ever since the vovkulaka had left them, they had pushed deeper into the forest proper, but were still leaving an easy enough trail to follow.

Their track had been straight and true for so long that Sarl almost missed their sudden turn to the southeast. He paused, scanning the vegetation ahead of him. It didn't appear to be the lair of a leshy, and he doubted there would be another threat in these woods that would make the wargs turn to avoid a fight.

So, they turned for a different reason.

Looking at the footprints after the turn, it took a few moments to notice that their stride had lengthened appreciably.

Now they're goin' full out! What happened? Were they called?

Sarl took a moment to take a sip from his water skin and to slightly loosen the straps holding his battle-axe to his back. It would rub annoyingly against him as he moved now, but his intuition told him he'd be needing it soon, and he didn't want to waste time later getting it unbound. Once this was done, he took off at a slightly faster pace than before.

After a short while, he reached the tree line again. He halted, scanning the overgrown meadow ahead. The wargs had pressed straight on through towards a small stand of trees on a slight rise, several hundred paces away. Sarl noted several farms in the distance, and he frowned at what he was seeing. The wargs were running full tilt directly into a settled area without any sense of caution, something they hadn't done before now.

He dropped his day pack and water skin next to a large oak tree to free himself of their bulk, and now he fully unstrapped his axe. Prepared for a fight, he stepped out of the tree line and moved quickly towards the hill in front of him.

He could smell the blood from over fifty paces away, which meant there was a lot of it. It was all human, as far as he could tell. As he reached some underbrush, he slowed his pace. It was almost impossible to be stealthy, as big as he was, but he tried his best to move forward quietly.

Suddenly, he caught the familiar metallic scent right in front of him where someone had previously disturbed the ground cover.

Sard me, the shapeshifter's back!

There was a small clearing in the middle of the trees, obviously a campsite of some sort. The devastation within the clearing gave him pause, even as well-traveled as he was. Scanning the area from the edge of the underbrush, he put his axe back in its place. He wouldn't need it, as any fight had ended a while ago.

The remains of several humans lay scattered about the area, and after a few long moments of looking through their day packs and meager supplies, he could only guess the number to be between five and eight. He surmised there had been a fight of some sort, and the wargs had been attracted by the scent of fresh blood. It certainly looked like a copious amount had been shed. Sarl could pick up the scent of the vovkulaka here and there around the clearing, with the strongest imprint being in front of the remains of the campfire. Some bodies may have been laid out on the ground here, but it was hard to tell. Either the vovkulaka or the wargs had made sure there was barely a trace of anyone left.

Tha shapeshifter must have attacked this group of humans, or vice versa, but why? A deal gone wrong? In his way? Just because? Makes no sense ta me. Whatever tha reason, the wargs had a feast when it was done.

Sarl could tell that the pack had broken out to the north after they had supped, apparently back to the forest as it bulged out to the east, sloping towards the river in the far distance. He was more interested in what the vovkulaka was up to, especially now that it was back. After some more searching, he could only find evidence of it traveling in one direction, heading towards a homestead that was set somewhat close to the hill. There was blood in this direction as well, although not as much as at the campsite.

He could see there were perhaps a half dozen figures standing near the main building of the farm, a large log-built structure with a stone chimney. As he watched, an individual came out of the building and walked over to the others, joining an already animated discussion.

It was never easy being the stranger in a crowd, especially a human crowd, but Sarl decided he had to approach the homestead if he was going to get any more information on what the vovkulaka was doing. If nothing else, he needed to inform the locals of the massacre he had just discovered. They didn't appear to be armed, so he made sure his weapons were secure but visible before walking down the hill.

As he approached, the group of humans were huddled together, deep in conversation. They didn't notice him, even when he got near enough to lob a rock into their midst. Deciding that wouldn't be the best way to get their attention, Sarl stopped several paces away and stood facing them, his arms crossed. After a few more moments, he coughed loudly and smiled without showing his teeth when they looked up in surprise. Two of them cried out in alarm, and the others seemed frozen in place.

"Afternoon, gentlemen! I'm lookin' for tha owner of this here farm. I need ta talk ta them." Sarl made a short bow while keeping eye contact with the group.

“Who...who are ya?” One of the two who had cried out, and who appeared to be the oldest of the assembled men, had recovered somewhat from Sarl’s unannounced entrance. He seemed wary, but not afraid.

“Just a trapper, headed north. But I found somethin’ on tha hill back there an’ need ta send a message to tha local lawman ’bout it.”

“Are ya kin by chance?” There was a hopeful tone to the man’s question.

“What?”

“Are ya kin of tha Madors?”

“Who are tha Madors?”

“Tha orc family that lives...er, lived here.”

Sarl’s eyes widened in surprise. “Orcs? Settled here?”

The old man’s shoulders sagged a bit. “Was hopin’ for a moment you was kin. Looks like they was attacked last night, an’ we...” He ground to a halt, a look of despair on his weathered face. “We don’t know what ta do.”

Sarl had continued to smell blood mixed with the scent of the vovkulaka as he had approached the farmers, and his body tensed as he looked towards the nearby building. The combined trail led straight towards the back door of the homestead, the same opening from which he had just seen one of the men exit. Without saying another word, Sarl strode towards the single-story structure. None of the locals attempted to stop him, although one of them yelped again in surprise when they caught sight of the axe on his back.

When Sarl stopped at the door and looked in, the first body he saw was a poorly dressed and desperately thin man. He seemed to be in his late twenties, although it was hard to tell from how emaciated he was. His dead eyes gazed at the ceiling, a surprised look on his face. But he didn't capture Sarl's interest for more than an instant, as he had already seen the other bodies strewn about the large room. A middle-aged female orc lay in a dried puddle of her own blood on one side of the dead human, and a similarly aged male orc with a sword impaled through his chest lay on the other side. But it was the little one curled up next to his father, looking almost asleep instead of dead, that caused Sarl's own blood to boil.

A guttural growl escaped his lips as he clenched his fists, attempting and failing to remain calm. He couldn't proceed further and instead wheeled around to face the group of humans huddled together some dozen paces away.

"*Who did this?*" Sarl bellowed, his rage threatening to overwhelm him. He advanced on them, his whole body visibly shaking while he held his fists in front of him, as if he would pummel all of them into the ground. "*Who did this ta my kind?*"

Two of the group broke and ran, while the old man fell to his knees, his arms stretched out. "Pl-Pl-Please, good sir, we don't know! We just found 'em a couple hours ago, we ain't even touched 'em! We..." He closed his eyes as Sarl towered over him. "Oh no..."

Sarl stared wildly at the remainder of the group, who remained rooted in place with fear. He wanted so badly to shake the old man apart, to tear them all from limb to limb, to burn the homestead to the ground, to find solace in violence like so many times before.

No, Siryy Vovk, these are not your enemies! Find your peace amidst the ruin of this world...

From the depths of the void came the tender whisper of her voice. He closed his eyes to stop the angry tears and followed it out of the darkness. Sarl shakily took in and let out a long breath, feeling the warmth of the afternoon sun on his face. *Yak khochesh, Soloveyko...*

Opening his eyes, he grabbed the old man and hauled him to his feet. "Who's tha human lyin' dead in there?"

The farmer desperately glanced over at one of the others in the group, a scrawny teenager with little more than some fuzz on his chin. Sarl, slightly under control now, recognized him as the one who had come from inside the building earlier.

"Tha-Tha-That'd be Igor, sir," the teenager said shakily. "He's from Myr. My older brother used ta run with 'im."

"What's Myr?"

"Town down that way. Maybe two leagues?" The boy pointed vaguely to the west. "Last time I saw him, he was beggin' at tha main gate."

"So then what's he doin' out this far? An' what's he got against my kind, huh?" Sarl demanded.

"We don't know, good sir, please believe me! Tha Madors been here five seasons, nobody ain't done nothin' to 'em 'fore now.

They be good people." The old man had found his voice for a moment but trailed off as Sarl looked down at him.

Sarl took another deep breath and tried to think. He looked back at the teenager. "This Igor, he run in a group?"

"At least when he was younger, yeah. Used ta be 'bout six of 'em that was together all tha time. Ain't never up ta no good. It's why my brother stopped runnin' with 'em 'bout a year ago an' came back to tha farm."

Sarl let go of the old man's tunic and took a step back. Part of a picture was forming in his head, that of a group of hungry thugs, not even worthy enough to be called bandits, raiding the farm for food and money. But he still couldn't place why the shapeshifter had been down here as well. *Why would it care 'bout a simple farmer? An' why would it attack those dumb shites up at tha campsite before or after tha attack on tha farm? Did they take somethin' it wanted? An' tha wargs didn't come down here ta feed, either.*

The salt from his tears was stinging his eyes, and he rubbed them with both of his hands while he tried to think of plausible answers to all his questions. When he looked up, he could see a simple one-horse wagon approaching. The driver appeared to be alone, and they were coming at a fast clip.

He glared around at the group, who had all stood mute while he had thought. "I'll be right back. Don't anyone leave."

Sarl turned and walked back to the log cabin. Taking a deep breath, he pushed forward into the building this time. The scent of the vovkulaka was there, barely noticeable beneath all the typical homestead odors, but definitely there.

Sarl did a cursory search of the large room, averting his eyes from a second child's body under the table, so as to not risk flying into a rage again. The space had been hurriedly ransacked, and he didn't see a money box, but there was no way of knowing who had conducted the search. If something important was missing, there was no way for Sarl to identify what it might be. Shaking his head sadly, he walked back outside into the sun.

The wagon he had seen approaching had arrived, and the driver had dismounted and was talking with the others. A seasoned woman, she was clutching the arm of the old farmer as she spoke. They all turned to look at Sarl as he reappeared from inside the cabin, their conversation dying away. He approached the group but stopped a few paces short, arms at his side, as calm as he could be under the circumstances.

"Right, then. Ya sent for tha law yet?" Sarl asked.

The old farmer nodded. "Yes, good sir, that's what Yana...uh, my wife here...came ta tell us."

Yana took a step forward and did a slight curtsy. "I sent our son ta Myr ta tell tha sheriff there, but it'll be a spell 'fore they get here. Are ya kin to tha Madors?"

Sarl shook his head at her. "Nah, ma'am, just a trapper comin' through these parts. Came down here ta report what I found on that hill ta tha law." He gestured behind him as he spoke. "So, it's good that tha sheriff's coming here."

She raised an eyebrow at this. “Pray tell, what did ya find on tha hill?”

“Bodies, ma’am. Well, what’s left of ’em.”

There was silence as the group took in this new revelation.

The old farmer finally spoke up. “Whaddya mean by ‘what’s left of ’em?’”

Sarl had decided before even approaching the humans the first time that he was going to say nothing about the shapeshifter. And, if the wargs had already moved on like he suspected, that wasn’t a reason to put the farmers more on edge by mentioning them either. He instead used a familiar lie. “Whoever they were, I think they were attacked by wolves. But it’s such a mess up there, I also think they were fightin’ each other ’fore tha wolves showed up. Lots of blood, an’ not much of ’em left. They’re...well, let’s just say you can’t tell who’s who.”

There was a low murmuring of confusion from the group.

“I ain’t heard o’ no wolf attackin’ nobody this close ta town, have you, Anitoliy?” asked one of the younger men.

The old farmer put his hand to his mouth and pondered the question briefly before answering. “Maybe if they was rabid, or maybe if there was enough fresh meat? Ya sure there was a wolf attack?” He looked at Sarl, who shrugged.

“Don’t rightly know, but there are wolf tracks leadin’ in an’ out of tha campsite up there. Not sure it matters since they’re all dead either way.” He looked at the teen again. “You said this Igor fella ran in a group? About six of ’em?”

The young man nodded quickly. “At least he used ta, sir.”

Sarl turned to the side and spat on the ground. *That’s got ta be his group up on tha hill then. Guess that shapeshifter saved me tha trouble of killin’ them.*

Yana looked at her husband. “What’s he mean ’bout Igor? Who’s Igor?”

“Some young fella from Myr, luv. Looks like he an’ his mates are tha ones that attacked Hernac an’ his family. We got no idea why.”

“Oh!” Yana made to go towards the homestead, but Sarl held up his hands as her husband tried to pull her back.

“Beg pardon, ma’am...Yana...ya don’t want ta go in there.”

“I can handle the sight of blood, orc!” she said curtly as she shook her husband off her.

“It’s tha kids...” It was all Sarl could do to not scream at the sky.

“What?!” She staggered back, the enormity of the tragedy sinking in. “What...what about Ruslana? Their mother?”

Sarl quietly nodded. “She’s in there too.”

“Oh...” Yana crossed herself and sank to the ground. “Why did they do it? Why...?” She faltered as her husband sat down next to her. She wrung her hands, staring into space. “But that means... Oh, Dovira...”

Sarl stared blankly at her. “Who’s Dovira?”

“Their eldest. She just turned sixteen,” answered the teenager.

Sarl looked back at the cabin. "She ain't in there."

"'Course not, she's at our house!" the woman snapped at him, then softened immediately. "My apologies, good sir. How would ya know that? Anitoliy found her over there this mornin'." She pointed at some large oak trees that stood nearby. "She's alive, but she won't say nothin'. It's like she ain't all there. That an'..." Yana's voice cracked, and her mood suddenly changed from sorrow to anger. "I don't believe it," she whispered, almost to herself, and she struggled back to her feet. "Why would they do that? How *dare* they do that!"

"What is it, luv?" The farmer tried to rise as well but couldn't.

Two of the other men hurried over to help him up as his wife marched directly over to Sarl, grabbing him by his tunic. He could sense the heat coming from her and remained silent as she searched his face.

"Are ya sure those bodies ya seen up there on tha hill were part of this?" She gestured with her head towards the cabin.

"Gotta be, ma'am. There be tracks an' blood all tha way between here an' there."

"An' they're all dead? Mutilated, ya say?"

Sarl was surprised at the sudden venom in her voice. "Yes, ma'am. Like I said, there ain't much of 'em left."

"Good!" She released him and took a step back, trying to settle herself.

"What's goin' on, luv?" Her husband was finally up on his

feet and came to her side, ignoring Sarl altogether. "Is somethin' wrong with Dovira?"

Yana turned to face him. "Ani," she whispered so low that Sarl could barely hear her, "there's somethin' evil afoot. I don't know why those boys decided they needed ta attack tha Madors, let alone kill 'em, but it's worse than that. I...I'm just glad they're all dead!" She put her hands to her mouth, clearly shocked at what she had just said.

"Yana!" A horrified look crossed the farmer's face. "Why would ya say that?"

"It's just that... Oh, Ani, I was cleaning tha poor girl up an' noticed..." She glanced over at Sarl and then back to her husband. "I think they *all* violated her! It's so bad...I don't think she can ever have... Why her, why Dovira?" She hugged her husband close as her voice trailed away, angry tears spilling out of her and onto his neck.

Sarl felt the darkness rising within him again, and it was all he could do to focus on everything he had seen and heard this day. He still couldn't string all the events together to where he could make sense of them. *Unless...*

"Yana," he said as gently as he could. "Did Dovira say anythin' to ya? Anythin' at all?"

"No, nothin'." Yana released her husband and quickly wiped her eyes with the sleeve of her blouse. "She ain't moved at all, starin' at nothin'. I left our granddaughter ta mind her 'cause I don't think she should be alone."

"I'm sorry ta ask, but was there anythin'...strange about her?

Her clothes, or maybe her skin?"

"Ha!" the old lady exclaimed sarcastically, and she put her hands on her hips. "Ya mean besides tha fact she's been *raped?!*" She glared at Sarl, and he looked away.

"Sorry, ma'am. Just tryin' ta work somethin' out." He bowed in apology and then turned to walk towards the oak trees where the young woman had been found.

The tall grass had been matted down under the tallest tree where Dovira must have lain for some time before the farmer discovered her. Sarl breathed in deeply, and his gut tightened as he confirmed what he had suspected and feared. The vovkulaka had been here with her. It must have been with her the whole time, both in the house and at the campsite. *She* was the object of its desire. So, it hadn't been the local thugs who had raped and mutilated her after all. Which meant...

He knew what he had to do.

CHAPTER NINE

The King and She

"You wanted to see me, Father?" Lianne did a slight curtsy in the doorway, purely out of habit, as the royal family dispensed with most formalities when alone with each other. She was happy for this respite in decorum, as she had heard some courts carried titles even into their bedchambers. She had wondered aloud in the past how someone could shout out "Your Royal Highness!" while in a station of passion, much to the amusement of Melina. Now, she fought to control the calm look on her face as she remembered the bawdy conversation that had followed that comment.

Her father, His Royal Highness King Elric Kalchik II, looked up at her and smiled. "Ah, my dear! Yes, come sit with me." He shuffled some papers and moved his lantern to the side of the small table he had been writing at while she entered the room and sat down in the chair opposite him.

The furniture in the small study was quite simple in nature for a king, but it was sturdy and performed its responsibilities well enough. The fireplace in the corner of the room was lit, creating shadows that danced playfully across the various ancestral portraits that decorated all four walls. It was providing a modicum of heat, enough to chase away the autumn chill.

Her father reached across the table and quickly squeezed Lianne's hand in a show of affection. "So, tell me, what part of our kingdom did Master Gregor lecture on today?"

"The southern counties, Father, specifically the ones that border the lands of Astrikhon."

"Was the lesson solely geographical in nature, or did he delve into other more interesting issues?"

Lianne smiled placidly. *Of course, he lectured on other issues, Father! I'm sure you gave the old man an agenda to follow.* "I knew the geography of the area well enough already, so he switched to a history lesson. I assumed this was because you have been discussing trade rights with them during council, and he wanted to provide me with some perspective on our long relationship with the Astrikhon kingdom."

Her father nodded. "Yes, indeed. I am glad he chose to do so, and I am gladder still that you surmised his reasoning. Did he go back in time before the last Grey Horde ravaged our lands?"

"No, he did not." Lianne had been disappointed in this, as she knew very little about the massive and semi-mythical orc armies that had crushed the eldar into near extinction and then held sway over various human kingdoms for almost a thousand years. Truth be told, she had never received any sort of formal education on the remaining orc tribes to the east. *Just drunken ballads and old wives' tales meant to frighten children into behaving.* "He only referenced it at the beginning of the lesson, that the Army of Man was the first time our two kingdoms were allies in any real sense of the word."

"A wise place to start. And no doubt he discussed how the

relationship has ebbed and flowed over the years due to mostly petty squabbles?"

Lianne briefly outlined several centuries' worth of broken treaties and border skirmishes for him, information he knew only too well. "He only delved into greater detail with the assassination of King Rurik Kalchik some eighty years ago."

"Hmm, yes. Definitely *not* a petty squabble, when a ruler is cut down by a neighbor."

"But that's just it, Father! Master Gregor stated that it was never determined whether the assassin had truly come from Astrikhon! That the evidence was circumstantial at best."

Her father was quiet for a few moments, his gaze first drifting towards the ceiling, as if looking for divine inspiration, and then to a particularly stern face that peered out from a painting to his left. When he spoke, it was in a sober tone. "Rurik the Peacemaker was—is still—a hero to many people in this country. It was, after all, during his reign that we truly began our long journey towards political relevancy and prosperity. But he also made many enemies, especially outside our borders. Astrikhon had much to lose when he was able to forge a lasting peace with Oircadia without their involvement. In their minds, it upset the balance of power in the region to be against them. If they did not strike the actual blow, they certainly condoned it." He sighed and refocused his look on Lianne. "In the end, it meant the same to our people."

Lianne leaned forward in her chair. "Regardless, Master Gregor believes that your great-uncle collaborated with Astrikhon and was the mastermind behind the...uh..." She faltered as her father raised his hand to silence her.

"My child, do not start down that tired and well-traveled path of lies and rumors. Duke Isialav was supposedly many things, but one thing I believe he was *not* was a traitor. Both the inquisition and our ancestors cleared him of any wrongdoing, and that was the end of it as far as the church and our family were concerned. There were many other issues to deal with at the time, obviously. But the courtiers loved to wag their tongues as much then as they do now, so the story of the 'Bloody Duke' spread to all corners of the kingdom and beyond."

He looked pensive as he continued. "You would do well to remember this unwelcome proclivity of the court in your dealings with them. Gregor should remember this as well." He stood up abruptly and walked the few paces to the hearth, shaking his head. "And by the Almighty, I will remind him myself." This last part was to himself, but Lianne's well-honed ears caught the angry murmur.

"My apologies, Father. Dredging up hearsay about the family's distant past was not my intent."

He relented slightly. "I know, my dear, I know. I say this mainly to remind you to think before you speak, as what is distant history for you may not be so far away for others. Even these protected walls have ears, and we do not need to raise old troubles to mix with new ones."

Lianne was taken aback by her father's warning. *Is he really worried about spies here?* She glanced behind her at the door to the room, which she had left open upon entering. *Shite, the guards! Is he worried one of them is listening?*

He turned away from the fire in time to see the direction of her gaze and the worried look on her face. He chuckled lightly, and when Lianne looked at him with an arched eyebrow, he returned her quizzical look with a somewhat rueful smile. "My apologies. I should not have chastised you so harshly just now, as we are quite safe from any interlopers here in this room. Justinian guards the other end of the secret route that leads here, and if he was a traitor, I would have been dead ages ago."

Lianne blinked rapidly, and once again struggled to maintain a calm look. *He misinterpreted what I was looking at! A passageway here? I thought Lucas and I had found them all months ago!*

"A secret passageway, Father?" she attempted to ask innocently.

"Come now, Lianne! Do you really think you and that servant girl of yours are the only ones who use the hidden passageways for spying on others? Ah, do not fret," he continued as she felt her face grow hot with embarrassment. "It pleases me that you discovered them and are already using them to your advantage. Knowledge is more precious than gold, and court knowledge is even more valuable than that."

"Well, yes, that is true enough." Lianne decided to press a bit. "Who else knows of these passageways? I have never dared ask anybody for fear of disclosing their existence."

"Who knows? Those that need to know," he answered rather obliquely. "I am glad you have the wisdom of your mother to stay quiet about such matters. Do you trust—what is her name, Melania?—that she will also remain quiet?"

"Melina, Father. And, yes, I trust her with my life!"

"Let us hope it does not come to that. But, fair enough." He paused briefly. "I assume you are aware that your brother knows of these passageways as well?"

Lianne hesitated in kind, but then nodded and came clean. "Yes, I know. Lucas and I have, uh, shared notes on what we have found."

He nodded, obviously unsurprised at this minor confession. "He came to tell me all about it the instant he discovered them, of course, with that boundless energy of his. I almost had to whip him to keep his mouth shut about them. Too boastful and eager to please certain young ladies of the court already, that one. Yes," he continued as he walked back to the table and sat down, "he would do well to learn some discretion from you."

"Lucas is still young, and I believe he will learn such things in time." Lianne was pleased with her father's compliment but felt she had to defend her brother at least a little.

"I trust you are right. But I did not request your presence to discuss your siblings or secret doorways."

He started to arrange the papers that were lying on the table between them and inspected several of the top documents closely. Lianne noted he had to squint his eyes to read whatever was written upon them. As for the news about another passageway, she put the nugget of information to the side for now but would not forget it. *Mel is going to be busier than she thought on the morrow.* And then, almost as an afterthought, *Who does Father have watching me?*

The king found what he was looking for and held up what appeared to be a proclamation. "No, the subject we must discuss involves matters of state. I believe you are ready for a diplomatic mission of sorts that involves the subject matter of Master Gregor's lecture today."

"Father!" Excitement and anxiety mixed together in both her stomach and her exclamation.

The man on the other side of the desk had stopped being her father for the moment and assumed the mantle of royal leadership. He looked at her coolly as he reversed the paper in his hand and formally offered it to her. She accepted it demurely and quickly scanned it.

After reading for a few moments, Lianne looked up, puzzled. "An investiture ceremony? For me?"

"Yes, my child. You will formally become the heir apparent come next Martius, on your birthday."

"Is this formality *really* necessary, Father?" She continued in a rushed manner before he could reproach her for being mildly insolent, "What I mean is, you and Mother have always supported me and have prepared me well for my future duties. The court has known for quite some time that this is your plan. There is no other strong claim to the throne outside our family, and Lucas cares nothing about the throne; all he wants to do is hunt."

Her father leaned back in his chair. "You would be surprised how quickly a young man's thoughts can turn to things such as power and authority. The thoughts of any man or woman, for that matter. But I do have faith that your brother will stand by your side and serve you faithfully. He loves you with all his being and would protect you to the last. No, this ceremony will be for the people, both within the realm and without. It is indeed a formality, but one that has played out over many generations of our family. I believe it is necessary to play it out once more for tradition's sake as a whole, but more importantly, to enforce your rights against those that would question the authority of a woman."

Lianne scoffed and this time let her insolence stand. "*Really*, Father? I thought that debate was settled by the Council of Basel years ago!"

"That was for religious positions only. Certainly, that is important, since the power of our throne ultimately comes from the Almighty One. However, the church typically does not meddle much in secular matters such as this, so long as the annual tithe and the appropriate number of acolytes are provided." He frowned. "Regardless, there are many who hold fast to the old ways, even if the old ways have been swept to the side by the march of time. You will, after all, be the first ruling queen of Perizidon. It will be important to follow all the rites for the investiture of the heir apparent, as I said, if not for you, then for others."

Lianne studied her father. There was a gap of some thirty years between them. She knew this was because his first wife had died without bearing any children and it had been several years after that before he had married her mother. Time had been mostly kind to him, at least until recently. There was only a touch of grey in his hair, and he still rode at the front of the fall hunting parties. Master Gregor had been his teacher many years ago and still compared all current students to her father's acumen. His extended time spent on the throne had given him much wisdom in the ways of politics, and very little escaped him in matters such as this. She sighed inwardly. He was, of course, right about the ceremony.

"Very well. I understand and agree with your reasoning. But what does Astrikhon have to do with my investiture?"

He fixed her with a stern look. "Come now, think before asking a foolish question such as that."

Her face felt hot again, although only slightly this time, and she thought for a brief moment. "You want them to attend?"

He nodded. "Very much so. We continue to work with them to slowly rebuild the old alliance. As you know, Symon has been at their court for several months now, negotiating various details on a wide-ranging agreement. Well, he returned last week with good news and a final version of the agreement that I signed last night. All that is left now is to send a delegation back to their capital with the signed document, and that delegation will also present a formal invitation to the investiture ceremony. An act of friendship, if you will. Symon assures me they will accept the invitation."

"And you want *me* to lead this delegation?" Lianne was stunned. This seemed too wildly important for her first diplomatic mission.

"Technically, the dragoman will lead the delegation, since he will be the senior diplomat, but Symon will, of course, be bound to obey you as the need arises. Hopefully, the need does not arise."

Lianne's mind raced as she thought of the potential reasons why she would be a royal appendage on a simple delivery mission. *Father wouldn't be sending me on a lark.*

"So, I am going...because you wish for me to be *seen*?"

"Yes, that is part of the reason. Having you present yourself to King Haldir and his court, before the ceremony, will give the appearance that we seek his acceptance, if not his approval, of your coming rule. I doubt he will be conceited enough to actually believe that we are attempting to curry favor with him at such a base level, but the gesture should still be appreciated. He is a vain man and likes to have his ego stroked."

"Still, if it is ultimately a meaningless gesture, then why do it in the first place?" *I am no bauble to be gawked at, Father! You know how I feel about this!*

"Part of the great game that is played, my dear. But beyond the machinations of old men, you truly do represent the future of our kingdom and, no doubt, the futures of both kingdoms will be intertwined as much as our pasts have been. Why not let the future of our kingdom offer an unsullied hand of friendship to their future?"

That's an odd phrasing. "Their future, Father?"

"Yes, their future ruler, King Haldir's son, Hadeon. He is your elder by roughly a year. The Astrikhon court does not have the same traditions we do, so he was proclaimed heir apparent upon his baptism, when he was just an infant. He was not part of the initial negotiations regarding this agreement, but Symon indicated he was at the final meeting, sitting next to his father. It is my assumption his grooming for rule is following the same trajectory as yours. Hopefully, there is common ground to be found and discussed between the two of you."

Wait... Oh Shades, please let it not be so! For a terrible thought immediately entered Lianne's mind.

"Father, these negotiations...they were matters of *state*, correct?"

"Hmm? Yes, of course. Primarily the disposition of troops at our respective frontier forts and taxes on the river trade. I will, of course, have Symon brief you on everything prior to your departure."

"Was the negotiation of my *betrothal* also a matter of state?" She trembled slightly as she asked the question, petrified at what the answer might be.

"What?!" He started to laugh before he looked more closely at her. He caught himself, quickly reached across the table, and took her hands up in his. "My eldest child and the pride of my life. Your mother and I would never demean you like that!"

Lianne's relief was immediate, and she squeezed her father's hands tightly. She was somewhat ashamed for doubting him in this matter, as he dissuaded the use of arranged marriages to resolve diplomatic issues within his own court. She knew that her mother had freely chosen him; she had boldly made the marriage request herself, for goodness' sake! But Lianne also knew that her father was correct in stating that the "old ways" died slowly for some. Melina had been promised to a local cobbler's boy some time ago, an ugly brute who threw rocks at dogs, and the poor girl had frequent nightmares about her future wedding night. *And I've seen the bruises her sister wears whenever her husband has been out drinking and whoring! She should never have been forced to marry that known lout in the first place.*

"I'm...I'm sorry, Father. I am overreacting."

As she slowly unclenched both of her hands, he deftly raised the right one to his lips and kissed it gently.

"No, my daughter, you are just a hopeless romantic."

She giggled as he released her. "Whatever do you mean?" *And how would you know? I've seen you and Mother together. Trust and respect to be sure, but romance? I do not believe it!*

"You simply wish to marry for love. That is difficult to do, even in the best of circumstances and with the perfect matchmaker in your service." He was looking around the room again, visiting the portraits one by one, as if seeing them for the first time.

Lianne followed his gaze as it stopped to linger on a small painting near the corner, almost lost in the shadows. It took her a moment to realize who he was looking at. *That's Father's first wife!*

What did Mel's mother say her name was?

The name clicked into place. "Forgive my rashness, Father, but are you thinking of Leysa?"

He turned to look at her, his eyes wide. "How did you...? Ah, it does not matter. Yes, I confess, I was thinking of Leysa."

"You...did you marry *her* for love?"

Her father suddenly looked very old, and he closed his eyes. He was silent for several moments before he pulled himself back to the present. He opened his eyes again and sighed deeply. "I will do your mother a great disservice if I speak on the matter at any length. It was many years ago and involves many people who have been in the ground for a very long time. But, yes, I loved Leysa dearly, and I was truly blessed that she loved me as well."

Oh my! Now I must know more about her! Lianne remained silent, hoping that her father would reminisce further.

But after a few more moments, he lightly slapped the table with his hands and stood up, as if he was fully clearing his head of old memories.

"Where were we? Ah yes, Hadeon. No, he is not your betrothed, although to give you fair warning, that issue was broached by his father during the initial discussions. While Symon would typically trade away his own mother if he thought it would gain him an advantage in a deal, he was smart enough to follow my lead and politely dismiss that idea, and it was quickly dropped."

Lianne grimaced internally. *Well, thank the Almighty that the dragoman is less of a snake than he lets on to be!*

Her father continued. “However, I do want you to meet Hadeon, but not for reasons of courting in the sense you were alluding to.”

She frowned. “I’m sorry, but I do not follow you.”

“You must court him for what he already is, the future leader of his country. His grandfather was a brutish laggard, who could barely read, and only lived to kill orcs and beasts of the forest. His father is a sullen prick, who has a sharp mind for trade but is vainglorious. Does this Hadeon take after either of them, or is he his own man? Will he look you in the eye when he speaks with you, or will he be too interested in the cut of your dress? Will he toast your good health, or will he ignore common courtesy? You will most likely be dealing with him, or against him, for several decades, so it is important to build an informed first opinion of him, as that will guide our kingdom’s relationship with him and his court. You will have reports from Symon and others to assist you, but you will be making the ultimate decision on how we commence negotiations on any future agreements. Just remember, there are many steps to this dance.”

Lianne smirked a bit at one of her father’s favorite phrases, but she also swallowed hard. *Heavy will be the crown upon my head.* “So, travel to be seen, but also to observe?”

A look of approval crossed her father’s face. “Exactly! Ah, you will make a fine queen indeed!”

“Hopefully not *too* soon, Father.” She openly grinned at him.

He smiled back at her. “I agree, my dear. Hopefully not too soon. I do not intend to become a spirit and haunt you for a while yet.”

She wrinkled her nose at him in a most un-queenly manner. He laughed at the facial expression she had been making since she was old enough to understand his sense of humor, and for a brief moment, she felt like a little girl again.

Lianne went back to reviewing the document her father had handed her earlier, reading through it carefully. She was vaguely aware of her father tending to the fire before he returned to the table. He sat once more, waiting for her to finish. The fire crackled and hissed in the background, but no external sounds penetrated the study.

“The investiture seems like quite the event,” she said dryly when she reached the end of the treatise.

“Mmm, yes. They always are. I am already clearing some of the woods to the south of the city so there will be room enough for the various royal houses and other invitees to mingle when they wish to do so.”

“How much space are you allotting each party?” Lianne already had many questions that were not addressed in the document she was holding. *How many delegations? Will each be afforded the same amount of space? Who will be housed next to each other? Where will the delegation of the Holy See be placed? Do we have to feed them? How long will they stay?*

“Roughly two hectares each. The assignment grid will be

discussed at the next council meeting. I believe we will be able to accommodate up to eight major delegations in the first arc, but Master Builder Kitko does not agree with my calculations."

She never does! Lianne detested the bad-tempered woman and couldn't wait to get rid of the miserable shrew when she ascended to the throne. *If no one has accidentally killed her on a construction site before then... May the Almighty forgive my evil thoughts.*

"Eight? How many delegations are you inviting, Father?"

"That is a good question, my dear. We already sent an invitation to Kostantine, of course, and it is understood that the Holy See will grace us with a high-ranking official. I have left it to Archbishop Dorjan to settle all those arrangements. Insofar as secular invitations go, I have the main list here." He took another document from the table and offered it to Lianne.

She held it for some time, studying it closely. *Kingdoms, fiefdoms, free cities, even the distant so-called Holy Roman Empire. God's bones, there are over three dozen names here!* However, she noticed that Astrikhon was not on the list, as well as a few more neighboring domains.

"You said the 'main' list, Father. I presume this not the *only* list?"

He smiled. "You are, of course, correct. Those are the invitations being sent out as a formality, to avoid being accused of snubbing some far off lord or lady who would never attend in the first place. If any on that list attend, and I assume a least a few will, if only to be seen by others, we will, of course, accommodate them. Nay, I am sure you noticed who was *not* on that list...those that must be dealt with carefully and with all due consideration. A priority list, so to speak."

"Like Astrikhon?"

"Like Astrikhon."

"Are you including Oircadia on this priority list?" She was genuinely curious.

Her father nodded. "Yes, indeed. Well, as best we can, at least. It is always somewhat difficult to know who to invite from their confederation. We already sent a delegation into their lands a few weeks ago. The archbishop was loath to send more missionaries into orc territory, but we had several rangers volunteer to go with the woman who was selected to make the attempt. We didn't know how long it would take to make contact with their court, but lo and behold, our small party was met by a warband barely a league past the Riphean Gap!"

"The orcs knew they were coming?" Lianne's stomach tightened just a touch. "Do they have spies or informants among us?"

"Most assuredly so, and apparently more active than we thought. Nevertheless, it appears to have worked out for the best. They took the sister's vestments and made her swear by our Almighty that she would not proselytize in their territory, but then they escorted our people straight to the current capital of the Choros tribe. They were given an audience with the khan, who lavished them with gifts and swore on their heathen gods that the peace between our nations still stands. He was honored to be invited to"—here her father hesitated, to clear his throat—"to your 'Day of Despoilment,' as he put it."

"What?!" *The Almighty preserve me, are the old wives' tales about the orcs actually true?*

"Yes, well, I believe something was lost in translation, as I am told our missionary was a bit taken aback by her gift and may have been distracted at the time."

Lianne cast a sideways glance at her father. "And what, pray tell, was her gift?"

"A naked female slave."

Lianne couldn't help herself and snickered.

"Lianne Kalchik, this is no laughing matter!" her father admonished her severely, but she could see the smile he was trying to hide as clear as the midday sun.

An instant later, they were both laughing like two drunken farmers.

After a rather long spell, Lianne was finally able to catch her breath. "What were the rangers given? Matching naked male slaves?"

Her father had resorted to dabbing his eyes with a handkerchief. "Oh no, they were given handsome horse bows. The slave girl was obviously meant to be a joke. The sister set her free immediately upon their return, but what has happened to her after that, I do not know. The archbishop was livid, of course."

"Of course." *That dried-out husk of a man loses more of the church's flock after every homily, what with his strict interpretations of sin. Again, may the Almighty forgive my evil thoughts. Ugh, I will have quite the confession come the Sabbath!* "But what of the other tribes in the confederation?"

"From what we can gather, there are still four main tribes. The Choros khan—Basik is his name—denied our delegation further passage through his territory but said he would pass along our invitation to the other khans at their winter conclave. One of the rangers stayed behind to act as an emissary and to attempt to negotiate terms for the size of their overall party that will attend." He chuckled. "The last thing I need is several thousand orcs showing up at our border demanding passage to the capital."

Lianne didn't think it was a laughing matter, but she didn't outwardly react to his last comment. "But at least this Khan Basik is coming?"

"That was his stated intention. It will be interesting to meet him. He is a direct descendant of the Great Khan Ellac, who made peace with our ancestors. Since then, the Choros tribe has honored that pact and has been mostly successful in keeping the other tribes in line. We owe much to the orcs in regard to trade, as well. If anything, they have been more straightforward and honest than some of our human brethren."

Lianne was certain she knew who her father was referencing. "So, that leaves Malorossiya and Rusgorod. Are they on the priority list as well?"

"Yes, our collective 'friends' to the west will be invited, if for no other reason than to not give their leaders yet another slight to complain about. Malorossiya will send someone, I am sure, but as always, they will take their lead from the Rus. As for that bitter old man sitting on his throne in Gavan, who knows if he will grace us with his presence or send any sort of delegation." He shook his head and muttered to himself, "If we were to snub anyone, it would be him."

Lianne pretended not to have heard the last comment. "Aren't you worried about letting a delegation from Rusgorod inside our lands? Won't they see many things they should not?"

Her father shrugged with an air of resignation. "If the orcs have spies among us, then no doubt the Rus have even more. If it ever does come to war between us, it matters little what a delegation might see on their travels to our capital, as I assume there is nothing in the way of fortifications they haven't already seen. They may not even care, as I am sure King Ioseb believes his own propaganda that claims one Rus soldier is worth five of ours. Of course, his army is also over ten times the size of ours, just to make sure. And in any event, I hope to avoid war."

Lianne snorted and didn't even try to keep her scorn concealed. "And a simple gesture like inviting that tyrant to the investiture will avoid war? Come, Father, surely you do not believe that!"

"Careful, child. You sound too much like Symon. No, not just the one simple gesture, but the fact that it follows in the wake of many other simple gestures. We trade honestly with the Rus as best we can, we provided grain when they were hit by famine several years ago, and we have attempted to resolve our border disputes fairly. When that one general of theirs raped and pillaged his way through their frontier villages and then begged us for sanctuary, we handed him back to them bound in chains without hesitation. Rusgorod has no legitimate reason to think of us as their primary adversary, and I aim to keep it that way."

"Mother thinks that old man is a viper!"

"Well, she would know best, wouldn't she? At the end of the day, her grandfather is a known threat, and while it may be painful to do so, one that we should be able to counter."

Lianne was unconvinced. "I just don't know..."

Her father looked at her. For an instant the shadows on his face fell away, and Lianne knew she was looking at true royalty. His was not just an inherited crown but an earned one. Handsome, regal, stoic, benevolent, just, wise, valiant. So many words were conjured up in her mind when trying to describe him. The words became indistinguishable from each other until they were forged into one simple title: King. It was a fleeting glimpse, but in it, she knew that she would always strive to emulate the best of him in her own way. To reforge those words into another simple title: Queen.

The king's rejoinder brought honor to his title. "Think of it this way, Lianne. Ioseb has isolated himself and his country these past forty years since he took power. I doubt he has anyone left that he can truly call an ally. Even Malorossiya is but a vassal state that is a millstone about his neck. What do you believe he will think when he comes to our capital and sees the full might of those who have come to pay you homage? How will he react when he sees you take another step towards your rightful place among the rulers of humankind? He will see that while he has built walls and sought to bully his neighbors into submission, we have built bridges and sought long lasting ties of friendship. You will build upon the foundation laid out for you, surely as I have done. He will see our future is bright, and that he has no future. I truly hope he comes to witness your celebration and leaves a wiser and humbler man."

"Do you think that is possible?" she asked doubtfully.

He smiled. "No. But one can be optimistic."

She sighed. "I will try to follow your lead, Father. Truly, I will."

"Good. Just...just remember to be careful if and when Ioseb comes here. While it has been many years since I saw him face to face, based on his interactions with others, he has not changed his ways. That means he is still rude and spiteful and will do his best to draw you out. On top of that, on a personal level, it pains me to no end that he does not care for you or your mother."

"I understand." Lianne said grimly. "Mother says, if I were a firstborn *son*, things would be better between the kingdoms. To this day, she blames herself for the rift." *In all truth she blames me, whether or not her accusation is spoken.*

Her father must have sensed her thoughts. "Nonsense, Lianne! Your mother's actions that brought her to Perizidon only widened a rift that was already there between the kingdoms. And the subsequent bitter animosity occurred well before even the *thought* of you was conceived. You could be my firstborn son, or my dog, or my favorite walking stick, and it would not matter to Ioseb in the slightest. If you are bound to me, then he loathes your simple existence with every fiber in his body and will attempt to see you eradicated."

"Surely that's a tad exaggerated, Father." Lianne arched her left eyebrow and gave him a knowing look.

He smiled at her and reached across the table to pat her arm. "Of course it is, my dear. But do not let my hyperbolic tendencies get in the way of the truth. I cannot stress it enough that you must be mindful around Ioseb and his advisors at all times. If he does not want to kill you, then he will certainly want to humiliate you. If he can make you look weak and uncertain now, it will be much easier to sow the seeds of discontent later, when it is time for you to ascend to the throne. And he may not know it, but that time may come soon enough, I am afraid."

Lianne sighed internally but kept a stoic look on her face. This time, she knew her father wasn't exaggerating. It had been kept quiet, under pain of death, but her father was sick with an illness that the apothecaries couldn't diagnose. They kept insisting that, if they could do a little bloodletting, that would help them ascertain the truth. But on this issue Lianne agreed with her mother; letting some leeches feed on her father wouldn't solve anything. *It's barely one step above an orc shaman dancing around a campfire with deer shite spread on his face, praying to some heathen god.* In any event, her father was tired all the time and could not retain weight, no matter how hard he tried. He still projected a strong image in court, and even the entire inner council was not aware of the issue, but Lianne knew this would not last forever.

It was the reason she feared the investiture ceremony...that it was really a placeholder for a coronation.

"Come, Father. You have already told me that you will not become a spirit for some time to come. We will face this tribulation and all others together."

"Fair enough. I accept your offer of an alliance." He stood up one final time and came around the table to embrace her.

Knowing that the conversation was at an end, she rose up to hug him back and then stood on her tiptoes to kiss him on the cheek. His beard felt coarse against her lips.

"I will take my leave, Father. Thank you for entrusting me with this knowledge and for the task you have set before me."

"Good night, Lianne. It will be a week or so before Symon is ready to leave, but I will have him send you the list of provisions for your review in the morning. Oh, and I need you to meet with another special envoy who may be joining the delegation. We can discuss that tomorrow." He bowed deeply to her, with an amused look on his face.

She curtsied in return, then turned to leave the room. She glanced back as she reached the door, and he had already turned away, looking at the portraits on the wall. *Looking at Leysa's portrait, no doubt! I must hear more about her when the time is fitting.*

It was well past Compline, and she hurried down the hallway towards the stairs and her chambers. *Wait until Mel hears where we're going!*

CHAPTER TEN

Sarl In Stren

The early evening moon was just starting to peek over the horizon as Sarl entered town. He had timed his arrival well, as he was less than fifty paces inside the wall when the church bells started tolling for what was locally considered sunset. There was a general commotion behind him, but he didn't bother to turn around. No doubt the watch was changing, and with that, the main gate was closing for the evening.

Sarl was certain that the guards would still let known people of good repute enter through the smaller wicket gate. They probably would let known people of *ill* repute enter, as well, if their captain wasn't around and the bribe was sufficient. But he was definitely not a local, and he had just endured dirty stares and rude questions about his reasons for entering town. No amount of coin would have gained him entrance after the gate was closed, and he was grateful to have barely saved himself from another cold night in the woods.

Although it seemed nondescript in nature, he vaguely remembered being in this settlement at least once in the past. The solitary mountain that loomed above the town from a few leagues away was memorable enough at least. As the peak commanded the horizon for quite a distance around it, he knew he had been in its general vicinity previously and that there was precious little civilization beyond the town to the north. There were enough forested areas in the nearby foothills that he could maintain his charade as a trapper, but with this being a river town, he wondered if he should switch out wolves for beavers in his banter to blend in a bit better.

In any event, his real prey had been in the area not too long ago, and he was keen to keep pace. Similar to other settlements to the south, the vovkulaka appeared to have entered the town while the wargs had skirted around the populated areas immediately outside the walls. Unfortunately, the trail had gone cold as he had approached the main gate, presumably because of all the traffic coming and going from the river town. Sarl was hopeful he'd at least be able to pick something up at the local tavern. If nothing else, it gave him an excuse to come into town and sleep on something other than tree roots.

The main plaza was already quiet, the various food and goods stalls closed for the night. Several laborers hurried past, too intent on getting home to worry about a random orc roaming the streets. As he approached the town hall, he noted that the building was made of stone, a bit surprising this far out from civilization. *That, I'd remember. So maybe I ain't been here before? Sard it, there's tha tavern. Time ta quit thinkin' an' ta start drinkin'!*

The tavern in question was directly across the plaza from the town hall, and unlike all the adjoining structures, was ablaze with light. As he drew close, Sarl could see through the windows that it was still just the early crowd inside. His stomach growled.

Multiple days of iron rations and eating on the move was not uncommon for him, but it didn't mean he liked doing it. A worn sign above the entrance announced that he was about to enter the Wild Boar, and without breaking stride, he pushed open the door and made his way into the main hall.

Several patrons looked up as he entered, but to them, he was just another disheveled trapper coming in from the Wilds for a night of carousing. There was hulk of a man sitting at the end of the bar, almost as big as Sarl himself, and he pushed himself off his stool as the orc looked around the room, letting his eyes adjust to the brightness. As the enforcer approached, Sarl could see that he walked with a slight limp. No doubt some unruly drunk had gotten a quick hit in when he had been looking the other way. *Means he should be a bit more careful now. He probably doesn't drink as much on tha job as he used ta do. Looks ta be strong as an ox, but probably is slow as one too.*

"Weapons in tha locker, friend. Collect 'em when ya leave." The man was sizing him up, same as Sarl was doing to him, with both seemingly coming to the same conclusion. *It'd be a bit of a struggle, but I can take 'im.*

Sarl smiled at the order, showing his teeth, and slowly unbound the battle-axe from his back as he continued to look around the room. Nobody else seemed to be wearing a long blade, so at least it appeared to be the same rule for strangers as it was for locals.

"All weapons, mate? Or just me axe?" Sarl patted the

hunting knife strapped to his thigh but didn't move to unstrap it.

The brute smiled, trying to menacingly show *his* teeth in return but only showing how many were missing. "Nah, keep yer little stinga if ya want. Jus' keep it in yer pants 'round me!" He laughed at his attempt at a crude joke, which Sarl chose to ignore. It was too early in the evening to start something, and he was hungry.

He carefully deposited his axe in what appeared to be a converted water trough and then went looking for an empty table along the far wall.

An older, wiry man stood behind the bar, watching Sarl cross the room as he poured drinks. Sarl shifted slightly as he passed near the counter, enough so that a small bag of coins could be seen attached to his belt. The tenseness in the bartender's shoulders lessened somewhat and, knowing he had a paying customer, he nodded quietly to one of the barmaids lounging nearby. She fell in behind Sarl, following him to the table he had selected. It was near, but not quite wedged into, the corner of the room, and Sarl sat down with his back against the wall. The bench creaked under his weight, but it had seen worse and seemed solid enough.

"What'll it be, luv?" The maid had yellowish-brown hair and looked to be barely twenty. She retained a strong hint of the pretty young girl she had just been, and Sarl was quick to note that her breasts didn't sag, and her hips bore no signs of child birthing.

He smiled at her rakishly without showing his teeth. "As big an ale as yer barman can pour an' that you can carry, miss."

"That'll be pretty big, luv," she responded quickly, and she winked at him mischievously. She, too, had seen the bag of coins.

"I'll wager yer right, seein' tha size of yer, uh, arms," Sarl said, while unabashedly looking directly at her chest. "Tell me, miss, how's tha goulash here?"

"Best goulash this side of tha mountain, luv."

Sarl knew that wasn't saying much, since there was nothing but a cold wasteland on the far side of the lonely peak, but he played along. "Then I'll take a bowl. Just don't skimp on tha meat." He winked back at her, then bobbed his head courteously. "If ya please."

"Oh, as ya wish, yer highness!" She smiled and then turned quickly, making her long skirt twirl just so. Without looking back, she sauntered off towards the kitchen.

Oh, she makes tha boys 'round here harder than granite, that's for sure! Sarl smirked to himself as he slowly disentangled his bulk from his pack. His hunting knife was prominently featured on his hip, in case anyone looked at him from the direction of the bar, and he rather hoped he would be left alone long enough to eat in peace.

The goulash turned out to be excellent, enough so that Sarl ordered two more bowls as the evening progressed and the tavern slowly filled. The ale turned out to be terrible, enough so that he only ordered a half dozen more to wash down the goulash.

The tavern was louder and rowdier by the time he finished

his dinner, as several dice games had broken out among the locals. From what he could overhear, passe-dix seemed to be the local game of choice over hazard or other, simpler, options. The barmaid, whose name he had learned was Katrya when ordering his second bowl of goulash, flashed him a wide smile as she walked past with a round of drinks for the table in the corner, and he raised his mug in a tipsy salute.

I gotta be careful, in case one of her regulars decides I'm trouble.

Katrya glanced at him again on her return trip to the bar, and he motioned for her to join him. She quickly changed direction and came over, but rather than stand over him, immediately went to claim the empty chair opposite him. It was impossible not to notice as she sat down that her bodice had loosened at the top. There was just the hint of milky white flesh beneath her collarbone, and it teased at all that couldn't be seen. Sarl was sure it had been done on purpose, either for him or for someone else. He was also sure it was having the desired effect on him.

I drink anymore, an' I'll wanna be trouble.

"What can I do for ya, luv?" Katrya asked. She had wiped her hands on her apron as she sat down, and now she crossed her arms on the table as she leaned forward to hear him above the crowd noise.

He smiled and tried to stay focused. "I think I'm done, Kat. I can't eat any more goulash an' I don't want ta drink any more of that beer yer servin'. What do I owe ya?"

Her disappointment seemed legitimate. “Why are ya leavin’ so soon, luv? Ya got lots of time if ya want it. Ol’ Bainor won’t kick tha drunks out for at least several more hours.”

“Who’s Bainor?”

“Tha owner,” she replied, and she gestured towards the wiry man behind the bar. “So long as they”—she waved her hands all around her—“don’t break nothin’, he lets them stay ’til tha wee hours.”

“Good money, eh?” Sarl chuckled.

“Oh, for sure.” She laughed as well. It was a kind and cheerful laugh that seemed out of place amid the crude din of the crowd. “An’ he splits it with tha help, too, so we don’t mind tha extra work.”

“Well, that’s decent of him, for sure. Hey, he don’t happen ta have rooms here, does he? For tha night, I mean.”

“Sure, luv, an’ he’s got a couple open since it ain’t Sobota tomorrow.”

Based on this comment, Sarl assumed that the day before the Sabbath was market day for the town.

“Good. I meant ta ask him when I came in an’ forgot.” Sarl jerked his head at the table next to him. “Gotta hope tha rooms are away from this lot, though. Ain’t this Bainor worried someone will complain ta tha law about tha noise?”

“Silly orc, tha law’s right over there!” Katrya pointed to a table on the other side of the room, where a middle-aged man was sharing a drink and a laugh with a young woman. “Nobody will complain if tha sheriff is already here! An' trust me, he ain't movin' so as long as he keeps gettin' his free drinks."

Sarl smirked as he looked over at the couple. "Fair enough. What's his name? I need ta talk ta him too."

"Sheriff Farkas...uh, Yuri Farkas. Why ya gotta go talk with tha sheriff? Ya ain't thinkin' of talkin' ta him now, are ya?"

He ignored her first question but turned to face her. "Ya sayin' that I shouldn't go over there now?"

"Well, he don't like bein' bothered off duty, an' he don't like strangers, even when he *is* on duty. Besides, he's with his second, an' nobody should bother him if he thinks he's gettin' a piece of her tonight."

Sarl laughed. "Fine, I get it. I'll talk ta him tomorrow mornin' when he's in a good mood." He looked at the young woman with the sheriff a bit more closely. Her auburn hair was tightly braided, and her long angular face fit well with the rest of her well-tuned body. Even from across the room he could tell she had muscles to spare. "Well, if he's still alive after that strong lass rides him inta tha ground!"

Katrya smiled, but her eyes flashed dangerously when she heard the backhanded compliment toward the other woman.

Noticing this, Sarl took a long, last pull of his drink, carefully composing his face before putting the mug back down on the table. "Well, since ya asked, Kat, I would stay a bit longer, but..."

"But what, luv?" She seemed distracted, and he noticed she was staring at the sheriff and his second.

"But I don't got no company with me, an' I don't wanna listen ta this lot yammer on 'bout points all night." As she turned to look at him, he nodded at the dice game at the next table, which was getting quite animated.

The barmaid smiled and started to rise. "Well, if it's company ya want, I can find ya whatever ya fancy. Boy, girl, ya can—" She broke off with an exclamation as he somewhat forcefully put his right hand on the table, palm down. His empty dishes rattled but didn't fall off onto the floor.

The tone of his voice contrasted sharply with his sharp and sudden action. "What I'm tryin' ta say, Kat, is that I'd stay ta have a drink with ya, if yer up for it. But then, I suppose staff can't mix with patrons when yer on duty, now can ya?"

"No, we—" She halted, then met his eyes as her face turned pink. After a few moments, she stuttered out, "I...I ain't for rent, luv."

"I don't wanna rent ya, Kat. I wanna talk with ya. Been a long time since I had someone ta talk with. Besides, I don't know nothin' 'bout this town, an' ya seem ta know all that's important ta know."

He couldn't tell if she was disappointed or relieved that he didn't want to pay to bed her. Katrya seemed about to shift her hand over his, but instead, she quickly rose to her feet. She wouldn't look him in the eye again as she fiddled with the strings on her apron.

"Well, thanks, but yer right, I can't drink with ya. Bainor's probably already sour that I spent this much time talkin' an' not workin'. Ya owe ten copper. Just pay at tha bar when ya ask for that room." With that, she turned and weaved her way through the crowd, disappearing into the kitchen.

Sarl watched her go and shook his head. *I'll never figure out humans. Especially the female ones.*

There was a loud cheer from his neighbors as he gathered up his pack and made to leave. As he stood up, he glanced over the top of the two men closest to him. Everyone around the table was thumping each other on the back or spilling ale as they knocked their mugs together in congratulatory toasts. Everyone except for one young man, who was seated at the far side of the table. He seemed frozen in time, staring straight ahead, as if dumbfounded at what he saw. Sarl couldn't see the dice, but he knew the look all too well. A sure thing had turned out disastrously wrong.

Sarl didn't stick around to hear what or how much the youngster owed the rest of the table. It didn't matter to him, and he was tired from many hard days in the Wilds. He made his way towards the thin man behind the bar, who looked up as he approached to greet him with a curt smile.

"Evening, good sir. Need another drink?"

Sarl stifled a yawn. "Nah, I owe ya for dinner, an' I'll take a room if ya got one."

"Very good. Let me get the ledger." Bainor glanced over at the enforcer, who was still seated at the end of the bar, and made some gesture with his left hand. It was obviously a signal of some sort, but Sarl didn't see any noticeable shift in the large man's position or demeanor. The tavern owner then disappeared into the storeroom behind the bar that appeared to double as an office.

Sarl turned around to scan the room as he waited for the tavern owner to return. As he did so, the young man from the corner table staggered up to the bar, obviously still traumatized from his loss.

The front of his shirt was wet, and he smelled of a mixture of bad wine and even worse ale. "Where's Bainor?" he called out.

"Whatcha need, Faddei?" It was one of the other barmaids. She was older and heavier than Katrya, and she looked like she had farmer's wife strength. She glanced over at the drunk as she poured a round of drinks, a mild look of disgust blending with just a hint of motherly concern.

"I need Bainor! I wanna complain 'bout how he lets folks in here with loaded dice!"

The older barmaid shook her head. "Maybe don't get soused before playin', ya ever thought of that?"

Faddei stared at her blankly. The thought had obviously never crossed his mind. "Where's Bainor?" he weakly mumbled to himself, and he looked around for the owner. His hazy gaze stumbled across Sarl, and the drunkard seemed to notice him for the first time. Faddei's head lolled back as he tried to look Sarl in the eye. "Whatcha lookin' at, *pes*?"

Sarl narrowed his eyes, but he stayed where he was. "I'm lookin' at a loser, I reckon."

"What?" The young man took a step back and steadied himself on the bar. "What'd ya call me, *pes*?!"

"I called ya a loser, boy, an' you're a piss poor loser at that if yer callin' everyone else a cheat." Sarl looked down at his right hand as he spoke, like he was checking his nails, but his body tensed for whatever idiotic action was about to come next.

Faddei turned several shades of purple, and now he managed to exceed even Sarl's estimate of idiocy. Bainor reappeared from the back room, and the drunk looked rapidly between him and Sarl. "I'm done with this shitehole, Bainor! First ya let cheats in, an' now I gotta take insults from this *pes*! It ain't right, an' I got half a mind ta fix things proper!" He tried to spit in Sarl's face but failed miserably.

Cursing in anger and embarrassment, he drew a small blade from a sheath that had been hidden in the small of his back. "I'll cut ya down ta size, *pes*!"

The enforcer was on his feet in an instant, moving quicker than his bulk would suggest.

As the older barmaid took a step back, Bainor shouted ineffectively at Faddei, "No daggers! No daggers!"

The room seemed to collapse upon itself, as all eyes turned towards the bar in anticipation of a show.

But, in the blink of an eye, it was over. Without even moving from his place at the bar, Sarl had Faddei's blade in one hand and his throat in the other, holding him at arm's length above the ground. The enforcer stopped a pace or two away from the pair, seemingly confused as to why the young human was desperately kicking his feet, both of his hands scrabbling at the huge fist that was choking him.

Sarl brought the struggling drunk closer to him so that they were face to face. He tilted his head slightly and hissed in the barely conscious man's ear as he continued to squeeze. "This *pes* don't bite, boy, but I do more than yer sorry barkin'! Ya wanna go from poor loser ta dead loser, *pizda*?"

"That'll do, stranger! Why don't ya put him down 'fore things get worse than they already are?" a voice rang out across the room, which had turned eerily quiet.

Sarl glanced over at the speaker. It was the sheriff who had addressed him from across the now-quiet room. He was still seated at his table, but the young lady with him had stood up, her hand on the hilt of her longsword. The rules regarding weapons didn't appear to apply to the law, although Sarl couldn't tell if the sheriff was similarly armed.

Sarl smiled with his teeth showing and looked back at Faddei. "Worse, eh?"

What was left of his conscience whispered at him from the depths. *C'mon, meat, ya don't wanna sit in a cell for killin' this shitehole.*

He sighed. "Fine, be that way." He lowered his arm and released the now-limp form.

Faddei fell to the floor like a ragdoll, his neck red but still in one piece. Sarl flipped the dagger in his hand so that he was holding it by the blade and offered it to enforcer. The hulk of a man looked at the tiny blade blankly. Sarl assumed that he usually started or ended fights, so having done neither in this case seemed to have him a bit confused about whether he should pummel Sarl or not. The enforcer looked over at Bainor for direction, who himself was still trying to process what had happened.

It was the older barmaid who was the first to recover. "Hey, uh, stranger! Next time, give us a moment ta take odds on ya!" She smiled at him, and several patrons seated near her at the bar chuckled nervously.

Sarl looked at the woman, trying to read what she was conveying with her eyes. He could tell that she didn't want trouble, but more for her sake or his, it was hard to say.

He calmly placed the dagger on the bar in a small gesture of peace, and she rewarded him by sliding a mug of ale already poured for someone else down to him. Catching it up, he drained in a single motion, ignoring the awful taste it left in his mouth.

He looked around the still silent room and grinned. "Think tha guy on tha floor just bought a round for tha house!"

Cheers and laughter erupted from the table in the corner, and the noise rippled out into the rest of the room. Within a few moments, several people were shouting out their orders for a free drink. Bainor, having recovered his senses, motioned at his servers to go ahead and pour. He gave a different signal to the enforcer, who came forward and hoisted the unconscious form off the floor. He easily threw Faddei over his shoulder and headed towards the main door.

The tavern owner turned to address Sarl, shaking his head as he did so. "You just stuck that lad in debtor's prison, 'cause I'm not fronting him the kind of coin you're spending for him."

Sarl shrugged. "Like I care. Now, what about tha room?"

"Ah, yes." Bainor returned to business just as quickly. "One room, one night?" Seeing Sarl nod, he continued. "Apologies for not havin' a bath, but I can have hot water and a basin sent up if that'll do."

"Aye, that'll do."

"Very well. Please sign here." The bartender turned the ledger around and offered up a charcoal pencil. "Your mark will do. It'll mean you're paying me a silver piece for a room with one bed for one night, plus hot water, and breakfast in the morning. I put what ya owe for tonight in that total as well."

Sarl could have signed the ledger, but instead, he dutifully made a large "X" mark where the other man was indicating. He dug a silver kopek out of his pouch and placed it on the bar next to the dagger. Bainor nodded and handed him two wooden markers. One had been painted green, the other blue.

"Go out the door you came in and turn right. 'Bout ten paces down will be a door with a single lantern, go in there and see the woman at the counter. Give her those markers, and she'll take care of you. Breakfast is in here, any time after Prime."

Sarl gave the man an informal salute and turned to go, noting that both the money and the weapon were no longer in sight. The enforcer, having disposed of his load somewhere outside the tavern, was back at his post. He intently watched Sarl retrieve his weapon from the converted water trough but remained silent.

As Sarl adjusted the straps that held the axe to his back, he sensed someone else standing a few paces behind him. He slowly turned and was not overly surprised to see the sheriff's second standing there. She had taken a neutral pose, with hands on hips, and her weapon remained sheathed.

The woman smiled, not too unkindly. "Evenin', sir. 'Fraid I gotta ask ya some questions 'bout tha lad ya just put in one of me cells."

Sard me sideways, I just wanna go sleep! Sarl blinked and thought for a moment before comprehending. "Ah, you're tha jailer then?"

"That I am, good sir. Kira Toth, at yer service." Her stance didn't change, and she didn't seem the least bit intimated by his size.

"Well, Jailer Toth, I'd say tha lad just slipped in his own filth an' I happened ta catch him a bit awkward, that's all. Think he fits tha role of bein' drunk an' disorderly, if I ever saw it."

Her smile hardened ever so slightly. "Oh, come now, orc. Those pretty eyes of yers ain't brown, but yer still full of shite with that rot. I'm gonna need a proper statement from ya."

Sarl sighed. "I ain't goin' nowhere tonight, so perhaps I can give ya a statement in the mornin'?" He hoped this was enough for her, because otherwise he didn't have the energy to either talk or fight his way out of the tavern.

She thought about his offer for a few moments before relenting. “Fine. Get ta tha town hall ’round Terce. If I ain’t there yet, then wait ’til I show. Tha guards will know not ta let ya leave town otherwise, so please don’t be stupid.”

“Fine, whatever. Tomorrow, town hall, Terce.” Without so much as a wave, Sarl turned and headed for the door.

***

As he lay awake in bed sometime later, Sarl couldn’t get the barmaid out of his head, and it confused him. Sure, she had been pretty and had a quick wit, but there was something more than that running through his head. If he were truthful with himself, he would have admitted that she reminded him of Elise.

His inability to fall asleep wasn’t helped by the fact that he could sense somebody outside his door. He had stayed quiet enough that, if they had wanted to attack him when they thought he was asleep, they would have made the attempt by now. But no attack had come. He decided if whoever or whatever was out there didn’t want to come in and assault him in the room, then it wasn’t worth his while to go out and confront them in the hallway.

Maybe that blasted shapeshifter has spies in town, an’ they’re just markin’ my location? Is that why it came ta town, ta meet up with someone? But I didn’t smell it in tha tavern, even though I’m sure it stopped there. So much for takin’ tha chance that it’d be in town tonight. Guess I’m back ta trackin’ tha pack tomorrow. They better not wander off too far.

Thinking about the weeks-long pursuit north brought him back to where it started, and the fact that he wouldn't be where he was now if he hadn't answered Elise's call for help. Thinking about her over the years had always helped center and calm his thoughts, but not since their last meeting. If anything, thinking about her now was having the opposite effect.

Sarl absentmindedly played with the talisman that hung around his neck, trying to put coherent thoughts together. A bluish-green garnet, it and its brother had been a treasured family heirloom that Elise had stolen from her mother in a moment of spite. She had tearfully given him one of the stones when she left their small village some five years ago for the priesthood. Originally fashioned in a thin solitaire ring setting, Sarl had since had it remade into a pendant on a silver chain link necklace that he kept hidden under his tunic.

He had left the village for good shortly after Elise had, and the stone was his only connection to her and his past. The connection to Elise was both figurative and literal as it turned out, as the stones had revealed a strange secret once they had been separated from each other for a time. At some point in the distant past, old magic had been applied to them, the knowledge of this being lost as they had been passed down through generations of Elise's family as nothing more than valuable gems. But even now, countless years since magic had gone the way of the eldar, the garnets called to each other across the leagues, a surprise that the two erstwhile lovers had discovered and taken advantage of on occasion.

So long as they wore their individual stones close to their bodies, Sarl and Elise would have a vague idea where the other one was located. They also knew from experience that deeply urgent thoughts could be conveyed across the expanse between them; it was why Sarl had known to head to Krov in the first place and why events there had played out as they had. He had long suspected that deeply passionate thoughts could be passed along as well by the stones' connection, but he had always resisted the urge to try. Now, he tried to push all thoughts of her, especially passionate ones, from his mind.

Barely on my mind? More like all the sardin' time… He tossed and turned, debating whether he should rip the pendant from his throat and cast it and Elise out of his life. And yet he knew he wouldn't. If she called to him again, even now, he would run to her like he always did.

At some point, he couldn't sense anyone outside of his door anymore, and he passed into fitful dreams.

***

Katrya had stood in the hallway for a very long time, thoughts racing through her mind as she debated what to do. Why was she drawn to this trapper? Sure, he had been marked when he came into the tavern, and she had dutifully played her part, but there was more to him than that. Perhaps it was because she sensed he had a story to tell, one that would take her far away from Stren and her troubles. Perhaps it was because he had treated her as more than just a piece of meat at the end of their encounter. Or perhaps it was just because she had never been with one of his kind, and his scent both excited and scared her.

She could hear faint rustling from his room from time to time, but she knew he was alone. What would he do if she knocked?

Eventually, she turned and ran, like she always did.

CHAPTER ELEVEN
The Prince Of Astrikhon

Prince Hadeon Sokolov of Astrikhon was tired, bored, and above all, miserable. The hunt was not going well at all. It was raining, which meant the dogs had lost the scent when the wild boar had gone to ground. Worse still, it was a cold, steady rain that had slowly worked through his outer garments and seeped into his bones. He was already chilled through and through, and he wondered if he would be able to feel his toes or move his feet whenever the call came to push forward. He shifted slightly, trying to find the last bit of dry material to place between him and the sky.

He could barely make out the men on either side of him, even though each was only ten paces away. The Master of the Hunt had called for the picket line to hold in place some time ago in the hopes that the mist would rise a bit, but so far, all that had happened was that everyone was now wetter and hungrier than before. At least Hadeon had halted underneath a sizable tree; some cover was better than none. Poor Aleksei, to his right, had been caught in the open and appeared to be on the verge of melting into the tall grass he was standing in. Hadeon would have just moved up to the tree line if he had been in Aleksei's waterlogged shoes, but as crown prince, he could get away with such ill-mannered discipline, while his manservant could not. Aleksei feared the whip from the Master of the Hunt more than the rain, so he remained where he was.

Trying to think of anything other than various forms of precipitation, Hadeon focused on the upcoming king's council meeting on the morrow. Dragoman Chumak, or the Pompous Prick from Perizidon, as he was derisively called by most of his father's advisors, would be the main topic of conversation once again. He would soon be back amongst them, bringing with him the signed trade agreement that both kingdoms had labored on for so long. Hadeon's father had grudgingly admitted that the agreement was a solid one and would help secure the kingdom's northwestern border for the foreseeable future, so the diplomat would be welcomed with the proper amount of formal civility and respect. However, the fact that the prick was bringing the Perizidon heir apparent with him was much more intriguing to the entire Astrikhon court, including Hadeon.

Obviously, the fact that the firstborn of King Elric II of Perizidon was a girl had been known ever since her birth. There had been some speculation that Princess Lianne would be passed over as heir when her brother came along several years later, but this idea had been squashed almost immediately by various foreign dignitaries. Reports from embedded court spies had long corroborated the fact that Perizidon would have their first ruling queen whenever Elric passed on into eternity. Personally, Hadeon found it curious that this had ever been thought a contentious issue, but then he knew from personal experience that old traditions faded very slowly. If this was true in both Astrikhon and

Perizidon, perhaps it was the same the world round.

What was maddening to his father was that Elric had always refused to negotiate terms for his daughter's hand in marriage. Even now, on the precipice of Lianne's investiture, Symon the Prick had made it quite clear this was nonnegotiable. In his father's opinion, this stubbornness had caused the discussions on the trade deal to drag out for months, instead of just weeks, or even days.

"By Jehovah's bones, that idiot of a king has the best card in the whole deck, and he refuses to play it! How can I trust a man who is either too stupid to know better or too besotted with his own daughter to use her to bring everlasting peace to the region?" His father had raged on the matter any number of times during his council meetings, and Hadeon was sure some version of this diatribe would crop up again tomorrow. He vaguely wondered if his father saw him in the same light...as a piece of livestock on which he was trying to fetch the best price.

***

Several months prior, Hadeon had been interested enough in the marriage issue to raise the topic during a lesson with Master Pavel. Where did he, as a prince of a neighboring kingdom, rank in terms of perspective spouses for the young princess? The don chuckled and asked how serious the question was to be taken.

"After all, Your Highness, I am no matchmaker and am not predisposed to know what fair maidens desire in this day and age."

Hadeon laughed as well. "Heaven help us both, old man, if I am coming to you for advice on how to woo women! No, my question is merely diplomatic in nature."

The don smiled. "Ah, so you did read up on our succession laws after all."

"Of course! When have I ever—uh, never mind. Yes, and I believe most, if not all, of the kingdoms around us have laws for this occurrence as well."

"You are correct, Your Highness. Such a happenstance of firstborn royals wedding each other would be rare indeed, but archaic as they are, the laws born out of desperation during the time surrounding the last Grey Horde still hold legal weight. As you know, it is tradition that the *possibility* of such an arrangement be proposed as part of any formal alliance, even if it is never acted upon." Pavel did not have to tell Hadeon this was one reason why his father's council held such enmity against Symon the Prick. He had immediately dismissed the possibility of marriage from the recent treaty negotiations, breaking said tradition.

Hadeon crossed his arms. "So, if such an arrangement is merely improbable, and not impossible, my question stands. If she does marry another royal suitor, or even just a nobleman from another kingdom for that matter, how would that impact the relationship between our two kingdoms? Could there be some newly created alliance that could threaten us?"

They had been discussing the first draft of the agreement with Perizidon and the impact on trade routes to the south before Hadeon had wandered off topic. However, like any good teacher, Master Pavel was willing to indulge his student's curiosity for a short spell.

"Very well, Your Highness. Let me see..."

It was a warm summer day, and the don had to take care not to let any perspiration drip on the large map that lay spread out on the table before them. It was centered on their own kingdom but stretched in all directions for several hundred leagues. After a momentary pause, he began gesturing at various realms and city states, speaking more to himself than to the prince.

"We can eliminate Myste altogether, as the doge believes himself unassailable in terms of both wealth and prestige. He would command too high of a dowry just to marry some third cousin of his. That wouldn't mean anything of substance to Perizidon. And Kostantine doesn't factor into this conversation unless the young lady takes a pilgrimage to the holy city and marries the Son of the Almighty for all of eternity."

Hadeon smiled at this, but said nothing, while the don slowly circled the large table to look at the world from different perspectives.

"Would they look internally? Perhaps, perhaps...although King Elric is wise and tries to keep his courtiers in equal standing. He would not provide one with an unfair advantage over the others without major concessions. I suppose those in his court and their progeny would know the young lady very well and would offer the best chance for her to marry for love...Pfah! For love!" At this, the don went quiet for a long moment. From the distant look on his face, Hadeon could have sworn the older man was reliving some long-lost relationship. If he was, there was no mention of it as he resumed his monologue on potential challengers for the hand of the young princess.

"The Bulgars are too far away. Malorossiya makes no sense; they're just a mindless puppet of Rusgorod, and nobody in their right mind would negotiate directly with them. Rusgorod has no recognized heir or other children to wed, and it's not like King Elric would do them any favors even if they did. Probably wouldn't piss on King Ioseb if he was on fire, by all accounts..."

"What?" Hadeon knew there was no love lost between the two kingdoms to the north, but did the two rulers detest each other that much?

The older man waved his hand to silence the prince, attempting to remain concentrated on the immediate question. "Yes, yes, the Houses of Kalchik and Geladze despise each other. I'm surprised the Rus haven't invaded their neighbor, truth be told. Hmm, perhaps there is some usurper lurking about in that northern wasteland who is looking to secure the throne for themselves? Could King Elric be more cunning than we give him credit for and be negotiating with one of the Rus generals? No, we've investigated all of them, and none of them have a strong enough backbone to act on their own. There's no one worth securing an alliance with by way of losing a beloved daughter, anyway."

Pavel fell into another protracted silence, drumming his fingers on the edge of the table. Finally, he looked up at Hadeon.

"Well, Your Highness, unless Perizidon sends emissaries to the four corners of the known lands, I believe that only leaves Vkraina to our west as a potential royal contestant for Princess Lianne's hand in matrimony. Besides you, of course. But their royal family's eldest son just turned seven last month, so I believe you would come out on top in any battle of the mind or body. Hopefully, the young lad isn't too charismatic." At this, he winked at Hadeon, who laughed good-naturedly in return.

Hadeon himself studied the map for a spell, trying to view the world from his northern neighbor's perspective. Perizidon's peace treaty with the orcs, as wretched as it had made Astrikhon's position for many years, had secured their entire eastern front. It had allowed them to think about financial matters other than their army and brought stability within their own lands. *So why would they have thrown that stability away by angering their large neighbor to the northwest somehow? Or were their relations always bad with Rusgorod, even decades ago, meaning they were merely attempting to shore up their western front by making peace in the east?*

He addressed his teacher, waving at the northwestern portion of the map. "Master Pavel, why is there such enmity between Rusgorod and Perizidon? It hasn't always been like that between them, has it?"

The don walked slowly over to the corner of the map that Hadeon had gestured at. The territory claimed by Rusgorod extended past the map edge, making it difficult to recognize the physical threat they might pose to anyone else. He glanced down for a moment as if to get his bearings before responding.

"Remember that Perizidon was once a territory of the old Rusgorod empire, breaking away when the strength of the Rus army was at its nadir and they could not, or would not, protect the regional capital of Velych against orc aggressions from the east. Ever since, the two kingdoms have never been too closely aligned, and they have clashed over border disputes numerous times over the years. Even before their current ruler, the House of Geladze has always wanted to retake the world one league at a time. But they always had bigger, and in their minds, *better* targets to go after than Perizidon. But things took a serious turn for the worse after King Ioseb's son Georgy died fighting the Polotsk far to their west some years ago and left the old man to raise his two grandchildren all on his own.

"There is only speculation and rumor as to what happened within his family over the next few years. It could have been as simple as total disinterest in the children's well-being, to something as terrible as outright abuse and incest. Believe what you will. The end result was that, several years later, King Ioseb's grandson, Nikita, died under mysterious circumstances, leaving him without a male heir. His granddaughter, Arina, fled to Perizidon soon after that to escape the tyrant. It is said that her nanny and several ladies-in-waiting paid for her freedom with their heads."

Hadeon shook his own head at this. "This story sounds very much like idle chatter one might hear at the local tavern, or perhaps tongue wagging between courtiers."

"You asked for a history lesson, Your Highness, and I am but passing along what I know of the matter."

Pavel seemed annoyed at being compared to a common gossipmonger, and Hadeon immediately bowed to his teacher. "My apologies, good sir, pray continue. I assume that Perizidon did not hand King Ioseb's granddaughter back to him, and that is the reason for the major fracture in relations?"

"That is correct, Your Highness. King Elric decreed that Arina could stay as an honored guest of the Perizidon royal family until she turned sixteen, at which point she could decide for herself the path her life would take. Let us just say that King Ioseb does not share such an open-minded opinion on the free will of the fairer sex; he was furious. If his armies had not been engaged to the west, fighting the Polotsk yet again, I believe he would have sent them into Perizidon after her right then and there.

"Soon after that, there was a botched kidnapping attempt to retrieve Arina for her grandfather. That only ended in humiliating Ioseb even further. Perizidon caught the Rus elite guard contingent before they even reached Velych and hung every single one of them as spies. The incident only served to harden hearts on both sides of the border. The last straw for King Ioseb was when Arina came of age and promptly married her protector, King Elric. She—"

"Wait a moment!" Hadeon interrupted the don. He thought for a moment, making sure he had the relationships correct in his mind. "I thought you said that Rusgorod has no heir to wed. Are you not saying now that Princess Lianne could hold claim to *two* thrones?"

"She could, Your Highness. But what I said is that Rusgorod has no *recognized* heir to wed. King Ioseb disowned his granddaughter long ago and would rather see her and her spawn dead than have his crown. He is known to have two children that are alive; they are both younger than his granddaughter, if you can believe it. But they are both bastards, so their claims to the throne would be tenuous at best at the present time. Beyond that, to our knowledge, he has not designated a courtier or general as regent, let alone assign any in the line of succession."

Hadeon found himself genuinely interested in the court intrigue unfolding before him. "Still, the princess has a claim to the Rusgorod throne through her mother, and a strong one at that. I suppose her father could claim it on behalf of his wife as well."

Pavel nodded at the prince. "Very true, Your Highness. However, King Elric has always been pragmatic about the situation. He has enough on his hands as it is with ruling one kingdom. And by all accounts, Queen Arina wants nothing to do with her grandfather and cares not a whit about his throne. They are both probably content with letting the Rus generals fight among themselves for the crown when King Ioseb finally passes on from this life. I do not know how the princess feels about the issue, or if she has had any serious discussions with her parents regarding her unique status."

"But King Ioseb would make war over this issue, even now? After, what, some twenty years since his granddaughter ran away?"

Hadeon frowned, confused at the Rusgorod king's motives.

Pavel shrugged and started to walk back around to the other side of the table. "He is a warrior king who has been slighted, Your Highness. It has taken the lives of many of his soldiers and vast sums of coins from his treasury, but he has settled many slights over the years with his army. Also, he knows of no other way to ensure that one of his bastards claims the throne instead of someone from his direct lineage."

"So, to your earlier point, why hasn't he invaded Perizidon before now?"

Pavel raised his hands to his chest, forming an arch by pressing his fingertips together. He almost appeared to be praying. "As far as I can ascertain, circumstances have always been against him. The Polotsk distract him to no end with their own warring ways. There was a peasant revolt within his borders that he had to put down about a decade ago. Then, when the Rus suffered from famine several years ago—one of their own making, by the way—King Elric won a massive diplomatic victory by delivering grain to them via Malorossiya. Perizidon would have had the full force of the church behind them if the Rus had invaded right after that. But the court of public opinion is fickle, and King Ioseb has been biding his time while other matters catch the eye of the Holy See."

"He cannot bide his time too long, can he? He is what, seventy years old?"

"Somewhat older even than that, I believe. But, of course, he will live forever. Or at least another decade or two." The don wore a wry smile on his face.

"Ah, of course he will." Hadeon grew silent as he studied the map again, returning to his original question of marriage and the making of kings, queens, and alliances. There were many more kingdoms farther west and south on the map that the two of them had not discussed, but he agreed with Pavel's assessment of the local marital terrain.

Except that he missed one potential contender.

"What about Oircadia?" Hadeon suddenly asked, tapping the large swath of land east of the Riphean Mountains.

"What about them?"

"Well, couldn't the princess marry one of their khans, or their version of noblemen?"

"You mean…really, Your Highness?!" The don seemed completely flummoxed by the suggestion.

Hadeon shrugged. "Why not? Out of all the human kingdoms, Perizidon has always had the best relationship with the orcs. And there is precedent for the two parties reaching a secret pact with each other. After all, Perizidon shook our kingdom to the core only a few generations ago with the peace treaty they negotiated with the orc confederation behind our backs."

"Behind everybody's backs!" Pavel retorted, as if the almost century-old treaty was a personal affront to his dignity. He scowled at the map and thought a bit before answering the prince fully. "You are both wise and correct to not eliminate the orcs as an adversary, even when it comes to seeking the hand of a princess in marriage. But that outcome does not seem plausible to me. The tribes have no formal representation at the Perizidon court, and while trade flourishes between the two kingdoms, they have never marched together on the battlefield. To my knowledge, there have never been any societal ties made between the courts. No, I do not see it." The don scoffed. "You might as well say she could marry a commoner!"

"Well, couldn't she?"

"That's what lovers are for, Your Highness."

***

The baying of hounds brought Hadeon back to the present, and he looked up in surprise. The rain had finally slowed to a drizzle, and the line of men had just started to move forward. Thoughts of the impending diplomatic event with the prick and the princess would have to wait.

He quickly checked his spear, attempting to wipe the shaft down so his numb hands could grip it more tightly. No doubt the Master of the Hunt would want to corral the boar in a way that Hadeon would be presented the best chance to skewer it, but personally, he was fine with anyone getting the kill. He just wanted to be dry again.

CHAPTER TWELVE

No One Expects The Holy Inquisition

Lianne mounted the stairs as quickly as she dared, at least in public. It was all she could do to not take them two or three at a time. Mother would be appalled at such an unladylike action, but she was late for a meeting and did not like to be so. Her sparring session had run long, so she had a valid excuse. Still, she had hoped she could reach the map room first and prepare for the meeting that was about to be held with a member of the clergy.

Father had briefed her on this particular church envoy earlier in the day, mainly so that she would mind her manners. *A grand inquisitor, no less! But Father didn't appear frightened when he spoke of her.* This had struck her as strange, since everyone usually acted as though inquisitors were akin to the *babayka*, except that they didn't scare just children.

"The inquisitor has requested my assistance," her father had told her, "with a small but delicate matter involving Astrikhon, no less. I did not inquire as to the nature of the request, but I did offer up that you and Symon were traveling to Boloto in the next few days."

"So, this inquisitor, he—"

"She, my dear. The inquisitor is definitely a woman." Her father had smiled, almost wistfully. He spoke in an odd enough tone that Lianne looked intently at him and noted a faraway look in his eyes. His posture had also softened ever so slightly.

The Almighty take me, Father, how many women do you have stories about? she thought. And then immediately followed that with, *For crying out loud, Li, it's an inquisitor! She probably saved his soul from something perverse, not that she did something perverse herself.* Lianne blushed at where her mind went so easily these days and hoped her father didn't notice how flustered she was.

He reached for his tea and hadn't seemed to notice her close inspection of his mannerisms. He looked up as he took a sip. "You were saying, my dear?"

"My apologies, Father. This inquisitor, she will not be coming with us as you originally thought?"

"It did not sound like it. She mentioned having business to the north to attend to in the immediate future."

Lianne felt like snickering. "So, Symon is to be a lackey for the church? How does he feel about that?"

Her father coughed a bit as he set his cup back down on the table. "No, the inquisitor specifically asked to speak with *you* about the matter."

Now Lianne truly was flustered. "*Me*? But I am not the official diplomat for our mission."

"And this is not an official request, or so I am led to believe."

"What kind of message would she want—"

Her father held up his hand, and out of habit, Lianne stopped talking. His gesture meant this particular line of questioning was at a dead end.

“My dear Lianne, I have known Grand Inquisitor Koval for some time now. If she wishes you to know her reasoning, she will tell you herself. Remember that our family has a rather...unique...history with the inquisition. Unlike most, we respect rather than fear them. This particular inquisitor has earned my respect and gratitude several times over. I would willingly perform this task for her, whatever it may entail, if she had asked me to do it. But she did not.”

Lianne pondered these words as she reached the second floor of the keep. There were two guards at the stairwell entrance. She assumed they had already been ordered to move away from the council room door. That meant the inquisitor was already inside, waiting for her. Standing next to one of the guards was Melina, wringing her hands and fidgeting. She had a nervous look on her face, and as soon as Lianne came into view, her maidservant hurried forward to meet her on the landing.

“M’lady!” she hissed. “Me thinks a witch waits for ya!”

Lianne glanced over at the guards and tried to shush her maidservant. “Melina, please!”

“I mean it, m’lady! She’s dressed all in black, an’ she has these terrible eyes that look right through ya! She ordered me outta tha room an’ it felt like she was touchin’ me soul when she did it!”

Lianne lightly scoffed at the notion. “All of that just makes her imposing. It doesn’t make her a witch.”

“I don’t know what a Imposin’ is, but if it’s some sorta monster, then you’re right!”

"What? No, I meant—" Lianne stopped and smiled. "Never mind, Mel. Trust me, please. Father says he has met with her before, and he hasn't been eaten or cursed, right?"

Melina seemed unsure about the cursed part, but she faithfully nodded her head. "Very well, m'lady. I goes where you go!"

Lianne smiled at Melina and reached out to squeeze her forearm in a reassuring manner. She then straightened and walked the few paces to where the guards stood at the edge of the landing. She vaguely recognized both of them as being regulars in the keep's rotation and wracked her mind for their names. The younger one cast a furtive glance in her direction as she approached, while the older one stared resolutely ahead, the epitome of military form and function.

"Guard Oldenfeld, is it not?" Lianne remembered the younger soldier's name first, helped by the recognition of a fading scar on the bridge of his nose. He appeared to be only a few years older than herself, and his face flushed at the sound of his name.

"Your Highness! I live to serve!" After a moment, he remembered to perform the king's salute.

Out of the corner of her eye, Lianne could have sworn she saw the smallest of frowns cross the other guard's face.

Lianne bobbed her head in recognition of the formal greeting. She knew protocol dictated that she ignore the guards altogether, as they were merely doing their duty, but she wanted any intelligence she could gather on the person she was about to meet.

"Well met, sirrah. Pray tell me, who waits in the map room?"

A nervous look came over the young man's face. "I don't rightly know, Your Highness. I've not seen her before. I, uh..." His voice trailed off as he lost his train of thought. He glanced at her again and visibly swallowed.

"Can you describe her for me, at least?" Lianne asked.

"She's not like anyone I've ever seen, Your Highness. I mean, not that she's overly peculiar looking. It's just that her eyes... You know how sometimes you feel like you're in a dream and someone just knows what you're going to do before you—" He halted as if he knew he was starting to blather on about nothing, and now he looked directly at Lianne, a wide range of emotions playing out across his boyish face.

She cocked her head slightly and looked at him with an arched eyebrow, trying to puzzle out what on earth his problem was. *The Almighty take me, is he going to faint?*

The older guard cleared his throat to interrupt the proceedings before his counterpart completely fell apart. "Beg pardon, Yer Highness. 'Tis a holy woman that awaits ya."

"I see." Lianne turned her focus to him. "Guard Kushmaul, isn't it?"

"Kushnir, Yer Highness. Ivan Kushnir." He performed the king's salute to perfection and continued to stare straight ahead. Both he and Lianne pointedly ignored the fact that Guard

Oldenfeld's halberd was swaying slightly as he fought to remain at attention.

Lianne bobbed her head again. "Guard Kushnir, how do you know she is a holy woman? Does she wear vestments?"

"She wears the uniform of the inquisition, Yer Highness. Black on black, dark as midnight an' tha souls she damns."

Lianne smiled faintly at the description. "How long has she been waiting?"

"Been waitin' 'bout an hour, Yer Highness. She ain't left tha room since she got here."

So, she would have beaten me here even if I had attempted to arrive early myself. Interesting. I wonder what she's been doing all this time. "When did she order you to change your position?"

"Straight away, Yer Highness, soon as she arrived." Guard Kushnir glanced at Lianne for the first time and answered her next question unheeded. "'Fraid we got no knowledge of what she's been doin' in there."

"I see." This was disappointing but not unexpected. Lianne didn't bother asking on whose authority the inquisitor had ordered the guards to relocate. Her position in the church would have provided some level of respect, and most people complied with the inquisition without question anyway. The potential threat of losing one's soul tended to have that effect.

The mild interrogation had not given her much more to go on, and she looked back at Melina, who was still hovering on the edge of the landing. The poor girl did not seem enthused at all about the prospect of seeing the inquisitor again, despite her earlier vow to follow Lianne wherever she might travel.

Lianne silently motioned her forward and strode off down the hallway, leaving the guards behind. She might have heard a heated whisper from one guard to the other to "get yer shite together!" but she did not turn around.

The two of them stopped briefly just outside the door of the map room so that Lianne could catch her breath and Melina could adjust her cape, and then they proceeded slowly into the meeting space.

CHAPTER THIRTEEN

Guess Who's Coming To Drink

Kozel hated crowds, especially the inbred muddleheads that seemed to congregate in every town market this side of Velych. He could hear them already, bleating out their wares to all that walked by, and he wasn't even inside the walls yet. And the smells—already his nose was being overwhelmed by the mixture of sweat, dung, and rotten vegetables that wafted through the breeze. He couldn't comprehend how they could stand each other. *Maybe that's why people in the Wilds don't like strangers. We don't smell like they do.*

He glanced up at the sky, squinting slightly. He had approached Stren from the southwest and was loitering in the shade provided by a single, towering birch tree that stood closer than it should have to the town perimeter. Even though it was still midafternoon, the sun's brightness was somewhat muted by the clouds that had been gathering steadily throughout the day. If he didn't go into town now, he might as well wait until after the gates were closed for the night. While things would be quieter if he waited, and probably less odorous, the delay would just bring more complications to the task at hand. He sighed, adjusted the hood on his cape to shade his eyes as best he could, and broke cover to make for the road into Stren.

Traffic wasn't very heavy at the main gate, but luckily, the guards' attention was being taken up by a shoving match that had broken out between two peddlers. The tin pans and other metal accoutrements on their packs bounced and banged together as they tussled, setting off a cheery melody that contrasted wildly with the foul words the men were hurling at each other. Everyone else in the vicinity had stopped to watch the show, and Kozel was able to maneuver behind the gathering crowd that was already cheering the combatants on and laying odds. Staying in the afternoon shadow being cast by the palisade as best he could, he slipped through without being challenged.

Having visited Stren numerous times before, he knew the town layout well. It meant he could avoid taking the most direct route to his destination, as that led through the main square and the multitude gathered for the market. Instead, he turned into the second alley to the left, where it was instantly quieter. He relaxed a bit, but he kept his hood up just the same.

Stren was a rather well-to-do town, especially for this far north in the Wilds, but most of the alleyways were still little more than narrow, dirt paths wandering between closely packed buildings. Kozel carefully made his way towards the river and the docks, turning several times and avoiding areas of mud as best he could. It didn't take long to reach his destination, a nondescript, two-story house with only two small windows and a latched door facing the alley.

He easily defeated the latch and let himself in, blending into the darkness within the back room. The windows were so dirty that he could barely see his hands in front of his face even at this time of day. He didn't bother lighting the lantern he knew to be hanging to the right of the door and instead moved quietly to the inner door that led into the house proper. Hearing nothing, he entered and made his way through what served as the pantry and cooking area where it was much lighter. There was a crude stairway leading up to the sleeping quarters, but he ignored this and instead went to a large table located in the middle of the ground floor. It was near the fireplace, which was cold and dark. There was little need for heat during the day this time of year, and the occupant apparently did not cook much at home.

Several chairs were sitting haphazardly around the table. They would have commanded a nice view of the main street through several large windows that faced that direction, but one window was boarded up and the other two were almost as dirty as the windows facing the alley. The front door was made of solid wood, and Kozel noted the set of iron brackets where a wooden beam could be placed to bar entry. He had reasoned on previous visits that if there was that much concern about intruders, then all the front windows should be boarded up and the back door made secure, but he let the thought pass. Faint noises of everyday hustle and bustle filtered in from outside, but other than that, the house was silent. Despite its shabby appearance, he knew it to be well built.

Kozel considered making some tea, but if he didn't expend more energy than he cared to, it would take forever to get water to boil. That, and he wasn't sure if there were even any leaves in the house. The room had a wood floor and other signs of the owner being fairly well off, but the pantry was bare of any food. There was a certain staleness about the place, like it had been some time since fresh air had been let inside. Someone was coming here regularly, but they didn't appear to be staying very long.

He decided to wait for the homeowner, at least until it got dark outside. If she hadn't come by Compline, he had several other places he could look for her. But one place involved a crowd, and the other two locations involved meeting more of the town watch than he cared to see on this visit if he could help it. Seeing her alone was why he had braved entering town during the day to begin with. So, he chose a chair at random and sat down at the table, rotating the chair so that it faced the front door. He also made sure there was space to draw his knives if the need arose. Not that he didn't trust her, it was just... He smiled to himself in the gloom. It *was* because he didn't trust her. *Because if I did trust her and that idiot sheriff, I would have just gone north to the mountain straightaway.*

Kozel must have dozed off, as he was startled awake by the noise of someone fussing with the front door latch. There was still a modicum of light coming down the stairwell from the second-floor windows, seeming to indicate the time was late in the day as opposed to early at night. He managed to roll his shoulders and stifle a yawn before the door opened and a young woman entered.

Kira busied herself with shedding her equipment, placing

her sheathed long sword on a hook on the wall and throwing her leather gauntlets on a small table next to the front door. As she started undoing her banded leather chest plate, she paused for just a moment before starting to unbuckle the straps running down the right side of her torso.

"Ya just gonna sit there?" she asked, without looking up.

Kozel said nothing and just exercised his fingers, as if his knuckles were stiff from the waiting. His hands looked like two spiders dancing at the end of invisible threads.

"I know who it is. I can smell ya from way over here," she continued. "An' besides, not many other folks are dumb enough ta enter me house with no invite."

Kozel smirked and broke his silence. "My dear Kira, but you *have* invited me here, at least in the past. Unless you are rescinding said invitation now? That would be a pity."

She said nothing as she continued to methodically undress, moving next to her greaves. If the light had been better, Kozel could have looked straight down the loose tunic Kira wore under her armor as she bent over. A small part of him longed to view her ample chest, as well as the rest of her sculpted body, but he chastised himself and briefly looked away. There was business to attend to, and that was that. This wasn't the time to indulge in human vices.

Her armor removed, Kira stood up straight, stretched with her arms above her head, and walked across the room past the table, continuing to say nothing to Kozel. She went into the back room from where Kozel had entered and came back after a few moments with a lit lantern and a bottle. She rummaged briefly through the shelves next to the cooking area and procured two clay mugs before returning to the table. Once there, she sat down opposite Kozel, forcing him to shift his chair so he could face her. After setting the lantern down, she poured a clear liquid into both mugs and roughly placed one in front of him. After raising her own in a silent toast, she threw it back in one gulp.

Finally, she smiled at him. "Sorry, Koz. I ain't used ta talkin' with nobody right after me shift. Need ta clear tha head of all tha nonsense I've been hearin' all day."

Kozel waved her comment away and picked up his drink. He was used to her brusque behavior and rather liked her no-nonsense approach to life. "Not to worry. If I was insulted that easily, there would be many more dead people waiting to be judged by the Almighty."

She snorted and poured herself another drink while he looked at the contents of his mug. He normally didn't consume alcohol, which he assumed this was, so he sniffed it tentatively before taking a sip. Curiously, there was no odor, and when he tasted it, there was somewhat of an earthy flavor that he couldn't quite describe. He felt a slight burning sensation as the liquid made its way down his gullet. Quickly, he drank the rest of his mug, matching the jailer's earlier action, and managed not to choke as the burning sensation grew in intensity.

"What is this?!"

Kira laughed. "It's just the local *horilka*, Koz. What's wrong with ya?"

He looked at her askance, and she grinned widely. "Fine, it's *horilka z pertsem*, so this one is bottled with hot peppers. Ya shouldn't drink too much at one sittin' if ya know what's good fer ya." She winked at him and threw back her mug for a second time, smacking her lips appreciatively. Her biceps and neck pulsated with each motion, and with her wide shoulders and hair pulled back in a tight ponytail she looked exactly like the fearsome warrior that he knew her to be.

"Hmm, I see." Kozel allowed her to pour him a second portion, but he merely held his mug in his hands. The horilka was horrible, as far as he was concerned.

Kira poured herself yet another mugful, but she, too, merely held it in her hands after setting the bottle down. She looked at him with clear, bright eyes, their dark green color visible even in the dim lighting.

"So, what are ya doin' back here so soon? Thought ya was muckin' things up down south fer several more weeks, or did ya lie ta me on yer last visit?"

"Why would I lie? Let's just say that things down south became a tad difficult, and I was unable to make contact with the cell in Krov."

She snorted at his comment. "Thought ya could get in an' out of anywhere. Ya losin' yer touch, or did they not have enough shadows for ya ta hide in?"

He shrugged. He was certain he could have forced the issue down south if he had wanted to, but what he didn't want to admit was that his foothold was tenuous at best in that part of the kingdom. The crown had a strong presence in both Krov and Molotok, with leadership that wasn't as susceptible to persuasion as in Stren or elsewhere in the north. Couple that with the commotion over some mishap in Krov with a young girl that led to additional night patrols, and some religious lunatic hunting wargs for the church throughout the region, there had been too many eyes focused on either town. It hadn't been worth the risk to push things.

"It is of little concern for the present. In any event, I was able to solidify matters in Myr on my way back north."

"No concern, eh?" Kira's eyes bore into him. If he had been a lesser being, he would have felt uneasy under her gaze. "Ya got me up to me eyeballs in conspiracy up here, an' it ain't no concern that ya can't build up support in tha south?"

"It's the north that matters the most. You know that." *Both according to the Rus plan and to mine.*

She downed her mug but did not pour a fourth serving. "Yeah, I do know that. Don't mean havin' more help would be bad."

"Besides, if anything is found out before you make your move here, it's that idiot sheriff of yours who will take the fall. Or, well, that drunkard of a mayor!" He added the last part in a bit of a rush, as he saw her tense when he slandered the sheriff.

She muttered something under her breath that even his ears

couldn't catch and frowned. "Yeah, 'bout Yuri..." She started to say something after a long pause and then stopped again. She seemed to be debating about having a fourth drink after all, as her eyes took on a faraway look. Her hand drifted to her mouth subconsciously, and for a moment, she looked extremely feminine.

Suddenly, it hit Kozel as to what the problem was. He laughed suddenly and loudly as he slapped the table.

"What's wrong with ya?" Kira demanded, startled at his outburst.

"What's wrong with me? What's wrong with you?" He tried to breathe, only partially succeeding. "Oh, Kira, my dear. Yuri? Yuri Farkas, your esteemed sheriff? Since when did you close your eyes and start thinking with your thighs?"

"What?! Why, ya shite eatin'..." She turned several shades of red and pushed her chair away from the table.

Kozel looked at her and immediately burst into another peal of laughter, tears rolling down his face so strong was his emotion.

A rueful smile slowly formed on the woman's face, and after a few moments she laughed too. "Okay, okay, I admit it! So, he's got a nice spindle, what's wrong with that?"

"Oh, nothing, my dear, absolutely nothing! I am glad you are getting pleasure out of your job, truly I am."

"Yeah, well...it's a nice side benefit, I guess."

"But you have to admit, Kira, he is quite the dullard. He'd be nowhere without you putting the right ideas in his head." *My ideas, actually.*

"But he ain't dumb, Koz! It's just...well, he just has a small mind an' only thinks 'bout small things." She sighed and sat down again. "Don't worry, he's still expendable. He ain't tha only spindle out there."

"Oh, don't be so ruthless. He doesn't factor into my end game, but if you want to rule from behind him while hiding in the shadows, that's up to you. You can sard him from behind too. I can arrange to get you a—"

"Stop it!" Kira tried to look angry, but her mouth betrayed her. "Whatever. Ya ain't here ta ask me 'bout how I spend me nights. Why ya riskin' gettin' seen here?"

"It's not that much of a risk, and I had to check on the testing up north anyway. I was heading to The Mountain"—he emphasized the name like a local would—"but I assume they'll still be a few days sampling the new vein. So, I figured I'd drop in for a short spell and get an update. How's recruitment?"

"Eh, okay. We got a couple more grunts from tha dregs of society, but if they make it through initiation, that's good enough. They ain't from around here, so they'll have no clue as ta what we're really doin' when tha time comes."

"What story are you selling them?"

"That if they last, they'll be paid ta be guards on tha boats or ta look for smugglers on tha river. Might just root out some troublemakers in tha longshoreman guild along tha way for good measure." She looked knowingly at Kozel, although he knew exactly what she meant without any added emphasis.

He was amused at the irony of the situation but just nodded and absentmindedly played with his mug.

The jailer continued. “So, that’s got us ta just under three dozen bodies. Only six of us know tha real deal, but there’s no reason why tha others won’t follow when ordered. Ain’t nobody up here in power that would say otherwise ’cept tha mayor, an’ she’ll probably be dead ’fore tha year’s out from all tha wine she’s drinkin’.”

Kozel hoped this wouldn’t be the case. He didn’t want the mayor to be replaced with someone competent. *We’ve got her completely isolated, and I doubt anyone would listen to her now even if she did sober up. If she dies, it will only make things harder for us.*

He repeated the number Kira had just told him. “Three dozen? Any chance of getting a few more before the fun kicks off?”

She pondered the question briefly. “Maybe? Assumin’ tha fun is still a couple months out, we’ll get a few more before long. But I think we can move with what we got if we need ta.”

Kozel nodded, more to himself. He agreed with her appraisal of the situation. She and the sheriff would have to hold the town just for a short while, and they might not even have to make a move until help was right outside the gates. In any event, there were no Perizidon garrisons of appreciable size within a week’s march of Stren. The troops stationed at Tuman were stretched thin just holding their own position. The longshoremen were the only local group large enough or strong enough to resist, and they could be neutralized or bribed beforehand.

“And your lover with the enormous spindle, is he still getting orders from abroad?”

Kira didn’t rise to the bait and only smiled as she replied. “Yeah, far as we know, they ain’t movin’ ’til early in tha new year. Guess they think tha snow will help ’em.”

Kozel didn’t think much of the Rusgorod invasion plan as he knew it. In his opinion, it was much too risky to try any large troop movements in the winter, when there was too much left to chance. Of course, he didn’t think the generals in question knew any other way except brute force. In any event, he just needed them to show up in great enough force to trigger a response from Velych. Given the circumstances that he was creating, that would not be an issue.

“Very well. And the weapons cache?”

“We should be set. Two stores located in town an’ one outside, just in case. Lemme get tha manifests for ya.” Kira rose, stretched again, and then quickly mounted the stairs to the upper level.

She returned shortly with several documents and handed them without comment to Kozel. They were written in cipher, but he knew what the various symbols meant and worked matters out in his head as he skimmed the document. Everything seemed to be in order.

“Any strangers come through town recently?” he asked as he handed the documents back to her. “Or any locals acting oddly?”

"We're all odd up here, Koz," Kira said in good humor. "Why else are we here?"

"Ha! Fair enough."

"Far as strangers go, there ain't been many, 'less you count those that come an' go with tha barges an' trappers that wander in 'bout once a season. Already told you 'bout those two new recruits we got. Oh, an' we had another one that I didn't recognize that came through this week." She paused briefly. "All three were orcs, come ta think of it."

"Hmm, really? What, are they all related to each other?"

Kira gave a short laugh. "Yuri sure thinks tha first two are, but that's just 'cause they got dumb names that sound the same. Nah, I doubt it. Tha one was just here, like I said, an' we caught tha other two a couple months ago."

"Caught?"

"Yeah. Pretty sure they was part of a group of bandits that were burnin' homesteads 'round tha region, but they never fessed up ta it. Yuri threatened ta hang 'em just tha same, an' they was smart enough ta pick a job instead of a stretched neck. They're workin' at tha docks now."

Kozel rolled his eyes. "They sound like solid recruits to me, Kira."

"Beggars can't be choosers. An' unless ya got some horse calvary ya ain't told me 'bout, then they're tha best we got. That other one...well, we would've taken him, too, but he wasn't interested. He was smart enough not ta cause trouble while he was in town, so we couldn't just nab him like some others. Claimed ta be a trapper, but I don't know 'bout his story. He was lookin' for somethin' or someone 'round here. I'm just not sure what, tho."

"What did he claim to be trapping, and what do you think he was tracking?" Kozel asked with mild amusement.

"Wolves for tha former, an' he wouldn't let on 'bout tha latter."

"Wolves? Around here, this time of year? That does sound suspicious." Kozel looked at his fingernails, becoming bored with the conversation he had initiated.

"Well, he actually said wargs, which is—"

"Did you say wargs?" Kozel started paying full attention now, and his skin tingled.

"Yeah... Wait, are ya sayin' there *are* wargs 'round here?" Kira sat up a bit straighter in her chair. "I thought he was jokin' with me! Should we be worried?"

"Yes. And no. I mean, it doesn't matter. This trapper, or whatever he is, can you describe him?"

Kira furrowed her brow. "Ain't nothin' special, really. Guess he's on tha tall side, even for an orc. No tattoos or scars, least none ya could see. 'Bout tha only thing that really stood out from normal was his axe."

"His axe?"

"Yeah, this big ol' monster he straps on his back. An' the way he carried himself, I'd say he's used it on more than wargs. It's why I told Yuri ta offer him a job."

"But he said no?"

"Said maybe later, after he finished some business to tha north of town. That's why I said he was lookin' for somethin'."

"Really..." Kozel leaned back in his chair, his mind racing. *Could this be the same person who was hired by the church to cull the wargs down around Krov? Almost nobody hunts wargs, especially alone. But why would he be so obsessed with them to come this far north in pursuit? Or has he been following me the whole time? But, surely, I would have noticed him if he was. Think, imbecile! Shite, is the church somehow aware of me and my plans? This could bollox everything!*

"Kira, when is the last time that traveling priest has been through here?"

She thought for a moment. "Three weeks ago. So, he should be back in one or two weeks from now. What's that got ta do with anythin'?"

"Tell me, do you know what people are saying to him in confession?"

"Uh, no, Koz. He keeps that quiet, 'cause, ya know, it's *confession*."

Kozel drummed his fingers on the table, thinking furiously. "And the rumors that keep tongues wagging at the tavern, are they still mentioning the lights on the mountain?"

"Yeah, though not as much now as in tha spring. Nobody has said they want ta investigate, if that's what you're worried 'bout. Koz, what is it? You worried that word 'bout what you're doin' at

The Mountain has leaked?" Kira was openly concerned now, and there was a hint of fear in her eyes. Kozel figured she had to know her life was in the balance.

He answered her truthfully. "I don't think anything's leaked. But there seem to be some strange coincidences afoot. This orc with the axe, is he still in town?"

"Nah, he left couple days ago. But I'm pretty sure he was travlin' light an' left some things with Bainor."

"Who's Bainor?"

"Tavern owner. Tha Wild Boar. Rents rooms too."

So, the orc's planning on coming back soon. "Interesting... Do you think you can get your hands on whatever that orc left?"

"Sure thing. Ya want ta see it tonight?"

"If I can get in and out of the tavern without too much trouble, yes." Kozel figured having to deal with all the odors of the tavern was just the price he would have to pay for information on the trapper.

"I'll bring his bags back here, no worries."

Kozel smiled. "Excellent! Thank you, Kira, that means more than you know."

She ignored his gratitude and stared at him with her piercing look. "Will ya please tell me what's goin' on in that messed up head of yers?"

Kozel looked at Kira, as if for the first time since she entered her house. She was strong and pretty, but most of all, he knew she was intelligent. If only she hadn't been born in the Wilds, she would be well on her way to being a general, or a master builder, or really anything she wanted to be. Instead, she was stuck in a backwater town as the second to a dimwitted sheriff whose only redeeming quality was that he had a large prick in his britches. It was why Kozel had offered her a deal in the first place, and it was why he knew she was all in, no matter what.

He leaned forward, his hands clasped on the table. "This may just be pure speculation on my part, but this orc may be part of my recent difficulties down south. What went on there certainly fits with the little he told you about what he's doing up here. It could just be pure chance that he ended up here, but he could also be here on behalf of the church." He decided not to tell Kira that he knew it was the same pack of wargs that the orc would have followed all the way north.

"The church? C'mon, Koz, he ain't no priest, that's for sure!"

"The church has been known to hire mercenaries for odd jobs that don't require religious training, so the fact that he isn't a priest doesn't change anything." *Although it does make me feel better personally.* "If he's on their payroll, then he could be after the wargs for them, or he could be looking for some obscure relic they think is buried up here, or he could be doing any number of things for them."

Kozel rubbed his chin as he continued. "It doesn't sound like he is meant to rendezvous with the priest who travels through here, so that makes me believe we aren't up against some sort of full-scale investigation. But I don't want him near The Mountain if I can help it. Hopefully, those rumors didn't pique his interest, as he doesn't sound like the kind who would be scared away by a ghost story. There's too much at stake to have some random person stumble upon our operations and ruin everything."

"Hmm..." Kira appeared in deep thought. "An' if he ain't here for tha church? Maybe he's just up here on some personal vendetta an' is lookin' for some*one* instead of some*thin'*? I know how you run, Koz. Did ya kill his mum?" She smirked and finally poured herself another drink.

"If I did kill his mother, it was a long time ago. And if I killed a friend or two of his recently, then they definitely deserved it."

"That sounds like a story, Koz."

"Yes, a short and bitter one."

After waiting a beat without Kozel providing additional details, Kira shrugged. "Fine, whatever. I'll grab tha orc's gear an' ask Bainor a few more questions 'bout him. This orc stopped a brawl at tha tavern 'fore it could start, so he'll stick out in peoples' memory."

"An orc *stopped* a brawl? Will wonders never cease."

"Ya ain't kiddin', but I saw it happen." She downed her drink as quickly as its predecessors. "Does this mean you're stayin' in town for a few days?"

"No, I believe I'm going to head north to The Mountain immediately. It will be good to see how alert the lookouts are, especially if someone is on the prowl in the area. But once I have the latest test results, I shall return. Perhaps this fellow will be back by then as well, and we can have dinner together."

"Ha! Fine, I'm washin' up an' then headed out. You're welcome to tha bottle." Kira rose from the table and headed back upstairs with her documents in hand.

Kozel watched her go, and once she was out of sight, he carefully poured the contents of his mug into the fireplace.

CHAPTER FOURTEEN
Theology and Politics

A slender woman, taller than Lianne had anticipated, was standing by the windows on the other side of the long table in the middle of the council room. She was indeed dressed in black from head to toe, including a hooded cape that hung about her wide shoulders. She wore her dark hair short, and as she turned to face Lianne, she subconsciously brushed a few strands of her bangs out of her eyes. Lianne found her to be attractive, but in the way one finds an experienced athlete attractive—strong, fit, and proud. Her face was slightly tanned but showed no lines or wrinkles. Her age was impossible to guess, other than she was older than Lianne by some years. *I need to ask Father how long he's known her, because she seems more like Mother's age than his.*

As Lianne advanced slowly into the room, she observed that the grand inquisitor's weapon, a nasty-looking blade, was lying on the table, along with a journal of some sort, a medium-sized satchel, and some nuts. The grand inquisitor herself moved away from the window as soon as Lianne and Melina entered but did not continue around the table to greet them. Halting after just a few paces, she stood patiently with her hands behind her back, a small gold and red brooch on her chest the only color noticeable in her uniform.

As Lianne stopped equidistant to the table, the grand

inquisitor gave her the king's salute, then bowed at the waist. "Your Royal Highness," she intoned, "I am Grand Inquisitor Moirne Koval. It is an honor to meet the daughter of Elric and Arina Kalchik."

In return, Lianne slowly performed a deep curtsy. "Grand Inquisitor, I am Princess Lianne Kalchik. It is an honor to meet a most holy defender of the one true faith."

The short but formal introduction complete, they stared at one another from across the table for a few moments before the grand inquisitor broke the silence.

"It pleases me to be in Velych and to see your father again. The last time I was here, you were still but a child who was not yet allowed in court. While your father and I have sought each other's counsel over the years, this is the first time I have had a chance to make your acquaintance."

"You have known my father for some time then?" Lianne asked. *Just how old are you, anyway?*

"Long enough to know he is a good king."

Lianne bowed her head in acknowledgment of the compliment while noting that her question hadn't really been answered. "I do apologize, but he has never mentioned your name to me until this morning, and he has given me very little to go on as to the nature of this interview."

Grand Inquisitor Koval gave her a short smile and made a slight shrugging motion. "He should be complimented that he has not mentioned my name. Most men lack such discretion when it comes to interaction with someone in my position."

Well, aren't you the braggard! "Men would boast of knowing an inquisitor in close detail?"

"You misinterpret my meaning, Your Highness," the grand inquisitor replied. "It is human nature to attempt to impress those around you with your knowledge. Knowledge of others, knowledge of the world around us, knowledge of information that no one else has. To be discrete with your knowledge implies wisdom, which I believe your father has in abundance."

What is it with the mutual admiration between them? What exactly is your history with this woman, Father? Ugh, keep your mind out of the gutter, Li! Concentrate!

"I am glad you hold him in high regard, Grand Inquisitor, for I do as well. You say he is a good king. I would say he is a better father."

The grand inquisitor bobbed her head in return, but Lianne got a distinct feeling of "we shall see how he did with you" coming from the older woman. She took it as a personal affront and tried not to be immediately annoyed by it.

Lianne moved to the table to try and mask her mood, and she decided to sit in the chair closest to the head of the table but not at the head itself. Master Gregor had, at one point in her studies, sketched out the convoluted protocols for seating arrangements and hierarchy of status between church and state at formal functions. However, Lianne considered this meeting to be informal, and it was still unclear what the subject matter would entail. So, she chose to be as neutral as possible for the moment.

Melina came forward with her and arranged her cape again as she sat down. The maidservant then bowed and moved to stand by the far wall.

The grand inquisitor had also moved forward, but while she approached the table, she did not sit down. At this distance, Lianne could now see what Melina had said about the inquisitor's eyes. They were an odd pale grey color and seemed almost animalistic in nature. She found them to be a bit unsettling, but not monstrous.

Lianne attempted to ascertain the reason for the meeting once again, this time more directly. "So, Grand Inquisitor. How might—"

"Inquisitor will do for my honorific, Your Highness. It is less of a mouthful, at least." She stared steadfastly at Lianne, and there was no trace of humor in her voice.

"Ah...very well. Inquisitor, how might I assist you?"

The inquisitor coughed lightly. "My sincere apologies, Your Highness. What I have to discuss with you is of a sensitive nature. Would you be so kind as to dismiss your servant girl?"

"But of course." Lianne was becoming more vexed each time the grand inquisitor deflected her question, but the request itself was expected. She had discussed the possibility of this happening with Melina the previous night. Now, Lianne turned slightly to face the girl and politely motioned to dismiss her.

Melina bowed silently again and then walked quickly out of the room, quietly closing the door behind her.

Inquisitor Koval opened her journal as Melina left the room

and now made a few short notes. Outside, it was a bright autumn day, but while the sun shone brightly through the windows, the angle was such that only the inquisitor's side of the table was illuminated. The table was wide enough that it would have been difficult for Lianne to read what was written under any circumstance, but the sunlight made the pages an indistinguishable dazzling white.

The inquisitor finished writing and, picking up the journal as if to consult what she had just jotted down, drifted back towards the windows. The beams of light made her black outfit fade into the grey stone wall whenever she walked through them, making it hard for Lianne to focus on her.

"Your father tells me that you will soon be on a diplomatic mission to Astrikhon?"

"Yes, Inquisitor. We intend to sail within the next week."

"He further indicated that you are going on a bit of an exploratory mission...to introduce yourself to their royal court and meet their heir apparent?"

Lianne nodded. "That is also correct." *Father really took you into his confidence, didn't he?*

"Do you think it odd that you do not intend to introduce yourself to the archbishop of Astrikhon on this trip as well?"

Surely Father told you this part as well. We certainly went round and round about it in council!

"It is supposed to be a short trip, and our dragoman did not think it necessary at this time. Formal introductions will be realized at my investiture next year, with a representative from Kostantine overseeing the ceremony."

"Ah yes, Symon. But what do *you* think, Your Highness?"

Lianne paused to consider her response. After a moment, she replied, "I will follow their court's lead. If they hold the church in high esteem, they will no doubt provide the means for a meeting with the archbishop while I am there."

"A politically wise rejoinder. Might I inquire as to what you would recommend if the tables were turned, and Prince Hadeon paid your court a visit?"

Lianne wanted to say she would keep Archbishop Dorjan as far away as possible from anyone still breathing but realized that response would not be politically wise in the least. "Assuming his visit occurs after mine, I would recommend we treat his presence as they treat mine in respect to meetings with the church or other organizations important to our realm."

She knew instantly that she had used the wrong term or phrase.

The inquisitor looked at her with wide eyes. "*Other* important organizations? Pray tell, Your Highness, who is as important to your kingdom as the church?" It was difficult to tell if the tone of her voice was playful or accusatory.

"I didn't say 'as important' as the church, Inquisitor!" Lianne quickly protested, as conflicting thoughts raced through her head. *Do not twist my words, wench!* competed with *Careful, Li, she's just trying to rattle you.* "All I mean to say is, proper introductions will be made based upon the situation we find ourselves in at the time." She continued somewhat defiantly, "The church plays an important part in all of this, of course." *But not the only important part!* was heavily implied.

The inquisitor continued to stare at Lianne. "Surely your father has had you educated in the basics of the relationship between church and crown?"

Lianne bristled. She did not like the implication that either she was a simpleton or had been given an incomplete education. "Of course, he has," she responded tersely. She closed her eyes briefly as she thought, then opened them and quoted, "'And He said unto them, render therefore unto Caesar the things which be Caesar's, and unto the Almighty the things which be the Almighty's.' From the book of Lucas, I believe. I apologize, Inquisitor, that I cannot cite chapter and verse for you."

The inquisitor nodded, ignoring the sarcastic tone of the last sentence. "Well said, Your Highness. Much better than most acolytes." She turned away to look out the windows again. "Most bishops, even."

She muttered the last part under her breath, but Lianne's sensitive ears picked out both the words and the sudden rush of bitterness in the inquisitor's voice. However, her voice returned to a neutral tone for her next question.

"But how are the requirements called out by our holy scripture defined and made reality in your kingdom?"

Lianne furrowed her brow. She hadn't expected to be grilled

about religion and civics, but so be it. After a short reflection to recall her studies, she replied. "Pontifex Gelasius laid out the basic tenet that there are two forces that rule our material world, the spiritual sovereignty of the priest and the executive power of the prince. Both forces proceed from the Almighty One. The prince is but one of the many sons of the Almighty, and as such, is guided by the priest and his authority in matters of the soul. However, the priest must obey the prince and his authority in all things secular. The prince receives his authority from the Almighty, *not* the priest." Lianne emphasized the last part of her summation, as it had been drilled into her by her father that, at least in earthly matters, when she became sovereign, her word should (and would) mean more than the archbishop's.

She continued. "This is why, at least in our lands, the county sheriffs determine the value of a person's property and the tax to be collected from it, but the priests review these assessments and perform the actual collection. From the collected taxes, a tithe is given to the church and the clergy for their operations. This allows for balance and harmony between church and state, as opposed to separation and discord."

Inquisitor Koval nodded again. "Indeed. That is how the theory goes, anyway. Although you forgot to mention the priest *also* receives his authority from the Almighty, *not* the prince." She matched Lianne's previous emphasis. "Regardless, both your father and Archbishop Dorjan are god-fearing men, who usually have the best interests of their collective flock in mind, so the established system here more or less works." She turned, raising her hands in mock surrender, cutting Lianne off before she could protest. "Your Highness, trust me that I mean no insult to your father. I have walked among your people and observed his administrative works over the years. He is a fair and capable ruler. But, like all men, he is not infallible, nor can he be in all places at all times. What I question is not the man, but the system—nay, the world—in which he resides. But let us return to the hypothetical. In your opinion, what is the primary threat to this balance and harmony?"

Lianne responded immediately, as Chancellor Emmanuel ranted on this subject at almost every council meeting when discussing the treasury. "Corruption within the system, Inquisitor. At the most basic level, the sheriff and priest conspire to hold money back for their personal use. Or the sheriff imposes a crushing levy on the tavern keeper who won't serve him free ale, or the priest forgets to collect taxes from the farmer's wife he's sarding in the confession box."

The inquisitor raised an eyebrow at the crude slang used, but Lianne pressed forward.

"And on and on, human avarice in all its forms. But this is why we have adjudicators and inquisitors, to judge and pass sentence on all matters temporal and spiritual."

The inquisitor seemed satisfied with this answer. "Mmm, yes, fighting corruption is one of the banes of my existence. If only the heretics would repent on their own so I could concentrate upon this particular task."

Lianne knew that her father could give two figs about heretics so long as they paid their taxes and didn't cause unrest, but she kept this to herself. *Does this inquisitor believe Emmanuel is skimming money from the royal tithe and Father is complicit? No, she just paid Father a backhanded compliment to the contrary. And she wouldn't be talking to me if she suspected this. She'd have the chancellor in thumbscrews and be asking him some very direct questions.* "So, Inquisitor, are you here to inspect our ledgers or to root out heretics? Or both?"

The inquisitor gave a short laugh with no trace of humor in it. "Personally, I leave the ledgers to the adjudicators. And while heretics no doubt infest this court like all others, they are not the primary reason for my appearance today."

Then tell me what you want! "Not to be discourteous, but this brings us back to my initial question: what is the reason for this interview?"

Inquisitor Koval walked over to the table and leaned towards Lianne. Her tone and features were serious, and she peered at her with an unwavering gaze. "Your father speaks very highly of you, Your Highness. So highly, in fact, that it borders upon boastfulness and exaggeration beyond mere familial devotion. I prefer to ascertain all facts for myself, and the immediate issue at hand is your true competence in matters of both heaven and earth. You will indulge me and my questions, will you not?"

Lianne flushed slightly, but did not avert her eyes, matching steel with steel. *The armored fist beneath the velvet glove begins to show itself. But I do not scare easily, Inquisitor!* She remained silent and waited for the other woman to make her next move.

The inquisitor waited for a few moments, then slapped the table with her left hand as she straightened, causing Lianne to flinch slightly. She sauntered back to the windows yet again, appearing to inspect the battlements. "I must advise you that I take silence as acquiescence, Your Highness."

Beyond irritated now, Lianne pushed back against the condescending statement. "Is that why some interrogations by the inquisition last until the person being questioned no longer has the capacity to talk? I do think it would be hard to form words, let alone an opinion, if you were unconscious or have quite literally lost your tongue. Easier to obtain the confession you seek, perhaps?"

Oh, that blow landed, she thought, for the inquisitor's shoulders had suddenly gone stiff. She turned slowly back around, her hands clasped behind her, the sun streaming through the windows making a bright outline around her profile. Her demeanor was calm, and to Lianne's surprise, no anger flashed in her eyes. Rather, nothing registered within them at all. Terrifyingly, it was as if the blank look represented the unholy abyss the inquisitor had no doubt damned souls to in the past. She did not advance towards the table but remained standing in place, coolly observing Lianne and the contents of the room all together.

God's piss, too far by half! Careful, Li, she can condemn even you to hellfire!

Lianne broke eye contact and folded her hands together on the table in a sign of supplication. A tactful retreat was in order. "My apologies, Inquisitor. My careless chatter goes too far. I did not mean to imply that you bring the Almighty One's wrath down on any who do not deserve it."

The inquisitor seemed to accept the statement as a direct and sincere apology to her person, as opposed to a royal sycophant pretending to bend the knee to the holy might of the church. She waited a beat before responding, her eyes slowly returning to their pale grey color. "No harm taken, Your Highness. I cannot speak to the overzealous nature of some of my brothers and sisters, but I can and do take responsibility for my actions and for those who are in my charge. All who come before me are judged fairly and impassively, for it is through me that the will of the Almighty manifests itself upon them."

The inquisitor then relaxed her stance and continued in a milder tone. "It does serve you well to question the character of those who would hold authority over your subjects, whether in this life or the next. Neither your father's teachings nor your own wit have failed you." At this point, she coughed slightly, and Lianne could see that the blank stare had been replaced with a twinkle, accompanied by a small, wry smile. "Just remember, Your Highness, that there are many steps to this dance."

Lianne blushed, and ducked her head so that the inquisitor could not see the childish grin on her face. *She definitely has been around Father in the past! He could have given me more of a warning about her tactics, but I suppose there is a test in every conversation.*

She regained control of her features quickly and looked up again. "Yes, Inquisitor. Thank you."

"Good. Now, before we take this conversation any further, I must ask who is standing in the hidden passageway on that side of the room." She pointed at the wall in question, and her smile grew wider at Lianne's reaction. "Please don't look so shocked, Your Highness. I am no stone smith, but I have observed that the interior wall of this room is several paces short of the external wall seen through these windows. This is an internal tower, so I seriously doubt the builders constructed one wall that much thicker than the rest for defensive or structural purposes."

Lianne's mouth dropped open, and it was all she could do to not burst out with an oath worthy of a stable boy. *So that's why she kept looking out the windows. She was gauging distances!*

She had to compose herself yet again. "It would be Melina, Inquisitor. My maidservant, the one whom you asked to leave the room."

"It is good to have loyal servants nearby. But, please, dismiss her completely. Hopefully, she has seen and heard enough to know I am neither witch nor assassin."

Intrigued, and realizing she must comply for the discussion to progress, Lianne did as had been requested. Standing up from the table, she quickly walked over to one of several large bookcases that stood against the wall in question. She rapped her knuckles on the left side of the bookcase and then pushed with some effort on the right side. The secret door that the bookcase was attached to swung silently into the corridor behind the wall to reveal her petrified servant.

Melina curtsied deeply, and her voice was both squeaky and shaken. "A thousand 'pologies, Your Highness! I dunno what I did ta alert that...that knight...of me presence, but I'm awfully sorry!" She was visibly shaking, and Lianne could tell she was on the verge of fainting.

She instinctively reached out and gently took Melina by the shoulders. "Mel, it's all right!" she whispered. "This one is sharp enough for the both of us, and she figured out the secret door all by herself. She didn't hear you, I promise."

Melina was visibly relieved. She took a step back and wiped away the tears that had formed on the edges of her eyes. "Thank you, Your Highness. What would you have me do?"

"Go out and make sure no one is listening at the other door." Lianne nodded her head at the closed door that led out into the known hallway. "If someone is there, make a racket, and the inquisitor will deal with them. If no one is there, then sit in the chair that guards the other end of this passage in the next room and let no one pass you, not even Lucas. I will come get you when we are done here."

Melina straightened up to her full height and pushed out her chest like a foot soldier at attention. "Yes, Your Highness! On me honor!" She curtsied again and then turned and scampered down the secret passageway to do the bidding of her mistress.

Lianne watched her go and then shut the bookcase.

"Are there many such passageways in this castle?" the inquisitor asked.

Lianne hesitated slightly before answering. "Yes, there are several more within the keep. Father will need to show them to you."

The inquisitor shook her head. "No, that is not necessary. Pardon my lack of discretion. Let us return to the matter at hand."

They both walked back to the table and sat down opposite each other. Inquisitor Koval spoke first, seeming to choose her words carefully. "Your Highness, please know that I hold your father in the highest regard and that I consider us to be friends. He has long attempted to do what is right and good. Not only has he taken his gifts received from the Almighty and increased them tenfold, but he has been charitable and generous to all. He has given freely from his personal coffers, as well as the kingdom's treasury, when it has come to providing for his subjects. Truly, the land and your people have flourished under his rule."

Lianne could sense the "but" coming from a league away. She remained silent and let the inquisitor play out her lines.

"Unfortunately, as you know, the church is bound to remain neutral when it comes to secular matters and the law of the land. We observe, we advise, but ultimately, the choices a king or queen makes for their kingdom are acts resulting from the free will the Almighty has accorded to us all." She looked directly at Lianne with clear, cold eyes. "It also means, Your Highness, that even when a friend may be in peril, I cannot intercede directly unless there is reason to believe the church is also at risk. Even an inquisitor can bend rules only so much."

"How convenient for you and the church." Lianne did not attempt to hide her exasperation at what she had just heard. *Is the inquisitor hinting at some unforeseen threat to Father, or to the kingdom as a whole?* Her hands were in her lap, and they balled into unseen fists.

"Convenience has nothing to do with it, Your Highness. Would you prefer that the clergy stick their noses into every decision made by your king's council? Or decide for the people when a ruler should be removed?"

Lianne was becoming more irritated by the moment. "Of course not! But I would hope the clergy would at least bring attention to what they know so that sound rulers can make sound decisions!"

"Which is exactly what I have been doing with your father for some two years now!" the inquisitor snapped in return. "He knows that the threat of an invasion grows in my mind like a storm cloud on the horizon!"

Lianne leaned back in surprise, taking a moment to let the enormity of what the inquisitor had just said wash over her. "Did you say two *years*? My father has known about an invasion for two *years*?"

"The *possibility* of an invasion, Your Highness. Rumors that make no sense, stories that cannot be tied together."

"But...but he has said nothing about this to me!" Lianne was having a hard time grasping why such a plot wouldn't have been exposed the instant it was detected.

"Why should he? You have only begun to learn how to govern this kingdom under normal circumstances. We thought there was time before you had to be given an advanced course in crisis management."

We thought...so something has changed. Also, we? Lianne swallowed her retort. Now was not the time to be argumentative. "Very well. Please enlighten me as best you can."

The inquisitor studied her, as if collecting information for a final appraisal. Finally, she nodded slowly. "I am sure you know there is no love lost between your father and your maternal great-grandfather, King Ioseb of Rusgorod?"

"I am well aware," Lianne replied with a tinge of bitterness. *Is my existence really the cause for all of this?*

It was as if the inquisitor was reading her mind. "Believe me, Your Highness, there was concern even before you were born that Rusgorod would attempt something underhanded to usurp power away from your family. Fortunately for Perizidon, the great famine created by House of Geladze's own ineptitude, coupled with your father's decision to publicly prop them up with grain deliveries, paused their plans for several years. Both politically and militarily, they were in too weak of a position to make any inroads here, especially with their never-ending sorties into the lands to their west. However, I believe their hand was forced some four years ago to try again."

Lianne thought for a moment and could not puzzle it out. "The birth of my sister?"

"No, Your Highness. The fact that the bridge your father commissioned over the Grumaius was nearing completion, far ahead of any construction schedule the Rus could have conceived."

Lianne was still confused. "The bridge? Even Master Gregor says it is truly a masterpiece in engineering, but I do not see how—" Suddenly, things fell into place. "Trade!"

"Exactly!" The inquisitor smacked the table with her open hand for emphasis. "The bridge and associated causeway have created a gateway to the east from your capital city. Already, trade between your kingdom and Oircadia has increased twofold from just a few years ago. Rusgorod, and other nearby kingdoms, if truth be told, have long been jealous of the stable diplomatic relationship that Perizidon has maintained with the orc tribes. Now, the economic ties between your peoples will soon be so strong that an alliance in a time of war will occur naturally, if only to protect your shared interests."

Lianne was glad that Chancellor Emmanuel was not in the room. He would have chided her over not seeing the obvious long-term economic benefits of the bridge.

She thought furiously in an attempt to make up ground. "So, this is why Astrikhon has reached a new trade agreement with us?"

"Correct, Your Highness. While the river trade has always

been strong between the cities of Velych and Boloto, the new agreement provides Astrikhon with an avenue to also trade with Oircadia and your kingdom easier access to Myste and the kingdoms to the south. Your father was somewhat generous in the terms of the agreement, much to the chagrin of your dragoman, but it was done with an eye to secure your southern border as quickly as possible. Your trip will bring a successful conclusion to the negotiations."

"So, Rusgorod is worried they will be isolated?"

"They have already isolated themselves to quite a degree. But, yes, having a neighbor they detest becoming stronger by the day will only make matters worse for them unless they act in the very near future."

"I realize I may be making things too simple, Inquisitor, but why can't they come to an agreement with us like Astrikhon has? Or with Oircadia, for that matter? We were in open war with the orcs at one time and yet were able to come to terms with them."

Inquisitor Koval sighed. "It is indeed simple, and yet it is not." She looked heavenward and recited, "'Pride goeth before destruction, and a haughty spirit before a fall.' If there ever was a living embodiment of that piece of scripture, it is King Ioseb and the Geladze ancestral line that has controlled Rusgorod for years. He and his kind have always ruled through brute force and intimidation."

"Surely, we have attempted to reach out to the Rus, as we have with Astrikhon?" Lianne asked. Although now that she thought about it, she could not remember any discussions in her father's council regarding diplomatic relations with their estranged neighbor to the northwest.

"It has been some time now, but yes, your father has certainly tried in the past. Unfortunately, your great-grandfather does not know what to do when approached with either friendship or cold logic. He personally rid himself long ago of any counselors who would tell him the truth. He is surrounded by sycophants and incompetency in all areas except the one that matters to this discussion: his army." The inquisitor looked down, as if she was inspecting the grain of the wood table they were seated at. "It doesn't help matters that he loathes your father."

Lianne could not understand the level of hatred that would blind a person to such an extent. "Why does he hate my father and this kingdom so?"

The inquisitor looked up, refocusing on the princess and the task at hand. "That is a story for another day, Your Highness, and one that should be told by someone other than myself. My time here is short, and we have yet gotten to the crux of our conversation, why I have asked your father for assistance."

Lianne absolutely detested loose ends and unfinished stories, but something in the inquisitor's demeanor told her that she would not receive satisfactory answers to her many familial questions right now. What troubled her the most was that there obviously was so much about her parents, her father in particular, that she did not know.

"Well then, Inquisitor, if you believe we are on the verge of being invaded, why are you asking my father for assistance? Should he not be begging you for your aid, regardless of the church's official position on such matters?" A horrible thought crossed Lianne's mind. *Is this some form of blackmail?*

"Again, it is not that simple. As I said, the threat of invasion, or some other nefarious act by Rusgorod, has only been hinted at to date. There has been no troop buildup at the frontier, and your father's spies have not noticed any increase in illegal activities that can be directly attributed to Rus agents. My belief that King Ioseb started putting plans into motion to undermine your kingdom some four years ago was just that, and only that, for quite some time...a belief."

"Then why are you involved so intimately in this issue? You have already said that you cannot help my father, even though he is a friend to you and an ally of the church." There was definitely something going on that did not add up in Lianne's mind.

The inquisitor began to answer, but then stopped herself, as if reconsidering how much to tell Lianne. After a short pause, she started up again. "I have been looking for evidence to support my beliefs and suspicions for some time now, as much as my normal duties have allowed. But I have searched for this evidence not only for your father but also for the church."

"For the church?"

The inquisitor nodded. "Yes. If I can link the threat to your father's throne to a potential attack against the teachings of the

Almighty, there are various boons that I can then immediately bring to bear in defense of both."

Politics know no boundaries, Lianne thought. "I think I understand. 'Unless there is reason to believe the church is also at risk,' is that it?"

"Exactly, Your Highness."

"And have you found something?" Lianne asked hopefully.

For the first time in their entire conversation, doubt seemed to cloud the inquisitor's face. The beams of light coming through the windows had shortened as the sun's position in the sky shifted throughout their discussion, leaving the inquisitor and her side of the table in the same dim light that the rest of the room had been. Lianne could plainly see that the other woman was troubled by some inner thought.

"I will confess that it is still unclear to me," she admitted. "But there is some sort of evil that stalks the land, and not just in Perizidon. Reports from my fellow inquisitors across the region speak of increased demonic possessions, wargs and other foul beasts roaming where they should not, and all manner of evil spirits and monsters. Certainly, most of these claims are the product of simple folk's imaginations and their ignorance of the natural world, but the sheer weight of reports has increased significantly over the past several years."

"You think that Rusgorod is employing foul magic to further their means?"

Here, the inquisitor managed a smile. "No, Your Highness,

nothing that overt. The archbishop in Gavan has a difficult time gaining an audience with your great-grandfather on a regular basis, but there have been no occult sightings, and the church still receives the appropriate number of tithes and acolytes from the kingdom. What I fear is that some evil entity is aware of King Ioseb's scheming and has decided their plans align well enough with his to lend oblique assistance."

"Come again, Inquisitor?"

"Have you heard of the saying, *amicus meus, inimicus inimici mei*, Your Highness?"

Lianne translated the Latin into Common but frowned all the same. "'My friend, the enemy of my enemy.' No, I have not heard of it."

"It is an ancient proverb from lands far to the east of here that the inquisition has employed on a number of occasions. Essentially, you may not agree with either one of two combatants, but you will help one to overcome the other."

"Hmm...and then turn on the second?" Lianne wasn't sure how this would help matters.

The inquisitor seemed to shrug with her eyebrows. "Perhaps, but there is no need if your intended goal has been reached. And that is what I am worried about here. Neither kingdom would openly embrace the Unholy One and the evil it represents, or so I believe. But, if the Unholy One can deploy its minions such that one kingdom is weakened or destroyed, the power of evil only increases with the anarchy, death, and overall suffering that would occur as a result."

"So, if you prove there is indeed infernal activity afoot, that still assists my father against Rusgorod?"

"Yes, in that it will allow the inquisition to openly initiate a widescale investigation into all manner of things in all kingdoms and regions we believe are impacted. This would, of course, include Rusgorod. To deny access to an inquisitor in such a case would result in immediate excommunication of the ruler and all those deemed to have influence with him or her."

"This assumes you are correct in thinking Rusgorod is not in direct collaboration with the Unholy One and my great-grandfather still cares about his soul," Lianne mused. *And going by all the stories I've heard about him, it wouldn't surprise me if he was the Unholy One himself!*

The inquisitor was seemingly unmoved by the possibility that King Ioseb had forsaken his eternal soul for earthly gratification. "Regardless, I trust we would gain access to what is important. The inquisition might be initially thwarted or delayed, but it has never been denied the truth in over a millennium of operations. Many secrets would be brought into the open, and any plans your great-grandfather might have against Perizidon would be laid bare. He could not hope to succeed in the face of being a known belligerent on the side of Chaos, whether that was his intent or not. If he attempted anything at that point, all nations would rally under the banner of the church in a holy crusade against him."

Lianne wondered if the gathering of such a force would be

in time to stop a concerted attack on her lands, but she pushed tactical thoughts to the side for the time being.

The inquisitor continued. "In any event, I came to Velych to provide your father with an update on my findings and to research some documents in your cathedral's library. I meant to travel to Boloto next for some general inquiries with the local clergy, to perform additional research, and to visit with another trusted friend. This is why I considered accompanying your entourage when I learned of your diplomatic mission to Astrikhon. However, this changed during my recent audience with Archbishop Dorjan."

"Oh, really? What did His Excellency have to say?" *And how did he stay awake long enough to tell you anything worthwhile?* Lianne gave up asking for forgiveness for her prejudiced thoughts against the archbishop.

"Not much, truth be told. But he had several reports from outlying parishes that he deemed important enough to show me, and I am grateful to him and the Almighty that he did. One was a report regarding a vovkulaka sighting to the west. Not much by itself, but it coincided with the culling of a large pack of wargs that had ranged a hundred leagues farther south than it should have. The last part of the report indicated that it was thought the shapeshifter was traveling back north with the remainder of the pack and that the local parish had hired some sort of bounty hunter or mercenary to go after them. Somewhat irregular, but sensible, given that there was no inquisitor or knight in the general vicinity."

Lianne pondered this briefly. *Surely a monster straight out of childhood bedtime stories isn't really on the prowl within the kingdom? And to refer to it so matter-of-factly too.* Still, it felt to her as if the inquisitor was grasping at straws in an attempt to prove her case. "My apologies, Inquisitor, but that does not seem like much to go on."

"Agreed. By itself, it makes for an interesting story, and that is about it." The inquisitor leaned forward in her chair and spoke rapidly. "However, the second report came from a rather studious priest, whose assigned flock is scattered across the northern counties of your kingdom. He has been collecting stories and rumors for several years now and only recently cataloged them all with cross references to certain known events. I have reviewed both his data and his calculations, and I believe his methodology to be quite sound. His conclusion, which I trust implicitly, is that there is something amiss in the area believed to be where the vovkulaka is heading."

The sense of anticipation coming from the inquisitor was infectious, and Lianne also leaned forward. "Yes? Where exactly is that?"

"In the area around the mountain you know as Mount Iklo."

It was as if lightning had come down from heaven and struck Lianne squarely in the chest. "*The Mountain?!*" she practically squealed as she leapt from her chair, the hair on the back of her neck standing at attention.

She surprised both herself and the inquisitor with her reaction, and they stared at each other for a moment, the inquisitor with wide eyes and a look of amusement and Lianne with heavy, gleeful panting.

"Your Highness?" the inquisitor asked cautiously. "Is there something wrong?"

"My apologies." As she continued to talk, Lianne hurried over to a map case that was against one of the side walls of the room. "I cannot explain it. It's just that, out of all the locations in the kingdom that I have not set eyes upon, that mountain is the one place that intrigues me the most!"

Opening the top drawer, she hurriedly pulled out the large map depicting the overall kingdom that Master Gregor often used in his lessons. She came back to the table to stand by the inquisitor, who had risen to her feet, and laid out the map in front of them. There, in ornate crimson lettering, the name of the mountain called out to her like a beacon.

"Call it a childhood fascination, but I have always felt there is more to that mountain than has been documented!"

The inquisitor quickly scanned the map. "Well, by all accounts, not many eyes have been cast on the mountain for quite some time. I asked your father about it, and there have always been more pressing issues than to send an expedition to investigate a barren peak full of ice and snow. But, yes, my newfound interest seems to match your childhood fascination. I have decided I will head north immediately to further investigate these two reports."

"Let me go with you!" Lianne blurted out the words before she could catch herself.

"Your Highness!" the inquisitor exclaimed with surprise. "Control yourself!"

"I...I'm sorry, Inquisitor," Lianne stammered, her face burning with embarrassment. All of a sudden, she no longer wanted to be a princess with diplomatic duties. She wanted to be a young girl on an adventure. It felt impossible now that just a few days ago she was excited to be going to Boloto to meet with another royal house. With this revelation, it all seemed dull and grey compared to scaling the mountain that had fueled so many of her daydreams.

But, deep down, Lianne knew it was an impossible request. If she hadn't already felt the weight of her future crown upon her, the revelation of the potential eradication of her kingdom before she ever ruled it was quite sobering. She attempted to swallow the bitter pill of maturity as best she could.

The inquisitor's features seemed to hold some empathy. "Trust me, Your Highness, I feel your pull for adventure. After all, that is one reason why I joined the army so many years ago. But duty and responsibility call to all of us, and I would have you be my proxy in Boloto, if at all possible."

Lianne knew it was more of being told what to do, as opposed to being a truly open request, if not from the inquisitor, then from her father. "What would you have me do?" She managed not to sigh as she asked the question.

The inquisitor gestured at the satchel that was lying on the table. "I have various messages and reports to pass on to the archbishop in Boloto. He is a longtime ally who has always supported my work, both officially and unofficially, and he is aware of this quest of mine. I would ask that you carry these documents to Boloto and personally deliver them to the archbishop. He will give you an audience, I am sure of it, but just in case, I will provide you with a personal signet that will gain you entry into any room in the cathedral. He will no doubt have advice, and potentially other documents, to send back to me. Bring these back with you to Velych. If I am not here, share them only with your father. He will know how to contact me or will safeguard the information until I return."

Lianne felt as if the floor had been dropped out from under her, so underwhelming was the request. "I will fulfill this task, Inquisitor. But"—she could not contain her overall disappointment—"all of this just to tell me I am to be a glorified errand girl for the church?"

Inquisitor Koval laughed clearly and loudly, and the twinkle in her eye returned. "At the most basic level, yes, Your Highness. I am sure this feels like little more than fetching and delivering. However, the documents are quite critical in nature, and I certainly would not hand them over to just anyone. You have proven yourself to be your father's daughter, and something more as well. You have gained my trust in this matter and in general."

Lianne didn't fully believe that the inquisitor was kissing her arse with platitudes just to make her feel better, but the thought did cross her mind. She made a slight curtsy in acknowledgment of the compliment as the other woman continued.

"I also believe that knowing the reasons behind the task is extremely important in this case, especially as they relate to your family and your kingdom. I wish I could answer all the questions that have been raised in your mind, but I must depart as soon as is feasible. Just know, Your Highness, that I would prefer to have you as a willing accomplice as opposed to a suspicious adversary, both in this simple task and in all things."

Lianne grudgingly nodded. What the inquisitor said was true enough, in that performing the delivery would be easier knowing the reason behind it. *And, if Father trusts this woman, who am I to think otherwise?* She calmed herself and formally acquiesced. "I would serve at the request of the church regardless of my personal thoughts, but I thank you for taking me into your confidence, Inquisitor."

Strangely, the inquisitor extended her hand as if they were memorializing a pact of some sort. With only brief hesitation, Lianne grasped it with her own. The woman's grip was firm but not overly so.

"You bring honor to your family, Princess Lianne. You have my pledge of support, and I will guide you as well as I can in all matters henceforth."

It's still just a bloody message. Lianne swallowed hard and managed to force a smile.

CHAPTER FIFTEEN
Working The Docks

Uptar was in the middle of yet another dream when he was again rudely awoken. This time at least, it didn't involve getting deluged by a bucket of foul-smelling water, but the smack to the head wasn't all that much better.

"Hey, Uptar! Tha guards say ya need ta go see tha dockmaster!"

Uptar groaned at the disturbance. He had fallen asleep while sitting at the bunkhouse's table, his head laying on his crossed arms. Even with the hit, he didn't lift his head but merely turned it slightly so he could glare through barely open eyes at the young man standing next to him.

"What tha shite, Ostap! Why'd ya do that?"

The other prisoner shrugged. "All I know is I was told ta wake yer sorry ass up. Sounds like they got a new job for ya an' that brother o' yers." The young man turned and wandered off towards the toilets without another word, leaving Uptar alone with his tired thoughts.

Uptar remained motionless for several moments, trying to will himself to sit up. It wasn't even worth it to yell after Ostap that the damn brother joke was getting dumber by the day. Finally gathering himself, he pushed away from the table and stood up, bleary-eyed and sore.

This week it had been four straight days of standing waist deep in the cold river, lashing logs together to form the large timber rafts that were floated south from Stren. He rather hoped that the dockmaster wanted him to do anything that didn't involve getting in the water. The log drivers were insane, and he had almost had his head caved in twice. He couldn't tell if they were trying to kill him because he was still new or just out of general spite.

He passed Umuk as he made his way to the door leading to the outside. The other orc was sound asleep in one of the top bunks, no doubt dreaming about logs, as he went about sawing some loudly. Uptar decided not to bother waking him and kept walking. If it was an easy task, there was no sense in sharing it. On the other hand, if it was a difficult or dangerous task, then he'd try and convince the dockmaster to give it to the other orc while he wasn't there.

Uptar reached the door, rubbed his eyes, and then knocked loudly. Immediately, he heard the latch being undone from the outside, and the door swung open on creaking hinges. Two guards were standing in the sunlight, and they all just stared at each other for a few moments before he stepped outside.

"Ostap tell ya who wants ya?" One of the guards asked the question in a bored and sullen tone. His face carried the pockmarked signs of being a smallpox survivor, but beyond that, Uptar didn't care to tell the difference between the two humans.

"Tha dockmaster?"

"Yup." The guard gestured towards a squat-looking building

that sat closer to the water. "Git."

The other guard closed and barred the door while the first fell in behind Uptar as he started walking in the direction indicated. Uptar paid little attention to the hustling dockhands who swirled around him. Some were wearing the same simple tan prison garb that he was clothed in, but most were freemen toiling away by choice and wore their longshoremen vests with pride. It was busier today than it had been, as some of the fall harvest had already arrived from outlying farmsteads, and there was nowhere to put it. Several large flatboats lay at anchor in the distance, farther down the river, and there was a general ongoing rush to clear the dockside to make space for them. Uptar wondered if he was about to be told he was trading his wood for wheat.

Upon reaching the shipping office, he turned to look at the guard, who just gestured for him to go inside. Upon entering, if anything, there was more chaos within than without. One boat captain, red in the face, was arguing about slip fees with a tired-looking woman at a side table. Another captain was complaining to an irritated little man at another table about his actual cargo not matching the manifest. Meanwhile, various clerks ran about with their ledgers, calling out numbers to each other that made no sense to Uptar. The low-hanging ceiling seemed to add a sense of urgency to all the action within the room.

Uptar could see the man called Bartosh in the back of the office, inspecting documents that were being brought to him, and giving orders in response. He had only met the dockmaster directly once, on the first day he had been brought to the docks to work, but the old man was a familiar face to anyone doing business on the water in Stren. It was Bartosh who gave the work crews their orders in the morning, controlled the payroll, oversaw slip rentals, prioritized who got unloaded first, and dispensed dockside justice. His kingdom was small, but he was certainly the master of it, regardless of what the longshoremen might say.

Over the years, the dockmaster had developed a unique set of rapid hand signals that he would use for the majority of his directions. The system helped him retain order amidst the din of the docks, and others had started using it as well. After almost two months of service, Uptar had seen enough orders to understand most of the basic movements. *Move ship now...Get money first...Unload cargo...*all came in rapid succession from Bartosh to the various clerks and messengers as Uptar approached him.

There were some dozen people waiting to see the dockmaster, and Uptar pushed his way into the middle of the group. If there was any grumbling or cursing that he'd cut the line, it was lost in the background noise, and nobody challenged him to move to the back. Uptar waited what he considered to be patiently, as several men and women ahead of him were given orders before he presented himself.

Bartosh looked him up and down, taking a few moments to recognize him. Then the hand signals flashed in front of him. *Outside door...*and a few more that Uptar didn't understand. He tried repeating one of the gestures back to Bartosh with a quizzical look on his face, but the old man just shook his head in annoyance.

"Vykhod' nadvir i chekay mene bilya dverey!" Bartosh spoke in a raspy voice that was hard to hear given the circumstances, but his knowledge of the orc dialect was better than most.

Uptar raised his eyebrows, as he hadn't known the old human could speak his native tongue, but he nodded and turned to go back the way he had come. The dockmaster was already conferring with the next person in line.

The guard was waiting for him when he got back outside, and Uptar shrugged in response to the unspoken question about what was going on now. "Was told ta wait here," he grunted, and then he leaned up against the wall of the building in what shade there was.

The guard seemed about to say something, but then he also shrugged and claimed another piece of the wall on the other side of the entryway.

Uptar looked down at the ground, trying to assess his current lot in life. Since agreeing to work for Yuri, he and Umuk had been on the docks every day, doing every shite job imaginable. It was true that they were clothed, fed well enough, and had a roof over their heads, but they were locked in their bunkhouse whenever they weren't working and were closely watched whenever they were out and about. He knew Umuk had been looking for a way to escape, the same as he had been doing, but none had presented itself as of yet. The one failed attempt he had witnessed several weeks ago had not ended well. The dead body of the prisoner had been strung up as a warning even after she had been killed by an arrow to the head.

Workdays usually lasted from dawn to past dusk, and of course, nobody had mentioned one word about "movin' up" as the sheriff had put it. Uptar hadn't even seen Yuri since they had started working. He was alive, which was better than the alternative he had originally been given, but he still had no real prospects for the future.

He had already been waiting a while when he saw Umuk approaching from the bunkhouse, accompanied by another guard. A familiar frown was on the other orc's face, and he squinted in the sunlight as he looked around him.

He stopped several paces short of the door and looked defiantly at Uptar. "Ya seen Bartosh yet?"

Uptar nodded. "Said ta wait here for him."

"If we gotta wait for him, then why did this *malen'ka suka* wake me up early?" Umuk looked like he was going to kick one of the guards, but instead, he just grumbled to himself and fell in beside Uptar along the wall. He squatted beside it rather than leaning against it, and it amused Uptar to think about the other orc taking a shite right then and there. At least it would have represented his general mood.

Yet more time passed, with various clerks and dockhands coming and going, but with no sign of the dockmaster. Even the guards grew restless as the sun traveled higher in the sky and the shadows shrank.

Finally, Bartosh appeared at the doorway, still looking annoyed. He didn't seem surprised to see Umuk there along with Uptar, and he motioned for them to follow him before turning with an air of authority that assumed they would do as they were told. The guards fell in behind them, and everyone proceeded towards the boats. Bartosh walked quite slowly, and Umuk and Uptar were reduced to taking half steps so as to not bowl the old man over as they moved through the crowd of workers. The dockmaster was given a wide berth as he walked, and judging by the short bows and tips of caps from those he passed by, it was more out of respect than fear.

The procession gradually worked its way down the quay, passing flatboats of various sizes, until they reached the end, where a decent-sized ship lay at anchor. Its long body lay close to the water, and its shape and implied purpose contrasted wildly with all the other vessels in the port. There was one large mast amidships, but its main mode of locomotion was a series of oars along each side. There was a high level of activity on and around the ship, and there were two more guards armed with short bows posted at the foot of the gangplank. They came to attention as they saw Bartosh approaching.

The dockmaster stopped short of the gangplank and turned around to look at Umuk and Uptar. He looked them up and down, nodding his head, and then addressed them in their native tongue.

"So, the brothers are finally in front of me again. As I told you on your first day, I care not where you hail from or what you did to end up with me, only that you would work hard. And so you have. Perhaps you have not proven yourselves to be loyal quite yet, but you have proven yourselves to be capable. Which, for my current purposes, is good enough."

He paused, at which point Umuk made a point to spit on the causeway. "We ain't brothers, old man! Why does everybody keep sayin' that?!"

Bartosh rolled his eyes and sighed. "I don't care, you dumb *pes*. And don't interrupt me again, or you'll be building timber rafts for the rest of your short and sorry existence."

The Umuk that Uptar knew would have tried to crush the man's skull for either his tone or the insult, but now he just growled and said nothing more. Uptar wagered they might be able to reach the dockmaster before taking an arrow to the face or a sword in the back, but even at this close distance it would be a draw at best. He figured even Umuk wouldn't be dumb enough to take those odds. He tensed but remained silent as the dockmaster continued.

"Now, while the threat of death put you here and has kept you in line until now, I would exchange that threat with the potential for advancement. And coin. I offer you the chance to join the crew of the *Vydatnyy*, the largest ship to ply the northern reaches of the Gruminus. You will join as free men, or free orcs, as it were. You will no longer sleep in a locked bunkhouse, and you will be paid a salary of two denga a day. The ship will be your life. You will swab, you will row, and you will fight. Most important for you, I imagine, is the latter. Because with the fighting, you will be entitled to a share of any plunder taken by the ship to supplement your income. Questions?"

Umuk had rudely coughed when the salary had been mentioned, and now he gave a short, mocking laugh. "Two denga? *Two* denga?! Latrine diggers make more than just a few copper pieces, ya cheap *svolota!*"

Bartosh shrugged, ignoring the insult. "If I had latrines to dig, you would be at the top of my list to stick in the hole. As it is, you can row for a bit of money or lash logs together for free. Your choice, but you will need to make it now."

Umuk fell silent, obviously fuming. After a moment, he put his hands on his hips, the perpetual frown still on his face. "Ya said there'd be fightin'?"

The dockmaster smiled. "You will be patrolling the river, imposing law upon the lawless. Very few smugglers give up their wares quietly, and negotiations have been known to go awry very quickly. There are no true soldiers on the *Vydatnyy* save for the captain and steersman, so the rowers fight as needed. Most appreciate the exercise and the monetary rewards. Besides, you will not encounter a ship's crew larger than ours anywhere on the river."

Umuk smirked, as if bashing a head in was the most pleasing thought in the world at that moment. "Fine, count me in."

Bartosh looked at Uptar. "You as well?"

After a very slight hesitation, he nodded. "Sure. Beats log work anyways."

The dockmaster nodded to himself, as if he had known the

end result all along. "Very good. Your sentences of penal servitude are hereby considered at an end. I will inform the sheriff and complete the appropriate documentation. Your employment with me begins immediately, with terms being, ahem, negotiated approximately once every season. You are, of course, welcome to flee into the Wilds if you wish to break our agreement, but I doubt you will get far with no provisions or weapons. And you will be killed on sight if you are ever discovered after deciding to run. That decision, of course, is entirely up to you." He turned back around to address the guards by the gangplank, switching to Common.

"Please escort these two fine crew members to see Captain Ruslan. When he is done giving them instructions, escort them to their new quarters and see they are properly outfitted. One of you report to me when they are settled."

The guards gave Bartosh the king's salute but remained silent as he made to leave.

He signaled to the remaining two guards to fall in behind him, but he glanced at Umuk and Uptar one last time and addressed them again in their own language. "To quote an ancient tyrant, '*Hard work has set you free, so don't shite on this opportunity.*' I don't want to have to talk to either of you again unless it's to promote you." He turned away and began his slow shuffle back to the shipping office.

CHAPTER SIXTEEN
The Devil In The Details

Kozel sat at the table in Kira's house, turning a silvery grey rock over and over in his hands. Unlike at his last visit, he had made tea for himself, but then he hadn't taken more than a sip of it. The mug now stood on the table, mostly full of lukewarm liquid, while the fire in the hearth burned low and he remained lost in thought. Kira was either upstairs asleep or away, yet again, at Yuri's. He hadn't bothered to check when he had let himself in about an hour ago.

His trip to The Mountain had brought satisfactory results. More than satisfactory, truth be told, in his opinion. He just knew what had been found wasn't what had been hoped for by others when the news had originally broken that a hidden source of metal ore had been found. *But that's what happens when you chase myths and legends,* Kozel thought. *You're always disappointed in the end.*

How a Rusgorod scouting party had stumbled across the cave in the first place was unknown to Kozel. He assumed they had been driven into it by one of the many storms that slammed against the north side of The Mountain. Having been to the location himself several times now, what he did know is that it would have taken a minor miracle to discover it by chance, the narrow opening looking like little more than just another cleft or crack in the mountainside. If there had ever been a formal survey party sent to

The Mountain from Perizidon, or even by the eldar race in ancient times, Kozel didn't fault them for not making the discovery.

In any event, the Rus scouts discovered a fairly sizable cavern beyond the narrow entrance, large enough to house a half dozen men or so for a short period of time. They had marked the location as a potential storage room for future raiding parties and then moved on. No doubt their focus would have been mapping potential invasion routes around The Mountain, not geological formations within it.

How long ago that first scouting report was, Kozel didn't know. He also didn't know how long ago some miner's son, now a private in the Rus army, had sheltered in the cave on a subsequent scouting trip and sent home samples of what he thought was silver. Whatever the lucky coincidences or chances of fate that had brought to the attention of King Ioseb that there might be hidden natural treasure in The Mountain, it didn't matter. What did matter was that a royal decree was immediately issued for a proper assessment of the lode.

Testing by the alchemists had confirmed that the samples brought back were iron ore, not silver, but any disappointment had been swept away by the stunning proclamation by one of them that "light iron" had been discovered. The announcement was heavily disputed by the rest of the Rusgorod royal academy, but the chance that a source of the fabled metal had finally been found only drove the demand to determine what exactly was under The Mountain.

Like anyone who grew up listening to tall tales told by their ancestors, Kozel knew the stories well. Soft, malleable, and lightweight, the eldar race had supposedly discovered the silvery white metal they knew as *euncheol* deep in the earth and had created great weapons and armor from it. The metal had helped make their armies nearly unstoppable for a millennium, and they had guarded both the locations of their mines and their smelting process closely.

Ever since the ascendance of the "lesser races" of orcs and humans, their own kings and generals had lusted after the legendary metal. The orcs called it *lehke zalizo*, and the humans called it "light iron" or "silver iron." Regardless of the name it went by, the metal continued to evoke thoughts of glory and empire. The ancient eldar weapons that lay in various royal treasuries around the known world hinted at what could be if the metal could be rediscovered and forged again. Lost to the vagaries of time, all anybody could guess was that the eldar mines were far to the southeast in what was now the barren wasteland of their homelands. But many a miner had failed to find even a pebble of the mythical ore, and many an alchemist had wasted their lives and their master's fortunes attempting to recreate it.

Once the Rus geological survey team had reached Mount Klyk, their name for The Mountain, their exploration had been performed at a frenzied pace. Initial digging made it appear that a major vein had been found, heading at a steep downward angle towards the center of the earth. Testing had led to the conclusion that an iron ore of extremely high purity had been discovered. The alchemist who was part of the survey team had predicted as high as eight parts out of ten in the samples they had studied to date. Unfortunately, they had also determined that the metal did not appear to be the fabled *euncheol* after all.

The news had not been surprising to Kozel when the Rus captain in charge of the local operation had briefed him just a few days ago. He had believed for some time that the tall tales about the silvery white metal were just that. He had been in enough treasure vaults and handled enough ancient weapons to know better than to chase myths. The eldar race may have been expert forgers and blacksmiths, but in his opinion, the metal they used was nothing more than crucible steel. A high-grade steel, to be sure, but nothing that couldn't be recreated by others with enough training and artisanship.

Having said that, he did remember the disappointment he had felt long ago when he hefted his beloved hunting knives for the first time. Beautiful and wicked, their blades were so thin they should have shattered just by looking at them. If any weapons could be made from light iron, it would be them. But he knew their balance and form were that of normal steel, despite what the cowering lord, whose treasury he was standing in, had babbled about them being an ancient family heirloom taken from an eldar prince. That the knives could cut through just about anything, Kozel had determined just a few moments later, as did the decapitated lord. Thus, the knives had served him extremely well over the years, and he lovingly kept them polished and sharp. But he had known from the moment he took possession of them that they were not made from the stuff of legends.

So why had he initially reacted with hope and anticipation when he had heard of the Rusgorodian secret mission that was investigating a mysterious vein of ore discovered within The Mountain? It was hard to admit, but after all these years, there was still a small piece of wonderment and belief in miracles inside him. It was a very human trait, and one that he detested. Yet still it persisted. And so, he had been afforded the opportunity to relive the disappointment of his knives once again. He had departed The Mountain in a sour mood, albeit knowing he was being childish about the situation. At least no one had lost their head this time.

When he felt he couldn't brood on the past any longer, Kozel shook himself out of his self-pity and stood up, dropping the rock on the table. Tossing back the now-cold liquid in his mug in one gulp, he went over to the fire and built it up again to boil new water. This being done, he added new leaves from the pantry to the tea pot that hung by the fireplace and waited impatiently for them to steep. A bit of honey would have been ideal, but it wasn't his kitchen, so he figured he couldn't be overly demanding.

As he waited for his tea, he began thinking about how he could spin the discovery to the old man back in Gavan. No doubt the news of what had actually been found was already working its way back to the Rusgorod capital city. Kozel wondered idly how quickly the alchemist who had stated light iron was present would be shown the error of his ways. King Ioseb wasn't necessarily crazy, but he typically did not take bad news all that well. He certainly didn't suffer fools.

Not that Kozel feared for his own life, like most men did when they brought bad tidings to the Rusgorod court. He was far beyond the reach of the king, and in any event, he believed their schemes intermingled with each other enough now that he was indispensable. It was more a question of timing, as Kozel didn't need the fool to lose focus at this critical juncture in the overall plan.

Kozel took a moment to breathe in the vapors rising from his mug after he filled it, this particular mixture of spices making his nose tingle. The warmth spread through him as he drank deeply, and he sighed in contentment as he poured another serving. He would have to remember to compliment Kira on her tea selection, especially since he was sure she stuck primarily to ale and horilka when she imbibed.

He looked at the piece of ore on the table thoughtfully. While Rusgorod had some gold mines and a few other raw resources, they did not have a suitable source of iron within their borders. It was true that they had forced Malorossiya into paying tribute to them in iron ingots, among other valuable trade stuffs, but this was not enough to satisfy the high demand of the Rus army and fuel their campaigns in the far west. This, in turn, meant that the merchants in Myste and their doge had grown extremely wealthy by selling weapons and armor to the Rus over the years.

Kozel smirked at the thought of this need for outside

assistance. It also meant that Perizidon and others knew exactly what was being shipped north, as the merchants were more than happy to sell copies of their manifests. King Ioseb hated that anyone knew anything about his business, especially King Elric and his ilk, but he had raged at the doge through letters and proxies for years, to no avail, about the selling of information to his enemies.

But now, since the size and purity of the vein could be confirmed, Kozel knew there was a veritable treasure trove of high-grade iron tantalizingly close to the Rusgorod border. He had no doubt that it would take several years before enough iron could be mined and smelted to make a difference in the production of armaments. But he personally had the time to wait, even if the king did not, and he felt that whoever held the mountain could hold sway over the region for the foreseeable future. If the Rus held the mountain, they could become self-sufficient in equipping their men-at-arms, and their brute strength would only grow. The high-grade iron would be enough; the old bastard didn't need the legendary *euncheol* to fulfill his desire of bringing Perizidon to heel.

This meant that taking and holding Stren as a strategic stronghold was paramount. Kozel was confident that Yuri and the cohort he was building could seize the town, but the Rus army would be needed to hold it. If this happened, even if Perizidon decided to stand and fight, most of their northern counties would be in the hands of the enemy for quite some time as the armies bludgeoned each other to death over several years of campaigns. It would be enough time to bring materials taken from the mountain into play.

Kozel smiled. He knew he could sell the strategic value of The Mountain to Rusgorod, adding a legitimate reason for invasion alongside the wild machinations of an old man. Also, placing a small contingent of soldiers at the mine to guard it while mining equipment and laborers were brought in would not alter the overall focus or direction of the planned invasion. It was a solid recommendation, one he knew could be incorporated into overall planning with little argument.

Pouring himself a third mug of tea, Kozel wandered to the front of the room and gazed out through the dingy windows at the main road that traveled past the house. It was well past dawn now, and the town was starting to stir. He had come back to share some of the information he had obtained with Kira and to see if she and Yuri had raised any more recruits since he had been gone. But he was impatient to be on the move, so a quick note would have to suffice. The gates would be open soon, and he would be able to escape into the Wilds without raising an alarm with the guards.

Both the warg pack and that insufferable orc were somewhere to the west of town, and he still needed to figure out what was going on between them. It would also ease his mind considerably if he could confirm that the orc wasn't up here to meet with the local priest. His cursory review of the greyskin's belongings he had left with Bainor during his last visit had not offered up any tangible evidence one way or another.

Kozel turned away from the windows to look for some

paper and a writing instrument. As soon as he could scribble a note to Kira, he would be off. Nothing would stand in the way of his plan. Not Rusgorod, not Perizidon, and certainly not some damn trapper with a big axe.

CHAPTER SEVENTEEN

The Wandering Priest

"I keep tellin' ya, Father, tha bull was killed over a month ago! Why should I have ta pay full taxes on it?"

Father Malachi looked up from his ledger and slowly shook his head. He knew the farmer was being ignorant on purpose. The Chernenko family had been working the land for at least three generations, and Petro himself had gone through this process many times before. There were already ten head of cattle accounted for in the final tally, yet he remained belligerent over this last one.

"For the same reason that has always been in place, Brother Petro. The sheriff assessed the value of your household and your belongings last year when the bull was alive. You are paying for last year's assessment. Next year, this particular animal will come off your inventory, and your overall value will be reduced accordingly."

"But tha bull in question didn't just die! It was butchered by wolves, an' I got nothin' ta show for it!"

Malachi struggled to maintain his composure. "So you have already said. And as *I* have already said, in the eyes of the crown and the church, how one loses an asset has no bearing on how the tax is assessed or collected for the time it was in your possession."

"It ain't fair, Father!"

It never is, is it? Malachi sighed inwardly and said nothing in return. The farmer fumed on the other side of his kitchen table as

Malachi looked at him, silently counting the moments. When his count reached twenty, he raised his quill and made an exaggerated motion of dipping it into his ink pot.

"Very well, Brother. I will mark you in arrears, and you can challenge the ruling within the next thirty—"

"Fine! Fine! Take all my hard-earned coin!"

Malachi stopped short of writing anything down as Petro began to rummage through his coin purse. After several moments, he produced several silver kopek and copper denga pieces, selected a specific number of each type, and tossed them on the table. They clinked and clattered unceremoniously down among a somewhat sizable number of coins already assembled in between the two men.

Malachi quickly calculated both the added and total amounts in his head. Petro had still shorted him a couple copper denga, but he decided it was close enough. If such things really mattered, then the Almighty would remember the affront come Judgment Day.

Malachi made several marks in his ledger and then bowed his head over the tithe. He normally didn't pray in Common, but he made it a point to do so now. "Almighty One in heaven, you have given us riches beyond measure. We can only return a fraction of what we owe you; but we ask, Almighty One, that you will bless our offerings and help us to use all your riches wisely in your service and for your glory. Amen."

He snuck a peek across the table as he crossed himself and formally accepted the coins. Petro sniffed and acted oblivious to what had just been said, but his wife, Ivanna, was trembling with rage and was staring daggers at the farmer. Malachi hoped that, next year, there would be a bit more humility shown for the many blessings the Almighty had showered upon Petro and his family. Excessive pride and avarice had not been sins the farmer had admitted to earlier in the day when he'd had heard confession.

After filling out the receipt for payment in full, Malachi pushed the slip of paper across the table. "Thank you both, Brother and Sister Chernenko. I am done with my official duties, but I would be remiss if I did not ask if you have any other need of my services while I am here."

"We would be honored if you stayed for dinner, Father," Ivanna said quickly, and Malachi had the distinct impression she had just kicked her husband under the table to keep him from protesting. Petro's face grew stonier than it already was, if such a thing was possible, but he said nothing.

"I thank you kindly, Sister, for your hospitality. But the road is long, and I must travel some distance before nightfall if I am to make it to the next homestead."

"Well then, at least take some sustenance for the road!" she insisted.

Malachi smiled and bowed his head in gratitude as she rose and went about gathering some freshly made biscuits and a bit of bacon. They would be a welcome substitute for the hardtack and jerky that were his normal meal while traversing the Wilds. As she worked, Malachi's mind went back to something Petro had mentioned several times during his tantrum.

"Brother, about the death of your prized bull. What do you mean when you say it was butchered by wolves?"

The farmer had an exasperated look on his face, but after glancing back towards his wife, did his best to control his temper. "Just that, Father! When my eldest discovered tha carcass, its innards were all gone, an' it had been bled dry!"

"Innards? As in, everything?"

"Aye, Father!"

Malachi was neither farmer nor trapper, but he had been around many of each throughout his years. "That is not too unusual, is it? Wolves typically eat everything from their kills if they have the time, I am told."

"All tha choice organs to be sure, but tha intestines? Tha stomach an' what was in it? That's not normal, Father!"

"Hmm...I assume there were markings or prints around the body?"

"Aye, Father, quite a few. Like a whole pack had been feedin' on tha poor thing."

Malachi reopened his ledger, but to a different section. He consulted some older notes that included some hand sketches and measurements he had made. "The prints...could you estimate their size?"

Petro nodded. "Bigger than usual, Father, 'bout the size of me hand." He held up his right hand, which was heavily calloused and dirty from many years of manual labor. Malachi estimated it to be half again larger than his own.

"Could you tell which direction the wolves came from and left?"

"Well, I don't remember seein' any tracks comin' in, but they mighta come out of tha ravine to tha west. Ain't much dirt down there ta mark. They left goin' north by northeast."

"You said there was no blood at the scene?"

"No, I said he had been bled dry. There was blood all over tha ground and leadin' away from tha body. But it looked like there weren't a single drop left in him. I tell ya, it ain't natural, and it ain't right that you're treatin' it like he just died of old age or somethin'! The stud fees were gonna be—"

Malachi was flipping back through his notes as Petro talked, nodding his head but not really paying attention to the farmer argue for the third time why he should be compensated for the loss of his prize bull. After a few moments, he found the entry he was looking for. A sow and her calf had been killed in a similar manner to the south. If the collective memories of the storytellers could be trusted, the deaths had happened less than a week apart from each other. It was the size of the paw prints reported at each scene that had left an impression in his mind. He smiled grimly at his witticism and crossed himself again.

"Is something wrong, Father?" Ivanna had finished wrapping his meal in a rough homespun towel and was standing by her husband whom she had interrupted midsentence.

Malachi looked up from his ledger and shook his head. "No,

Sister, I was just writing some notes about your unfortunate loss. To, ah, ensure it is recorded correctly for future visits."

As Malachi slowly made his way east towards his next stop, he ruminated on the gathering list of odd happenings that his parishioners were telling him about. The cattle attacks were fairly low on the list, truth be told. Due to the size of the prints, he had originally thought the first attack to be a bear instead of wolves. *But bears don't hunt in packs. So, larger than life-sized wolves? Wargs, or some other monster from the old times?* To his knowledge, no humans had been attacked, so while there was cause for caution, there wasn't cause for alarm. Just yet, anyway.

Caution was always top of mind for Malachi regardless of what might be lurking amongst the trees. While he was used to the remote vastness of the Wilds, he was never comfortable traveling alone with a large amount of money in his lockbox. Priests who worked in more urban areas could rely on people coming to the nearest church or monastery to remit payment to church and crown, but Malachi did not have this luxury. If taxes and tithes were to be collected, he had to go to each individual homestead in his parish. However, Malachi truly believed that his primary purpose for being in the church was the saving of souls. He would have visited each homestead regardless.

By custom, he was afforded protection by every able-bodied parishioner in the Wilds within half a league of their front door, and he could dispose of his collected coins in the larger towns and villages along his route. But this still meant that he was vulnerable to attack on the days he was in the wide spaces between the small points of civilization. Through the grace of the Almighty, and a bit of luck, he had never been seriously harmed.

As part of his general responsibilities, Malachi had dutifully logged all the reports of strange lights in the sky, snippets of infernal chants wafting on the night breeze, and cursed crops he had received from the superstitious over the years. But it had only been recently that he had studied what he was writing down. There had been an uptick in overall reports over the past two years, almost double what could be described as typical. Supposed werewolf and vampire sightings had cropped up recently, especially in the western part of the parish, and someone had been outright murdered in Stren this past spring.

The recovered murder weapon had been a cruel-looking knife with runes of the old gods carved on its handle, immediately starting rumors of witchcraft being involved. The local sheriff was supposed to be handling the murder investigation, but Malachi was certain it was going nowhere. He had passed all his observations along with his last two quarterly reports to his superiors, but no new orders had yet worked their way back to him from the archbishop's office in Velych.

Several hours later, he had worked his way through Ivanna's biscuits and was nearing the next homestead. After the Chernenkos came the Shoikoses, and then the distance between parishioners shrank considerably as he began to near Stren. Malachi was confident that he would reach the Shoikoses prior to Vespers, and he felt blessed that they were his last stop of the day. Hannah and Mykola would welcome him warmly and would graciously have him spend the night under their roof. Their children were always happy to see him, and the eldest daughter would no doubt challenge him to a game of chess after evening prayers. Malachi's mouth watered in anticipation of the warm stew and freshly baked bread smeared with honey that would be washed down with just enough ale to send him to bed a content and happy man. He knew that, if he had chosen a different path in life, he would have aspired to live and love like the Shoikos family did.

Letting earthly temptations get the better of him, Malachi lightly flicked his whip across his nag's rump, urging her into a slow trot. His small wagon creaked and bounced along the slightly rutted dirt path he was following, and as he crested the next hill, he could see the Shoikos homestead directly ahead of him, less than a league away across a shallow valley. The scene seemed too picturesque to be real.

The cry of a nearby wolf shattered the tranquility of the moment, and Malachi instinctively pulled on the reins as he looked around wildly. The nag had also heard the howl and ignored the apparent order to halt. Whinnying in fear, she leaned forward, trying to conjure up speed from days long past. As the wagon sped up negligibly, Malachi spied two black bodies running just inside the tree line to the right. They were moving parallel to him, and as he watched, the rear one seemed to bark out a warning. They both veered deeper into the underbrush.

There was another howl, behind and to his left, but this time it was answered by another that sounded like a beast was coming at them directly from behind. Malachi, somewhat under control now, didn't bother with turning around and looking for his pursuers. He gave the reins to the nag to let her run as best she could, figuring that every step brought them closer to the homestead and relative safety. Bending slightly, he quickly rummaged through a storage space that had been built into the seat of the wagon and drew out a crux decussata. Unlike most of its brethren, this one was made of steel, and the two diagonal pieces had sharpened edges that were tipped with silver. A handle had been fashioned directly under the crosspiece, and when Malachi grasped it, the saltire-shaped dagger felt balanced in his right hand. It only measured approximately four palms across, but the ugly weapon could be extremely effective if the user had been trained properly.

Malachi glanced to his right again as he readied himself. The two wolves that were pacing him were back and had been joined by a third. The late afternoon sun illuminated them briefly as they darted between the trees. Their eyes flashed red whenever they looked over, sharp teeth exposed as they ran with their mouths open. There were more howls, still behind but closer.

"Nam etsi ambulavero in medio umbrae mortis, non timebo mala, quoniam tu mecum es!" Malachi intoned the words of the ancient psalm given by the Almighty to protect those walking in the shadow of death, and he did his best to clear his thoughts for the coming fight.

The wagon had reached the valley proper now, and within it the sun was already below the horizon. The path sloped gently downward and widened due to the trees that had been cleared for firewood and fencing this close to the homestead. It meant that, despite the dim lighting, Malachi could clearly see the three wolves angling in to attack. The nag saw them as well and screamed in terror as two of the beasts launched themselves at her flank, while the remaining one took aim at him.

Malachi timed his thrust perfectly, catching the wolf at the base of its mouth with the right prong of his dagger as it lunged to grab him by his neck. Its momentum threw them both off the wagon, but he turned with the weight so that he landed on top of the beast, padding his fall. Claws tore into his travel robe and skin as the wolf spasmed while he tried to disentangle himself from it, and wrenching the dagger free, he was able to roll to the side. The mortally wounded animal fixed him in its gaze, and he could feel hatred fill the space between them. It attempted to howl, but only a gurgling sound came out, blood cascading out of the gaping wound.

Malachi was vaguely aware of a larger struggle to his left, and out of the corner of his eye he could see that the wagon had been tipped on its side by the combined force of the three attackers. The poor nag was also on her side, legs kicking to no avail. Even if he could have helped her, there was no time, as two more wolves came up from behind, and he was forced to turn and face them.

The newcomers paused some ten paces away, sniffing the air and catching the full scents of horse, wolf, and human blood that were combining to form an overpowering stimulant. One sat back on its haunches and gave a mighty call, the sound echoing through the valley, while the other began pacing from side to side, edging ever closer to Malachi. Its red eyes shown out from its black mask of a face, like glowing coals from the fires of the abyss.

Malachi could no longer hear his horse struggling, and he assumed her attackers would also be at his throat in a moment. He slowly retreated towards a large oak tree to try and limit the angle of attack by what he assumed would be four beasts at once.

"Nihil timeo in hoc mundo, jam enim pro alio salvatus sum!" He called out more as a challenge to his foes as opposed to offering up a last prayer of respite. There truly was nothing to fear, as he was at peace with the Almighty. Calmly, he braced for the onslaught and a fight to the death.

Abruptly, there were scuffling noises from the other side of the wagon, and then the sounds of breaking bones and yelps of pain. The wolf who had been edging closer to Malachi paused and looked in the direction of the disturbance, its ears flattening against its skull as a low growl escaped its mouth. The second wolf, having already heard several responses to its call, turned towards the sounds as well.

"Prykhod'te do mene, moyi tsutsenyata!"

Malachi recognized the harsh dialect of the orc tribes to the far east, but he had no idea what was being said.

Striding out from behind the wagon came a large greyskin, smiling widely and snapping his teeth like a wild animal. His battle-axe was covered with blood. As the orc drew closer, he bellowed out his own challenging howl at the two wolves in front of him.

Malachi sensed movement to his right and shifted to put the tree between him and whatever was in the brush. Two more wolves burst out into the clearing the trail ran through, barking and snapping at each other.

The orc continued to advance, but he moved in a short arc that cut the distance between him and Malachi while maintaining a common front to the beasts.

“Hrayte zi mnoyu, suky!” The orc feinted towards the wolf closest to him as he shouted his challenge, and when it jumped back, quickly reversed his swing.

His axe missed a second wolf by the merest of whiskers. It, too, jumped back, growling and hissing, eyes ablaze. The remaining two turned their combined gaze on Malachi, as if they were silently trying to will him to walk forward into their clutches.

“Away, foul beasts, away!” Malachi called out, as he held his crux decussata in front of him. Like the orc’s weapon, it dripped wolf blood that stained both his robe and the ground.

The menacing greyskin had reached his side, only glancing at him briefly. “Let ’em come, Father, let ’em come! Don’t shoo ’em away like mangy strays! They took tha bait, now we gotta make ’em pay!”

The four beasts began to pace back and forth in unison, just out of the swath of the orc's axe.

The orc crouched low, as if to spring forward and attack, but he seemed to be looking beyond the combatants immediately in front of them. Malachi peered into the trees in the direction the orc was looking. He blinked rapidly and shook his head, as if he didn't believe what he was seeing. It appeared that a large wolf was staring back at them from some thirty paces away, except that it was standing upright like a man. It gestured at them with its right foreleg, and its challenging howl was guttural and vicious in tone.

"Aye, Father, ya see it too? That vovkulaka is what's drivin' these wargs! He's what I'm after, an' he knows it!" The orc raised his head and shouted, "Don't ya, suka blyat'? Stop sendin' yer minions an' face me, ya *pyzda*! Povertaysya v peklo, volokhatyy demone!"

Malachi's chest tightened when he heard the orc refer to both wargs and a shapeshifter in the same breath, but before he could say anything, the four charged together in a rush.

They covered the ground between the groups in an instant, but the orc was ready and timed his counter perfectly. His axe whistled through the air and effortlessly shore off the snouts of two of the beasts, causing them to fall in a heap at his feet, writhing in soundless agony.

Malachi had just enough time to brace himself as the other two plowed into him. His raised dagger caught one in the chest, but the other one sank its cruel teeth deep into his left thigh.

Malachi screamed as his entire body instantly felt like it was on fire, and he could feel the warg bite down harder, his leg tearing away, his life over, his service to the Almighty at an end...

***

Already the priest's wound seemed to be festering, yellow pus and bright red blood oozing out of the gashes in equal amounts. As Sarl worked, the priest tried to rouse himself and screamed in agony. He had to put a knee on the man's chest to anchor him in place.

"C'mon now, Father! Ya fought tha good fight, but we gotta patch ya up before tha second round starts!"

"Water...water!" The priest pointed feebly at the upset cart and its contents that lay scattered on the ground around it.

"Okay, okay, gimme a moment!" Sarl finished the tourniquet and then quickly crawled the few paces over to several chests that had spilled open upon impact with the ground. He didn't see anything that looked like a waterskin, and he glanced back at the priest in the hopes he could give additional instructions.

"Holy water...holy..." The wounded man tried to gesture again, but his strength was rapidly fading.

Sarl scanned the items around him a second time and caught sight of a small, cylindrical vessel. It was silver in color and was adorned with a crucifix. He picked it up and noticed it was tightly capped. Unscrewing the cap, he could tell there was liquid inside it.

Quickly making his way back to the priest, he offered him a drink from the container.

"*Stultus*..." The priest turned his head away. "On the leg..."

Embarrassed, Sarl liberally sprinkled the holy water on the

wound. There was a hissing sound, and the priest screamed again, but the amount of pus immediately reduced in volume. Sarl emptied the entire contents of the tube, and the priest writhed underneath him. Despite the obvious pain, some color came back to his face, and he seemed slightly more lucid.

"Book..." The priest waved in the direction of the cart again.

"Huh? What? Ya want yer bible? I don't think yer ready for last rites just yet, Father!"

"Not funny...no, my ledger...can't leave it here..."

Sarl went back to the chests, and this time easily found the item he was looking for. A large, leatherbound journal that had seen much use was lying on the ground, quills and ink pots scattered about it. There were holy symbols on its front and spine, and when he picked it up it seemed lighter than it looked.

Brushing it off, he brought it to the priest, who grasped it firmly against his chest.

"Thank you...Brother Orc..."

"Save yer breath, Father. We gotta get ya ta safety 'fore those wargs come back." Sarl looked over at the ruined remains of the nag and hoped she had gone quickly. "Looks like we're footin' it. I figure we make towards that farm just east of here an'—" He turned back to Malachi and found him passed out from blood loss and trauma.

"Well, shite! Guess I'm luggin' ya."

***

Maryska did her best not to cry as she tended to the priest. She considered him to be family, a well-traveled uncle who would tell her stories of the large world outside her valley and who always made time to play chess with her. Now he lay mangled on her parents' spare bed, passed out from the pain of his injuries. She knew by what she could overhear from the conversation in the front room that both her father and the large greyskin who had brought the priest to their door did not think much of his chances. Her mother had rushed out to collect herbs with Artyom and Fedir acting as her escort, but Maryska had seen the worried look on her face and knew she shared the others' opinion.

The bleeding had mostly stopped, and the tourniquet that the orc had applied had been loosened, so the priest was out of immediate danger. She had carefully peeled back his robes and undergarments and was now flushing the deep incisions in his thigh with *aqua ardens*. The cuts hissed in anger with the application of the distillate, the liquid turning a dark red as it ran off his leg onto the rags she had placed on the floor.

She knew the main concern now would be whether the leg should be amputated, not only because of the grievous wounds but also because of the fear of *skaz*. Even her father had gone pale when the orc spoke of wargs being on the prowl this close to the farm, as they were surely infected with the dreaded disease. Maryska would hate to see the priest lose a leg, but she would never forgive herself if he lost his mind instead while under her care.

She heard the front door of the house close, and her father immediately came into the room. He had brought more rags with him, along with a small paring knife and a small bottle of what she assumed was medicine. She knew that he meant to cut away parts of the damaged skin and flesh immediately around each wound so they would not fester, and she shifted to one side so he could inspect the leg.

"Where did the orc go, Father?"

"Back to the attack site. He wanted to collect the priest's belongings before it gets too dark. He'll be back though, as he'll be staying here tonight."

"Is that safe?" she asked in alarm.

Her father snorted. "Maryska, if that brute wanted to murder us then he would have done so already! He may be from a fallen race, but we should reward his charity with our own. Father Malachi would already be dead if it were not for the greyskin carrying him here."

"Yes, Father." She had finished applying the *aqua ardens* and carefully soaked up any remaining fluids from the priest's leg.

He inspected her handiwork and nodded. "Good. Could you fetch the lantern and hold it close for me?"

Maryska did as she was told, and her father began probing the deepest wound with his knife. She noted that he had washed his hands, and the knife shined brightly in the light of the lantern, as if it had been dipped in liquid and wiped clean. Father Malachi groaned at his touch and shifted slightly.

"Does he have a fever?" her father asked, not looking up as he continued to probe.

“Yes…” Her eyesight blurred briefly as she fought back tears once again.

Her father shook his head and mumbled something under his breath that she could not pick up. He glanced down to the foot of the bed, noting that she had already strapped the priest’s leg to the frame. “Good girl. Your mother taught you well. Keep an eye on him while I work. We may need to restrain him further.” He bent over the leg again and began to cut some skin away.

Maryska heard noises of several people coming into the house and reasoned the other family members were back. Her mother poked her head into the room, taking in the proceedings at a glance and nodding at Maryska with a quick smile. Then, she was gone again, and Maryska could hear her calling for her younger sister to come to the kitchen.

She turned back in time to see her father open the small bottle and carefully wet the edge of a clean rag with the contents. It had a silvery white color and appeared to be odorless. She had never seen her parents use it before.

“What is that, Father?”

“It is called *lunares medicina*, my dear. Very valuable, very precious. It is supposed to help stop the spread of *skaz*, the Almighty willing. It also happens to contain silver, which, if our orc friend is correct about the wargs, will help protect against their evil nature.”

He wiped the wound he had cut skin away from with the moistened rag, and the edges immediately turned black. Father

Malachi groaned again but did not move.

"However did you get such a mighty potion?"

Her father gave a short laugh as he picked up the knife again and moved to the next gash. "Would you believe, from Father Malachi? It was some years ago, when you were but a babe. Your mother was anxious about all sorts of strange maladies and insisted we be prepared for the worst. This is one of several arcane medicines that Father Malachi was able to procure for me on one of his trips to Velych. Thanks to your mother's planning, we may now have a chance to save his life. Just, uh, don't remind her that she was right yet again." He looked over at her and winked, and despite the seriousness of the situation, she wrinkled her nose back at him and grinned at the old family joke.

The process of attending to Malachi's wounds was long and arduous. Maryska stayed in the room when her mother came in to apply herbal ointments and dress the deep cuts. Not only did she feel it her duty to see the entire surgery through, but she was also admittedly nervous being around the orc. He had come back with the priest's belongings, as well as news. Her father spoke with him in the front room in a low tone for quite some time before ordering the boys to serve him supper.

Once the orc was settled at the family's dining table, her father came back to the priest's side. Her mother had just finished the last wrapping, and the two of them held hands with Maryska and prayed over Father Malachi as he would have done for them.

"Bless the Almighty, O my soul, and all that is within me,

bless his holy name. Bless the Almighty, O my soul, and forget not all his benefits: Who forgiveth all thine iniquities; who healeth all thy diseases; who redeemeth thy life from destruction; who crowneth thee with lovingkindness and tender mercies..."

When they were done, her father continued to hold onto their hands and addressed them as equals. "The orc brings bad tidings indeed. The rest of the pack are still on the prowl nearby. He could smell them and thinks their number to still be more than a dozen. I have secured the cows in the barn, but I am afraid the other animals will need to fend for themselves tonight. When the morrow comes, he will leave for Stren to bring word of the attack. Hopefully, the sheriff will send some of the town watch our way."

"Why did the wargs attack poor Father Malachi in the first place?" Maryska's mother spoke in a low tone, worried but firm.

"I don't know. The orc said—"

"What is his name, dear? He is a guest after all."

Maryska's father nodded at her. "Of course, my love. He calls himself Sarl but did not give a surname. I don't know if the tribes use them or not. No matter, Sarl said he has been tracking the pack for some time now. According to his story, they ranged far to the south, and he was hired by another parish to get rid of them. He claims to have killed over a score to date."

Maryska scoffed at this. "Well, either he is a mighty warrior or a mighty braggart!"

Her father looked at her with a firm gaze. "Child, give him the benefit of the doubt. We all heard the baying shortly before he appeared with Father Malachi, so there are wolves of some sort in the vicinity. Both of their weapons were filthy with blood, and not each other's, so something or someone attacked them both. And finally, he was brave enough to go back to retrieve Father Malachi's belongings after dark and came back unharmed."

Maryska swallowed, regretting her instantaneous judgment of character. "You are right, Father. Forgive my outburst."

He smiled at her gently. "Do not fret, Maryska. Perhaps this Sarl is both a warrior and a braggart, and we are equally right in our opinions. Regardless, he did not have an answer as to why they attacked, only that they have attacked other homesteads to the south." He looked at her mother and squeezed her hand. "I believe we are safe for the night. The orc and I will take turns with a watch, and I will have the boys and Maryska sleep with you, Ariana, and the baby. We will set wards and alarms around the property tomorrow; it is too late and too dark to do that now."

Maryska looked at Father Malachi and finally allowed her tears to come.

***

Sarl sat by the fireplace, nursing a mug of ale. He had volunteered to take the first watch, and the rest of the household was quiet. The farmer and his family had treated him well enough, especially given the circumstances. The younger children had been more curious than afraid, and he had even allowed the boys to hold his hunting knife and the priest's unique weapon.

He idly held the curious dagger in one hand even now. It

was much too small for him to use, but he had always had an appreciation for fine craftmanship and the flair of the unknown. It would also be useful to know how to counter it.

The mother and eldest daughter had been the most aloof, polite, but avoiding eye contact, and only being in the same room as him for as short a time as possible. He didn't blame them. According to the old tales that men told about the orcs, he should have already disemboweled the farmer and raped both of them twice.

He shook his head in amusement and finished his drink. A half full jug stood on the table, but for now, he placed his mug on the floor next to him, stretched out to his full length, and warmed his toes.

He felt badly for the priest, but he only partly blamed himself for what had happened. Yes, he had baited the pack towards the road after staking a freshly killed buck, smeared heavily with his own blood, for them to smell and find, but how was he supposed to know someone else would stumble into his trap right when it was sprung? Even then, if the church had provided even the most rudimentary of horses to the priest, the wagon would have made it to where he had been hiding. As it was, he had spent precious time running up to the point of attack and had lost the element of surprise. Worst of all, he had to let the vovkulaka slip away while he dealt with the injured man, so it had all been for nothing. He knew he wouldn't be able to use the same trick twice.

Sarl absentmindedly fingered his talisman as he stared into

the fire. For the briefest of moments, he had thought of leaving the priest to his death to pursue the monster. If he had done so, he assumed he would have had to attack the rest of the alerted pack head on before even getting to their leader, which made no tactical sense. Besides, the priest had fought bravely and had taken down two of the wargs himself. That alone made him worth saving in Sarl's eyes.

He looked at the dagger in his hand again and reminded himself to give it back to its rightful owner in the morning if he was awake.

In tha morning... Sarl scowled at the dark room as he rose to help himself to the contents of the jug. He was now duty bound to head back to Stren in the morning and report the attack. He had also told the farmer that he would return with or without town watch reinforcements, in the event the priest could be moved to town. It just meant more time lost in searching for the vovkulaka.

Furthermore, Sarl wasn't sure what to do about the priest's ledger. He had a vague notion of how humans conducted business in this realm, but the concept of taxes was beyond him, and looking at all the numbers in the book had made him cross-eyed. The farmer had advised handing it over to the sheriff, but Sarl wasn't sure if he could trust the man, let alone his second. He decided he would leave it here, with the rest of the priest's religious trappings, in hopes that he recovered.

As for tha priest's lockbox... Sarl took a large swig directly from the jug, wiping his chin with his shirt sleeve. He had conveniently forgotten to tell the farmer he had retrieved it, let alone that he had buried it near the western border of the farm. No doubt someone would remember it at some point. If the priest regained consciousness, he would certainly ask about its whereabouts. Sarl might even volunteer the information under the right circumstances. He hadn't made up his mind. *But for now, what they don't know won't kill 'em.*

There was a solitary howl in the distance. It carried far and wide in the still night air, but there was no discernible response. Sarl lay back down in front of the fire, confident that his troubles were over, at least until the morning.

CHAPTER EIGHTEEN

Moirne On The Move

The morning after Moirne's interview with the princess was cold and wet, making a dreary start to her travels. As she headed towards Velych's northern gate, the grey sky did not foretell any break in the weather for the day. Her waterproof cape was well-made, however, and there had been no change in her plans to account for bad weather.

She had left her church uniform and armor in the cathedral's priory, having decided it would be better to travel incognito for now. Her attire under her cape was fairly nondescript, but her noble-looking steed still marked her as someone who was more than just a poor traveling merchant. As such, while Moirne did not expect trouble this far south, she kept her sword prominently lashed to her back to give any miscreant fair warning she was not an easy mark.

The guards at the gate were too busy staying dry to do more than make note of her departure, and she lightly prodded her horse into an easy jog as she cleared the portcullis. The road was made of flagstones for roughly half a league outside the city, and even in the gloom of the overcast day, they shone brightly in the rain. Traffic was still heavy despite the weather, especially the inbound carts and wagons, and Moirne deftly maneuvered around various slow-moving obstacles as she proceeded forward.

Eventually, the homesteads and farms that crowded close to the capital road began to spread apart, and the number of fellow travelers began to dwindle. The road became a mixture of mainly gravel and a bit of mud as it continued north, paralleling the Grumaius River. It remained relatively wide and in decent condition due to its constant use as a towpath, and Moirne was able to urge her horse into a working trot. Despite the weather conditions, the mare reacted positively and eagerly stretched her gait.

At regular intervals, Moirne would pass teams of donkeys dutifully marching forward, pulling flatboats of various shapes and sizes upstream. The drivers' songs maintained a cadence of sorts, but they sang more to pass the time than to direct their beasts of burden. Most would simply wave or salute as she passed by, as opposed to calling out for some sort of conversation. In any event, she had nothing to say to them and kept to herself as much as possible.

Most of the flatboats heading north up the river were lightly loaded so as to not unduly burden the donkeys, but some manner of cargo was almost always carried so the return trip was not completely unprofitable. In contrast, their brethren headed downstream rode low in the water, heavily burdened with cut timber, quarried limestone, or other raw materials from the Wilds. They slipped past in the middle of the channel on their way to Velych and other ports farther south. There was the occasional sloop or other sailing vessel that would pass, going in one direction or the other, but, as Moirne knew, they were used much more to the south of the Perizidon capital where the river was wider.

Traffic on the river was heavier than on the road, and as she kept going north, there were fewer and fewer travelers on foot or horseback. Random hamlets dotted the countryside on the western bank of the Grumaius, but the eastern bank was almost entirely bereft of life. It had been over a thousand years since eldar barbarians had swept out of the east, burning all before them, and even the orcs had not threatened to invade through the Riphean Gap in several generations. Still, old fears never truly died in the Wilds and merely mixed with new ones to solidify legends into facts. Anyone who lived east of the Grumaius was considered an adventurer or a bloody fool. Even the garrison town of Stina was barely occupied, serving mainly as a forward base camp for the army, as opposed to being a bustling center of commerce.

The day passed peacefully as most had in these parts for the past decade, ever since King Elric had successfully mounted a campaign against the so-called Bandit Lord of the Wilds. The king had fulfilled his pledge to safeguard travelers (and their wares) along the important trade route from Velych, all the way north to Stren, and the kingdom as a whole had profited mightily ever since. The small watch houses that had been constructed along the road every two to three leagues between Velych and Tuman during the Time of Troubles were no longer needed, and now they stood locked and bereft of life. These days, they were only occasionally used by royal messengers or the odd military patrol, and they were no longer stocked with provisions.

Moirne's status within the church hierarchy afforded her the ability to access the watch houses, and she did so at one she arrived at around Sext to get out of the rain and to let her mare rest and graze for a spell. She herself did not eat, and after a short prayer, merely brought a chair to the doorway and sat looking out at the road, smoking her pipe. The few donkey teams and travelers that passed might have looked at her oddly, but none chose to greet or challenge her. She was either somebody important, or somebody imposing, or both, and it was not worth the trouble to find out.

She had spent most of the morning deep in thought, and her melancholy mood persisted as she watched the rain turn into a fine mist. Try as she might, she could not put her fingers on more clues to help solve the mystery laid out in front of her. She knew she was right about Rusgorod, and she was fairly certain there was something more going on than their old king's hatred for Perizidon and his need to correct perceived slights. But if the Rus were going to invade, when and where would they do it? If there was some other malevolent presence at work, who and why? She had no real proof, just ghost stories and secondhand reports. If she answered to anyone other than the Almighty and the pope, she knew she would be hard pressed to argue why she was wasting church time and resources on this investigation. But her gut very rarely led her astray, and it certainly felt sour at the moment.

The afternoon journey was much of the same, other than it being slightly less wet, as the mist eventually just became a low-lying cloud. The foggy conditions didn't seem to concern the donkeys headed upstream, although Moirne assumed most of the boats headed downstream would need to anchor or draw up to the shoreline earlier than they would like. As for her own travels, she estimated she could make it about halfway to Tuman, the garrison town located at the confluence of the Grumaius and Gruminus rivers. She could have made camp with some of the flatboat drivers, as they typically grouped together at night for safety in numbers, but she knew she would not be welcome. The regularity of the watch houses made it much easier to decide how far to travel for the day in real time, although she did have one in particular that she was aiming for. It was situated in a very remote stretch of the road where the flatboat drivers were loath to stop for the night, and it was highly doubtful she would need to share it with anyone else.

Moirne made it to the location in question around Vespers. The watch house was located within a heavily forested area, and the trees crowded up against the roadway for some distance on either side of it. She sensed old magic nearby, as if the woods were hiding some door to the past when gods and titans walked the earth. The feeling was certainly fainter than the last time she had traveled through these parts, but it still lingered. For tonight, it would serve her purposes.

During the Time of Troubles, this part of the road had been known as being a natural place for an ambush, and the trees and undergrowth had been cleared away for some fifty paces around the watch house when it had been in regular use. Nature had reclaimed the ground over the past decade, and now the structure seemed like it was about to be consumed by the woods. Several saplings were growing immediately adjacent to the door, and the exterior was mostly covered up by thick foliage. Overall, the watch house looked and felt more like a cave than a building.

Ignoring the old hitch post near the door, Moirne carefully walked around the structure, tamping down underbrush and weeds to make room for her mare to stand out of sight from the road. She was able to clear enough space directly opposite the building's doorway for her horse to stand, and the canopy overhead was so thick, it might as well have been a small stable. After watering and tending to the mare, Moirne carried her saddle into the watch house and made a cursory inspection of the interior. While a few of the watch houses had fallen into disrepair or been vandalized over the years, most were still in decent shape. Fortunately, this one was in the majority.

Built out of stone, with a wood floor and slate roof, the watch houses were sturdy and had been created to provide shelter from both the elements and potential attackers. Some of the more advanced designs had cellars or bolt holes, but these were usually considered a luxury that the common soldier either didn't need or didn't deserve. Four small sleeping quarters, each with two bed frames, were located away from the door, along with several small storage spaces. The main room served as office, kitchen, dining room, and living room all in one, with a large fireplace dominating the center. Small windows that could serve as arrow slits in an emergency lined all four walls, although these had been filled in and covered when the houses were closed. Whatever had served as an outhouse at this location was long gone, and Moirne had already had to make do with what the river offered.

The furniture, sparse as it was, was still in good repair, and there were even some tools, a simple lantern with candles, and a bit of rope in one of the storage spaces. Almost a full cord of firewood was stacked along one wall, and the fireplace looked extremely inviting on such a wet and dreary day. Unfortunately, Moirne was positive the chimney cap would be overgrown and blocked. At best, all the smoke from a fire would be forced back into the room and choke her. At worst, escaping embers would start a fire overhead and burn everything down around her, the rain notwithstanding. She consoled herself by changing out of her damp clothes and hanging them over several of the chairs to dry out.

There was enough light with the lantern to read and write by, and after a simple meal of bread and salted pork, Moirne busied herself at the small table with reviewing some case documents she had brought along with her. With all the windows blocked, the house was stuffy, and her pipe smoke didn't help matters. She left the door open a crack for a bit of circulation, although the wind was mostly still.

After an hour or so of reading, Moirne stretched and went to look outside. The weather had cleared as she had hoped, although with the new moon, the night was still quite dark. After putting her documents away, she collected some of the firewood from the wall and brought it outside. Dumping it near the edge of the road, she went back inside the watch house to retrieve the lantern and then went about gathering dead wood and brush from around the nearby forest. Even with the day's wet weather, the denseness of the trees had kept most of the undergrowth dry. Within due time, she had constructed a rather large pile of kindling and medium-sized branches, and she even managed to drag several sections of a fallen tree out to the road.

The roadbed was soft enough from the rain to allow Moirne to quickly dig a shallow depression in the middle of it with her boots, making sure she was positioned in an area where there were no overhanging trees. Within this space, she went about constructing a bed of kindling and pine needles before placing pieces of wood in an angled position above the bed, creating a cone-like structure. Using her flint and steel, she started her bonfire, and the dry firewood went up in a rush. Quickly throwing on more dead branches, the flames soon were above her head in height, both they and the smoke being generated going straight up into the still night air. She watched in silence, continuously feeding the fire so that her signal beacon remained as large as possible.

After about a quarter of an hour, she let the flames slowly die down until there was nothing more than hot embers left. These she doused with water from the river, and they hissed and spat at her in protest of their short life. In just over an hour, the show was over, and she retreated to the house to wait for a response.

Moirne dozed fitfully on and off for several hours before

some barely perceptible change in the night noises coming from the forest brought her back to full alert. She could sense someone nearby, just outside the house. No doubt they were inspecting the remains of the fire. Moirne quietly opened the door and relit the lantern. Placing it to the side of the table so she could view the entryway, she also relit her pipe and sat down again.

After several long moments, a hooded figure stepped quickly through the door. It was as if coming inside was like they were taking a plunge into an ice-cold lake. Better to take the shock to the body quickly, as opposed to easing into it. Their shadow seemed to shimmer in the light of the lantern, and they advanced to the middle of the room where the fireplace stood. Moirne could tell they were smelling the air, which had the suspicious odor of smoke upon it.

"It's my pipe, not the hearth," she said simply.

The figure turned towards her, studying her carefully. Moirne remained seated and made no move towards her weapon.

"It's a nasty habit, and it will be the death of you," came a female voice, chiding but not unfriendly.

"I suppose you are right. But even I am allowed a small vice or two, am I not? If nothing else, to prove I am human?"

"Hmm, is that really something you wish to do?" The other woman pulled back her hood as she advanced again, this time towards the table and into the full light of the lantern.

She had tight dark curls for hair with a pearl white complexion that showed no age or blemishes on her face. Her hazel-colored eyes twinkled with a mischievousness that played against her years, and she wore a smirk pressed upon thin, red lips. Most notable though, were her pointed ears, briefly visible when the motion of removing her hood pulled her hair back with it. Numerous silver earrings flashed in the light before her long tresses fell back into place on either side of her face.

Moirne rose to greet the eldar with a warm hug. "Aerysiel, my old friend. I am glad you are still here, alive and well!"

Aerysiel returned the hug before pulling back and looking Moirne in the face. "Of course, I am still here! The forest still needs me, perhaps more now than ever."

The two of them were more or less the same height and build, their silhouettes playing with each other in the flickering light of the lantern. If they couldn't pass for sisters, then being mistaken as first cousins would not be a stretch.

"You seem to be continuing to do a good job reclaiming this area, at least!" Moirne gestured around and behind her to call out the wild growth that surrounded the man-built structure.

The eldar sniffed, and subconsciously rubbed her nose with the back of her hand. "Here, perhaps, but my spies tell me that men from Tuman constantly nibble at the northern edges of the wood, looking to expand their hold. It is inevitable that humans will waste what Nature has wrought, just like my kind did so long ago."

In her younger years, Moirne would have immediately launched into a debate regarding how Nature was merely part of the Almighty's overall creation, but now she merely gripped the shoulders of the other woman and smiled. "We shall see, Aery, we shall see. Nevertheless, I was hopeful that you would be in this area at this time of year and would come to investigate a, ahem, 'minor disturbance' on the road."

Aerysiel laughed, the sound of it light and cheerful. "Hmm, yes, your signal was seen up and down the river from at least a league away, probably farther up in the hills. You are correct, word soon reached me about both the bonfire and that someone was taking shelter in the old human house. I, of course, did not know it would be you, but I am glad that it is." Reaching up, she took Moirne's hands in hers and gently pried them off her shoulders, bringing them down between them. She smiled, and after a quick squeeze, gently released them back to Moirne. "But come, your need must be urgent if you are willing to risk a stunt that could have anyone, or anything, come pay you a visit. Sit, and tell me everything. At least"—she laughed again—"as much as you have a mind to tell me!"

They sat at the table and, in a hushed tone, Moirne briefly discussed the reports she had received in Velych and her suspicions about possible relationships between events. She did not reveal the source they came from, as that would be irrelevant to the eldar, and she did not discuss any potential Rusgorod connection.

Aerysiel listened intently, then nodded. "Yes, I have heard the reports of wargs and other beasts ranging much farther abroad than usual this past year, both from the north and from the mountains to the east. There was even a pack of mangy *sobaky* that came through the gap a few months ago, but luckily for them, they went north instead of through my lands." She spat on the floor in disgust. "I will never understand why you humans decided to trust the orc tribes! They will be your downfall!"

It was a tired refrain that Moirne had heard many times in the past. This time, she decided to let the dogs of ancient history lie, even if they were not sleeping for the eldar. "What of the vovkulaka, Aery? Have you heard any stories about it?"

The other woman frowned. "Not specifically that one, but I have heard there are shapeshifters about these days. You must remember that the treants and leshy keep most undesirables out of my woods, so I do not see the same level of taint that other parts of the land may suffer. But..." She paused.

Moirne waited a beat before prodding gently. "Something feels off to you, doesn't it?"

Aerysiel sighed. "Yes, something feels off. Most of the treants have slumbered for many years now, but the pace of their lack of responsiveness has accelerated." She smiled wistfully. "The one time they are fast at something, and it is their own demise! But the leshy concern me even more."

"How so?"

"They seem...well, more selfish? I suppose that is the word for it. It is always hard to read the minds of the spirits, but they seem less inclined to save the lives of ailing flora and care more about protecting their realm."

"Is that not what you want them to do?"

Aerysiel rubbed her nose with the back of her hand again and looked unsettled. "Yes, but they should know that, if they sacrifice themselves for the forest, they merely return to Nature and can be called upon to inhabit a new body. I think they are afraid that there will be no one left to call their spirits back."

Moirne frowned, as this was a touchy subject between herself and Aerysiel. Monsters such as the leshy were considered abominations by the church, since they were not the creation of the Almighty, but rather derived from corrupted old magic. They were not even considered sentient beings, like treants, as they did not appear to have any moral sense about them. Being soulless in the eyes of the church, they were doomed to the void under any circumstance.

She decided to change the subject slightly. "And what about the forest in general, Aery? The natural flora and fauna?" She tried not to emphasis *natural* too much, and the eldar ignored her gibe.

"The forest is well enough. Whatever is bothering the old world has not impacted the new one as of yet." She sighed again. "I should be happy, or at least satisfied. Overall, Nature continues to find balance within itself. She appears to be able to evolve with the age better than I can." The shadow of a death long awaited passed over the eldar's face briefly, but then she brightened again and laughed at herself. "Listen to me! You should tell me to go drown myself in the river with such a gloomy outlook!"

Moirne laughed as well. "Never, my old friend! But I would have you be happy, so let us talk about more pleasant topics."

"Yes, let's!" The eldar leaned forward eagerly, putting her elbows on the table and clasping her hands as if in prayer. The movement made the sleeves of her cloak fall back, revealing tattoos of intricate patterns of leaves that spiraled around both her forearms. "I must admit, I never grow tired of your stories about the world's distant places. Tell me, where have you traveled since we last saw each other?"

They commiserated almost until dawn, their laughter and voices drifting out of the watch house and into the forest. Their words were much too hasty to understand for the treant who was standing guard, but it was glad that its mistress was happy. The mare had warily regarded it for some time before drifting off to sleep, and no other creatures dared come close enough to bother it or the occupants of the house.

The treant and the eldar slipped back into the depths of the woods with the coming of the sun. Several hours later, the only signs that anyone had been present were the trampled down underbrush behind the house and a roughly circular charred piece of ground in the middle of the road. Moirne did not have much more intelligence now than yesterday, and the sour feeling in her gut continued to grow as she headed north towards Tuman and beyond.

CHAPTER NINETEEN

A Study In Sarl

Early in the morning after the warg attack, Sarl hurried on his way back to Stren. There had been a brief discussion with the farmer about whether he should be accompanied by Maryska or one of the boys to add validity to his story, but Sarl had argued they would just slow him down. Time was of the essence if he was to make it back to the farm by that evening with help. Besides, he already had all the proof he needed to validate his story. The head of one of the wargs he had killed was rolled up in a sheet that was currently slung over his shoulder, and he also had the priest's weapon with him. If Sheriff Yuri, his second, or the town guard wanted more evidence than that, they would need to send someone to the farm to gather it themselves.

Unfortunately, time was not of the essence regarding treatment for the priest. Father Malachi had never awoken from his coma, and now lay still, as if already dead. His breathing was shallow, and his skin felt hotter than the surface of the sun. If there had been any sort of medical assistance available in Stren, the risk of moving him would have been taken. But the family knew that Hannah's healing skills were as good as, if not better than, anyone else within several days' travel. When Sarl had left the farmhouse, she was standing vigil over the unconscious man, applying cool, wet rags to his forehead and chest while offering up prayers of intercession.

Sarl moved at a fast clip, and he had been in the region enough over the past several weeks that he knew where he could deviate from the worn pathways and take shortcuts through the countryside and other farmsteads. Several dogs, and one farmer, challenged him along the way, but a few swift kicks and one cold stare were easy resolutions for clearing his way. Slightly winded, he was trotting through the western gate of Stren before midmorning had arrived.

Sarl made a beeline for the town hall, not wanting to be held up at the gate while he explained his package. There was an immediate challenge from the guards as he passed their station, which he ignored. When he glanced behind him, he saw two of them stumbling out into the road after him, struggling to draw their swords. Sarl grinned and resisted the temptation to wave at them as he picked up his pace.

A series of whistles rang out from the direction of the gate as he entered the main square, but there were no guards present at the town hall entryway to waylay him. He strode inside the building, looking for, but not seeing, the sheriff or his second in the immediate vicinity. He decided to approach the nearest clerk, who looked up from his ledger in bewilderment as the large orc entered his peripheral vision.

"Can I help—"

The clerk was interrupted as the guards who had been giving chase burst into the hall, adding to the growing confusion.

Sarl was already in the process of unslinging the warg's head from his back, and he continued to ignore the guards. Always one for a flair of the dramatic, he unrolled the sheet that was wrapped around the head in one motion, allowing it to land solidly on the clerk's desk with a heavy *thump*.

"I got an assault ta report!" Sarl bellowed over the clerk's cry of alarm at seeing the mangled remains appear in front of him, seemingly out of thin air.

Sarl shifted slightly to his left as he spoke, to allow the guards to see the hideous visage, and they recoiled enough that he now had space to react if they decided to try and seize him. The other clerks in the room were on their feet now in various states of surprise, and several moments later, two more guards appeared at the foot of the stairwell that led to the second floor, apparently in response to the commotion.

Sarl scowled at the growing audience. "Where's tha sheriff?! I gotta problem out in tha Wilds an' need—"

"All right, all right, that's enough!" A female voice cut Sarl off, and Kira appeared from the stairwell behind the guards. Her hand was on the hilt of her sword as if expecting trouble, and the noise from the clerks died away as she advanced into the room. She slowed as she saw and recognized the intruder, but her hand remained on her hilt.

"So, orc, yer back! An' yer causin' trouble again already?"

"I brought ya trouble this time, jailer!" Sarl gestured at the desk. "One of several wargs I killed a couple leagues west of here, but not before they attacked yer travelin' priest!"

There was a momentary shocked silence as everyone took in the news. "What did ya say?" Kira asked sharply, her eyes narrowing as she looked closely at the head. "Wargs attacked Father Malachi?"

"Aye, near tha Shaimos farm."

"Who? Ya mean tha Shoikos family?"

"Whatever. That Hannah woman with her man an' her brood. Like I said, tha priest got attacked near their farm last night, an' I came ta report it an' ask tha sheriff for help. Pretty sure tha pack is still out around there."

Kira had come up to the desk and was fingering one of the warg's fangs, but she was listening to Sarl as he spoke. She looked up at him with probing eyes. "So, where's tha priest? Why ain't he with ya?"

"He ain't dead, at least not when I left this mornin', but he ain't doin' that well either. His leg was almost torn off in tha attack!"

There were several muted cries from the clerks at this, and one of the guards crossed himself.

Sarl continued. "That Hannah woman is tendin' ta him. We decided we'd kill him if we moved him."

"Why'd they attack him in tha first place? Malachi ain't one ta go lookin' for trouble." Kira continued to stare at him, searching for any cracks in his story or demeanor.

Sarl shrugged. "Dunno, I was in tha area huntin' for tha pack an' heard tha ruckus. Came up right as tha priest offed one of tha beasts with this." He held up the crux decussata that he had purposely left unclean.

There was an audible gasp from the nearest clerk, as not many laypeople knew of the existence of such an ugly holy weapon. He offered the weapon to the jailer, who took it without comment. Her eyes continued to follow him.

Sarl could sense sympathy for the priest in the crowd. Shaking his head, he continued his story of half-truths. "I was able ta help him get a few more, but one got through an' bit him in tha thigh. Even that didn't stop him. He kept fightin' 'til tha rest retreated 'fore he passed out from blood loss. From what I could tell, he had been tryin' ta lead tha pack away from tha homestead."

Kira looked only partially convinced at his story, but the rest of the crowd muttered appreciatively. They drank in the news of their heroic priest, who now lay at death's door after protecting his flock. Many a heartfelt prayer would be offered up to the Almighty for Father Malachi that night as the story spread through town.

The jailer coughed to get Sarl's attention. "I assume these are tha same wargs ya talked 'bout huntin' tha last time ya was here? Tha ones from down south?"

Sarl nodded. "They gotta be. But they seem ta have doubled back for some reason, 'cause I thought they were still headed north. It's my fault for not catchin' them before they got tha priest." This at least was true, although not for the reason being conveyed by his contrite look.

Apparently, he had said enough to make Kira believe at least the framework of his story, and her hand finally moved away from the hilt of her sword.

She sighed and shook her head. "Well, ya got tha rest of tha priest's property with ya?"

"Nah, I wanted ta travel light ta get here quick an' ask for help as soon as possible. Tha Shoikos family wants protection sent their way, if possible before night falls. If ya got someone with medical skills, I'd send them too. I left tha priest's ledger an' everythin' else at tha farm in case he wakes up." Sarl had decided he wouldn't be able to lie about the whereabouts of the ledger, but he deliberately stayed hazy as to whether he knew about the priest's lockbox.

In any event, the jailer didn't press him for any details. Instead, she gave the warg's fang one last jab with her finger before taking the head in her hands and repositioning it so that it was facing the door leading out to the main square.

The head stared cruelly straight ahead at everything and nothing, including the two guards who had come from the city gate. The look in their eyes seemed to harden as they stared back, and their stance visibly straightened. This monster had attacked one of their own, and they were finding the resolve within themselves to do something about it.

"Mykola Shoikos an' his family deserve protection," Kira announced, her voice strong and clear so that everyone in the room could hear her. She turned to one of the guards behind her. "Olena, go find tha sheriff. He should be comin' back from tha Kravchenko farm soon enough, but we need him now."

The guard saluted and ran past Sarl.

Kira turned back to look at him again. "How many wargs do ya wager are still out there?"

Sarl thought for a moment. "At least twelve, maybe even a score."

"Think ya got tha alpha?"

"Yeah."

She looked at him sideways, as if sensing hesitation in his answer. "Yeah, but?"

Sarl wasn't sure if she would laugh him out of the hall or not, and at the last moment, he decided it wasn't worth mentioning the shapeshifter just yet. If someone else saw it and reported it, he felt that would help matters immensely, or at least make any future explanation easier. That, and he couldn't quite bring himself to trust either the jailer or the sheriff just yet.

"But nothin'. Hard ta tell who's leadin' who with all tha howlin' they do."

Kira seemed to be thinking about something, and there was a brief pause before she responded. "Right. Well, soon as tha sheriff gets back, we'll form up a squad ta go help ol' Mykola. If yer comin' with us, I suggest ya get somethin' ta eat. It'll be an hour or two 'til we leave."

Sarl thought about telling her that he was leaving immediately. However, the chance for some quick goulash made his mouth water. *An' maybe that barmaid will be workin' tha day shift too. I can always outrun tha jailer's squad back ta tha farm if they're takin' too long.* He shrugged nonchalantly. "Sure thing. Ya want me ta take that with me an' dump it somewhere?" He pointed at the warg head.

The jailer smirked. "Nah, we'll keep it here. Ya know, fer evidence."

***

A short time later, Sarl sat at the bar of the Wild Boar, grumpily poking at some weak gruel. Goulash wasn't served until the evening, according to the equally grumpy barmaid who had served him. The ale was the same as his last visit, which meant it still tasted like cooked cabbage. *No wonder this place is deserted,* he thought to himself as he choked down some day-old bread. The sparse lunchtime crowd didn't even warrant the enforcer checking people's weapons at the door, something that Sarl and several other patrons had conveniently forgotten to do. If there were any ongoing dice games, they were much quieter than when he had been here over a week ago.

Suddenly, he caught a familiar metallic scent at the edge of his olfactory senses, as if it were coming from a nearby room. It was faint enough that he didn't think any of the humans around him could detect it. *But that means it's been here! Or maybe it's still here, somewhere close? Sard me, did it have tha nerve ta follow me ta town? If it's takin' tha time ta track me, then why didn't it attack yesterday?*

It had been a question he had been thinking about on and off ever since the fight, or at least since he had gotten the priest to safety and his berserker-like state had dissipated. Even after he had killed the last of the wargs in the immediate vicinity of the horse cart, there had been at least six more in the underbrush that could have continued to attack. He could have fought them off if he had abandoned the priest and used the wagon as a shield, but it would have been tough going, and he doubted he would have emerged unscathed. And that would have still left the vovkulaka to deal with.

It had approached to within less than twenty paces, enough to observe the small battlefield littered with warg corpses and the mangled priest. The remaining wargs had continued to howl and yip at each other, circling ever closer to their prey. And then, just like that, the shapeshifter had barked out a command in some infernal language that Sarl didn't understand, and they had all melted into the underbrush as the twilight had deepened.

At the time, his only thought had been to save the priest, and he had rushed the unconscious man immediately to the nearby farmstead. But when Sarl had come back to fetch some of the priest's belongings and weapon, there had been no sign of the vovkulaka or the pack. The horse's corpse had been dragged off somewhere, but it did not appear as though anyone had rummaged through the cart itself. The money box and Malachi's religious accoutrements had been left undisturbed, as had the priest's weapon where it had fallen on the ground. The only explanation that Sarl could come up with is that the shapeshifter had been affected by the presence of the holy man or his kit and had been loath to approach too closely. Not being a holy man himself in any sense of the term, Sarl had collected what he had come for and left quickly without performing a wider search of the area.

All of this swirled around in Sarl's mind as he fought the temptation to immediately turn and look around the room. Instead, he breathed deeply through his nose as he pretended to take a drink from his empty mug while raising his free hand to signal for a refill. It was impossible to determine which direction the scent was coming from, but he was confident that he was not imagining it.

His thoughts were interrupted by the still grumpy barmaid as she roughly set his new drink down in front of him, the ale sloshing onto the bar.

She looked down at his uneaten meal and then back up at him. "What's tha matter, yer majesty? Our porridge not to yer likin'?"

"I think ya gave me pig slop by accident, miss," Sarl said in a dry tone, a smile tugging at the corners of his mouth as he winked at her.

Her mouth twitched as well for a moment, and then she laughed. A woman probably in her late twenties, she bore the marks of a hard life, but overall, seemed stronger for it, as opposed to beaten down.

Sarl smiled broadly and picked up the new mug. It still smelled like rotten cabbage, but he did his best not to show too much distaste as he took a long pull.

The barmaid's tone was much lighter than before. "All right, luv, ya got me. I'm sorry we ain't got no goulash for ya, but tha main cook don't come in for a few more hours. If you're here tonight, I'll make sure ya get yer fill."

The fact that the shapeshifter might be nearby had Sarl reconsidering what he was going to do. "Fair 'nough. Hey, does Bainor got rooms open for tonight?"

"He sure does, luv. He'll be in here when tha cook comes, I'll tell him ta save one for ya. What's yer name?"

"Sarl Blackmoor, at yer service!" He bowed his head and saluted her with his mug.

Smiling, she gave an exaggerated curtsy in return. "Bohdana Panchenko at yers, good sir!" She looked at his bowl again. "Ya want me ta just take it?"

"Yeah, I ain't gonna touch it. No compliments ta tha chef."

"Fine, fine, I get it, luv." She gathered up the full bowl and the two empty mugs as she talked. "Ya want anythin' else?"

"Just a question for ya. Do ya know Katrya? Is she workin' today?"

Bohdana's mood immediately soured again, and a dark look came over her face. "Why do ya want ta know 'bout that shrew?"

Oh, shite. Think quick, meat! Sarl coughed and tried to look embarrassed while he lied about the first thing that came to mind. "She, uh, arranged somethin' for me tha last time I was here, an' I just wanted ta see if...well, uh..."

The barmaid snorted. “Somethin’ or some*one*, luv?”

He held up his hands in mock surrender. “Ya got me, Dana. Some*one*.”

Her face flushed slightly at the spur-of-the-moment nickname, and her overall demeanor softened just a touch. “She don’t work today. If ya really need help with *that*, then anyone workin’ here can help ya.”

“Anyone? Even tha brute at tha door?” Sarl smirked and nodded in the direction of the enforcer.

Bohdana nearly dropped the dishes in her hands as she let loose with a hearty laugh. “Yeah, sure, luv! I dunno if you’d like what Ernest would send yer way, but if ya really want ta ask him, I ain’t stoppin’ ya!”

Sarl laughed as well, and whatever tension he had triggered within her when he had mentioned Katrya seemed to be gone. “Well, Dana, maybe I’ll just deal with ya instead.”

She winked at him. “Watch yerself, luv. Someone might get tha wrong idea ’bout what you’re sayin’. Now, is there anythin’ else?”

“Nah, I’m good for now. What do I owe ya?”

“I won’t charge ya for tha porridge, luv, so just two copper. An’ maybe I’ll see ya tonight.”

Sarl left the tavern in better spirits, despite the fact that he was still hungry. He stood for a moment outside the main entrance, trying to pick up the metallic scent again, but the slight breeze and the multitude of odors coming from the square made it impossible.

However, he had already made up his mind; he was staying in town for the night. If the sheriff was going to send a squad to the farm, the family would be safe. Besides, he had the sneaking suspicion that, if the vovkulaka was in town, there was a good chance the pack would leave the outlying homesteads well enough alone.

There wasn't much he could personally do for the priest, whether he stayed here or went back, but he had thought of one item he could offer. Subconsciously touching his talisman through his tunic, he made for the small chapel he had seen near the west gate. He assumed it was locked since the priest was away, but that wouldn't stop him.

***

"So, he's the one that just reported the attack on the priest?" Kozel asked the jailer from the shadows of the small room.

"Yeah, that's him," Kira replied.

Both of them were being careful to stand back from the window that was above the tavern's sign, but the orc never turned to look behind him as he sauntered off across the square towards the west. He was easy to pick out among the sparse crowd, even as he drew farther away.

Kozel felt the pit in his stomach growing. He already knew who the orc was before Kira had come to tell him about the warg attack, but her confirmation still made him more uneasy than before. *How in the blazes does the church know what's going on? Who talked?*

She continued. "He came inta town 'bout an hour ago from

a homestead a couple leagues west of here. Came straight away ta make his report an' brought evidence too. Soon as Yuri gets back, we're formin' a squad ta head out back tha way he came ta protect tha farmer an' see ta tha priest." She looked over at him. "Ya don't want me ta try an' stop that, do ya?"

"No, no, no. It is a prudent move to make." The attack on the priest had been an unwelcome turn of events, even if it seemed to confirm the orc really was up here to meet with him. Kozel cursed himself and looked up at the ceiling. *What am I missing? Think!* He tried to keep the worry out of his voice. "Did the orc bring the priest's ledger back with him?"

She snorted. "Nah, he made some shite excuse 'bout travelin' light ta get here quick. Like a book would slow him down."

That's a small break in my favor, but he could have easily read it last night. But then to not bring it here, does that mean the orc knows enough to not trust Yuri with it? This last thought made the pit in his stomach grow even larger. "We have *got* to get that ledger and figure out what those two know. Can you personally go with the group that's headed to the farm and secure it?"

She wheeled to face him, alarm written all over her face. "Whaddya mean, what those two know? I thought ya said before that tha orc wasn't up here ta meet with tha priest! Now yer sayin' they're workin' together?"

"Well, maybe I was wrong before!" Kozel snapped. He hated to be wrong, and he inadvertently let some of his anger at himself leak out.

Kira swallowed hard. "Koz, I know you ain't been tellin' me tha whole story, an' that's fine. But ya gotta tell me what we're up against now! If tha church knows what we're doin', then ya know they're gonna warn tha king's men!"

"Which is why we need that ledger!" Kozel tried to control himself, as he knew none of this was her fault. She was scared, and he really didn't have any solid answers for her. His nostrils flared as he breathed out slowly, attempting to slow his heartbeat.

As he did so, Kira turned away to face the window again, her arms wrapped around her torso as if hugging herself for comfort.

"Look, Kira. There's very little that I haven't told you, and the small part of the plan you don't know is for your own protection. I don't know how much the church knows about what we're doing, but the fact that they sent a mercenary to investigate instead of an inquisitor means they only have general suspicions at best. Trust me, I know their system and how they do things."

While Kira didn't turn around, her stance seemed to soften as he talked.

He moved forward until he was standing next to her, looking out the window. The orc was at the far end of the plaza now, and as they watched, he turned right and disappeared from view.

Kozel continued. "If we can get a look at that ledger, then we'll know what the priest knows. And whatever he knows, the orc will know only that much or less, right?"

Kira huffed somewhat dismissively. "Unless tha orc brought information with him from down south ta share with tha priest."

"Mmm, doubtful. If that were true, there would already be more signs of preparations down south, either from the church or the state. And I saw nothing of the sort just a few weeks ago. What's more likely is that he brought questions from a superior that he hoped the priest could answer. Again, the ledger is the key."

"Unless the priest didn't write anythin' down an' just told this orc what he knew."

Kozel grinned. Kira had always been good at finding holes in a story or theory. "Again, doubtful. The last I saw him, the priest was in a state that precluded long discussions, and I—"

"You *saw* tha priest? *When*?" There was surprise and more than a bit of anger in her voice now as she wheeled on him again.

He coughed lightly, kicking himself for the slip. "Uh, last night. I witnessed the attack on him."

Kira's hands balled up into fists, and Kozel took a step back, wondering if she would actually strike him.

Instead, she blinked slowly, clearly seething. "What tha abyss, Koz! Why didn't ya tell me this?"

"If the orc hadn't reported the attack, I would have. Just not as publicly as he did."

She looked like she wanted to choke him, and it took a moment to compose herself. "So, ya saw these wargs tha orc keeps talkin' 'bout?"

"Yes, I saw them." *Too much of them, truth be told.*

“He said they ’bout bit tha priest in half ’fore he chased ’em away.”

“A bit hyperbolic, but mostly true. He had to carry the priest off the field, as the holy man was bleeding out from a deep leg wound and was unconscious. Like I said, I doubt they had time to talk.”

“So, what, tha wargs just stopped attackin’ and allowed him ta walk off? That don’t make sense, Koz!”

“Between the two of them, they killed over a half dozen beasts in the space of just a few moments. Wargs aren’t stupid enough to make a bad situation worse.” He decided not to tell her that they had been called off. *In any event, the way that orc was fighting there would have just been more dead wargs with no change to the outcome. I’m not sure I could take him in a fair fight, if it came to it. Of course, I would just make sure it wasn’t fair.*

Kira shook her head. “I don’t like this one bit. An’ how am I supposed ta get tha ledger if that orc’s nosin’ around when we go back?”

“Go without him. I’m sure you or that boyfriend of yours can make up some reason to keep him here in town tonight.” When she looked at him skeptically, Kozel continued, “It’s not like you haven’t done it before.”

“But what about tha priest?”

“What about him? If he’s dead or unconscious, then the ledger must be handed over to the local king’s representative for safekeeping, until a member of the church clergy comes to collect it. With the mayor out of commission, that's you or the sheriff. You'd have all the time in the world to read the ledger. And if the priest is alive and conscious, then he's duty bound to give you his statement on what happened. That, no doubt, will shed more light on what he knows and what he's told the orc. Besides, he'll be weak and tired so soon after the attack. Just wait until he's sleeping to take a look at the ledger."

Kira slowly nodded and rolled her shoulders to undo some kink created by nerves. It was a good enough plan for now, and she was regaining a bit of confidence. "Fine, I'll go. What are ya gonna do?"

"I'll see if I can detain our 'friend' a bit longer than one night. We need to keep him close by until we figure out exactly what he's up to."

"Ya ain't just gonna kill him? Wouldn't that be tha simplest thing ta do?"

"Mmm, maybe the simplest thing, but not necessarily the best thing. Not yet anyway. I need to know who will come looking for him if he disappears. I'd really like to know if he's a pawn or a rook." *Besides, if I wanted him dead, it would have happened already.*

"Don't be smarter than ya have ta be, Koz."

He smiled wolfishly as he turned away from the window. "Don't worry, my dear. I'm no cat, and curiosity won't be the death of me."

***

Sarl was drunk, and it felt wonderful.

He had commandeered the corner table all for himself when he had come back to the Wild Boar, glowering at the regulars who wandered over about an hour later ready to set up their normal dice game. Being dinnertime with the larger evening crowd, the tavern's normal rules were back in effect, and Sarl's axe was safely tucked away in the weapons locker. But the men remembered what he had done to their friend without it, and after a few moments of staring, they had wandered off to find another table. Other than Bohdana, nobody had bothered him since.

Now, three excellent bowls of goulash later, Sarl was leaning back in his chair and enjoying a bit of people watching. The barmaid had easily persuaded him to switch from the cabbage-smelling ale to a local horilka after only one drink, the sweet honey aftertaste hiding the effects of the hard liquor. After several mugs, even as a large orc, he'd begun to feel the effect. It had been quite some time since he had managed to get himself drunk, and it was the first time he could remember where he was drunk and not engaged in some sort of brawl at the same time. It was downright pleasant, and for just a moment, he forgot all about the shapeshifter, the dying priest, and anything to do with wargs.

The nearby fire had been stoked high to fend off a surprisingly cold night, and the locals were all worried about an early frost. Sarl found himself almost caring that the local apple harvest could be ruined, and he settled an argument by agreeing with an old farmer that it was guaranteed to frost within six weeks of hearing a bush cricket. He bought a round of ale for the table next to him and gladly accepted their return purchase of yet more horilka for himself.

At some point in the evening, someone realized that Sarl had been the one who had brought news of the warg attack on the priest, and soon, any number of locals were pressed around his table peppering him with questions. After a few retellings of his story, it was as if Father Malachi had called fire down from heaven itself to smite wave upon wave of the evil beasts, collapsing from his injuries only when he knew the nearby homestead was safe from further attack. There were a few that crossed themselves nervously and wondered aloud if religious wards should be set up around town, but most raised a mug to the valiant priest and swore they would have stood by his side to the last.

"Ya say he ain't dead? Hey, can ya make someone a saint if they ain't dead yet?" The young farmer who asked the questions looked around inquisitively. He was shouted down immediately by the others gathered around the table.

"Shut yer yap, Stepan. We don't want him dead, an' tha Almighty don't want him yet anyways! Hey, orc, where'd ya say Father Malachi is at?"

Sarl took another swig of horilka and attempted to focus on one of the two crowds of faces looking at him. "He's with tha Shoikos family. They're tendin' his wounds an' whatnot."

There was a general muttering of approval. "Ah, Hannah Shoikos will set him right if anyone can! She's a right saint herself!"

"Ol' Mykola sure got himself a winner there, that's fer sure.

Hope his cattle's all right with them wargs runnin' around, though. That calf born this spring is still nursin', I reckon."

"Hey, speakin' of teats, have ya seen Maryska an' her—"

"Shut up, Stepan!"

Somebody pushed the young man away from the table, and a minor scuffle ensued that was out of Sarl's line of sight. Normally, he would have tried to watch the fun, but he wasn't sure if he could stand up. Instead, he took another drink and pointedly ignored the comment about Mykola's daughter.

"Tha cattle are fine. Tha farmer locked them up in his barn 'fore we stood watch last night."

There was a general nodding of heads, and a couple side conversations broke out. One in particular caught Sarl's attention.

"What's our fearless sheriff doin' 'bout this?"

"Ain't ya heard? His bitch led a squad out ta tha farm this afternoon ta set wards an' patrol tha area."

"Figures that he didn't go hisself, that—"

"Shut it, Vasyl!" somebody hissed in a warning tone. "We ain't all friends here!"

"Well, if that sardin' sot of a mayor would get off her arse an' do somethin', then we—ah!" The man called Vasyl had been viscously jabbed in the ribs by two others at the same time, and he doubled over in pain.

One of the jabbers looked at Sarl nervously to see if he had been listening. He had been, but he just shrugged.

"Oh, don't worry 'bout me. That sheriff of yers ain't doin' me no favors. I was supposed ta go back to tha farm with tha squad, but he an' his second got me under 'town arrest' or some silly shite. Don't want me ta leave 'til they figure out how true my story is." He took another drink. "Least I ain't sittin' in a cell."

There was more general nodding of heads, and someone pushed another mug across the table to Sarl. He idly wondered if more than just a few of the rabble of drunks around him shared his general uneasiness about what the sheriff was up to.

"That's all well an' good they sent a patrol, but I don't see how that's gonna help Father Malachi." It was the old farmer who had been right about the bush crickets that spoke up from the next table. He shook his head as he looked into his drink. "Soon as I finish, I'm goin' ta tha chapel ta pray fer tha Almighty ta heal 'is faithful servant."

His statement had a sobering effect on the group in general, and their earlier celebration of the priest's mighty deeds turned more contemplative.

"He...he always prays over tha sick an' anoints them with holy oil. Who's gonna do that for him? Who...who would say last rites for his soul if it came ta that?" The full weight of the situation fell upon the group as they pondered whether their newly minted saint would be forced to spend eternity in purgatory. There was sniffling from one of the younger, more emotional, men, but nobody made fun of him.

Sarl had been enjoying himself mightily up until now, and he frowned at this last statement. He was rather annoyed that the lively drinking appeared to be over, but he decided not to call out the old man as a killjoy. Instead, he decided to be optimistic for a change. "Don't ya worry, that priest is a tough one. 'Sides, I went to tha chapel this afternoon an' filled up several bottles with holy water. Gave tha bottles ta that Kira woman an' told her ta have tha farmer's wife use it on tha priest's wounds."

A feeling of relief swept through the crowd, and several people raised their mugs in appreciation while others slapped his back.

"Oh, that's good thinkin', that is."

"Father Malachi's gonna be all right, I reckon!"

"Thank ya kindly, orc!"

"Yeah, good on ya, orc! Guess I was wrong 'bout your kind being nothin' but thieving dogs!"

There was some nervous laughter at this last remark, and Sarl sighed inwardly. He turned towards the speaker with a retort at the ready. "Well, allow me ta make amends for my race, sirrah! Don't want ya ta think too highly of us, now. As soon as I'm done huntin' tha wargs, I'll be back ta loot an' pillage tha town, don't ya worry." He stared meaningfully at the middle-aged merchant who had made the atonal remark as he downed the remainder of his drink.

The man's face went white, and the conversations around them died away.

Sarl put down his mug and looked around. In an instant, he had turned back into an outsider. He was back in his element, and he laughed roughly.

He knew he was past drunk now, and it was glorious. He could barely taste the honey in his drink anymore, and both his sense of smell and touch were starting to go numb as well. If they wanted a brawl, it was time to go. He wouldn't feel or remember a thing tomorrow.

"Shite, man, I'm kiddin! I meant ta say, I'll only loot yer shop an' leave everyone else alone! Maybe I'll show yer wife a good time too, eh? That any better for ya, suka?" He smirked, showing his teeth, and he loudly slapped the table.

There was a bit more nervous laughter, and suddenly about half the group needed to go outside and take a piss, while the other half decided to help the old farmer get to the chapel.

To Sarl's everlasting disappointment, the merchant turned and hurried away, almost bowling over a young woman standing behind him.

Sarl's vision was fairly blurry, and he couldn't quite make out who the woman was. The large chandelier above the bar was directly behind her, creating a halo around her head that made it impossible to see her face. As the slim but shapely form advanced toward him, his heart rose as he wondered what she was doing here.

"Elise?"

CHAPTER TWENTY

Lianne In The Map Room With The Tomes

It was well after Compline, but Lianne was still in the map room with her hands on her hips, attempting to come to terms with the large stack of books, maps, and scrolls spread out before her on the large table. To the amusement of Gregor and irritation of Symon, she had gone into the archives the past several days and laid hands on every single document she could find listed in the index regarding Astrikhon. Treaties, royal proclamations, drawn and redrawn border maps, campaign notes with tallies of battles won and lost, reports from spies embedded in their court, annual trade reports...the amount of information was staggering. She supposed the sheer quantity made sense in that the two human kingdoms had survived as uneasy neighbors for several centuries. But the specific information she was seeking was not jumping out at her from the mass of assembled documents, and she was beginning to feel overwhelmed.

It had taken roughly a day for Lianne to get over her disappointment about not being able to travel to see The Mountain with the inquisitor. Ultimately, her practical nature won out, and she had turned her mind to the issue at hand. While she had general knowledge of the kingdom to the southeast, there were any number of details she wanted to learn before setting foot in a foreign court.

Unsurprisingly, there had not been much about court customs in the archives, beyond a small booklet that had been published a century ago by the wife of a traveling merchant. She had made a great fuss about the serving of a very strong coffee at breakfast and had some amusing anecdotes regarding local church traditions, but there was nothing earth-shattering about the royal family themselves or what negotiations her husband had with them. It had been a quick afternoon read and was one of the few documents that Lianne had already dispensed with. She had since reasoned that anything in the archives on the issue would be outdated anyway. She would just have to lean on the ladies-in-waiting she took with her to make quick friends with their local compatriots. They would need to wrangle tips out of the locals on Astrikhon court fashion and etiquette before the first grand ball.

More important was that she hadn't found, much to her annoyance, any specific documents related to the time of her ancestor King Rurik Kalchik, better known to her kinsfolk and future subjects alike as The Peacemaker. He had been the one who had struck the deal with the great orc tribes that made up the Oircadia confederation that instantly brought stability to Perizidon's eastern front, albeit at the cost of his own life via assassination less than a year later. But despite many fingers pointing at Astrikhonian spies or mercenaries being the killers at the time, there were no reports about an investigation into his murder in the archives. Equally as curious was the absence of the actual peace treaty with Oircadia.

Based upon her general history lessons with Gregor, she already knew that Astrikhon had the most to lose due to the peace treaty Rurik had obtained with the tribes. It meant the full wrath of the orcs was focused solely upon them for the next decade. Only the reemergence of the Black Death, or some similar malady from the great inland swamp that lay deep within orc territory, had saved the human kingdom from utter destruction. The disease had swept through the ranks of the Choros tribe's army as it besieged Boloto, forcing them to withdraw. Other orc tribes, sensing weakness, had turned to infighting, giving Astrikhon the respite it needed to rebuild defenses and rearm. While the perceived frontline was still patrolled heavily by the humans, there had been no major raids from either side for several decades now. But as far as Lianne knew, there had been no formal peace treaty between the tribes and Astrikhon.

All of this, she had thought, would be cataloged in great detail. Yet there appeared to be very little in the archives from that time in history regarding Astrikhon, save drawings of the border defenses between the two human kingdoms and several papers detailing the resumption of trade some fifty years ago. If the old stories were true about Astrikhon being behind the assassination of King Rurik, there was nothing to this effect in what Lianne had found. There was nothing about the assassination at all, truth be told, and that was enough to make her suspicious.

To date, Gregor had been of little help. He continued to insist that Astrikhon was behind the king's murder, as well as any number of other calamities that had occurred with Perizidon territory in the years that followed, but he offered little to no evidence to support his position. He had referred Lianne to several documents, but when she told him that she couldn't find them, he merely suggested she wasn't looking in the right place.

What would he be hiding? And why? Lianne wondered as she rubbed her eyes, giving up on conjuring the truth by merely staring at all the documents piled on the table.

Melina had brought some port and a simple charcuterie board up from the kitchen some time ago, and Lianne wandered over to the small side table where it sat to nibble on some hard cheese. Her servant, who may have stolen a sip or three of the port, was dozing in a chair nearby, but there was no reason to wake her.

Lianne smiled at the recent memory of her telling Mel about the upcoming trip and the girl's eyes lighting up with pure joy upon being told she was to accompany her mistress. Her excitement had been contagious, and it had done much to get Lianne out of her foul mood about not being able to see The Mountain.

Taking off her cape, Lianne draped it across her servant's silent form and lightly kissed her on her forehead before turning back to the main table.

Some unknown amount of time later, Lianne was studying a ledger regarding arms shipments when she heard a commotion from the corridor outside the room. There was the hurried slapping of bare feet on cobblestones, almost drowned out by a cacophony of metallic sounds and an order to "Halt!"

Melina bolted upright, her eyes as big as saucers as she realized she had been sleeping, and she grabbed the cape as she stood up with a crimson face. Both she and Lianne turned towards the door as a shaggy-haired youth burst through the opening, a large grin on his freckled face.

"What are you doing up at this hour?" Lianne stood as her brother entered the room and struck a motherly pose as she admonished him. But her grin almost matched his as he continued to bound forward. She was almost always happy to see him and raised her arms in greeting.

Rather than hug her, though, Lucas made a quick sideways move and ran behind her, grabbing her shoulders and turning to face the door from behind her, as she gave a short shriek of surprised laughter.

As the young prince hid behind her, the two soldiers who had been guarding the stairwell at the end of the hallway came running into the room. One of them immediately came to a halt and stood at attention at the door frame, but the other continued to advance into the room, struggling with his halberd. Not looking where he was going, he tripped on the edge of a rough cobblestone and went down in a heap a few paces from the royal siblings, his weapon flying out of his hands and skittering to the side.

Lianne did her best to suppress a laugh, and she could tell by the hiccuping going on behind her that Lucas was doing his best to do the same.

"Yer Highness! I 'pologize fer tha intrusion!" The soldier at the door practically shouted his greeting, desperately trying to convey to his compatriot that he needed to cease and desist his advance. "Sorry ta say, His Highness didn't alert us ta his intentions, otherwise we woulda—"

He stopped in midsentence as the other soldier managed to get to his feet. Still dazed, he stepped forward while trying to get at his weapon. It was only then that he looked directly into the eyes of Lianne, and that stopped him dead in his tracks. His face went white and then changed to a deep red in an instant, and he, too, now stood at attention, his halberd still on the floor next to him.

Lucas broke the sudden silence, his voice taking on an injured tone. "Dear sister, you must protect me from these unsavory characters that call themselves guards! I only wanted to visit you within the safe confines of our family abode, yet they tried and—"

"Lucas, enough!" Lianne turned and frowned at him, and this time, she meant the motherly admonishment as she started to feel there was some gravity to the situation.

He immediately went quiet and stood meekly behind her, looking like the young rapscallion that he was.

As she turned back towards the guards, there was the sound of yet more footsteps in the hallway, these coming at a dead run. Two more soldiers appeared, swords drawn. Lianne recognized them as being normally assigned to the throne room. They were older than the first two, with one of them balding and with salt in his beard.

Quickly assessing the situation and noting the royals in the room, the two newcomers stood at attention at the door, placing their swords across their chests in salute.

"Yer Highnesses! Are ya safe an' unharmed?" It was the bald one who spoke in a calm voice, and Lianne knew him to be a long-serving and well-regarded sergeant. None of the other three seemed to hold any rank, and out of them, she only recognized the one closest to her.

"Yes, Sergeant, we are well. I commend your men on their instant reaction to what they thought was an intruder. My brother should apologize for his unruly behavior that has caused this commotion." She looked back and glared at Lucas, and after a moment's hesitation, he stepped forward.

But before he could speak, the sergeant coughed politely and sheathed his sword. "'Tis I that must make tha 'pology, Yer Highness, and 'tis I that will accept whatever punishment your father decides ta mete out when I make my report to tha captain."

Lianne looked at him with a confused frown. "Whatever do you mean?"

"I mean, Yer Highness, that it was my responsibility for assignin' these two louts, who musta fallen asleep at their post. Or at tha very least, they weren't paying close enough attention ta their job of protectin' Yer Highness. That they let anyone near ya without a challenge is a most serious offense!"

Lianne could see the fear in the eyes of the young soldier closest to her, and he appeared to be trying to hold back tears. She sighed inwardly. She, of course, knew exactly what the sergeant meant, and publicly defending the soldiers and their carelessness would probably only make matters worse.

"I see, Sergeant. Well, my brother is no assassin, and he holds no knife to my throat. A lesson for all of us to be more on guard, myself included."

"Yes, Yer Highness." The man bowed stiffly, and then turned his attention to his wayward man. "Dane Oldenfeld! You 'pologize ta tha princess for intrudin' inta this here room without her leave an' then get yer sorry arse outta here on tha double!"

The guard visibly swallowed, and his face changed back to an ashen white color. Lianne remembered interacting with him on several occasions recently, including before her recent interview with the inquisitor, and his awkward non-responses to her questions beforehand. As young as he was, she had speculated it meant either he had a relative higher up in the ranks or that he was especially talented at some aspect of soldiering. But something just seemed wrong about him being in a uniform, she thought, albeit not unkindly. *He doesn't seem made out to be a soldier. He seems to not fit their mold. Maybe it's just the way he looked at me the last time I saw him?*

While Lianne was used to all sorts of people gawking at her at countless public events, she knew it was against etiquette for soldiers on guard duty to do so. While she personally thought it was silly how seriously senior officers took this and other minor mistakes the guards occasionally made, she did understand their underlying reason. *After all these years, they still don't want another*

King Rurik incident. 'Vigilia sui, societatis, circumstant,' indeed.

Now, however, the guard wouldn't look Lianne in the eye even for a quick moment. Instead, he gave her the king's salute and stood stiffly as he stared at some unknown point on the far wall.

"May Her Royal Highness forgive my reckless action! I live to serve, and I serve at the will of yourself and the king!"

Lianne folded her hands in front of her and struck as neutral a pose as she could. She tried to think of how to dismiss him as kindly as possible, given the circumstances. "Thank you, Guard Oldenfeld. My brother and I are happy to have you and all the other soldiers in my father's service at our sides, both in good times and in bad. Go in peace."

He saluted again and, gathering up his weapon, scuttled quickly out of the room. His partner saluted Lianne in turn and disappeared after him, as did the soldier who had arrived with the sergeant.

Lianne observed that Melina had quietly backed into the shadows of the room so as to not be seen by the older soldier, who was otherwise alone in the room with them.

His shoulders appeared to sag just a bit as the others left, but he remained at attention. "Permission ta speak freely, Yer Highness?"

"Of course, Sergeant. Sergeant Verchirka, is it not?"

He bowed again. "Rostyslav Verchirka, Yer Highness. I live to serve." He stepped forward into the room proper but stopped several paces away from Lianne and her brother. "I beg yer forgiveness for this incident, Yer Highness, an' I would ask that ya go easy on tha boys. They're good lads, even that bloomin' idiot Oldenfeld. If ya gotta assign blame, I would ask that ya pin it on me."

Lianne's eyes widened slightly. The older man was serious. *They must be in more trouble than I thought!* "Sergeant, please. While I did not see what happened, it is my assumption that my brother snuck down the stairs from the third or fourth level and then scampered by them before they could react." She again looked at Lucas, who seemed to finally grasp the seriousness of the situation.

He bowed formally to her and the sergeant before responding. "Uh, yes, dear sister. It occurred exactly as you say, and they had no time to react to my, uh, rash behavior. I shall endeavor to act in a more mature manner in the future."

If the soldier was annoyed with the prince and his behavior, he was too wise to show it. "I 'ppreciate what Yer Highnesses are tryin' ta say, but tha whole reason we got guards posted there is ta keep ya safe. They ain't there ta look pretty; they're there ta be alert at all times for any hint o' trouble. *At all times*." He emphasized the last three words by smacking his open left hand with his right fist.

Sergeant Verchirka paused, cleared his throat again, and then continued as he stood as erect as possible. "I have ta report tha breach ta tha captain, and he has ta report it ta tha king. His Majesty will no doubt ask ya for yer side of tha story. I would ask that ya blame their lack of trainin' ta put tha focus on me, an' me an' tha captain will handle their discipline separately."

Lianne looked at her brother. While she knew there were rules and discipline for a reason, especially with soldiers, the soldiers in question were still very young. They were barely older than she was! Their careers were not going to be ruined for her sake, and she knew what she needed to do.

She looked coolly back at the sergeant. "Well, Sergeant, I have no idea what you are talking about."

It took him a moment to respond. "Yer Highness?"

"You heard me. I rather think that, if Father asks me about any incident that you and the captain might claim to have occurred tonight, I will have to tell him the same thing. That I have no idea what you are talking about." She looked at her brother. "What about you, Lucas?"

He looked back at her like she was crazy. "What are you talking about, Li? You know that—ow!"

She pinched him rather hard and glared at him, trying to make him understand her thoughts. He didn't, but now he knew well enough to play along.

"I mean, of course, dear sister. I have no idea what anyone is talking about."

Lianne smiled and turned back to the old soldier. "Well, there you have it. I seriously doubt that Father will take the captain's word over mine or my brother's, so the captain will stand accused of lying to his king. Which means you will be accused of the same serious action. I do not want that to happen, so I would suggest that, whatever incident you believe happened here, stay between you and your men. If you decide to punish them for some misguided and mysterious infraction...well, that is, of course, entirely up to you."

The sergeant had been listening closely, and he slowly nodded as she finished. He attempted to keep both relief and a smile off his face and mostly succeeded. "Yes, Yer Highness! I fully understand an' will strike all thoughts of nonsense from me head immediately! I apologize for disturbin' ya, an' I will take my leave."

"Very good, Sergeant Verchirka." She smiled and bowed, and he quickly returned the gesture. He wheeled and left the room, making sure to stare at the corner where Melina had hidden herself as he exited.

Lucas watched the soldier leave and then looked at Lianne with a confused look on his face. "I don't get it, Li."

"Silly! He doesn't *have* to report what happened. He just felt it was his duty to do so! And what would happen to him and the guards if you or I complained about the lapse in security, and he hadn't reported it? I gave him an out. If you and I don't say anything, then he doesn't have to either!"

"So...they won't be punished? I am sorry, Li, I didn't mean to get anyone in trouble!"

Lianne nodded, but she furrowed her brow at her little brother when she replied. "Who knows if he decides to punish them, but that's up to him now, not whatever code of rules he'd have to follow with a formal report. And I know you didn't want to get them in trouble, but you have to remember what Mother tells us all the time!"

Lucas squirmed a little. "I know, I know, consequences... Consequuntur ad actiones tuas, tum ad motus actionum tuarum."

Lianne would have ruffled his hair in the past, but lately he had grown annoyed at the gesture because it made him feel like a little boy. *And I did just admonish him for being too childish; no need to immediately treat him as one.* She gave him a quick hug instead. "Thank you for playing along. But why are you down here anyway?"

"Oh, right. Mother told me to tell you that it's well past the time of night when young ladies of good repute should find themselves in their bedchambers saying their prayers." He smirked. "Or something like that."

Lianne sighed heavily. "Or something like that..." She looked at the pile of documents. There were only a few more days before she was supposed to leave, and there was no way she would be able to read everything she wanted to before the trip. She resolved that she would just have to take some of the less fragile items with her to study while in transit.

"Fine. Although, my retort to Mother would be that it's also well past the time of night when young boys of *questionable* repute should find themselves locked in their bedchambers while *others* pray for *them*!"

"Ha-ha, very funny!" Lucas stuck out his tongue at her and then turned and ran out of the room towards the stairs he had come from. "Night, Mel!" he called out to the shadow by the door as he left.

Melina came forward out of the dark corner, still clutching Lianne's cape. She looked at the door and then at her mistress, seemingly debating on what to say. "Erm...so, is m'lady retirin' now?"

"Yes, I better get upstairs before Mother decides to come down herself to fetch me. I'll take the cape. Just clean up the room and go to bed yourself. Oh, not the map table," she added hurriedly, as she saw her servant look at the huge stack of documents in horror. "Leave all that alone. I mean just the side table and whatnot."

"Ah, thank you, m'lady! Good night!"

"Good night, Mel." Lianne got to the door before turning one last time. "Oh, and Mel? No more port for you tonight, please." She smiled and winked at her maidservant and then left before Melina could react.

***

Captain Dragan Muromets had a headache, and his sergeant was only making it worse. *Is it too late for coffee? God's nails, I could use something stronger than that, the way tonight is going*. It was all he could do to not rub his eyes in front of his subordinate, who stood stiffly at attention, staring at a space several hands above Dragan's head. He steepled his fingers in front of his face and closed his eyes briefly, making it look like he was deep in thought.

Sighing deeply in exasperation, he finally looked up to respond to the report that Rostyslav had just given him. "I'm sure you're aware, Sergeant, that we just can't stand by with our spindles in our hands and let that little reprobate get away with that performance? I don't give a tinker's damn what Her Royal Highness said to you!"

"Yessir," the sergeant responded calmly. "It's why I told ya 'bout tha incident in tha first place."

"This is about discipline, Sergeant! If she's going to lead our entire army someday, she had better figure that out. And right quick, too!"

"Yessir. I know, sir."

Dragan paused before he said something totally out of line about the princess. He knew she was intelligent and a quick study at both sword and strategy. He had no doubt she had the makings of a fine commander-in-chief. *It's just that she's been coddled her whole damn life, and now she coddles everyone around her. She's too damn nice, and it's going to get her or her men killed! And that she was nice to that Oldenfeld piece of shite... Sard me sideways, why did it have to be him?*

"What was Oldenfeld doing at that post in the first place, Verchirka? I thought he had so many demerits he was washing chamber pots for the next month."

"Uh...same reason as always, sir. Special request through—"

"Through the dragoman's office. Why did I even ask?" Dragan finished his sergeant's sentence for him and sighed again.

Rostyslav did not respond to the obviously rhetorical question, and his face gave no trace to his opinion of the young soldier in question.

Dragan seethed as he tried to decide what to do with Dane Oldenfeld. *How can I teach him or the princess about discipline if the whole bloody court is allowed to run roughshod over my rules and regulations?* He had already pressed the king as hard as he dared that the council members should not be allowed to treat the royal guard as their playthings. At least there had been some improvements in how members of the city garrison were elevated into a posting at the castle in the first place. *Oldenfeld would have never made it in here under the current system, no matter who his uncle is,* Dragan thought grimly. *But that doesn't help me now. He's probably here until he gets someone killed. Or perhaps...*

He rose from his desk and made his way over to a large side table covered in documents. He immediately located the one in question and skimmed the proposed list of names of soldiers and their assignments for the upcoming diplomatic trip back to Astrikhon. He looked over at Sergeant Verchirka, who remained at attention.

"Remind me, Sergeant, how did Guard Oldenfeld do in the fall tournament?"

"In tha common tournament, Guard Oldenfeld placed first in sword and shield, second in archery, an', uh, I believe tenth or so in wrestlin'. If memory serves, sir, it was tha wrestlin' score that kept him from bein' named tha people's champion."

Thank the Almighty for very small favors! Still, the sword and archery scores matter in a fight, never mind his lack of manners, court awareness, or spit and polish. That's the argument to be made if anyone questions this decision. And I doubt anyone will...

Dragan returned to his desk to fetch a quill pen. Quickly, before he could change his mind, he added Dane's name to the bottom of the list of soldiers being allotted for the mission. Under the assignment column, he carefully wrote "Personal guard attachment, Dragoman Symon Chumak."

Still looking at the list, he spoke to his sergeant once again. "Sergeant, who was assigned with Oldenfeld this evening?"

"That'd be Guard Fedorak, sir."

"Very well. For inattention on duty leading to a breach of royal protocol, assign Oldenfeld and Fedorak to digging that new latrine ditch on the south side of the main wall."

"Yessir. Confined ta quarters at all other times?"

Dragan looked up, keeping his face calm. "For Fedorak, yes. For Oldenfeld, he is to report to you in full gear tomorrow night after Vespers. I believe he in particular needs some practice in guard duty, so you will afford him the opportunity to guard the middle of the parade ground from Compline to Lauds."

"Yessir."

"And, for *your* failure to adequately drum into Oldenfeld's head the meaning of discipline before now, I expect you to personally check on his well-being throughout the night. Perhaps you can instill some change in behavior in him. Is that understood, Sergeant Verchirka?"

"Yessir." There was no hesitation or change in pitch in the sergeant's voice.

"Very well. Dismissed!"

The sergeant gave Dragan the king's salute, wheeled perfectly, and marched out of the room. As soon as he was gone, Dragan sat back in his chair and closed his eyes. Coffee was probably a very bad idea this late at night, but since he was still awake, he might as well try and catch up on some paperwork. He gave himself a moment of reflection before calling for an orderly.

That sarding prick Chumak! He thinks he can continue to shove his nephew up my arse? Fine, two can play that game, Dragoman. Oldenfeld will be afforded every opportunity to create a diplomatic fiasco for you on your trip to Boloto. That's something even you wouldn't be able to hide from our king.

You want your relative elevated? Be careful what you push for, my lord.

CHAPTER TWENTY-ONE

In The Soup And On The Sauce

"Hey there, luv…" Elise called out to Sarl as she slowly advanced toward him.

He smiled widely as his heartbeat quickened, wondering but not caring why she was in Stren of all places. As she drew closer, she was still backlit by the chandelier, her long tawny hair swept to one side.

Bleary-eyed and not very sober, he didn't dare stand up to embrace her so, instead, offered her his hand. She took hold of it, willingly falling into his lap as he gently pulled her forward. She was able to get out a surprised "Oh!" before he leaned over to give her a short kiss.

She pulled back, laughing. "You *are* drunk, aren't ya?"

Wait. That's not…

Her hair was in his face, or at least that was the excuse Sarl told himself as it took a moment to clear his sight. He found himself staring into the twinkling blue eyes of Katrya, the barmaid from his first visit to the tavern, the impish look on her face turning cloudy as he continued to look at her, trying to comprehend who she was in his muddled state.

Sard me. It ain't Elise.

"Kat!" He was lucky that it came out more as an exclamation as opposed to a question, but she still frowned.

"Who'd ya think it was, ya dumb oaf? Yer 'Dana' perhaps?" The name was spit out in a mocking tone.

"Who...? Oh, Bohdana!" He was a tad slow in remembering the nickname he had given the barmaid who had been serving him the whole night, and the storm clouds on Katrya's face didn't clear with his hesitation. "Nah, Kat, she ain't my type. She was just servin' me goulash."

"That's not all she wants ta serve ya," Katrya muttered, casting a glance back at the bar.

"What's that?"

"I said, I see she's gotten ya into tha local liquor, luv. I can smell tha honey on your breath."

"I think ya can taste it on my lips, too, Kat," Sarl said as gently as he could, given his current condition.

She blushed a bit at this, and the twinkle returned for a brief moment. Then she frowned again, apparently for a different reason. "I assume Dana ain't told ya that you're drinkin' a hole in that coin bag of yers, has she?"

Money was the last thing on Sarl's mind. "Nah, I just came ta—"

"You're up ta twenty silver, luv! That many kopeks...that's a couple weeks' wages for most 'round here!" She had leaned in to hiss this into his ear, seemingly self-conscious for him regarding the money he was spending.

"Huh." Sarl had been overcharged plenty of times in places a lot worse than this one, and it usually ended badly for both parties.

But the food and drink had been quite good tonight, the cabbage-smelling ale notwithstanding. Besides, he had the money to cover the outrageous tab. He didn't like being gouged, but he wasn't going to let it spoil his evening. "Well, now you're here, an' yer presence is priceless! So, I make out fine in tha end anyways."

Katrya rolled her eyes with seemingly as much exaggeration as she could bring to bear. "Nice one, luv. Speakin' of silver, is that what that tongue of yours is made of?"

"Wanna find out?" The words spilled out of him, surprising them both.

She stared at him for a long moment, taking in his features. Sarl didn't consider himself the best-looking specimen of his species, but he wasn't a hunchback either. He idly wondered what humans in general thought about how orcs looked.

Katrya must have decided he passed muster because she leaned in again, and the impish look had returned. "Yes," she whispered. "But not here an' not yet, luv..."

He felt a warm feeling in the pit of his stomach, and it wasn't the liquor. She sat up straight, looking around the room. Most of the patrons had gone back to ignoring him, and the old farmer at the adjacent table had left. They were relatively alone in their corner of the world.

"Where ya been all night, anyways?" Sarl asked.

She was distracted for a moment before turning back to him. "Hmm? Oh, it's my night off, an' I usually don't come here when I don't have ta. I see enough of tha place as it is!"

"Oh? Then what brought ya here now?" He winked.

"Not yer bein' here, that's for sure!" She snickered at his crestfallen look. "Oh, c'mon, luv. Girl's gotta get paid, an' Bainor gives out coin every six days, don't matter tha day of tha week. But"—she cast him a sideways glance—"maybe I ain't sorry there was a bit extra waitin' for me here."

"So now ya wanna spend time with me, huh? Why tha change of heart from tha other week? Ya seemed right quick ta run then."

She crossed her arms, shaking her head. "Ah, yeah, you're right. It's impossible for anyone ta change their mind 'bout anyone or anythin'."

Women! Human women! With a bit of exasperation in his voice, he retorted, "Kat, I don't claim ta know ya, but ya gotta admit it's odd ta go from not wantin' ta talk ta be sittin' in me lap an'—"

Katrya took his face in her hands and kissed him squarely on the lips. As he responded, her mouth opened, and her tongue probed forward tentatively, catching his sharp teeth before he could think to open his mouth too. She pulled back slightly at this but held the kiss for a long moment before breaking off.

"Never thought I'd say this ta an orc, but ya talk too much." She smiled. "'Sides, I told ya last time that I was workin' an' couldn't talk. And now"—she shrugged—"I ain't workin'."

Sarl felt like he was getting whiplash from Katrya's apparent mood swings, or maybe it was that he couldn't read her true emotions at all. *Or is there somethin' else goin' on? What's she playin' at?* His head was swimming in all the alcohol he had consumed, and it was difficult to think straight.

"Well, if ya ain't usually here on yer night off, where are ya?"

"Don't tell Bainor, but I usually hang out at tha Oar House down by tha docks. Not as classy as this place, but cheaper."

Even as drunk as Sarl was, he couldn't help but laugh. "Tha *Oar* House? Really, Kat? Really?"

She laughed too. "Don't blame me, I didn't name it! And no, I don't turn tricks there, if that's your next stupid remark!"

He held up his hands in surrender. "I would never say that! All I gotta know is if their ale is better than tha piss here."

"Not really, but, ah, they got good chowder. I'd say least as good as tha goulash here. 'Sides, I think ya need a bit more food in your belly an' less drink. Less horilka, anyways."

"Ya askin' me ta go there with ya, then?"

"If you're up for walkin', luv." She slid off his lap and stood up quickly, turning to see if he could manage to get himself upright.

The warm feeling in his stomach continued to grow, but Sarl wasn't sure if he would be walking or crawling out of the tavern. "Uh, why don't ya wait for me outside, Kat. I, uh, need a bit of time ta gather my belongings. Might be better if we don't leave together, anyways." He remembered that his status with the locals was back in the gutter, and she might have any number of sweethearts or lovers watching them.

She might have had the same thought as she looked around

the room again, nodding to herself. She turned and winked at him as she replied, “Well then, I’ll give ya ’til tha count of one hundred ta meet me outside.”

“How fast ya countin’?”

“I guess you’ll find out, won’t ya, Sarl?” She made an about-face, twirling her dress just so, and headed towards the door.

“Shite, woman...” Sarl closed his eyes and slowly counted to twenty. It was only then that he shakily rose to his feet and made his way to the bar. Various people marked his passage, but nobody stopped him.

Bainor noted his slow approach and was waiting for him, an amused look on his face. “Well, good sir, I see that you’ve been having a pleasant evening with us! Is there anything else I can get you? The personal effects you’ve stored here? A room, perhaps?” He paused and then added, “Perhaps another drink?”

“Ha! I better lay off tha drink! Any more an’ I’ll be sleepin’ on yer floor. But I’ll take a room, an’ ya can bring my things there, if ya please.”

Bainor smiled curtly. “Very well, sir. I’ll get the ledger.” He made his normal signal to the enforcer and then disappeared into the back room.

Sarl gripped the edge of the bar with both hands, trying not to sway, and closed his eyes to concentrate on this task. Suddenly, he felt a gentle touch on his arm and smelled the slight aroma of roses. He opened his eyes and glanced over, managing a weak smile once he discerned it was Bohdana who had approached him.

She smiled back at him. "Sarl, luv, ya don't look so good."

"Dana, luv, I think ya know why I don't look so good."

She laughed and squeezed his arm good-naturedly. "Ah, yeah, tha horilka. I suppose I should have warned ya 'bout tha kick."

"An' tha price, woman! Hope ol' Bainor gives ya a rich cut."

A look of confusion crossed her face. "What are ya talkin' 'bout, luv? That liquor ain't that much more than tha swill you was drinkin' already!"

Now Sarl was confused. "But, she said—"

"She said? Who said?"

"Katrya..."

Bohdana's face grew dark at the name, and she crossed her arms. "Oh really? She's here? An' what, pray tell, did she say ya owed me?"

Sarl was too far gone to read the room, let alone a human he barely knew. "Twenty silver, pretty sure."

Bohdana's face went white with rage, and she slowly formed fists as she lowered her hands to her sides. It looked as if she was barely containing the impulse to strike him. "That little bitch! That's tha game she wants ta play?" She looked around the room, vainly looking for the other woman.

"I don't..." Sarl started to say something and then wised up a bit and stopped talking. He closed his eyes again and focused on standing absolutely still.

"Uh, sir?"

Sarl opened his eyes, unsure of how much time had passed. Bohdana had been replaced by Bainor, who was standing in front of him on the other side of the bar. He shook his head and wondered what Katrya's count was at now. *Probably a thousand, ya dumb dog.*

"Sorry, I was, uh, thinkin' 'bout somethin' else. What do I owe ya?"

"Dinner, drinks, a room..." The thin man looked up. "Apologies for not havin' a bath, but I can have—"

"Yeah, yeah, hot water an' a basin sent up. That'll do."

"Very good, sir. With what you owe for tonight plus breakfast on the morrow, that'll be three silver."

"Three? *Three*?!" Sarl threw his head back and roared with laughter.

The enforcer stood up upon hearing the outburst, and Bainor had a somewhat frightened look on his face when Sarl got himself back under control.

"Sir, I'll have you know the rates here are very reasonable, not to mention that you drank—"

"Nah, nah, I'm sorry. I got it, no worries." Sarl wiped a few tears from his eyes and undid his coin pouch. It took some fumbling around, but he managed to put three silver kopek coins on the bar.

Bainor studied him for a moment before shaking his head and turning the ledger towards him. Sarl put a large "X" where indicated in the book and then took the two markers the man offered him.

"Thanks. I know where ta go." Sarl turned to leave, and then suddenly, a thought occurred to him. "Hey! What if I wanted some, uh, company for tha rest of tha night? Can ya do that for me?"

Bainor smiled knowingly, leaned towards Sarl, and spoke in a conspiratorial tone. "Ah, good sir, but of course! Let me know your preferences for a companion, and I shall see what I can do. The rate will depend upon, ah, the age and cut of meat you hunger for and the duration you will be dining. If you know what I mean."

Sarl knew what he meant. "I'm just wonderin', that's all. For next time. Gimme a range."

The bartender looked a tad annoyed and straightened back up, but he had an answer at the ready. "Low-end quality cut for an hour would be fifty copper."

"An' tha best? For all night?"

"All night? Well..." Bainor thought a moment. "That would be about twenty silver, good sir! But if you're serious, we might be able to nego—"

"All right, all right, thank ya. Like I said, maybe next time." Sarl was smiling and laughing to himself as he gingerly made his way over to the weapons locker to retrieve his axe.

The unseasonably cold air hit him like a bucket of ice water as soon as he stepped outside, and he breathed in deeply as his head cleared slightly. He looked around to find the street empty and was about to curse his fortune when a short figure emerged from the shadows to his right. Katrya had a shawl around her shoulders but still snuggled closely as she came up to him, using his bulk as a windbreak.

"I was beginnin' ta wonder if ya had passed out!"

"Almost, but not quite!" Sarl replied with a chuckle. He put his arm around her, and it felt right to do so. "Nah, had ta figure out what I owed with yer boss, an' I spoke with our friend Dana 'fore I left."

"Oh, really? What did Dana have to say?"

"Not that much, though I don't think she's too happy with ya."

"Me?" Katrya looked up at him, feigning surprise.

"Well, ya might not of called her a *cheap* whore, but ya still called her a whore."

Katrya laughed loudly and clearly against the wind. "Oh, she'll get over it. It ain't tha first time we've called each other names. I'm just glad ya figured it out and didn't give ol' Bainor twenty silver!"

"True enough, Kat. Guess I'm savin' my money for somebody else."

She hooked her arm around his neck, bringing his face down so she could lightly kiss his cheek. "I told ya before, Sarl, luv. I ain't for rent." She brought him closer and nipped his ear with her teeth. "Ya got me for free," she whispered.

The warmth in his gut started to seep downward. "I...I, uh, got a room above tha tavern," he managed to stammer out.

She shook her head. "Don't shite where ya eat, luv, an' don't sard there neither. C'mon, I got a place nearby, an' it ain't tha Oar

House." She grabbed his hand, and they moved off across the square together.

"Hey, what was yer count at?" Sarl asked as he let himself be led towards an unknown destination.

She laughed again. "I forgot ta start!"

A pair of eyes followed their path, flashing red in the moonlight.

CHAPTER TWENTY-TWO

Hadeon Harried By History

Aleksei hated the archives. They were dark, dusty, and full of books he didn't care one denga about. But worst of all, they were located on the opposite side of the castle from the kitchen and food stores area. So long as the prince spent his free time looking for moldy tomes nobody had seen in decades, Aleksei would have little to no excuse to loiter near the pantries and attempt to pinch food and scullery maids alike. The one particular maid he had in mind, Maria, was always open to him sampling her pie, and it drove him crazy just thinking about her.

Hadeon was currently ignoring him and everything else in the large room they were in, lost in thought as he pored over yet another old document. Aleksei sighed. The prince had been spending an inordinate amount of time in the archives recently. It wasn't like he couldn't have ordered whatever map or ledger he wanted to review up to the royal study. The lighting there was better, the chairs were more comfortable, and the kitchen was in the same wing. However, the prince preferred to be in this remote section of the castle, isolated from most courtesans and their politics, in order to concentrate on the task at hand. It was a fair point in favor of the archives, but not enough to sway the vote in Aleksei's mind.

He assumed that the prince's fascination with the archives

and their contents would be over once that arrogant diplomat from Perizidon had come and gone, since Hadeon seemed to be focusing on the historical records between the two kingdoms. But the arrival of the Perizidon delegation was still at least a couple weeks away, and that was assuming they had good traveling weather. Aleksei found himself wishing for something he wouldn't have thought possible, that the old prick would arrive early.

Like everyone else in the Astrikhon court, Aleksei was eager to see the Perizidon heir apparent much more than the stuffy diplomat. He was careful not to mention any excitement over the princess and her impending arrival around the extremely jealous and quick-tempered Maria, but he couldn't help but be caught up in the frenzied anticipation. The rumors about a match between prince and princess alone were keeping many a courtier up late, but her appearance was also seen as the penultimate royal stamp of approval on the negotiated trade agreement. Only a visit by her father would have meant more to King Haldir and his constant need to be the center of attention.

Thank the Almighty that the prince hasn't inherited the suffering vanity of his father! I'm getting too old to bend over and kiss his arse, in any event. But, still, he could do with a bit more self-importance and sense of position. Maybe then I wouldn't be stuck in this social dungeon! At the very least, I wish he would listen to me and invest a bit of time researching fashion trends and court etiquette. We will only have one chance at a good first impression with the young lady.

As Aleksei watched his master from a few steps away, Hadeon looked up, rubbed his eyes, and slapped the table in apparent disgust. Carefully rolling up the yellowed parchment he had just reviewed, he set it aside and made a mark next to its name in the small personal ledger he had taken to carrying at all times. He then slouched in his chair in a most unprincely manner, staring up at the dark, arched ceiling.

The scribe who had been assisting him made to come forward to retrieve the document, but Aleksei silently warned the girl away with a quick hand motion. The prince hated to be disturbed when he was thinking over some matter, whether it be important or not.

After several moments, the prince shook his head, yawned, and glanced over at Aleksei. "What time is it, Alex?"

"At least an hour after Compline, my lord. If I may remind you that you have yet to take sustenance this—"

The prince looked away and interrupted Aleksei with a sound of disgust, slapping the table again as he did so. "Arrgh! What am I missing, Alex? Why can't I find any documents related to the Time of Betrayal?"

"My lord?"

"Are they cataloged differently for some reason? Does Master Pavel have them locked up somewhere safe? But, no, he told me they were here!"

Aleksei did his best to maintain a placid look on his face, masking the confusion going on in his head. "I… Forgive me, my lord, I know not what you speak of. The Time of Betrayal?"

The prince fully turned in his chair to look at Aleksei in mock shock. "Oh, come now, Alex, surely you have at least some small measure of education about our kingdom's history? No? I am talking about the time when Perizidon stabbed us in the back and made peace with the damnable orcs!"

Aleksei flushed angrily, but he was sure the reaction was mostly hidden by the dim light where he was standing. *Why would I bloody care about something that happened almost a century ago? Let alone know the insipid name that the don no doubt thought up to convey a sense of theater for himself.* He bowed stiffly to the prince.

"I am sorry, my lord, I attempt to leave history where it belongs. In the past."

The prince smirked. "Methinks that you would state something altogether different if I wished to learn what my grandparents wore to the royal ball celebrating their marriage."

"Of course, my lord. I would remind you that important events such as that are always memorialized in oil on canvas. You need only visit the hallway on the third level by the—"

Hadeon laughed. "Fine, fine. A point for you, my good man. And a poor example on my part. Never mind my rant. I will quiz Master Pavel about it." He sighed and half turned back towards the table, remaining seated. He began to drum his fingers on the chair's arms and seemed to be looking around for something in particular.

Aleksei coughed politely. "Perhaps then, it is time to call it an evening, my lord?"

The prince glanced back over at him. "You truly hate this place, don't you, Alex?"

"There are certainly better places to be. In my humble opinion, of course."

The young prince snorted and looked up at the ceiling again. "There is nothing humble about you, Aleksei. But that is what I like about you, after all. You are arrogant enough to keep irritating courtesans away, and your presence ensures that my mother believes I always have a minimum air of decorum about me."

Aleksei decided to accept the backhanded compliment. He really had no choice in the matter. He bowed stiffly again. "I live to serve, my lord."

***

Hadeon kept his face turned away from his manservant so the older man couldn't see his satisfied grin. Hadeon loved getting under his skin. Aleksei was almost as pompous as the prick from Perizidon, just without the age and diplomatic prestige to back it up. In the end, the prince didn't altogether mind the attitude, as the man was loyal to a fault. But forcing him to stay in the archives while Hadeon carried out his research would only build character. Or remind him of his station. Either reason worked in Hadeon's mind.

That the research was proving futile was certainly building Hadeon's own character regarding patience. While the amount of information regarding the long-standing and ever-changing relationship between Astrikhon and Perizidon was frankly staggering, the fact that there were some glaring holes in the historical documents was becoming very evident. The primary hole that was bothering him was there was next to nothing about the events surrounding Perizidon abandoning their alliance with Astrikhon, nor the subsequent desperate campaign that Astrikhon waged alone against the orcs. There were many a ballad and stirring novella about the Miracle of Boloto that occurred when the orc army had been decimated by disease just outside the city gates, but it was as if a whole decade of misery had been expunged from the collective memory of the nation.

Hadeon had started his research several days ago, once it was known that Lianne, the Princess of Perizidon, was certainly coming to the Astrikhon court. For whatever reason, he had a vague notion that it would be important to understand what their ancestors had done and said that had driven such a wedge between the kingdoms. More specifically, he knew the stories about Astrikhonian spies being behind the assassination of Perizidon's king right after their peace treaty with Oircadia still held sway among their populace. If this trade agreement was to be the foundation for a new age of improving relations, he wanted to be able to put the old rumors to rest once and for all. The fact that the archives presented no information on the matter, good or bad, was becoming quite disturbing to him.

He eyed the stack of documents on the long table that the archivist scribes had assembled for him. They seemed to mock him, daring him to find the needle of information he wanted in their proverbial haystack of words, graphs, and exhibits. *But it shouldn't be a needle; it should be the whole damn loom!* Time was growing short if he was going to locate anything useful before the royal visit, and he knew he had been shirking some of his duties to spend time with these books. He would have to quiz Master Pavel more closely on what the old don knew about this time period and the associated events. Their next session was supposed to be in two days, but Hadeon would summon him on the morrow instead. *But, for now...*

"Just one or two more ledgers, Alex. I shan't be long."

Hadeon swore he heard a muttered curse escape from the manservant's lips, and his smile grew as he picked out a large volume at random from the stack closest to him.

Aleksei coughed politely again before Hadeon could open the ledger. "If it pleases you, my lord, might I fetch you a cold plate from the kitchen?"

Hadeon relented a bit and nodded. "That is an excellent idea! A bit of red wine, too, if you please." He waited a beat before turning around in his chair, and his timing was impeccable as his manservant had just reached the door.

"Oh, and Alex? Do hurry back with my victuals. I give you leave to pry a kiss out of that lovely scullery maid you yearn for, but there won't be time to try and milk her tonight. There's a good man."

Aleksei turned crimson, and his jaw went slack for the merest of moments before he remembered himself. He bowed hastily and fled the room without saying a word.

Hadeon managed not to burst out laughing as he motioned for the scribe to come forward and assist him with some more light. The scribe wisely said nothing.

CHAPTER TWENTY-THREE

Love and Acrimony

Sarl and Katrya made their way forward in a somewhat haphazard fashion. Sarl was feeling better in the fresh air, but it was going to take more than a walk in brisk weather to sober him up. He did his best not to lean on the young woman. If he slipped, it would end badly for her.

The plaza ended, but a wide cobblestone street continued out from it. As far as he could tell, it headed directly towards the docks.

"Hey, we're really not headed to tha Oar House, right? Ya ain't tryin' ta pawn me off on someone there?"

Katrya snickered. "Ha! If I wanted ta dump ya, I woulda let Dana keep her hooks in ya. Least she wouldn't give ya tha great pox like most of tha tramps down at tha docks."

"Well, I guess she's a high-class whore for sure, then!" Sarl chuckled and continued to try and walk in a straight line.

The pavers went right up to the buildings that lined either side of the street. However, most had storage units, trading stalls, or various types of paraphernalia stacked up against their walls that kept pedestrians from crossing directly in front of any one doorway. The end result was a much narrower, clear passageway than had been intended by the original town planner. In most places, there was barely enough room for even one lane of traffic in either direction. Grooves from all the oxen carts headed in the same direction had been worn into the cobblestones over time, so at least the lanes were well-defined.

The street surface sloped slightly towards the middle from either side, with a short, narrow trough running the length of it, forming a centerline of sorts. The trough had been built to carry away whatever filth happened to land in the street, but it relied on rainwater to push everything towards the river. It hadn't rained in several weeks, meaning the trough was full of trash, human and animal waste, straw, and mud. The smell was rather horrific, even with the night breeze, so much so that it even pierced Sarl's addled olfactory senses. He gagged involuntarily.

Katrya looked up at him, a bit of concern showing on her face. "C'mon, luv, just a bit farther. But if you're gonna flay, do it in tha street!"

He managed to swallow the bile that had risen up into his mouth. "What a wonderful place you've takin' me to, Kat! What an incredible smell you've discovered!"

"You're an arse, ya know that, right?" She grinned at him as she said it.

"Always, Kat. Always." He grinned, as well, as he looked up to take in the surroundings.

Unfortunately, taking his eye off where he was going even for an instant had immediate consequences. Barely upright as he was already, Sarl stumbled over one of the ruts in the cobblestones and careened forward. He was able to put his hands out in time, so he didn't plant his face into the roadway surface, but he still wound up sprawled out on the ground. His hands were scraped and bloody, although he was still numb enough not to feel them or his knees, that were no doubt scraped as well. The only saving grace was that he missed landing in the trough by the merest of distances.

Trying to regain his breath, he had the presence of mind to breathe through his mouth. He might have passed out otherwise. He carefully rolled on to his back, away from the trough, to find Katrya standing over him, hands on her hips and a large, toothy grin on her face. He noticed for the first time that her teeth were perfectly straight, a minor miracle of dentistry in a backwater town such as Stren. They flashed a brilliant white in the moonlight and seemed to light up the rest of her features. The breeze was from behind her, and it lofted her long hair over and around her shoulders. He could tell that she was doing her best not to laugh at him.

"Couldn't get enough of my incredible smell, huh? Ya just had ta get up close an' personal with it?" Seemingly more for moral support than anything else, she held out her hand for him to grab onto so he could stand up.

He reached out and, grasping her forearm, pulled her down to him instead. There was no resistance on her part.

"Up close an' personal, yeah." He held her face in his rough, skin-torn hands, smudging her cheeks with blood. She didn't seem to mind.

She leaned forward, and he guided her in slowly as they locked lips, this time their tongues intertwining with each other as she carefully avoided his teeth. The warmth emanating from his gut grew in intensity as they kissed passionately in the middle of the street. The smell emanating from the trough no longer mattered.

After some unknown passage of time, Sarl felt the presence of someone else, several paces behind them. He broke contact with Katrya's lips, gently bringing a finger up to her mouth as he craned his neck to see who it was. It appeared to be the night watch who had stopped to admire the unfolding show.

Seeing that they had finally been noticed, the leader of the squad of four men cleared his throat and stepped forward. "Well, sirrah, I understand ya may not have coin for a room, but could I at least suggest that ya wallow in tha mud of a back alley instead of ticklin' tha teeth of that trollop here on tha main road? Hmm? Hey now, who's that with ya?" He took another step closer, motioning the man carrying the squad's lantern to come forward.

Katrya slid off Sarl, but even his bulk wasn't enough cover for her to not be recognized once the full strength of the lantern was cast out onto the street.

The squad leader snorted. "Well, well, well. Ya certainly get around, don't ya, Kat? This big lug payin' ya ta sard in tha street or somethin'?"

"Shut up, Mykhailo," she said as she moved to sit on her knees, facing him. "It ain't your business."

"I suppose not, I just didn't know greyskin meat was on yer

menu."

The other three guards laughed at this. Oddly, in Sarl's mind at least, none of them had their weapon drawn, and they were all in relaxed stances. They certainly didn't seem to be expecting any trouble out of them.

"Shut *up*, Mykhailo!" Katrya stood up, fists clenched.

Sarl slowly moved into a crouching position. It wasn't his fight just yet, and in any event, it didn't look like the watchmen were aiming to start anything. Even in his current state, he was able to reason that, if everyone stayed calm, they would just be a story told to the other soldiers back at the barracks later that evening.

Mykhailo stared at the two of them for several long moments, as if making his mind up about something. Finally, he sighed heavily and took a step back, motioning for the lantern to be shaded. "Ya do what ya want, Kat. Just find a room ta do it in. I don't wanna see ya tha rest of tha night." He looked at Sarl again and seemed about to say something to him, but he just grinned and ordered the squad to move on.

Katrya watched the four men leave, her fists still clenched.

"So...friend, family, or other?" Sarl asked once the watchmen were out of earshot.

Katrya remained motionless, staring at the receding party. Sarl stood up, wiping his hands on his pants as he did so, and waited for her to respond. She was shaking slightly, and he decided he didn't need to know if she was crying.

Eventually, she turned around. "Acquaintance. Used ta be a

friend. We grew up together, so he knows my sister too."

Sister? Interestin' detail, Kat. "Ah, I see. Nothin' like people that know yer whole history."

All sorts of emotions played across her face. "Exactly."

He shrugged. "I get it. It's one of tha reasons I left my small village an' don't plan on ever goin' back."

"Oh? One of tha reasons?"

"Yeah. I might've killed someone too."

Katrya's eyes widened slightly, but she didn't seem overly surprised. After a moment's reflection, she replied, "Huh. Well, did they deserve killin'?"

"Oh, absolutely. Just nobody else was willin' ta do it. Which is why I had ta leave afterwards."

She came over and patted him on the chest. "Well, I would leave here if I could. It ain't that small of a place, but it's small enough. Ya stay here long enough, everybody is up in your business." She sighed.

"An' yer up in theirs?" he asked pointedly.

She looked up at him, seeming to debate what to say before slowly replying, "Let's just say that, in Stren, it's even easier ta sell secrets than yer body. An' that's all I really care ta say 'bout that."

Ha! That means I was right tha first time I met ya, that ya know everythin' an' everyone I need ta know around here. Sarl chuckled. "I got no secrets worth sellin', Kat, an' I can wait a bit 'fore ya ta trust me with yer own."

Katrya raised up on her toes and pecked him on the cheek,

then looked around. "C'mon, let's go 'fore another one of me old boyfriends comes 'round tha corner." She took hold of his hand again, lightly squeezing it, and led him down the street.

After another fifty paces or so, she steered them to the left side of the thoroughfare, towards one of several nondescript two-story buildings squashed together between two narrow alleyways. This one didn't have anything piled up in front of it, which afforded a view of the street from several good-sized windows that stood to the side of the door. They were shuttered at the moment, but it appeared the smaller windows on the second floor were not. No light was visible from either floor, and the house was silent.

Katrya fumbled a moment with the door's latch before it gave, and the door swung noiselessly inward. She advanced into the doorway and then spun around quickly, holding the frame with both hands at head height. The action caused her shawl to shrug off and fall onto the wooden floor of the house. There was only inky blackness behind her, waiting to swallow her up.

She looked up at Sarl and smiled invitingly. "So, Sarl, is this what ya came back ta Stren for?"

He answered by moving forward and picking her up under her arms in a tight embrace, and she reciprocated by locking her legs around his waist. He slowly walked them both into the house, his eyes quickly adjusting with the dim light coming in from the street before Kat reached out to push the door closed behind them. He managed to make out a single large room with an unlit fireplace before the darkness enveloped them. Only a thin shaft of light coming from a staircase going to the second floor was visible once the door was shut.

"Let me bar tha—oh!" Katrya gave a quick yelp of pain mixed with pleasure as Sarl turned and, still holding her, pushed her up against the door and kissed her deeply.

He could feel her legs and arms embrace him tightly, and he was extremely conscious of his teeth as her tongue darted around them once more. His hands had slipped down her back when he had pushed forward, and now he held her buttocks in one as he used the other to support his weight against the door so he didn't completely crush her. The door creaked with their movements, but it was solid enough and was in no danger of collapsing.

"Upstairs..." Katrya managed to get out after a bit, slipping out of his grasp to make sure the door was bolted from the inside.

As she did this, he quickly dropped his satchel and weapons on the floor, picking her up again when she turned around. She worked her arms and legs around him to their former positions and kissed his neck, and he dutifully made his way towards the shaft of light and then up a simple set of steps.

There was a single sleeping area on the second story with a low bed up against one wall and a small writing desk opposite it. Moonlight shone through the two windows that faced the main street, creating long shadows behind them as they made their way towards the bed. It was unkempt, with a number of rough blankets tossed to one side of the simple straw mattress. It was as if someone had just been sleeping in it that afternoon and hadn't made it up again when they left.

He fell back into the bed with her on top of him, the frame complaining loudly at the rude introduction. As they continued to kiss, he shifted slightly so they were lying next to each other, his hand slowly moving up her thigh. He lightly stroked her through her dress, and she responded with a faint sigh and pressed up against him closely. He nipped at her neck and misjudged slightly, drawing blood.

She gasped and sat up, looking at him sharply and then laughing when she saw the look of mortification on his face.

"Ya gotta tell me now if you're a vampire, luv," she said, rubbing her neck.

"I—" Sarl started to apologize, but she immediately put her finger against his lips. He caught up her wrist and kissed her palm, then slowly sucked the blood off her fingers, lingering on her pointer.

That elicited another quick sigh before she broke away and stood up, moonlight cascading across her body.

Slowly, she undid her bodice, and her dress fell away as if it were an unneeded skin. Her undergarments joined the dress on the floor, and she stood before him in the moonlight, unafraid and unassuming. He had never seen anyone so beautiful in his life.

She saw the look of wonderment on his face and smiled. "You have entirely too many clothes on, luv."

She came to him as he clumsily struggled out of his clothes, kicking his boots off and throwing his tunic and undershirt away in such haste that they disappeared down the stairs into the darkness. She straddled him as he undid his belt, her tawny hair just covering her breasts, and it was only then that he realized that something was wrong.

He was numb to the point of dysfunction.

Panicking a bit, he raised her up off his waist to embrace her closely, but she wasn't nearly as drunk as he was and understood what was happening.

She smiled and cupped his face tightly, kissing him. "Ya can use your hands if ya need ta, luv...or I can help."

He grunted and kissed her between her breasts, then moved on to her left nipple. It and its twin sister stood erect, from the cold or the excitement he couldn't tell, but she pulled back slightly as his lips encircled it. So, he kept moving south, rotating their bodies as he went so that she was now lying on her back on the mattress, and she didn't stop him as he reached her stomach. It was smooth and flat, pointing the way towards something even more pleasurable.

She was clean-shaven, seemingly recently, as it felt as though there were bumps on her inner thigh from the use of tweezers or some concoction unknown to him. As he centered himself, he idly wondered if her pubic hair had been curly, and he was immediately conscious of the fact that he should have taken up the offer of the hot water and basin at the tavern before coming here with her. She tasted a bit on the sweet side, and while she wasn't overly wet, she still moved in time with his tongue, raising her hips slightly as he teased her a bit.

From experiences a long time ago, he knew he enjoyed giving more than receiving, and although he had never been brave enough to ask if he was any good, no one ever seemed to complain. He made sure to not to nip her with his teeth as he probed a bit deeper inside her, his nose still numb enough to not be able to provide any hint of whether he was hitting the mark.

He reached up to lightly pinch her nipples, but she grasped his hands and held them flat against her breasts. She had gone quiet, but was, by no means, stopping him, continuing to move in rhythm with his touch.

After a time, he moved back up and she kissed him desperately. He wanted her so badly, but try as he might, he couldn't mount her. His sweat and his talisman hit her chest as he struggled above her until she leveraged herself on top of him again. He held her close, playing with her hair as she played with him, their heartbeats racing each other as their bodies intertwined. He wanted to scream in frustration. It had been so long since he had enjoyed another's touch, he thought he would have exploded after just a moment of foreplay. He would have given anything to be inside her, but it wasn't meant to be.

Sometime later, she still lay on top of him, toying with his necklace while he held her closely. His head had stopped spinning, and his senses were starting to return to normal, so he noticeably jerked when she put her ice-cold feet on his calf muscle.

"Ya need ta warm me up," was her simple request, so he

grabbed a blanket to throw over both of them and then gripped her even more tightly to him. He hadn't a clue what she was thinking about, and he dared not ask.

Finally, Katrya raised her head, propping it on her bent arm as she looked at Sarl with a slight smile on her face. "Ya sure messed up me hair somethin' good."

"Least I did *somethin'* good..."

She bent over and kissed him lightly on his forehead and then went back to studying him. After a long while, she asked in a low voice, "Who is she, Sarl?"

"Who's who?"

"Whoever gave ya this, that's who." She held up the pendant that hung on its silver chain. "Ya promised ta somebody, luv?"

"No...not really."

She eyed him curiously at this but didn't say anything as he took the pendant from her and inspected the bluish-green stone as if looking for an impurity. He let it drop back onto his chest, and it was as if a millstone had landed on him. He winced at the memories.

"She gave it ta me when she went away."

"Ah...who'd she leave ya for?"

"Tha church."

"Oh my!" Katrya considered this unexpected response.

"Yeah...oh my, indeed."

"How long since she went away, luv?"

"Five years."

"Five years?!" Katrya looked at him in shock, then giggled.

Sarl felt his face grow hot but said nothing. They were both quiet for a while as she played with his chest hair.

Finally, she shook her head and looked him in the eye. "Ah, Sarl, I didn't have a chance, did I? Not until ya get this straight, huh?" She poked him gently in the heart. "Or maybe just this..." She poked him gently in the temple.

He couldn't and didn't answer this, but he was fairly certain it was both.

"So, she a childhood friend?"

"Yeah."

"An' she knows your secrets?"

"All of 'em."

"An' she left town, but ya felt ya had ta leave too?"

"Yeah...too many memories. An' that whole killin' thing."

"Ha! Yeah, that too." She was silent for a bit, as if she was thinking about what to say next. "Ya think she'll come back to ya, is that it?" Katrya finally asked.

"I...I don't know. Nah, probably not. Think she would've done it by now if she was gonna do it." It wasn't worth getting into Elise's promise to her parents and all the other heartbreak that had happened years ago.

"So why don't ya get rid of tha stone, then? Start fresh?"

"Never was a reason ta do so." A small part of him wanted to say *until now*, but he still had little clue as to the game she was playing.

***

Katrya put her head back down on the orc's chest, her hand finding his and their fingers interlocking. Sarl's breathing slowed after a while, but she could tell he was still awake by the way he shifted position at regular intervals. She felt warm and safe pressed up against him, but she knew the moment was fleeting. Soon, a storm of her own making would break, and she desperately tried to make up her mind as to whether she should warn him.

Why do I care at all 'bout an orc I barely know, who can't even get it up for me? What's he done for me other than make me smile a couple times? Is it as simple as he ain't forcin' me ta do somethin' like everyone else is doin' ta me? That he treats me like...I dunno, like a person?

It was some time before she found the nerve to speak again. "Sarl?"

"Hmm?"

"Ya ever had an itch ya couldn't scratch?"

He shifted again underneath her, and he breathed in deeply through his nose. As he exhaled, she could feel his grip on her tighten briefly before he let go of her hand. She glanced up and saw that he was staring at the ceiling, a bemused look on his face, both of his hands behind his head.

"Sarl?"

"Yeah, I heard ya, Kat. Not sure I know what ya mean."

"I mean, like ya knew there was somewhere else ya should be, but ya don't know where? Or there's somethin' else ya should be doin', but ya don't know what?"

He looked at her, the slight smile on his face holding steady. "Ya mean, like somebody wantin' ta leave their home but not knowin' where ta go or what ta do?"

She smiled back at him. "Yeah."

He breathed in deeply again, his nose twitching. "Sure, I know how that feels."

"But..." She struggled with the words, trying not to give away too much. "But even without knowin' how it's gonna end, ya know ya gotta do somethin', anythin', ta start ta get out of where ya are now?"

He stretched, arching his back, then disengaged himself from her briefly to move into a sitting position. Facing the stairs, he wrapped a blanket around his shoulders and leaned back against the wall. At his invitation, Katrya leaned up against him, pulling her own blanket around her. She curled up tightly, shoving her feet under his thigh to stay warm. Sarl put his arm around her and hugged her close, but he didn't answer her question.

She stared into the inky blackness that the stairwell disappeared into, wondering how much time they had left.

***

Sarl took one more deep breath. Now that his senses were returning to him, he had to be sure about the metallic scent he was picking up all around him. *It's been here, I know it! How in tha abyss did I not make tha connection until now? I knew Kat was leadin' me on for some reason, but this? Did it know somehow that she was tha perfect honeytrap for me?*

He did his best to ignore the fact that Katrya smelled like lavender, maintaining her likeness to Elise in his mind even to that small of a detail. But even as he chided himself for his carelessness, there was also some grim satisfaction in knowing the confrontation he had wanted since reacquiring the shapeshifter's scent near Myr was about to happen.

He decided he needed to force the issue with Katrya and figure out what she knew before it was too late. A larger part of him than he cared to admit held out hope she was an innocent pawn in some greater game that was afoot.

"Kat, that somethin' ya think ya gotta do..." He paused briefly, then went all in. "I have ta know who ya think ya gotta give up ta get out."

"Whaddya mean, luv?"

"Is it me ya gotta give up or get rid of?"

"What?" Her form shifted against his as she looked up at him, puzzlement in her voice.

He cupped her chin and looked directly into her eyes. "I can smell it, Kat. It's been here in this house before, an' I assume it's on its way now. You gonna tell me what's goin' on?"

Confusion reigned on her features. "What are you talkin' about, luv? What can ya smell?"

"C'mon, I ain't that stupid! I know ya wanted ta lead me on for some reason, an' I played along 'cause I sorta like ya. So, fine, ya got me ta come here, bully for ya." He let go of her chin, but neither one of them looked away.

Fear started to take over her confusion, and her mouth moved, but no words came out.

All of a sudden, he growled, the rage that had been growing inside him starting to escape. “But of all things, I didn’t think ya was workin’ for that suka blyat’!”

The words washed over her, apparently with no meaning, and she stared at him helplessly. “I don’t...I don’t follow ya, luv...”

“How much are ya getting’ paid ta serve me up on a platter, Kat? Twenty silver ’cause I’m ’bout ta get it up tha backside like a good whore? Or do I only rate fifty copper? Or were ya just promised a way outta town, is that it? Which is it, *luv*?!”

“Sarl...” Tears formed at the edge of her eyes, and she looked down at her hands.

He tried to keep his rage in check, breathing in and out rapidly as she rocked back and forth. An extended silence encompassed them and their separate thoughts.

Finally, with some effort, he quietly asked, “What are ya gettin’ for bringin’ me here, Kat? At least tell me what it’s worth to ya.”

She finally looked up at him again, the look of a cornered animal plain for him to see. “I...I’m getting’ nothin’, okay? You don’t understand. I had ta do it...”

He snorted. “I ain’t worth much, Kat, but I’m worth more than nothin’. Any trapper will tell ya that orc skins will fetch ya some good coin on tha black market.” He rubbed his left forearm as he spoke, as if confirming the thickness of his skin was within proper tolerances.

She balled her fists but placed them against his chest rather than striking him forcibly. “Nobody said nothin’ ’bout skinnin’ ya, let alone killin’ ya! All she said was ta get ya here an’ that someone was comin’ ta talk with ya. That’s all I know, Sarl, I swear it!”

“She? Who’s she?”

“My sister...ya know, Kira?”

“Who?”

Katrya huffed with exasperation. “Tha jailer?”

Sarl did a double-take and looked at her for a long moment. “Kira Toth...Yuri’s second. She’s yer sister?”

“Well, yeah, of course, she’s... Wait, ya didn’t know that?”

They looked at each other, bewilderment reigning on both sides of the conversation.

Finally, Sarl broke the confused silence. “How in tha abyss would I know that, Kat? Oh shite, c’mon, woman! Seriously, Kira an’ Katrya? Why’d yer mum name ya with tha same—”

“Shut it!” She glared at him, and it was obvious he had struck a nerve. “It ain’t that uncommon, an’ I’ve already heard every stupid joke ’bout our names from that idiot Yuri!”

Sarl wasn’t about to get into a debate about how strange some human customs seemed to him. He continued to stare at her, the mental framework of what he thought he knew crumbling and reforming. “So...okay then...”

He trailed off, trying to put back together what he thought

he knew. She remained silent, hands now back in her lap, seemingly unsure of what to make of his confusion. He looked around the room and then up at the windows, still trying to stay calm.

"Kat, where are we? I mean, whose house is this?"

"My sister's, though she ain't here that often, so I use it a lot."

"An' she told you ta bring me here tonight? I mean, exactly here?"

"If I could entice ya, yeah."

There's no way tha jailer would have known about Elise. Guess I'm just an easier mark than I thought. "Why here an' not a room at tha tavern?"

Katrya shrugged. "She just said somebody wanted ta talk with ya somewhere quiet, where nobody would see 'em come an' go."

Or me come an' go. Or not go, as tha case may be. He wasn't sure about the "no killing" part of the conversation between the sisters. "Somebody... So, not Yuri?"

Katrya made a short raspberry sound with her lips. "Why would he care if anyone saw tha two of ya talkin'? Anyways, he'd just haul ya in himself, if he wanted ta talk. An' before ya list off a bunch of other names, I don't know who she was talkin' 'bout."

So it's gotta be yer sister who's in with tha shapeshifter, not you! But why? Is it workin' for her an' Yuri, or are they workin' for it? An' why are ya doin' this for yer sister, Kat? Unless...yeah, that's gotta be it.

Sarl shifted so that the two of them were facing each other on the bed. "Let me guess. I ain't special at all, least not tha first time we met. Ya put tha mark on *any* stranger that comes ta tha tavern for yer sister, don't ya?"

Katrya looked out the window at the moon. "Yeah, somethin' like that..."

"Just you, or everyone that works there?"

"Pretty much everyone. Bainor will point someone out, an' then tha girls try an' pick up information on 'em. If Bainor thinks it's worth it, he'll pass things along ta either Yuri or my sister, an' they'll decide if they want ta talk further ta someone. There's coin in it for everyone."

"What does Yuri wanna talk 'bout? Jobs?"

Katrya nodded. "Yeah, mostly. He's always lookin' for help, either for tha town watch or on tha docks. Usually, he wants tha ones that are both strong an' smart, but he'll take strong an' dumb if he has ta."

"Tha docks? Thought tha longshoremen controlled all that."

"Sure, they control tha loadin' an' unloadin' of goods. But there's guard duty an' a lot of other things that go on down there that tha dockmaster controls."

This gets more an' more interestin'. Yuri must have a deal with tha dockmaster ta supply him with bodies. But why would the shapeshifter care 'bout controllin' tha docks? Think, ya dumb dog, think! If Yuri can control tha docks an' tha local swords, too, then maybe...

"Ya said they recruit for tha town watch as well?"

She nodded her head. "Yeah, but that only started in tha last couple of months. An' there are a couple new faces in tha guard that I never seen before, so they musta got them from somewhere else."

"Well, do ya know if they have the same deal at other taverns that they got with ol' Bainor?"

"It's really only tha Oar House besides tha Wild Boar that caters ta tha type they're looking for. Tha whores there are tha ones who pass along information 'bout strangers. But tha folks they recruit from there are usually just tha strong an' dumb ones."

Sarl smirked as the pieces of the framework started to reassemble in his mind. "Okay, Kat, okay... If ya had ta guess, how many strangers have decided ta stick around these parts an' work for Yuri in tha last year or so?"

She thought about the number briefly. "Oh, at least thirty by now. It's startin' ta cause issues with housin' an' whatnot." She had been looking out the window all this time but now turned around to look at him. "Why do you care 'bout all this, anyway?"

Sarl ignored her question and instead covered his face with his hands, his fingers rubbing his temples as if to remove the last vestiges of alcoholic haziness from his brain. Yuri had offered him a job the last time he had been in town, although he couldn't remember what he would have been doing for the sheriff. *It feels like ol' Yuri is tryin' ta build his own little private army, but ta what end? And what about tha checks an' balances in tha system? Where's tha mayor?* Sarl didn't know the intricacies of Perizidon law, but he knew enough to realize something was off in how the town appeared to be operating.

"Kat, where's yer mayor? I don't recall seein' them around tha town hall or anywhere else."

She laughed. "Yeah, an' you won't. Mayor Freya only comes out of her house if her wine supply has fallen below a full barrel, an' Yuri makes sure that never happens."

"Who signs all tha royal decrees then?"

"Yuri an' my sister take turns doin' it. They'd probably let ya sign somethin' if ya really wanted ta."

"An' tha church? Yer priest don't care 'bout his tithe?"

Katrya actually crossed herself before answering. "Father Malachi is a good an' honorable man. It don't surprise me none that he took on those wargs ta save those poor little Shoikos girls from harm. But he's *too* good an' honorable, 'cause he trusts Yuri ta do what's right. Yuri makes sure tha tithe gets paid an' some acolytes get recruited so nobody else comes sniffin' around, but after that, it's just lip service."

Sarl let the inaccurate version of the priest's story go unchallenged and just shook his head. It was just too easy for these shysters to make coin and gain power. *Sard me sideways, maybe I should sign up with Yuri after all.*

Katrya pressed him again. "Sarl, why do ya care? Why are ya askin' me 'bout all this?"

"Why are ya tellin' me 'bout all this?" was his rejoinder.

Katrya swallowed hard. She hesitated as if she were about to say something but then shook her head. "Nah-nah-nah, ya gotta go first, luv. I've said my piece for now."

Sarl nodded. "Fair enough." He was fairly certain now that she didn't know anything about the shapeshifter. Nothing that would help him solve his mystery, anyway. It didn't mean he was going to put all his cards on the table, but he could drop a few hints as to what was in his hand.

"If ya know about tha priest an' tha warg attack, then I assume ya know I've been huntin' those same wargs?" She nodded an affirmative and he continued. "I been chasin' those damn beasts for almost two months now. They ranged too far south, an' I was hired by some locals ta make sure they went back north an' either stayed north or became dead. Easy 'nough, right?"

"I suppose. But if it's easy, why's it takin' so long?" Katrya's moxie was quick to return.

"Ha! Right you are, Kat, right you are. There's somethin' else goin' on. Someone or somethin' is controllin' tha wargs somehow. Usin' them as scouts, maybe. I don't really know."

"Scouts for what?"

"That's just it, I don't know. But they've done some things that ain't normal for a pack of wolves or wargs ta do, enough that it's kept me interested in them longer than just chasin' them away would have."

Katrya seemed confused, as if she didn't know quite what to

make of this or why it mattered. “Okay. Are ya just guessin’ that someone is leadin’ them, or do ya know for sure?”

“I know for sure. I’ve seen ’em with tha wargs.”

Her eyes widened suddenly with enlightenment. “Okay, this person that yer talkin’ ’bout with tha wargs, is that who ya say ya can smell in here?”

Sarl nodded. “Sure as you’re sittin’ there.”

“Which means my sister knows them.” Katrya shivered. “So...are ya sayin’ my sister knows what the wargs are doin’?”

“I dunno. I didn’t know yer sister was meetin’ with this, ah, person ’til just now, so I don’t know how everythin’ she an’ Yuri are doin’ ties in with tha wargs. I assume she ain’t said nothin’ ’bout this to ya?”

Katrya shook her head, a worried look on her face. “Nah, she ain’t said nothin’ ’bout this, an’ we’ve been workin’ together for a long time too.”

“Workin’ ta do what? Ta leave?” Sarl looked Katrya squarely in the face, trying to read her mind.

“It’s complicated,” she said evasively, and then, as if to change the subject, she tentatively sniffed the air, slightly raising her nose as she did so. “What do ya smell, anyway?”

“Metal, I presume?” The new voice floated up from the first floor, the amused tone being followed by a light, friendly chuckle.

Katrya gasped and looked at the stairwell, while Sarl cursed himself for dropping his weapons at the front door.

Preparing for the worst, he called down to the vovkulaka in

his native tongue. "Yakoho bisa, suka? Ty khochesh pohovoryty zaraz?"

The voice came again, this time with a somewhat injured tone. "Please, good sir, there is no need for name calling. But, yes, I have gone to some trouble to arrange a private conversation with you, and I would be honored if you joined me down here. Uh, but if you could kindly put some trousers on first, as I do not share the young lady's desire to see your genitals."

Sarl moved to get out of bed, but Katrya grabbed his arm. "Is that tha man who yer talkin' 'bout? 'Cause I don't smell him if it is!"

He answered in a low voice. "That's him. But he ain't no man."

"What do ya—"

He put a finger to his lips. "He can hear ya, Kat. Ain't that right, suka?" Sarl didn't raise his voice beyond normal conversation level as he spoke to the shapeshifter again.

There was a cough and what sounded like a heavy sigh.

"Yes, of course I can. Sarl, isn't it? Please, I have been rudely eavesdropping on your conversation with young Katrya for some time now, and I would prefer to have you say things to my face as opposed to behind my back and a level away."

"Just be patient, suka!" Sarl winked at Katrya. "Start makin' a fire so we can see each other, an' I'll be down 'fore yer done."

"Fine, fine," came the muttered response, and immediately there were sounds of wood being tossed about.

Sarl leaned forward and whispered as quietly as he could in Katrya's ear. "I don't fully know what Yuri an' yer sister have been doin', but they're playin' with fire if they're dealin' with what I think is waitin' downstairs."

Katrya looked at him in alarm. "My sister's in trouble?"

"I dunno yet. I assume yer sister wants ta leave here as bad as ya do, yeah?"

She nodded in the affirmative after a slight hesitation. She reached out and grabbed his hand. There were so many things they had to say to each other, but they had run out of time.

Sarl sighed. "Fine, lemme see if I can figure out tha price of his ticket for ya. Just trust me when I tell ya that some things cost far too much ta get."

He kissed her on her forehead and then rose to his feet. He graced Katrya with a view of his backside as he bent over to grab his pants. As he put them on, he looked over at her and grinned.

"Kat an' Kira, huh? Sorry, I just don't see tha family resemblance."

She shook her head and seemed to ready herself for the punchline to a joke. "Yeah? An' what of it?"

"An' nothin', luv. I just think you're too pretty ta be that bitch's sister." He winked at her again and turned to walk down the stairs.

EPILOGUE
The Mountain

It was still cold on The Mountain, but now there were some who could attest to this through recent experience. The advance party of roughly twenty Rusgorod soldiers had been busy setting up a base camp on the northern slope of Mount Klyk, the name they knew it by, for over a month now. Even though the calendar said it was still late fall, the weather had turned decidedly nasty over the past week, making for a better incentive to work faster than any whip could be. Trees had been cleared, a shallow ditch had been dug, and day by day, the wooden palisade grew. Shelters meant to hold an entire company had been started as well. The camp was not supposed to be more than a temporary waypoint once the army pushed farther south, but for the time being, it was to be both a storage depot and a forward operating base and had to be protected as such.

Reinforcements would trickle in every few days or so, bringing more supplies and gear with them and slowly growing the invaders' ranks. Work was hard in the camp, but not as hard as the arduous journey each soldier had taken to get to the camp in the first place. In order to avoid being seen by the Perizidon frontier forts and the patrols that extended out from them, the Rus had traveled in small groups of three to four through the barren icy wasteland that lay far to the north of The Mountain. Believed to be impassable until just a few years ago, it was an extremely dangerous route. Perhaps one in ten did not survive the journey. With the coming of winter, it would only become more perilous, and the Rusgorod generals fretted about the growing losses even before the first battle. But their mad king insisted he had the men and resources to spare, and his schedule would not be delayed. All must be ready to advance on Stren by the start of the new year.

Yuri had experienced the cold of The Mountain as well, having been called north by the insufferable Rus captain in charge of the forward basecamp to be questioned and scrutinized on local readiness. Yes, he would have his force trained and ready to go by the date the captain's schedule dictated. Yes, the mayor was still incapacitated, or at least inebriated. Yes, the rumors about lights on The Mountain and things going bump in the night were keeping the locals nervous and close to home, far away from the northern slopes. Yes, there had been a random trapper or two who had gotten too close to the camp's location, but they had been taken care of and no one was the wiser. Accidents happened in the Wilds all the time, and if anyone was reported missing, then, of course, the sheriff would assign someone to investigate right away. If he didn't forget to do so...

Yuri toyed with his food as he sat at the Wild Boar, moodily wondering what Kira was doing. No doubt she had made it to the Shoikos farm by now and had set up camp nearby. She would be gone several nights, investigating the warg incident, and he already missed her terribly. Truth be told, he missed her fit body against his in bed more than anything else, and he was half tempted to make a quick trip to the docks to visit some old friends at the Oar House to satiate his hunger. But that bitch of a sister of hers would probably rat on him out of spite, and it wouldn't be worth the hassle that would create.

As he waved at Bainor for another drink, the sheriff decided he could hold out for at least a couple days before seeking solace in another whore's arms.

Kira's argument that one of them needed to go on the expedition to keep the men in line had made sense, even if he didn't like to be apart from her. None of their recent recruits had any proper training through the army and would have to be drilled on even the basics of camp protocol. He had never thought that they would have to be more than a basic brute squad to keep the local population in line, but she had aspirations of melding their men into a real fighting force. Personally, the last thing Yuri wanted was for their local militia's fighting prowess to ever be tested.

It was why he suffered the Rus captain and his long list of questions. With surprise as an ally, he was certain he, Kira, and their armed contingent could take the vital parts of town. But to hold them and to operate the town smoothly after the takeover, he would need constant patrols and heavy security at the docks and town hall. That meant he needed a Rus army garrison stationed in Stren. He knew that Rusgorod was just using him and the town to gain a critical foothold in the north once their full-scale invasion kicked off, but that was just fine. Under the Rus system of governance, they would need a regional governor to control things once the fighting was over. Who better than himself to fulfill that role? He would do anything to make himself appear to be indispensable, and so far, it had been working.

The attack on the priest had been distressing, and not just because Yuri genuinely liked the man. It was true that Father Malachi was as loyal as they came, to both church and kingdom, and would have turned Yuri in to either authority the instant he figured out what the sheriff was doing. But the priest was a soothing presence for the local population and gave them an outlet to report all the strange incidents they thought were happening out in the Wilds. Also, the attack meant that there was an increased chance, no matter how small, that the church would send someone to investigate the incident. And that would lead to some damn inquisitor demanding answers that Yuri was not in a position to provide truthfully, and that would only lead to disaster.

And so, he had done as Kira had suggested and dutifully sent a report north that detailed the incident with the priest, advising on the minor risk factors that it brought. He was already assuming that a simple report would not be enough, and he would have to travel to The Mountain yet again to see the captain. No doubt he would have to explain why he didn't have the resources to provide bodyguards for every single representative of the kingdom who wandered through his county.

At least he could claim credit for the orc who was already hunting wargs in the area, even if he was a loose thread that might need cutting sooner or later. Kira had told him that she was handling that issue and had made sure the trapper wouldn't leave town until she got back. Yuri had played along and hadn't asked too many questions, but he would prefer to either recruit the orc or get rid of him completely. *Because even one loose thread might be enough to unravel my beautiful tapestry!* Yuri grinned at his own poetic nature.

He, of course, wouldn't let on to the Rus captain that factoring the orc into the plan had been the idea of his second. Yuri almost always took credit for Kira's ideas, because they were usually amazingly simple once he thought about them for a bit. He knew he would have arrived at the same common-sense conclusions himself, given enough time, so they might as well be his ideas as far as anyone else needed to know.

Sooner or later, Yuri knew he'd have to get rid of the jailer. She was too smart, too strong, and too fearless. If she didn't want his job already, then she certainly would in the future. He just needed to squeeze as much out of her as he could before that fateful day, both in and out of bed.

The sheriff congratulated himself on his deviousness, downed his mug, and motioned for yet another drink. He could never get enough of Bainor's delicious ale.

The Mountain, as always, watched impassively from a distance.

BOOK TWO PREVIEW

The Inquisitor

"What I mean, Your Excellency, is that I have already sent for my primary suspect, so that I may interview them immediately. However, I consider this a mere formality, as I expect I will arrest them and charge them with the murder of Lady Toth's lady-in-waiting. Tonight."

Basil was confused. He blinked and shook his head. *But the accused was arrested almost a month ago! Brother Ezekyel sits in his cell even now! What is she going on about?*

Moirne gave a small smile at his muted reaction. "Yes, I understand this may seem a tad, ah, confusing. I assure you, Your Excellency, that my methods are sound, and my mind is certain. I will, of course, allow the suspect to plead their case, and if you had not sought me out tonight, then I would have requested an audience first thing in the morning to provide you with a full briefing. You are most welcome to stay for the interview and draw your own conclusions, if you like."

"Who, may I ask, is being brought in?"

"Lady Varissa Toth herself, Your—"

"*What?!*" Basil jumped to his feet, hands at his face. "God's nails, woman! What have you done?"

"My job, Your Excellency." Her tone was even and her gaze firm.

www.ingramcontent.com/pod-product-compliance
Lightning Source LLC
Chambersburg PA
CBHW060553310726
48982CB00008B/1108/J
* 9 7 9 8 9 8 9 8 7 5 4 0 5 *